CW00792818

Mike Ledwidge is a new author and should not be confused with the American Author of the same name. Hence M S Ledwidge has been used. This Mike Ledwidge does not write detective novels, perhaps due to the fact that he was a police officer in England for nearly 30 years and 'Coals and Newcastle' spring to mind. He now runs a small training business delivering Restorative Justice training courses, mainly in the UK and Central America. Mike has studied extensively and has a great love of science and he delights in the opportunities for imagination that the SF format offers.

He apologises for the lack of an aerial picture of the Iron Age fortress, but it has been impossible to locate one before this first print run.

He gives his profound thanks to his niece, Bridie France, for all her help with proof reading this book for me, and in particular controlling his desire for an excess of the use of apostrophes to 'emphasise' certain words. (Ooops! That's twice in one page)

This book is dedicated to Dr Helen Elizabeth Taylor (Lizzie).

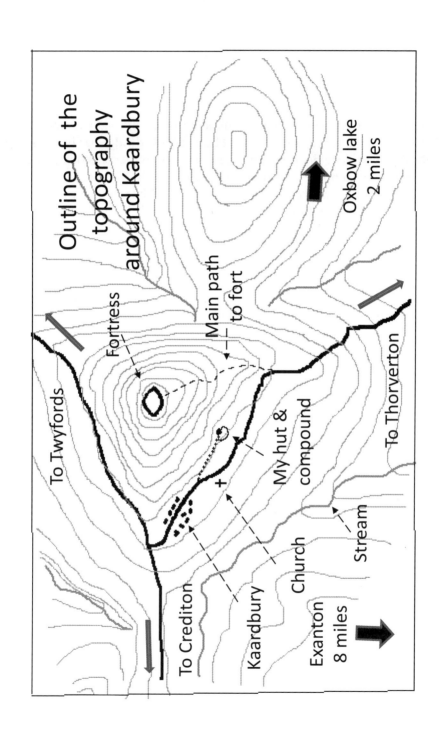

Outline of the topography around Kaardbury

Oxbow lake
2 miles

Fortress

Main path
to fort

To Twyfords

My hut &
compound

To Thorverton

To Crediton

Kaardbury
Church

Stream

Exanton
8 miles

The 'All Can Come' Fortress

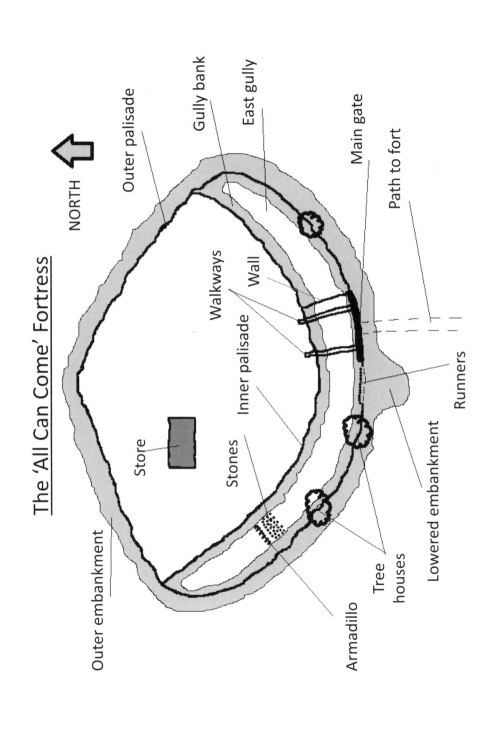

NORTH

Outer palisade

Gully bank

East gully

Main gate

Path to fort

Walkways

Wall

Inner palisade

Store

Stones

Outer embankment

Runners

Lowered embankment

Armadillo

Tree houses

Bill Marlin
Almost a Legend

By M S Ledwidge.

Published by Ledwidge Publishing copyright © 2015

Prologue;

The microlight thrummed under my hands. My knuckles were white with the force of my delighted grip. It was a bright midday and the ridge of the broken forest of the North Downs slid alongside me like the furry back of some sleeping monster. The air was crisp, and I felt as if the world was mine! I knew I should be flying a bit higher, after all I did not want to create too much of stir until I was a great deal further south west. But I could feel the ridiculous grin on my face that did not seem to want to go away, and the Z450 swept along like a majestic medieval dragon, its shadow five hundred feet below, jumping from tree to tree.

This should not be much of a surprise, as a dragon was exactly what it was supposed to look like. A great deal of money had been spent making it into probably the most expensive microlight in history. The wings were bigger than the standard ones used with the Z450, and were connected directly to the body unlike most other microlights, with the back edge of the wings serrated into a series of curves, giving the appearance of the stretched skin found between the fingers of a bat's wing. The front of the microlight had been shaped, as far as aerodynamically possible, to look like the head of some crocodilian monster, with large oval floodlights facing outwards and down as if they were it's eyes. I sat in the centre of the beast with the rearward facing propeller in its own safety cage behind me, blowing a windsock of a tail backwards into the sky, the tip of which flipped back and forth like that of an angry cat. On each side of my central seat there was an area about one metre wide and two metres long to which were strapped all the provisions and equipment I had painstaking put together over the last five months. From below, these looked like the thighs of the dragon. They narrowed backwards towards a knee joint where they angled sharply forward and downwards to the landing gear. The wheels were disguised so that they appeared to be the feet of the dragon held in permanent readiness to strike, like the talons of a bird of prey.

There had, of course, been a compromise with the feet, as the mechanics of retractable wheels, which is what I had originally demanded, would have been excessively heavy and prone to weakness. The one thing that I could not afford was a craft that fell apart on landing. But a clever use of bright floppy plastic claws covering both sides of those 'extra large' wheels created something like the desired effect. The sides of my cockpit were substantial, using stainless steel tubing and a high quality steel mesh. Over this was stretched a canvass cover, made at considerable cost, to protect me from arrows or pointed weapons. After all, I did not want to give anyone the title of 'dragon slayer'. A curved plastic removable windshield provided further protection from the front and sides whilst allowing me to see well enough to fly. When the microlight was on the ground, to avoid interference and damage by the locals, I could remove the windshield and close the cockpit with a folding lid. This had one of those electric locks on it that would have required a team of oxen to pull open.

The colour of the craft had been more difficult than I had anticipated. I had always wanted the dragon to be red, but I had changed the colour at least half a dozen times before I was happy with the mottled deep crimson of choice. The skin of the beast was patterned just like the scales of a lizard, paler on the belly than the back. There were a couple of additional features that the control committee had not discovered, which still gave me a bit of a thrill to think about.

In all the microlight and the equipment cost close to two million pounds sterling. This sounds a lot, but you have to put this into context. These 26 days were not only a once in a lifetime opportunity, but this opportunity was available to only one person in the world: me, Bill Marlin. Despite the cost of this trip I would remain a very rich man, for although it would be fair to say that I would probably not continue to be described as one of the top 10 richest men in the UK, by the time I returned to the 21st century, I was still going to be worth a bob or two.

I had led a charmed business life, but I suppose for every thousand failures there is one who succeeds most spectacularly. I had been fortunate to be that one in a thousand, although the reality of life is that I would not be telling this tale if I had been one of those failures. My business had been built on computers and the dot-com frenzy of the 1990s. A successful computer business with many UK outlets, a good software team and an effective search engine all meant that by the time I sold my business in 2002, at the age of 35, I was a billionaire. By this I mean an

English billionaire of a thousand million, not an American one of a mere hundred million. I sold the business for a number of reasons. The one I was most happy to publicly declare was that I was going to spend time with my newly born daughter. This resulted in the usual plethora of cute 'dad and baby' pictures in many newspapers and magazines. I was a celebrated entrepreneur and was even offered an OBE for services to industry.

The truth was, of course, a little different. I can now confess to being, to say the least, somewhat arrogant, something which tends to come with meteoric success, and great wealth. When introducing myself to people I used to say "Hi, I'm Bill Marlin – Computer Wizard! 'Bill' as in 'money', and 'Marlin' as in 'big fish'." I was also something of a ladies man. I had sold the business because I wanted to experience all the thrills available in life before I was too old to appreciate them, and I had set about doing this to the full. I tried everything, including trying to set a couple of world records in aeroplanes. I dabbled in a number of exciting and dangerous sports, but still, in my view, managed to avoid taking unreasonable risks. This was because, as I said in confidence to my friends, I wanted to live to enjoy my money rather than leave it all to my wife, from whom I was becoming progressively estranged.

In 2005 my wife filed for divorce, and despite the fact that we only became married in the same year as I sold my business, my lawyer advised me that I was likely to lose half my fortune to her. I was also told that the chances of getting custody of my daughter, Maud, were close to zero. I ranted and raved, and cited many cases of friends of mine who had been clearly discriminated against by the old fashioned and sexist court system in the UK, but to no avail. At that moment I had full control of my money – yes, my money – which I had earned the hard way over the last 23 years. But unless I managed to spend it without accruing new assets, my wife was going to get her somewhat avaricious hands on half of it. So, whichever way you look at it, the bottom line was that the cost of this venture, and the considerable loss from my personal fortune it involved, was significantly influenced by my anger towards my, soon to be ex, wife.

As luck would have it on Thursday 15th of September 2005 I was invited to a celebrity auction. It was a lavish affair held at the magnificent premises of the Mansion House in the banqueting hall of the Lord Mayor of London. I was not even sure what the auction was going to be about, but having just left another stressful meeting with my solicitors, and also after having consumed more than a couple of shots of good quality malt from the bar in the back of my Bentley, I got my driver to drop me outside the front of Mansion House before he drove on to park, and eat, elsewhere.

<u>Chapter One;</u>   Before.

How do I start this story? Probably one of the strangest true stories ever written and I suppose in some odd way I should view myself privileged to have been involved. But at the time that was probably the furthest thought from my mind. Survival was almost certainly the biggest driver, my survival, under the most extraordinary and extreme circumstances. Survival where there was no other help from my affluent reality, only the humanity around me, and the meagre items I had with me from our modern world.

What did I gain from the experience? Well perhaps we should start with what I lost. I lost 17 years of my life for a start, but I suppose I could also claim to have gained those 17 years in a way I could never have hoped for. I certainly lost a great deal of money. Many hundreds of millions of pounds sterling, although by the time I was able to do the tally I did not really care. Along the way I probably lost a lot of anger, and I suppose I gained some skills that had vanished in the aeons of time. I also suppose, if I am to be honest with myself, that the greatest gain I made was 'me'. In truth I was a bit of a bastard really, and over those 17 years I came to understand the real meaning of life, and in some small way contribute to the life, literally the life, of others. Yet, for me, the greatest loss of all was the simplest and most important of all things.

This story started in the Mansion House, hired by that group of strange individuals called the 'Einstein Group'. I arrived in my usual limousine, partially drunk. It had been another of those very full days for me. I had sold my business three and a half years earlier, in 2002, for just under a billion. I mean a real billion with 10 digits and I had earned that money the hard way, on my own. I had had little social life in my twenties as I took my computer business from a few bright ideas and a good search engine in the early 1990s, to a global success. I had met my wife by chance, well I had thought it was by chance, but the truth was my face had become known as one of the most successful businessmen in the UK and I have since found out that my wife had probably targeted me very carefully.

Without much social life I had met her at a conference in 2000. She was working on one of the presentation stands for Microsoft, she was gorgeous, and could talk about computers with confidence. Before I knew it I had been whisked off to her bed, and we enjoyed an enthusiastic and somewhat gymnastic affair. She claimed to hate the smell of condoms, and she swore she was on the pill, but within four months of that first meeting she announced that she was pregnant.

What was I to do? I did try to persuade her to have an abortion; I did not want to start a family with her because, despite the physical attraction, I was not sure I could handle the prospect of living with her for the rest of my life. But after the usual arguments I was convinced that I would be seen as a real shit if I either managed to persuade her to have an abortion, for which she could need therapy for the rest of her life, or if I simply failed to do the right thing. (Which of course meant the right thing in religious terminology and the terminology of her family.) So it was I married her on a crisp January day at the beginning of 2001 with the promise of being a good father to the bump under her expensive wedding dress, and that I would find some way of spending enough time away from work to make our relationship a reality.

It took me four months to decide that I could not run the business and keep my promise. I had reached the stage where I believed that my business had peaked in value, and there was a growing plethora of competition. I decided I could sell the company and walk away with more money than I would ever need. I could then start to do all those things I had missed out on. So I began by making a bucket list.

It took me less than a year to sell the business. I was pleasantly surprised at getting £950,000,000 for it. (As I said, just under 10 digits.) The celebration parties were huge and filled most of the UK business press for over a week. By then the baby, 'Maud Charlotte Marlin' was 11 months old and I was able to take her first birthday party seriously. Very seriously. Perhaps too seriously, as far as our neighbours were concerned. After all, how many people hire in their own circus, elephants included, for an infant's birthday. It cost me over 20k to remove the tyre ruts from everyone's front lawns. Anyway, Maud had her mother's red hair, and at the age of one, could walk, and even talk – a bit – and she did love the elephants.

That was a domestic high point. I suppose that in retrospect I have to carry a significant chunk of the blame for how things went downhill. In truth I had not really been ready to marry, and certainly not ready to marry someone who in the back of my mind I never forgave for trapping me by lying. She has always claimed that she was on the pill, but a couple of years later I was reliably informed that my wife had confided her plans to one of her best friends prior to the deed. As to whether this was the truth, or just bitchiness from that 'so called' best friend, I will probably never know.

The meeting with my lawyer that morning had not gone well. There apparently had been this court case; Logan verses Logan, in which everything was split 50-50. The lawyer was pessimistic, to say the least, about me retaining the bulk of what I had earned, despite the unfairness of it. On top of that I would almost certainly have to surrender custody of Maud to my ex. Apparently when it comes to children it appears that the courts are allowed to be very discriminatory indeed. In fact, since she had walked out, my wife had already started to use my little girl as a bargaining chip. Being a bit of a sad bastard I even worked out in my head that there was a real possibility my ex would get about a million quid for every shag we had ever had together. I wonder how many women have done that same trick, yet have the temerity to look down on prostitution with distain. 'Fuck me' I thought, and I most certainly had been.

I am saying this not so much out of hatred of women, but to give you some idea of where I was coming from that night. My lawyer had told me that anything and everything I owned would be included in the financial calculation for the divorce. The only chance I had of reducing the 'pay out' would be to literally lose, or give away, lots of money very quickly. Or to spend it immediately on something that will become worthless before the divorce is finalised. Oh, and I would have to make it look like it was not deliberate.

Chapter Two; The Auction.

As I slid across the seat to clamber out of the limousine I noticed a stain
on the thigh of my trousers, just above my inside left knee. I swore
profusely, and realised that this was some of the single malt that I had
been drinking. I had spilt some when the driver braked sharply coming
onto Cheapside, but I had mistakenly thought it had missed my trousers
and ended up on the floor. I suppose that is the price you pay for drinking
warm malt, and having a chauffer who has a predilection for driving too
close to other driver's arses. (Not appreciating that it was I who had asked
him to get me to the dinner on time, and that our lateness was due to my
tendency to leave everything until the last minute). In retrospect, very
retro-spect (by a couple of decades or so) what I said to him, as I got out
of the vehicle, was well out of order. I do, of course, now believe his
parents were married at the time of his birth, and even though I continued
to employ him even after the time when it was decided I would never
return, it was inappropriate for me to advise him he was no longer
employed in the terms I used. Especially as it was I who was too drunk to
realise that trying to hold the cut glass tumbler between my knees, in a
moving vehicle, was somewhat stupid.

I breezed up the steps into the Mansion House. I was vaguely aware of a
good number of flash photographs being taken, but I had become so
immune to this by now that, even without the alcohol, I would probably
have not taken much notice of them. Bit of a sad way of making a living
really, hounding celebrities in the hope to find them in a compromising
position, or in a distressed state. They always made me think of vultures.
Despite not actually chasing her that night, it is a shame they never had the
balls to apologise for being one of the underpinning causes of Princess
Diana's death.

There were the usual minions (I would never use that term now of course,
but I was a bit of a shit then), who ushered us into a reception room
where champagne was the order of the day. I think I got through four or
five glasses in the 20 minutes we waited before being sat at our tables in
the main hall. The champagne had been at the right temperature, but the
size of the main hall, and the known fact that warm air rises, resulted in

the temperature in the hall being cooler than many would have liked. I saw a number of those present asking for their coats to be retrieved from the cloakroom. I don't mind the cold; I have been accused of having ice in my veins on more than one occasion. I even had to have special quilts made for the bed at home so my wife (soon to be ex) could sleep under the 1000 tog Eskimo half whilst I slept under the half more suited to the tropics. Yet despite this immunity I still took the opportunity to give the head honcho a bollocking about the heating.

There were eight of us at the table. Two were academics. One was an elderly woman in her sixties with a startling shock of grey hair which appeared to have been let out of its cage for the evening. I suspected in her laboratory she kept it tied up in a bun, or ponytail. But tonight, possibly for the amusement of her hairdresser more than anyone else, it looked like a cross between an 'afro' and a privet hedge. The other academic was a bespectacled forty year old male, with three chins and a dinner jacket that was obviously from a less gravitationally challenged era in his life. The jacket also had a strange iron shaped discolouration on one lapel. The other five occupants of the table were two couples, one from industry and the other from finance. In both cases it was the serious looking balding half of these couples who were the financial big cheeses. In the case of the financier the word balding is a bit excessive, and receding gracefully would be more diplomatic. Of their ladies the financier's wife was a lady of similar age to him, about 50, but with the striking features of someone who was a real aristocratic beauty in her time, and who would still be reckoned as 'posh crumpet' so long as the lights were low enough to blur the little tell tale signs of age. The industrialist's wife was a good 10 years younger than he was, and a good 20 pounds heavier. She looked as if she had been a real cheery 'life and soul of the party' type in her day, but she was intense and snappy with her husband which shadowed her attempts to be all fun and smiles with the rest of us.

Apart from me, the other member of the table was a woman in her mid thirties who had clearly been chosen as my counterpart to make the numbers even. She was reasonably attractive with shoulder length dark hair that fell with that heavy bounce when she turned her head suddenly. She wore spectacles that made her look academic, but it turned out she was an heiress of some sort. Daddy's money was in property and shipping, but her real passion was archaeology. She didn't have the appearance of an archaeologist, but I looked at her hands and could see the strength in them, and the sensibly short nails. Given her broad shoulders and firm jaw, it flashed through my mind, somewhat unkindly, that she may have been a very attractive male transvestite. But when she spoke, she clearly was not. I quite fancied her really. By the end of the meal I fancied her a great deal.

My first course option was a very reasonable pate, chased down by the first half of a good heavy flavoured bottle of Rioja. Then to my disgust the fish course was delayed whist the opening speeches were made. I had come across this approach to 'after dinner' speeches before. The idea was that because what was to be said was so boring, a small portion of the speech had to be inserted between each course to prevent us falling asleep. So for the next fifteen minutes we all sat there listening to the credentials of the eminent speakers we would have to hear through the rest of the meal. To my dismay the corpulent academic from my table was to be included, and when introduced he half got up and bobbed his head up and down in recognition of the scant applause rippling around the room. All three of his chins moved like rubbery jelly, and he turned a mottled pink colour for a few moments. I heard something about his recent breakthrough in relation to the work on 'worm holes' whatever the hell they were. So he was presumably a lot brighter than his exterior implied.

The salmon was a bit dry so I called the waiter over and advised him to get me more of the sauce, pronto, as I got stuck into the second half of the Rioja. It appeared from the Archaeologist that she had heard that there was some sort of incredible opportunity being offered that night to the highest bidder. She went on to wax lyrical about the research possibilities if a trained archaeologist (like herself presumably) were able to take this so called 'incredible' opportunity. I remember something being said about there being worm holes all over the place all the time, but the problem was firstly to open them to a diameter greater than a few nano-microns, and the other was to work out where they would go. I then went on to hear that this 'Einstein Group' had found a way to do both.

My main course was a rack of lamb. I was not usually tempted to eat a great deal of lamb, as it can tend to be a bit fatty. But tonight I thought it might delay the onslaught of my intoxication, so I attacked what appeared to be most of one of the beasts, on a plate about half a metre across. I failed to clean the plate, but looking around the table I appeared to have beaten the rest of them. Even treble chins had barely touched his food, but that may have been due to his nervous checking through speech note cards as it appeared he was up next.

During this main course money was discussed. On looking round the cavernous room I could see that money was probably the main theme for its occupants. That, and the academics, plus a few hacks who were always up for a free meal. There were a couple of TV cameras at the back of the room, so someone was recording the evening for the public, or posterity, or both. It appeared that the main reason for people being invited to tonight's soirée was the size of their bank balance. Not much point in me being there then, I thought, I am about to lose half of it.

Three Chins got up and, after a somewhat nervous start, began to speak surprisingly passionately about the work they had been doing. I watched the Archaeologist listening to him as if in a trance. The look of rapture on her face made me slightly jealous, and in my defence this may have been a contributory factor in my later behaviour. It appeared that these worm holes allowed us to go back in time, but that the state of the world at the present could not be changed. So if someone, or something, went back into the past, then during the time since, everything has to be able to 'heal' or 'adjust' back to exactly as it is now. The power requirements were therefore exponential. We could produce enough power to travel back 1000 years, but to travel back to last week would require all the energy in the sun. He tried to explain it a bit more; I was on to my second bottle, and trying to get Archaeologist to share it with me. "If a person going through a worm hole appeared a week ago on a street in London, for only a few seconds, they may make one pedestrian delay crossing a road whilst another few cars pass by. That pedestrian is then walking along the street perhaps 50 or 100 metres further back than they would have been. Everything that person then does is slightly different from what should have happened. Everyone they come into contact with, the time they get into their car, where they are in queues, all changes. The ripple effects are huge and there would be no time to repair those changes before the present arrives. So nature makes it impossible to do this by requiring huge amounts of energy to open these 'recent past' worm holes."

I thought this must be a load of bollocks. But despite my difficulty in concentrating I was trying very hard to understand what was being said. In retrospect the main reason for this was that deep down I thought that if I was able to converse with the Archaeologist, in a way that made me sound knowledgeable about something she was clearly very interested in, I might manage to get into her knickers. This sounds rather shallow, and it most certainly was, but I had had my fill of females throwing themselves at me for clearly money and power reasons. Since my wife had left I had been inundated by unsubtle approaches, some of which I had succumbed to. But I had abstained for the last couple of months hoping to start a real relationship with an 'equal' and here was someone with lots of money, a brain, and very, very reasonable looks. I tried to visualise what she would look like if she spent a tenth of the time most women I knew did on her appearance. I realised that despite the lack of make-up she had a strikingly good bone structure, a fabulous smile and was genuinely beautiful. I decided that I would let her know that at some stage during the evening. Well I had to start somewhere, and you never knew your luck eh!

Three Chins carried on, "The trouble with opening wormholes is that we have to calculate when and where they will interface with. At any point on the planet there are a number of possible wormholes, but there is such a range of time that has already passed only a tiny fraction of these interfaces end up at a point in time during the last 3000 years. We have to limit our interest to the last 3000 years or so because, as erosion and the build up of soil and plant material progress so quickly, it becomes progressively more and more difficult to pinpoint the right place for a return journey. If we add to that continental drift of about four centimetres a year, you can start to see the problem. Just think how deeply buried a Roman road becomes in just 2000 years! If we had a 'return wormhole' at present day ground level above an old Roman road, the returnee would have to build a gantry to the right height above the level of the actual road two thousand years ago, and about 80 metres from where you would expect it to be, to be able to get through the wormhole in the few seconds we can hold it open. So when you start with only that tiny fraction of interfaces in the right time frame, then have to find ones where it would be reasonably easy to find the return point, and then add the complication of needing two geographically close enough together to enable a researcher to travel between the two interfaces in the time available, you start to run out of possibilities. If you then add the complication of providing ever increasing levels of energy, you can see how difficult this project has been."

Three chins waffled on a bit longer, then returned to our table all flushed, with all three false mandibles bobbing again to the applause. The dessert was nowhere near as good as the rest of the meal, so I left mine virtually untouched and made a point of giving the waiter a hard time yet again. (As I said, at that stage of my life I was a bit of a shit really).

So then we moved on to an older speaker. He was a man in his late fifties with a short cropped grey beard and a very dapper appearance. He looked more like a mountain goat than the quite brilliant scientist that he presumably was. "Every time we travel back into the past we affect the level of energy required to open the next interface. We have successfully opened 16 so far, and used eight of these to enable researchers from the present to travel back into our past." There was a dramatic silence and I was not surprised. Bloody hell! I thought, if they are telling the truth then this is not just some theoretical bullshit, could this be real??????

You could have heard a pin drop.... Then after what seemed like an age, Mountain Goat continued, "We have, of course, had to use these interfaces in pairs, otherwise we could not have returned researchers to the present day. So of the four human trips that have already been undertaken we have sent someone back for twelve hours into the early Tudor period, followed by two and a half days in the time of Queen Elizabeth the 1st. Then just over five and a half days in 1068, two years after the battle of Hastings, and finally a further 13 days in the year 371, during the Roman occupation. In every case the traveller has returned safe and well, and they have all been given a clean bill of health. All three of our time travellers are here with us tonight." Again, a silence during which you could have heard a gnat breaking wind. A chair was pushed back close to me, and I saw Privet Hedge stand up only a few feet away. I was aware of another chair moving off to my left as a middle aged man got to his feet and a shuffling of feet close behind me. "Professor James Vincent, Doctor Ruth McDonald and Doctor Paul Brown are our three intrepid explorers.

Professor Vincent of our team took the first two trips, this was followed by Doctor McDonald who witnessed five and a half days of the reign of William the Conqueror, and Doctor Brown went back to sample the Roman occupation. Neither Doctor McDonald nor Doctor Brown were associated with the project. Both are independent researchers in their own right, nominated by an independent panel, and chosen at random from the 11 suitably qualified volunteers who put themselves forward. Their role has been not only for the purpose of historical and scientific research, but they have also performed a number of validation tasks."

By now there was a growing hubbub of quiet discussion amongst the tables. Mountain Goat was forced to stop speaking and wait whilst the noise quietened down. He went on to explain a number of these validation tests. One of them I remember in particular involved the burying of pieces of oak wood soaked in pitch that had items implanted in them. "The remote location of these was known so that they could be recovered in the present time. It had been proved by a number of other eminent and independent observers and scientists that they have genuinely been buried there for the last 950 and 1,730 years respectively. They have been recovered from under a compacted soil which had been proved to have remained undisturbed for many hundreds of years. The pieces of oak have been carbon dated and proved to have been of that age, yet from the implants in them we can prove they were cut from trees felled in this country less than two years ago."

Archaeologist was aglow; you could see the shine in her eyes, the excitement radiated from her like heat from a furnace. She could not stop speaking when the cheese and biscuits arrived. You could almost hear the possibilities jumping round in her head. She was firing questions at Three Chins and Privet Hedge as if there was no one else on the planet, let alone at the table. Three Chins was almost slavering at the level of intense passionate interest focussed on him. Privet Hedge on the other hand was much more serene, and after a few minutes I was able to draw her into a separate conversation, leaving Archaeologist and Three Chins arguing over one of the other tests that had been used.

"What was it like then, a thousand years ago?" I asked Dr, (Privet Hedge), Ruth McDonald.

"You would be surprised at how like today it was. People are still people after all. I had to spend time on the language before I went because it was so different, but life was very busy for everyone, just getting on with everyday survival."

"Was it dangerous?"

"No not really, I was well away from where King William and his army were. People knew about the defeat at Hastings because the survivors had returned home. We also knew that William had used his army to rape and pillage all over the South East. But I was in the Midlands heading north to reach my return point in time. It was only 42 miles, but it took me most of the five days to get there."

"Where did you sleep?"

"Oh, mostly I slept in the woods ... I did go into a number of villages, and I did sleep one of the nights in a mill stacked with sacks of flour and grain. I did not want to be noticed too much. I managed to take about 14 hours of video which is being cut into a film. Most of that was of life in the villages, but I had to have the cameras hidden, so some of it is with a static camera I had built into a piece of wood I could set down on the ground, or stand against a building. The other was built into a woven basket of a contemporary design, so I could walk up to people and talk to them whilst filming."

"How did they react?"

"They did struggle to understand me. They thought I was from another country, or Scotland. But we did manage to understand each other well enough. I was able to negotiate the purchase of some food with coins we had made copies of, although of course most buying was done by a bartering process."

We were interrupted by the return of the first speaker, the one who had introduced everybody. He looked more like a businessman then any of the other speakers. He was about 40, with broad shoulders and a shining bald patch surrounded by sensibly short cropped hair. I did note that he had not made the fatal mistake of trying to paste strands across the top of his head. His suit probably cost more than the clothes of all the other speakers put together.

"So here we come to the focal point of the evening. We are here to give one of you a 'once in a lifetime' opportunity. An opportunity so unique that unlike travelling in space or climbing Everest, you will possibly be the only person ever to do this in the history of mankind." He paused for dramatic effect, but it was not necessary, he really did have everyone's undivided attention, even mine. "We have found another pair of wormholes. They are in the year 831, and they are 26 days apart. This is in the time of the Saxons and will be a very exciting time in our history to experience. There are no known hostilities in the locations of either of the interfaces, nor at any point near to the route of the journey between them. Because of the increase in energy required every time we send someone through a wormhole, our project is now drawing to a close. Without significant further funding what is seen as merely an interesting, but not very useful, scientific anomaly will be history itself. We cannot change the present by travelling into the past; that we now know. The more we travel in the past the harder it seems to be for time to heal all those small changes we inadvertently make. The way that this time/wormhole equation seems to control us making changes to the past, is to make it progressively more difficult for us to go there. So this may be the last trip ever made. That is why we are offering this opportunity to the highest bidder. The money we make from this auction will fund further research, and we hope will enable us to travel back to our past again, at some time in the future."

That was the time I started to look around the room again. I was thinking about the other people there, but in a way that fuelled that growing ball of excitement and fear in my guts. I realised that I was going to bid for this, I knew that I was going to be the one who won this auction. In retrospect there were probably a number of elements to my motivation. Firstly there was the alcohol, and if ever there was a good reason to limit the amount you drink, then this was an excellent example. There was also the growing realisation that this was an opportunity to blow some of my money, yes my money, before that bitch could get her hands on it. This was what my lawyer had said, wasn't it. "Spend it on something that will be worthless by the time of the divorce." Just think how pissed off she is going to be! I thought. But that evening there were two other incentives. One was Archaeologist, because if there is one way to impress a woman it is to be happy to part with large sums of money on a whim. They would prefer themselves to be that whim, but she had been so very interested in the whole evening. And lastly there was the pure bloody excitement of it. Think about it! Going back to a time of swords and shields and battles!

Going to a place so far removed from our safe sanitised world that I would be literally surviving on my own, reliant on no one, accountable to no one. I had taken a few risks over the last four years in my pursuit of excitement, but the thought of this was pushing adrenalin round my system so fast I thought I would literally take off.

It transpired that the auctioneer was a gentleman from Sotheby's, a man with considerable experience in such matters. He was in his mid forties with that florid appearance and a pink shirt. I appreciate the modern predilection for such colours, and that it should not be seen as effeminate, in fact it is supposed to show one's confidence in one's own sexuality, but it was just 'not me'. I have some good friends who are gay, and good luck to them, but to me 'Pink Shirt' was trying too hard to be trendy, and ended up looking more like an embarrassed pimp. "Can I start the bidding at one million pounds?… five hundred thousand then?" He had started, but my mind had been off into the dark ages already. "Thank you sir, five hundred thousand I am bid, do I hear six? Thank you, seven? Thank you, eight?" Now he started just nodding at the bidders as the numbers climbed. It rose through five million without slowing down, and the increments were now a million a time. "Do I hear eight million? Thank you, nine?" It slowed to almost a stop at 20 million when I decided to enter the bidding, "Twenty two million," I heard myself say. I felt on fire.

This was when another bidder entered the fray. He or she was on the end of a telephone, and there was a lady dressed in a severe black business suit standing beside a table near the back of the room off to my far left. On the table was a laptop, and attached to the laptop by a thin cable was a mobile phone. I assumed that this was a secure satellite link like the ones I had used many times in my business. I wondered who was on the other end of the line. Another member of the audience dallied briefly in the bidding at thirty million, but myself and the satellite link carried on upwards. Poor old pink shirt was sweating rather profusely. This was probably only partly due to the bright lights focussed on the lectern from where he was choreographing the bidding. We started grinding to a halt at about sixty five million. The whole of the room had been completely silent for some time now. I felt as if I was in a tunnel and all else was blocked out. After my last bid there had been a significant pause, then suddenly black suit, with a somewhat squeaky voice, shouted out "Seventy …

seventy million." There were a few audible intakes of breath. I waited for what seemed and age, Pink Shirt didn't even say anything, he just looked at me. Then I heard it. The voice I heard was quite clear, and surprisingly calm. The voice said the words quite slowly, and not particularly loudly. "One hundred million." Pink Shirt blanched a little, then said to the bidder, "Can I confirm your bid as one hundred million?" It was only then that I fully realised who the bidder was, because he was looking directly at me. Ooops!

So that was that. Whoever was on the end of the phone line chose to bow out at that point, and after what appeared to be an inordinately long pause and the usual final words about any other bids, and the 'going once, going twice' bit, his gavel came down on the portable podium, a small circular wooden plinth on top of the lectern. There was an explosion of noise, mainly applause, but there were one or two rather vulgar vocal 'whoops'.

The rest of the evening was something of a blur. I was congratulated by what appeared to be most of the people there, some of whom wanted to shake my hand, others patted me on the back as they passed and some were satisfied with saying something appropriate from the safety of the other side of the table. Pink Shirt and Mountain Goat approached me and said that they would contact me in the morning. The hubbub went on for ages, and Three Chins and Privet Hedge tried to have deep and meaningful conversations with me, the contents of which I only vaguely remembered. As the numbers started to thin out I was approached by Mountain Goat again and invited to a little 'soirée' they were going to have in one of the upstairs suites in their hotel. I turned to Archaeologist who was deep in conversation with three chins and asked her if she would like to join me.

It was about three in the morning when the little party we had broke up. There had been music, but little dancing. The conversation was focussed on the experiences of the three previous travellers, and the prospects of my visit to the ninth century, in the autumn of the year 831. Archaeologist was actually a very nice lady as well as (on reflection) being pretty damned gorgeous, and I warmed to her considerably as a person, not as just someone to 'bonk'. So much so that I felt a little guilty about making arrangements for myself to sleep the rest of the night in a room at the hotel, and discretely offering her a place to 'lay her head', so to speak. I was even a little surprised to have the offer accepted.

Chapter Three;   Planning.

I woke up the following morning at about 10 o'clock. Snuggled into the crook of my left arm was the Archaeologist. I usually find it difficult to sleep with someone in my arms, but we had managed it. We had also managed to overcome the inhibiting effects of too much booze, and make surprisingly passionate and sensitive love for over two hours before we fell asleep. I awoke with my customary 'dawn horn' which was noticed by Archaeologist and promptly taken advantage of. Even in her half awake and somewhat dishevelled state I was genuinely surprised at how good she looked and smelt. She also seemed to be actually really enjoying herself.

Over breakfast we discussed the preparation for my 'trip' and she seemed very keen to help. It occurred to me that it was going to be very useful to have someone with her knowledge helping me. There was also the added bonus of the possible extra extracurricular activity she may well be willing to continue to be involved in. The trip was almost nine months away and I had naively thought that I could start preparing a month or so before I went. Archaeologist, who I now know as Elizabeth Jane Montgomery, now know to me as Lizzie, and to her friends as 'Monty', tried to explain what I would need to do to prepare. It sounded like I had committed myself to nine months of very hard work involving everything from learning sufficient Anglo-Saxon to be able to communicate, to equipment preparation and survival training. She even started talking in excited terms about the possibility of me burying 'stashes' of items of Saxon pottery or jewellery in 'perfect condition' that could be recovered on my return. Most pottery from that era, apart from a few items found in graves was already smashed or broken. Apparently what was usually found in digs was literally their 'rubbish', broken pots and discarded fragments or shards.

That first morning over breakfast I started to formulate another idea in my head – one that perhaps had been lurking at the back of my mind during the auction of the previous night. I was a little surprised to be genuinely pleased to have been successful at the auction for all the reasons I have described, including the fact that it had probably cost my (soon to be ex) wife 50 big ones, which was a real bonus. But I was an entrepreneur, a high flier in more ways than one, so there was a big part of me that revelled in a calculated risk. I was also paying a very great deal of money, so I wanted more from my trip than just academic research. My bid had left the Einstein Group very happy indeed. The auction had exceeded their wildest dreams, and I had probably funded at least another decade of research. Given how much I had paid for the privilege, I intended to get my money's worth.

I called my solicitor and had him meet us at the hotel that afternoon an hour before my meeting with the Einstein Group's legal team. I invited Monty along. I did not know her that well as yet, but we seemed to 'click' on a number of different levels and she had a depth of knowledge that may have been useful. Could I trust her? Well why not. She had to be more trustworthy than most of the other women I had met. She certainly didn't go to bed with me for my money as I knew her family was loaded. She may have done so just to be more involved in what she saw as the most exciting project ever, but I was hoping that it was already more than that. Perhaps that was my irrepressible vanity, which was a dominant feature of my character at the time, but I like to think we really had started to care about each other, even at that early stage. Monty, my solicitor Cyril (yes I know, poor bastard) and I sat in the breakfast room of the hotel and went through the document that I had asked him to prepare before he arrived. I appreciate that it was a Saturday, but when I have a tame lawyer who I have always treated with considerable generosity, I expect him to jump when I require him to do so. He came with a laptop and printer and we made a few alterations before I was fully happy with the wording. The document required the money I was going to give to the Einstein Group to be held in trust until the evidence to prove the time travelling process was real had been independently evaluated by my people. Given the unexpectedly large size of the payout from the auction, a scam of monumental proportions would still have been very worthwhile. You can persuade a lot of eminent people to lie if you can pay them enough. I appreciate that the Einstein Group had no idea that such a large sum would have been involved, but I was still not going to be had over. With this amount of money involved I trusted no one, especially not other people's lawyers. I also wanted control over what I did and what I took with me to the year 831. I was aware that some sort of controlling ethics committee was mentioned last night. In fact Monty remembered a great deal more about it than I did. But I was not going to have some egghead

28

tell me that for a price of almost four million quid a day I did not have the right to decide what I was going to be doing in Saxon England.

We met at 4pm. Last night's hotel had arranged for their small conference room to be available free of charge. The auction and subsequent news reporting on their doorstep had been very valuable publicity for the hotel, so this was a further opportunity to see their name in print. I insisted that the press stay well away until the discussions were completed. I had seen the morning's papers and the auction was headline news. There was a picture of me shaking hands with Mountain Goat that had found its way to the front page of most of the tabloids. That hand shake being something I only had a vague recollection of doing. But I had some important questions to ask before I would sign a cheque with eight zeros on it.

There were eleven people at the meeting. Myself, Cyril, Monty and my secretary Janet on my side of the table, and six people from the Einstein Group and their legal team. Also at the meeting was my personal friend and renowned divorce lawyer Arthur Stenning, who I had asked to be there to witness the proceedings. The discussions about my prepared agreement went rather more smoothly than I anticipated. They could see my concern over proving the reality of time travel, and despite the explanation and presentations the night before, they seemed to be quite happy for the evidence to be examined in minutiae. They were even happy for 90 percent of the money to remain in trust until the trip had been completed. Although they did insist that the trip would be deemed to have been completed even if I died of natural causes before I went, or if I did not make it back to the present time. Well, let's face it, there was always the possibility that I either would meet with some accident in the year 831 or even decide not to return because I liked it there. Yeah sure! But I agreed anyway. I liked the wording of the 'natural causes' clause, as it excluded death by accident before I left, so I hoped it negated the possibility of someone arranging an 'accident' for me, just to ensure the payout of the 100 million.

The biggest argument was to do with what I wanted to take with me. I insisted that I took whatever I wanted, but there was considerable concern over this. Their concern was that if I took something that could cause too

29

much change in the past, I would either be prevented from getting through the wormhole by a change in power requirement, which seemed to be natures way of controlling the level of potential 'time damage', or when I arrived in 831, 'nature', or 'time' would limit the damage I did to the past by finding a way to kill me off. I thought it was all a bit far fetched, but in retrospect despite the odd way it was explained, it does make some sort of sense. The present has to be exactly as it is. So whatever I would do in the past could not change how the present would become. We knew that this was at least partly controlled by the energy requirement increasing the closer the worm holes got to the present, but I suppose that an accidental death was as good a way as any of preventing someone like me from changing the past too much. I eventually accepted that I would not be allowed to take anything with me that was specifically for killing, such as guns or modern weapons, but that I could take non-lethal means of self defence. I also accepted that I would have to have what I took with me agreed by an ethics committee. But I was able to insist that both Arthur and Monty would be on that committee, and that so long as the power requirement allowed it I would be able to take items of modern technology with me. I promised that anything I was leaving there and was not going to bring back with me would be destroyed, or I would bury or sink it, so that it would be lost forever.

When all the papers were signed up we allowed the press in the door. They photographed me writing out the cheque, and then photographed the handing over, and the handshakes all round. There were two TV crews in the room so I supposed I would be on the news again. I had hoped to have become accustomed to less invasion from the press when I had dropped out of the business world, but a series of over publicised sporting style challenges, my separation and now the impending sticky divorce had accelerated their intrusion. I had resigned myself to things being bad over the next few weeks, but hoped that they would ease up a bit, over the coming months, as I prepared for the trip. At least when I arrived in 831 the buggers would be snookered for a few weeks.

That evening I took Monty to my London flat. Well it's a penthouse, really, and in a prime location in Docklands. It sits above the river and on a warm evening you can sit out on the balcony and watch the river traffic, or listen to the drone from the roads and the distant noise of car horns.

30

On cold ones there was a very realistic gas powered log fire. I decided to take two days off just to chew over the prospect and enormity of what I had signed up for. As the weather was still good I invited Monty to come with me to my house in Borrowdale in the Lakes, but she declined. She said she needed to get back to Italy to spend time with her father, and to plan for an extended stay in the UK so we could prepare for 831. "I have almost no clothes with me, and I need to keep some appointments I have made," she said. "I must tell the university that they will have to do without me for the rest of the academic year." She seemed to be taking my preparation for the 831 as a personal quest, and although I would have been happy to do it all myself, the idea of working with her pleased me. Besides, how was I going to deal with all that accumulated stress I was bound to suffer? So I went to the Lakes, and she went to Milan, and we agreed to meet at the offices of the Einstein Group as planned on Monday the 19th of September. Although of course that did not stop me from filling the time between that Friday night and our various departure plans on Saturday morning with some fairly strenuous bedroom activity. Well in truth it was shower room, living room, kitchen (only briefly due to the cold floor) and then the bedroom, activity. My best excuse was that it had been a while for me, due to my simmering anger towards the female race in general. Perhaps deep in my psyche I did not feel that Monty 'came' in the same category. (In the nicest possible way of course!) I also seemed to be in that advantaged position of following some poor performers. Her ex was an insensitive unemotional character and endowed to the point of sex with him being painful, and she had recently broken up with a boyfriend who drank to the point of embarrassment, and who after a skin-full was unable to complete the act in a suitable time frame, subjecting her to an interminable pounding. Whatever I was doing seemed to work for her, very well indeed ....

I remember a story told to me by a friend who was a police trainer. He used to run training courses with another sergeant week in and week out, and because their two courses were run in parallel and they each had different subjects to teach, they sort of 'coxed and boxed' their way through the programme. Whenever my friend was in his colleague's class teaching, his colleague would be in my friend's class teaching something different. He said that the colleague he worked with lacked sparkle and delivered his training in a boring monotone. This meant that whenever my friend entered a classroom there was a visible delight from the students. Following a poor performer always seems to make us look good.

My chauffer had forgiven me sufficiently to drive me to Keswick where I picked up my soft top Jag from the garage who looked after it for me. I had always left it with them ever since the lake incident, where some young shit had forced open my garage, taken the spare keys from the cabinet and driven the thing into Derwentwater. He had done it where the road meets the top of the lake in Keswick, near the new theatre. He managed to damage half of the rowing boats that had been pulled part way out of the water onto the gravel beach. The car ended up thirty metres out in the lake, with just the torn top of the roof showing. The little shit got caught because two of that evening's theatre goers were off duty detectives from Leeds. You can't beat bad luck, eh! Anyway I left Paul, my chauffer, to find digs whilst I drove down to the cottage. I spent the rest of the weekend fell walking, climbing and running in fine but windy weather. I have to admit I cheated a bit on the run. I find it hard work at my size doing the really steep uphill work, so on the second day I drove up to Honister pass, and left my car in the small car park by the old slate mine there. I then ran north up the slope towards Maiden Moor, zig-zagging to be able to keep moving on the steeper parts. The climb is not too long, and at the top, only three or four hundred feet above the pass, you can angle north east towards the brow of Maiden Moor, and then head down the ridge of Catbells. The whole run is about seven miles, but by starting at the top of Honister and ending up at the road near the west bank of Derwentwater (with a mobile phone to call Paul to give me a lift back to my Jag), I got the feeling of 'fell running' but spent most of my time actually running either on the flat, or downhill. I even had time for a couple of hours rock climbing on Shepherd Crags. I headed back to London on Sunday night, Paul drove and I made a few phone calls, then slept. As he dropped me off I reminded Paul that I needed to be picked up at 7am, as if he ever needed to be reminded, and then rolled into bed to continue my sleep.

Chapter Four; The Einstein Group.

The drive to the offices of the Einstein Group took over an hour. They were located in a big house just outside Epsom in Surrey, near a village called Headley. We drove past some sort of rehabilitation hospital which looked like an old country mansion, before turning down a long driveway that looked more like a farm track. As the house came into view I could see some early indication of the finance problems. The main building was a big old Georgian house, the sort that would have a dozen bedrooms or so. There was a clear need for some TLC on the old girl, but I recon they would get little change out of 200 grand for the work that was needed just to the outside of the place. Beyond the old house there were two new buildings. One was a small, and completely out of place, two story office block, with probably eight to ten rooms in it. The other looked like one of those aluminium sided farm buildings that could double for a medium sized aircraft hangar. With the front doors open I could see four vehicles inside, two of which were the size of large articulated 30 ton lorries. The two others looked like good sized recreational vehicles designed for 'off road' use.

We pulled into an open space on the gravel and mud in front of the house and trooped inside. I was with Cyril and Janet who we had picked up from Epsom railway station. Thank god Paul knew how to get to these places. I had not needed to read a map for years. If I drove anywhere on my own I now used a 'sat nav', but Paul used the old fashioned method, and always seemed to know exactly where he was. The front steps were a bit pretentious even for this building, despite their state of repair, with two sets, one on either side of a small covered balcony over the main entrance. Mountain Goat and Three Chins were there to greet us, and they led us into the cool echoing interior. The hallway was huge and vaulted, opening up into a space that was the size of a small house in itself, with a chequerboard of polished black and cream tiles. I could see from the reflection of light off the tiles that, on the routes across the hallway between rooms, the black ones had worn more than the cream. Janet's court shoes clip-clipped across the floor like the start of a flamenco dance, echoing all around us.

I was wondering where Monty was when I heard her laughter. There was a strange feeling of tightness in my chest at the sound. I passed the corner wall on my right as I followed Janet, and there by a doorway in the corner was Lizzie talking to a lady I had not met before. She turned and her laughter turned into one of those heart stopping smiles and a look of real delight in her eyes. She virtually ran the four paces it took to reach me, then she hugged me and kissed me on both cheeks, stopping just short of giving me a huge snog in front of everyone. "It's SO exciting" she declared, and pirouetted on her left foot to lead me by the arm into the room in the corner.

We sat in what appeared to be the main drawing room that had been converted into a boardroom with 10 large wooden chairs with high backs and thick arms that were probably of a similar age to the house itself. The table was highly polished and of an appropriate vintage. We sat and talked. At the beginning it was very formal, with details of exact times and locations of the two wormholes. I was quite surprised that the wormholes were not the same time apart in the present, as they were in the past. It turned out that although the time I would experience in 831 would be 26 days, four hours and three and a half minutes (or 628.05833 hours), the time between the wormholes this end was over eight months. So I would return to the present effectively seven months younger than I should be. The timing was only accurate to about two seconds, but as the wormhole could and would, they promised, be held open for almost 10 seconds, all I needed to do was literally fall into it. I should have plenty of time to get through, even if I was twenty or thirty metres away when the hole opened.

The outward journey would be easy. I would be pushed through the hole on a sort of sledge which was designed to take a drop of quite a few feet without either damage to the sledge, or injury to me. I would be deliberately sent through a hole that would be set at an elevation above ground in 2006 such that it would be certain to be above ground level at the other end. This pleased me as I did not want to arrive in 831 buried up to my neck in mud, or rock, or worse! It was planned that the hole would be opened just above the ground in 831 and the drop should only be between 12 and 18 inches. I should arrive in a pasture on the top of the downs less than three miles from where we were, one thousand one hundred and seventy five years ago. It all sounded so easy.

One of the problems seemed to be that finding holes was not too hard, but as I had heard at the Mansion House, finding ones in the last 3,000 years was like looking for a needle in a haystack, a four and a half billion year haystack. So finding one in the last 3,000 years was a half million to one shot. Having found one in the right time frame, let's say from the time of the Romans onwards, but before about 1700AD, there was then the problem of finding another one close enough to make a return trip. This was paramount, not only for the safe return of the time traveller as the longer spent in the past the greater the likelihood of the unexpected happening, but it seemed that there was a power link between the two holes. You could not get someone through a wormhole if the machine sending the traveller was not already programmed to create the return wormhole, and the greater the time between wormholes the more power required to make the jump. Oh! And on top of that, there was the need to find a return hole which was close enough to a clearly identifiable object that was in the same place up to two millennia ago. Otherwise how was a time traveller supposed to find the exact spot to await the return trip?

In my case the return trip was about 400 metres to the south of a Roman road, almost exactly three miles east of the old perimeter wall of Gloucester. The wall and the road had been in place during Roman times, and of course were still clearly identifiable. To be on the safe side I would be taken to the current position of the return site and familiarise myself with it. I would also be given various technical devices to assist in locating it, to within a metre or so, from underground rock strata and the remains of a Roman villa just to the north. The rock strata was also important as it prevented a large tree growing at the departure point. Opening a hole into the past and then bringing back a few cubic metres of solid oak instead of me, would be not be my preferred option. The fact that I planned to use a microlight did, in reality, reduce what was probably the main concern of the planners. Without the microlight I would have to travel on foot for the best part of 200 miles to get to the return point. Although this would mean only about eight miles a day, this still created potential issues with delays and would have required me to get there well ahead of schedule just to be on the safe side.

There were, of course, the various safety issues which had to be considered, but which to me provided the real 'spice' of this venture. It was known that there were minor and sporadic coastal attacks by Vikings at about that time, but this was over forty years before the main period of hostilities leading up to the battle of Edington between the Saxons and the Danes. Our historians knew that the area I would be travelling in was stable and civilised, and although I would need to be careful, the only real risk was from the occasional 'robber' – and I was going to be well prepared for that.

Given there is a risk of boring you I will summarise the meeting as one which gave me rather a lot of not particularly useful information about the science involved, but which had the benefit of 'firing up' Monty once again. We then went into some discussion about the constraints applied to all the travellers to date, their experiences and so on, followed by a considerable list of preparatory processes which I needed to embrace fully. This list included me learning enough early Saxon to communicate effectively, survival courses, research and data collection seminars, equipment training, dry runs, location visits and so on. I insisted that I would take a microlight with me. I was already a very experienced pilot of a number of craft, and the microlight would give me mobility that was over a thousand years ahead of its time. There had been a joke during the speeches at the Mansion House in which Mountain Goat had suggested, probably only in jest, that the winning bidder may be able to travel into the past and turn out to have been the creator of a legend. A legend we already knew about, or one which had yet to be discovered in some hidden ancient text. "Perhaps one day we will dig up a thousand year old statue that looks surprisingly like someone sitting in this very room."

That was the quote that had stuck in my mind, and I had thrown it back at them at the London meeting when they had baulked at the idea of me taking a microlight to 831. I was going back to the ninth century to create the legends of flying dragons, and I pointed out that this was really their idea. Well no, it wasn't, it was mine, but it made it very hard for them to deny me. After all if it went too badly wrong we all know how it was guaranteed not to make any difference to the 'here and now' anyway.

We broke for lunch, and then carried on. During the lunch break I was shown the tracker vehicles in the big barn. The two 'biggies' were the mobile wormhole portals which not only were used to open and close the wormholes, but were used for finding them in the first place. For some years now they had been travelling round the UK scanning for potential holes, millions and millions of them. Well, rather them than me.

We worked through until after 7pm, when we decided to call it a night and head off home. I took Monty, Cyril and Janet down to a restaurant in a place called Dorking. I had been there many years ago when I was looking for the location of the Strawberry South recording studio with an uncle who was heavily into a group called 10cc. At that time we had been disappointed to find the studio had become a rather rambling hardware store, but as we passed the place that evening it appeared to have been changed into a mews of houses built around a central courtyard. The restaurant was still there, but it had ceased to be French. Still, I was hungry and they sold wine to go with the much needed food. Isn't it interesting how when you are with someone very rich, the desire to put ones hand in ones pocket at the end of the evening seems to be considerably diminished. Monty was the only one suggesting we should split the cost. I, of course, would hear nothing of it. Besides I had plans for where she was going to put her hands that night, and it did not include a foray into her own pockets.

The following day we had meetings at Headley with a number of people relevant to the preparations. My linguistic specialist was, believe it or not, called Helga. Helga Cottle. She had started life in Belgium with the surname Stellesgrum, but made the challenging phonetic mistake of falling for one of the minor staff attached to the European Parliament, and then marrying him. Still, for a lass with a big arse she was very good, (or at least appeared to be), at languages, especially ancient Saxon. We also had the advantage of the earlier trips made by the academics we had first met at the Mansion House. Although there were literally hundreds of years earlier and later than 831 they did give us a greater understanding of accent and intonation on the language, so at least I would be understood, probably.

There were three kit specialists who talked through everything from clothing to lighting, and a young man who was apparently the talented protégée of some fellow who travelled the world training people in survival skills. He told me about their one week course in the Lake District, which would teach me everything from trapping skills, to making a fire with only a bootlace and a knife. Well I was up for some of that! The final meeting of the day started after lunch, and was on the data recording and historical opportunity associated with the trip. They accepted that I was the paying customer, but that this was a unique opportunity that would never be repeated. Probably their one most convincing argument was that after my return I would be in great demand for books and appearances relating to my 'incredible journey' into the past. It occurred to me that if my wife was too successful in fleecing me, then at least I would have an easy source of income for a few years. I resolved to get the divorce case over and done with as soon as possible after my return, so that any money made from this would be well out of her grasp. Given the load capacity of a large microlight I was going to be able to take with me far more kit that the previous travellers. Probably the biggest problem was deciding what not to take, and which pieces of research would not get done. Still, it was early days.

Over the next two weeks my life shifted into another gear. It was more like the early days of my business where every minute of every day was important, and had to be used to best effect. I found that the London flat and the Suffolk estate were being watched by the ever present paparazzi, so I got Monty to rent a secluded country house close to the Einstein Group at Headley. It was on the outskirts of a village euphemistically called Newdigate, and was surrounded by locations equally suggestively named, like Beare Green (better than Pink I suppose), Wallis Wood (she did), Seamen's Green, (presumably a medical condition) and Leigh, (pronounced lie). It is rather sad that these trivialities caused me amusement. But then again, I never did say I was a deep thinker. I saw nothing of my ex, or Maud, and I had Cyril and Stenning rattling cages all over the place, yet short of actually kidnapping my own daughter there appeared to be bugger all I could do about it.

So I threw myself into preparations for the big trip with gusto. I was really enjoying it. I had the money and contacts to get what I wanted, and to really get things moving. I had until the first week in July next year to get ready. This seemed to be a very long time, but it began to fly by. The first thing I did was to arrange a meeting with the owner of an American microlight business. I flew with Monty to the 'Big Apple' and gave him plans and specifications for the craft. I wanted three identical machines delivered in the UK before Christmas, so that we could use one for practice, one for spares, and one for the final trip. I also wanted an identical extra frame for a microlight, which no one would be told about, that I could have some work done on in private. We then joined in the 'outward bound' course in the Lakes.

We arrived wearing what we thought was appropriate gear, and in possession of a range of kit that we know we should not have had with us. We were dropped by Paul at a pub close to one of the bigger lakes, which was the meeting place for everyone. We humped our packs into the warm interior and purchased two pints of cider. I was unshaven for probably the first time in the last 10 years, and had had my usually dark hair heavily tinted to a lighter colour. I hoped I would not be easily recognised, but I got a very long look from the woman serving us. I managed to put on something that I hoped sounded like a 'west country' accent and went to sit in the corner by Monty. We were not the first there and spent half an hour with an elderly Australian lady and a hairy youth before the rest arrived in a bit of a rush. We totalled fourteen; twelve of us were participants, and the other two were instructors. Introductions were a brief handshake followed by a few words of dire warning about the course, before we trooped out and into two Land Rovers with bench seats. Monty was bubbling, and I was a little hung over. I hoped it was going to be an interesting week.

That first night we had to get our 'one person' tents set up in the woods in drizzling rain. I was already having misgivings about the course. I was used to a great deal more luxury than this, a GREAT deal more. But Monty was still effervescent with enthusiasm and she did point out that this was virtually a prerequisite for 831. We were politely advised to move our tents from under trees which may lose heavy branches in high winds, so after some delay we returned to the main campsite where a large cauldron shaped water container, with a lid on, was boiling for tea.

The main meeting place and focus of the campsite was under an old parachute that was suspended from the trees to create a cone shaped canopy above us, but which was sited high enough so that the edges were some two to three feet above the ground. This gave us a relatively dry communal eating (and I was to discover also a working) area, some 30 feet across, with a semicircle of rough cut logs, sat upright, as seating. Not as comfortable as I had hoped for to say the least. We started with cups of tea and introductions during which the various attendees explained their varied fascination with the outdoors. The one exception was a well known TV personality who appeared to have been sent on the course to prepare for some sort of documentary series, in which he was to 'rough it' on a televised journey around the woodlands of the European Union's newest countries. He was the only one who clearly recognised me from the start, and I suspected he was sent there to provide a running commentary for the press on my progress, or my mere survival, during the coming few days.

Monty and I lay together in my double sleeping bag talking about the characters on the course, and the description we had been given of the following day's activities. I began to realise how much Monty had started to mean to me, and how her being with me on the course made me decide to try to stick it out. She fell asleep in my arms, something she did not usually do, as when she was asleep she had a tendency to throw her arms and legs around a bit, like a five foot 10 inch preying mantis. Our best option after the delights of our usual goodnight lovemaking was for her to put her head in my left armpit, and cuddle my left arm whilst facing away from me. That night in the tent she claimed she was not afraid of the dark, and I sure as hell did not want her to get into the 'one man' tent we had pitched for her. I know she had spent literally years of her life on various digs around the world, in far from substantial accommodation, but that night I like to think she was cuddling up to me because it felt a bit safer holding the tree not the branch, so to speak. I fell asleep listening to the wind groaning through the forest, and the intermittent patter of light squalls of rain.

The morning started early and there seemed little reason to put on clean clothes, so we trooped up to breakfast still smelling of the wood smoke from the previous evening. It was a brighter morning and I availed myself of the latrine facilities which was a shallow trench some 100 metres away from the site across a stream and on the side of a wooded hill. Apparently it is far better to defecate into a trench no deeper than 18 inches as it all rots down much more quickly than deeper ones. All the biological activity in soil takes place near the surface, so crap in deep trenches takes years to rot down. Having thought about that fact, I worked out that it was better to stand up and piss first, before trying to squat and crap. This advanced method, that had I worked out all by myself, avoided me spraying the trousers around my ankles whilst in that squatting position. I was quite chuffed at working that one out. I then returned to camp.

We started a series of short lectures on a range of subjects, such as water purification, knives and fires. What was most impressive was watching Tim, the course leader, starting with just a piece of dry log, and with the use of an axe, a knife and a piece of cord, produce a flame in less than five minutes. He started with splitting the log to create a flat board, then shaping a smaller piece into a short 'drill' that looked like a half inch thick wooden pen. (Small dildo size to the less academic, or more adventurous, amongst us). He then made a bow out of a curved bit of a branch and the cord. Bracing the board on the ground with his left foot, he set the drill into the bowstring with a twist, and then put the wide end of the drill on the board holding the top of the drill onto a piece of wood in his left hand, which was braced against his left shin. A few sawing movements back and forth with the bow in his right hand spun the drill, caused a bit of smoke and burnt a dark ring in the board. He then cut a notch in the board into the centre of the burnt ring, apparently to catch the 'ember', and with about thirty seconds of further effort there was a cloud of smoke and he miraculously produced a glowing ember which he waived about a bit, to get it burning better, then put it into a fist-full of dry grass and set it alight. 'Fuck me', I thought. 'What a clever bastard!' I, there and then, decided to take a few cheap lighters with me to 831, along with a few boxes of matches. The chances of me conquering that little trick inside a week was somewhere between 'no hope' and 'Bob Hope', and one of them was already dead.

"This is the Hemlock Pine. It has leaves very similar to that of the Yew tree. The way you can tell the difference for sure, is the colour of the back of the leaf. Yew is green, and the hemlock is a blue-grey," droned Tim. We were walking through a piece of open woodland about a mile from the camp, selecting trees of importance.
"The Hemlock Pine is no relation to the Hemlock plant, but it is

important to be able to recognise the Yew tree."

I was looking across at Monty who was listening avidly.

"Why the fuck is that then?" I thought.

"The Yew tree is the most poisonous tree in the world" Tim continued, as if he heard the question in my head. "A few leaves made into a cup of tea is certain death. The seeds are very toxic. Although the flesh of the fruit, a tiny bud, is edible, it is very dangerous to eat. I have a friend who is a seriously good woodsman who didn't actually eat a seed, he only scraped one of the kernels along a tooth by mistake ... he spent six days in a coma."

"Fuck me" I thought. I knew there were yew trees in the year 831 and I knew that some of those Yew trees were still alive today. I started to pay rather more attention.

By then end of the course I had a range of skills that no self respecting billionaire should be without. I could set snares for small game, recognise edible fungi, filter and purify water, remove the breast meat from a pigeon without a knife, make string from nettles, and believe it or not, start a fire with three pieces of wood and a piece of cord. I was nowhere near as good as Tim at it, and Monty was better than me of course. But I could do it, eventually. I had also acquired a sore back from sitting for hours of the top of a log stool, (no not that sort of stool log), had blisters on my fingers in strange places and smelt worse than I have done since I was two years old. It took a week to wash the smell of the wood smoke out of my hair.

As I have said, right from the start of all this there was that comment about 'creating a legend' which had run around in my head from that very first evening at the Mansion House. I had Cyril get hold of an engineer who I had had dealings with in the early days of my business. His name was Harry Gill, and he was one of the best precision engineers I had ever met. He had a good sized workshop which he ran with his son near Canterbury. The place was full of lathes and drills, and he was able to produce almost anything out of metal, from complete engines to surgical instruments. I had number of very particular tasks I needed him to look into. There were some items he would have to get through a contact I had in the British Army, but at this stage I just need him to do some preliminary work. Things would progress more quickly when we had the microlights in the UK.

My work on the Saxon tongue seemed to go OK. Helga said she was pleased with my progress. I was never a great one with languages, but with the incentive of the trip I seemed to be able to apply myself more than I expected. I had a number of audio tapes I used every time I travelled anywhere. To make the most of our time together Monty even started to learn it with me. It occurred to me that Monty shared a more than passing resemblance to a well known actress of the time called Jamie Lee Curtis. She was the daughter of Janet Leigh and Tony Curtis, both well known film and TV stars of the second half of the 20th century. I know that popular parlance of the early years of the new millennium used the descriptive term 'actor' for both sexes, but I struggled with that. It seemed somehow to remove the gender allure from the fairer sex. Thankfully by the time I wrote this it had returned to a more realistic, and gender appreciative, form.

It was about this time that she had her hair cut short. I remember with heart grabbing delight the text she sent me from the airport after a weekend in Italy sorting things out at her university. She had written a paper on the sampling process required in forensic sedimentology and had been hoping to get it officially published. Her text read; 'Paper published! Hair cut pixie style! Can I come round with a bottle of bubbly, with no pants on? xx

I was becoming progressively more attached to Monty. She was very bright, and very sexy, and a great companion in every way. My only complaint was that despite the truth that I did not have any real interest in any other woman at all, she tended to see competition where it did not exist. Still perhaps that is the way with all women, and the reason that although they try to deny it, they are constantly in competition with every other female on the planet. Perhaps that is even the underpinning reason for the very lucrative cosmetics and fashion industries of the western world.

The data recording stuff was quite interesting. They wanted far more from me than that had been recorded in the other four missions combined. There were a number of reasons; one was that the trip was longer that the others, another was that with the microlight I would have the capacity to carry a great deal more equipment than ever before, (perhaps this was one of the reasons they let me get away with it in the first place) and, of course, technology was improving year on year, especially in computer data storage. Many people, by the time of my trip in 2006, had their own little computer 'memory sticks'. Few realised that their little memory sticks, which were the size of a cheap lighter, had eight or even sixteen times the data capacity of the world's largest computers in 1991. In 1991 the world's largest computers cost 17 million each, and had hard drives of a mere quarter of a gigabyte.

I was in a position to get the very best technological equipment available, and as I not only had the money, but still had strong links to the very best computer hardware providers in the world, I was going to go well prepared. The very nature of the trip almost certainly meant that this sort of stuff would have been readily available anyway, as who would not want the publicity of providing me with all their best equipment? Probably the biggest issue was personal protection. I really wanted to take everything from a decent hunting rifle to a machine gun and anti-personnel mines. But sadly what I would be allowed to take would be very limited.

It was accepted that whatever I did in the past could not affect the present. The argument was that the greater my interference with the past, the greater effort time needed to put in to 'heal' itself, and to end up with the present being exactly the same as it is now. The more damage to this 'time continuum' the more energy required to make subsequent trips into the past. There had already been a noticeable increase in the energy required due to the four trips that had been made so far. This was one of the prime reasons for the project currently faltering and why it had virtually ceased to be of any value to anyone. If there were going to be any more trips into history at some time in the future, there would need to be as little damage to the past as possible. That, or a whole new method of creating a great deal more 'power' had to be invented.

The other prime reason, and the one that grabbed my interest, was that the more damaging and interfering the equipment or weaponry I took with me, the greater the likelihood that the easiest way 'time' would solve the problems would be through my early demise during the trip. Yes, 'demise', as in never coming back, and leaving my bones in 831. I had no plans for suicide, although in one or two drunken moments it had occurred to me. It is interesting how research shows that women are much more likely to use the children of a marriage as a 'weapon' in a divorce process, and it was constantly on my mind that I had not been allowed to see Maud in months. Wasn't it Chaucer who identified that what women really want is control? (If you don't believe it was that obvious so long ago, I suggest you read his 'Knights Tale'.) I suppose when sex ceases to be a bargaining chip the manipulative female tends to play openly dirty, as opposed to the not so openly dirty tricks such as lying about birth control. But I must not rant too much eh!

The final compromise, given my need for safety when on the ground, was a pump-action shotgun, with non-lethal cartridges. These guns can fire small bean bags at sufficient speed to knock a man over. They also fired CS gas projectiles, and I would be allowed to take one box of shotgun cartridges filled with rock salt. These would not kill a human at 10 paces, but would hurt like hell. I was also going to be allowed to take a Varey Pistol to fire flares which I hoped would be very scary to the uninitiated. I was even being permitted to take some 'thunder-flashes' and 'nine-bangs' which were used by the police and military for disorientating the enemy during arrests and house clearances. I certainly did intend to come back. If nothing else my relationship with Monty was exceeding my expectations by a factor of at least 10. I was wary of the very idea of falling in love, especially given my recent mauling, but she was becoming very important to me indeed.

I was also concerned about my safety in the air. After all Smaug, Tolkien's dragon, was killed by Bard's well aimed arrow, and I was aware that the big bows of the 15th century could be fired with an extraordinary power. I knew a bit about this as I had tried all sorts of things over the last few years, and had a real interest in both science and history. The standard hunting bow of the 20th century had a pull weight of about 45 to 50lb. That is like lifting a 50lb (22.68 kilogram) weight attached to a thin cord and strung over a pulley with three fingers of one hand. Doesn't sound that easy, does it? Especially as once drawn back there would be a need to hold that position until target was in view, the arrow was well aimed, and then released. Historians struggled to understand how the bow became such a devastating weapon in the hands of the 'English Archers' of Crecy and Agincourt fame, until we recovered the Mary Rose from the bottom of the sea at the mouth of the Solent. Preserved in the mud they uncovered some 120 war bows made of Yew. From the diameter and length we were able to estimate the pull required to use them, and it ranged from 120 to 180 pounds! (54 to 81 kilograms.) These bows could only have been used by men who had spent their lives developing their bow pulling strength, like ancient power-lifters. The English archers of the Tudor period must have looked like lop-sided Arnold Schwarzeneggers (a famous body builder/actor at the turn of the millennium, who won Mr Universe a record six times).

I had no idea if bows of this power were in use as early as 831, but the last thing I wanted was to be shot down by a lop-sided gorilla.

A thick canvass type material made from Kevlar fibres was used to cover part of the craft. It was not bullet proof, but it was stab proof against even the heaviest powerful bow, at the shortest of ranges. The Kevlar cover protected the engine and the pilot from below and alongside the craft. The downward and forward view of the pilot was protected by the high density plastic windshield, and there was the fine titanium wire mesh stretched over the tubular frame of the seating area of the craft. As I have said, the body of the microlight could be locked against outside attack by removing the windshield and closing the cockpit cover, which was like a box lid, which had one of those electronic locks on it. The sort of lock that could be opened with ease by using one of those plastic cards waved close to the lock panel. But it was a lock which took many thousands of pounds of pull to open it by force. This gave me somewhere to store the most valuable kit when I was on the ground, and even somewhere I could escape attack if I was sufficiently desperate. Considering the importance of getting in and out of this cage I would be taking at least three of those access cards with me.

I had some other rather unusual contacts I had acquired over the years. The best computer systems were needed for a number of uses in the world of intelligence, both in policing and the armed services. These important contacts were ones I had taken a personal interest in. These were some of the contracts I had been most closely involved with, and I had nurtured them well during my years developing one of the most successful businesses in the UK. As a result I had some very good links to one or two of those somewhat secretive organisations who provided equipment that would simply not be available to a normal citizen.

The more secretive stuff was only known to myself and Monty. We discussed at length some of the extra options I wanted available. Monty was apparently only concerned with my safe return, and wanted me to take anything that may assist that to happen. There were a couple of the more extreme options she was dead against due to their dangerous nature. The last thing she wanted was for me to not return because I had taken something with me that was so 'transforming' of the past that the only solution that 'time' had to prevent the present from being different was to kill me off.

The language work carried on at a pace. Helga was a cruel task master, and everywhere I went we had those tapes to listen to and CDs to play. I got very used to talking to myself or with Monty on trips around the country. This was on journeys between all the meetings and briefings required in preparation, including the work on research and historical opportunities. I also travelled a great deal to satisfy my personal desire to spend as much quality time as I could with Monty. We worked hard at cramming as many exciting and potentially valuable experiences as possible into the few months we had. I did a lot of miles indeed. We spent three separate weeks in The Three Valleys and the Espace De Killy, sleeping in the chalet I had bought in the early years of my business success. It was a small four bedroom place built to a Swiss design in a tiny village 10 minutes drive from the slopes. I had an elderly French lady, Madame Dupont, who looked after it for me who fussed around the two of us like an old mother hen.

Things moved up a gear when the microlights arrived. All three were set up in a hanger at Redhill airfield. It is only a grass airfield, but it was close to hand being only 20 minutes from the Newdigate house. The work done to them, and with them, was time consuming and I found I had to make frequent visits there. After they arrived I arranged for Paul and Monty to take the extra frame secretly to Harry Gill's workshop. There was work that I needed doing on that frame which only myself, Monty and Harry needed to know about.

We then travelled to America to show Monty the Grand Canyon. We travelled there by commercial 747 as it was just easier at the time. We had fun conversing in ancient Saxon for the first half of the journey. The air hostess thought we were from some Baltic state, or from Scandinavia. Monty was better than me at the lingo. It appears that women are better at languages than men. It is one of those evolutionary things, as apparently they needed language more than men to build relationships as part of their role as nest and community builders. To do this it has been discovered that they use both sides of their brain. Men use only one side of their brain for speech and so when speech is affected by something like a stroke, men are much less likely to recover their speech than women. (Perhaps that is why women are so good at nagging, eh!)

Anyway, we had fun on the flight, and Monty was literally drooling during the low level, and highly illegal, helicopter flight I managed to arrange down the length of the canyon section of the Colorado. We even took time out to drive to the Arches National Park near Moab, and climb Angels Landing in Zion National Park. Now there is a view to savour. I remember doing some climbing in the Zion valley about 8 years ago, and they have a 1400 foot, vertical rock wall that runs along the top end of the valley that looks like it was created with a knife. Thankfully, I was never sufficiently stupid as to try and climb it.

The last thing we did on our little trip was to spend an hour walking up 'The Narrows' – a deep narrow canyon that had been cut by the river at the head of the Zion valley. For long sections of the walk you have to wade through the river itself, with the 500 foot rock walls reaching vertically upwards on either side. Most people wear shorts, but my Monty, my Lizzie, was completely unabashed and stripped down to a T-shirt and high cut knickers. Following that bum along that river, with every man and boy we passed on the way so obviously jealous, was delightful. Some were mesmerised into open mouthed stares, virtually tripping over their tongues. It was an experience, and memory, that brings a smile to my face, and a twitch elsewhere, even now.

During our trip to the USA we stayed in an interesting mix of accommodation. Some of the hotels were definitely five star plus, but we did take some rooms that were a little less in terms of quality. Monty did not seem to mind at all. As she had said, many of the places she had stayed on archaeological digs in some of the more backward regions of the world were mere huts, or tents. There, her washing facilities were often bags of water suspended from a frame with a simple watering can nozzle providing the shower.

One evening we were sitting in a Jacuzzi that, believe it or not, was actually located in our bedroom in one of these hotels. I say sitting, but it was a little more complicated than that, as I was sitting on the bottom of the Jacuzzi, and Monty was sitting on my lap. (Literally as 'on' as is possibly achievable between red blooded consenting adults.) She was giggling and playing with one of those scrubbing things made from the fibrous structure of a dried marrow type of plant. This body scrubbing device which is called a 'loofah', was an unexpected source of silly fun, and she was giggling in a way that made my heart swell in my chest (amongst other things). That was when Monty raised the loofah out of the suds and announced that it looked just like the microlight. I supposed that given the lattice wire frame of the craft, before the canvas skin covered everything, there was some faint similarity. Monty was surprisingly flexible, and had been able to manoeuvre herself round to be sitting facing me without ever 'losing contact' so to speak. She sat there and held my head in her hands as she looked at me almost nose to nose. She had just about stopped giggling and had discarded that fibrous weapon into the agitated water behind her. "Look at it this way" she said, "us academics love naming things, so as I did not get to name your todger I sure as hell want to be the one naming anything else you get to ride in." Looking deep into her eyes, despite the mild fuzziness of the view due to my difficulty focussing at a distance of only few inches, I realised that I had found someone I could, and very much wanted to, spend the rest of my life with.

Anyway, from then on that is how she referred to them. For her they were re-named 'Loofah' one, two and three. Hence, when I eventually left for the dark ages, I was in a form of transport named after a dried plant we had been using for playful adult fun, during a delightfully bubbly form of sexual activity, in a bedroom, in a hotel, in Las Vegas.

We discussed my plans ad nauseam. My intention for the 831 trip was to travel up and down the Cornish peninsular, buzzing villages with the microlight, and then landing to see the reaction. I intended to capture the effect on the local populace using the video cameras I would take with me. But I decided that the first thing I should do when I got there was to try to land near my departure site, and make sure that I could find the exact point for my return to the 21st century. To make things even easier I had already arranged to get hold of some special bits of kit for pin-pointing a location. Which in my case was the location of the return 'time-gate'. I also intended to spend some time in the air over south Gloucestershire during the coming months. This was to help me pick out visual markers, such as hills and rivers, that would not have changed much in a thousand years, and should help prevent me from getting lost in a time when 'sat nav' would definitely not be an option.

There is a great deal more detail that could be added in describing the process of preparation. But it is time to get on with the story proper. The temptation to elaborate, especially about the time I was spending with Monty, is one that I will have to control. This was the first time in my life that I had felt like this about anyone and had not believed that such depth of feelings were possible. She was bright and clever and sexy and silly and fun and absolutely gorgeous.

A week before departure we were at my apartment in London and I was getting up to make a belated breakfast for us. My question, "How would you like your eggs done" was followed by her usual response which was "fertilized please" and then "OK, fried please," so I padded downstairs in my dressing gown. We had had our 24 hour 'naked day' in the flat the previous week, but I had never possessed any pyjamas, so I was better dressed than usual. I put the kettle on to boil and started the eggs. Monty came down in a splendidly silly all-in-one multicoloured 'romper suit' which was her preferred alternative to a dressing gown, and promptly put the tea cosy (the one my mother had made by hand and insisted I use to 'brew' tea) on her head. She then sat at the breakfast counter facing me, with her hands up in front of her like a dog, and said "breakfast please" which she followed with a panting sound with her tongue out. I realised I loved her completely, absolutely and completely. All of a sudden I did not want to go. I did not want to leave this woman, ever. Even for that once in a lifetime, unrepeatable, unique trip that no one else would ever have the chance to do.

But, hey ho, I was a twat, and stupid enough to go anyway.

After the run along the downs I headed slightly south of north west, up towards the Gloucester area. I hoped that it would not be too difficult to find now that the landscape below me was so different. At top speed, even fully loaded I could do about 80mph, so the journey was only going to be just over an hour. I eventually took the microlight, which was now officially named 'Loofah', up to its maximum safe altitude of about 10,000 feet. I suppose technically it should have been called Loofah (3 and a half), as Loofah (1) had been used for practice, and all those reconnaissance flights. Loofah (2) had been used for spares, some of which were now strapped on the side boards along with my kit, and Loofah (3) had had its frame swapped for Harry Gill's modified one, three days before the flight. The modified frame had been tested with the rest of Loofah (2) during preparations for the time-trip, from an airfield in the south of France. I had hoped that the 'flight and fire' practice we had down there would go unnoticed, and it had worked. Up here, at 10,000 feet, a mile and a half from the ground, I would be only a speck seen from below, and the noise of the engine would be hard to hear, especially if there was a moderate wind down at ground level. At this height it was surprisingly cold, and I could tell that the air was considerably thinner. But I knew it was still quite safe for me, from my skiing and climbing trips I suffered virtually no altitude sickness below 15,000 feet. Still, in my glorified shopping basket it still felt like a bloody long way up.

During the hour run up to Gloucester my mind wandered quite a bit. The fascination at seeing the landscape below me, completely transformed from the one I had seen a number of times on those practice runs, started to fade when I got to the stage where I had absolutely no idea exactly where I was, and could not work out what bits of the modern landscape would eventually be superimposed on which bits of the greenery below. There was no Reading, no M4, no Swindon. My mind wandered to Monty, and how I felt about her. In all my life I had met only one other woman I had believed I could have spent the rest of my life with, and she had turned out to be a rather clever gold digger. I have sufficient vanity in myself, (well plenty in fact), and an even more sufficient conviction of my soon to be ex's limited thespian qualities, to believe that it had not all been acting. So Monty was a true revelation. I had to admit to myself that I loved her. The last thing that I had given her was a letter, along with a copy of my latest will. The letter was mostly in poem form, and at last it declared my love, and it was the first time I had ever actually said it to her. I was already missing her, and I had been in 831 barely four hours.

The first few minutes after arrival had been taken up with getting over some considerable nausea caused by the drop through the worm hole. I threw up a bit, and then felt quite a lot better. The 'sledge' with all my kit on, was about six feet wide, and 12 feet long. The nose and underside of the sledge had a sort of stiff corrugated cardboard outer layer, of about nine inches thickness, that collapsed on impact, and this was glued over a layer of inflated rubber ribs. I had been sitting in a seat shaped harness, strapped amongst the equipment near the back of the sledge. As anticipated I dropped only a couple of feet, and the buffer on the front of the sledge, combined with soft soil and a couple of small bushes, took all the impact out of the landing. Yet the disorientation I experienced convinced my body that I had just bungee jumped from somewhere up in the outer atmosphere.

The sledge was mainly wood, and designed to rot away in a few years. I spent about two hours constructing Loofah, followed by a good three quarters of an hour strapping all my kit onto it, and making various checks. I had arrived on the North Downs, and there was plenty of room for me to take off from a slightly bumpy slope only 50 metres from where I dropped through the worm hole. This had of course been what we had hoped for, but it turned out to be even better than expected. I had anticipated ferrying the separate parts of Loofah a distance of up to half a mile to get to the more open 'down land', and a good take-off point. I even had a small collapsible wheelbarrow for the task. As it was, my 'runway' was still rather short, because of a number of significant trees on the steep slope below. Trees whose upper canopy was at eye level with Loofah as he slowly took shape. I know most vessels are given a female gender, but with a name like Loofah, Monty had insisted it had to be male.

Anyway, despite the trees, the slope down towards them was sufficiently precipitous, and with the engine flat out I was sure to have enough lift to get clear. I knew where I had arrived in terms of the geography, and there was supposedly no habitation for a few miles in any direction. But I wanted to get into the air as soon as possible, and get a good view of what the dark ages landscape looked like. Over the trees below me I could just see the flood plain of a small river, which would eventually be called The Mole, as it wound its way along the valley below me. Beyond that I could see a procession of ridges, starting with a thickly wooded hill about a mile away, then others, each lighter and fainter than the last, until a faint line on the horizon, probably some 20 miles away, which had to be the South Downs.

I wanted to get somewhere I felt safe before I spent time playing around with some of the hidden aspects of the microlight. As I have said, I had made some interesting adjustments to Loofah that I wanted to get to play with, and from those unusual military contacts I had made over the years, I had been able to bring some rather inappropriate bits of kit.

So it was only about three hours after arriving in the year 831 that I went through another belly-swooping experience as I dropped off the North Downs and then pulled Loofah out into the open air, scraping through the top leaves of a large oak. As I climbed through the air I could feel the microlight as it thrummed under my hands. My knuckles were white with the force of my delighted grip. It was bright midday and the ridge of the broken forest of the North Downs slid alongside me like the furry back of some sleeping monster. The air was crisp, and I felt as if the world was mine! I knew I should be flying a bit higher, after all I did not want to create too much of stir until I was a great deal further south west. But I could feel the ridiculous grin on my face that did not seem to want to go away, and the Z450 swept along like a majestic medieval dragon, its shadow five hundred feet below me jumping from tree to tree.

I was pulled from my reverie by the recognition of the steep valley down which the A417 would eventually run near Birdlip. It was in front of me to my left, which was excellent news, and told me I was only slightly off line for Gloucester. I swung the nose of Loofah to the west and there below me in the distance was the town, strikingly identified by the visible lines of Roman construction still showing through the gradually consuming amorphous sprawl of ninth century Saxon occupation. I turned south and then east, looking for the Roman road that should run below me towards

Cirencester. I realised I had flown virtually directly over Cirencester without even looking down. The place had an ancient amphitheatre and everything. I would need to be very careful that I did not simply get lost up here.

I spiralled down and down until there it was – a dark line with visible habitation along sections of the road, it was still clearly the main thoroughfare into Gloucester from the east. I could see the track towards the old Roman villa leading to the north and made a decision to find a safe place to land, and get myself sorted out. Flying away from habitation I stayed to the eastern side of what was probably the original flood plain of the river Severn. There was a low wooded hill in front of me with open pasture beyond. I could see a few goats, and the ground looked pretty even. Swinging in from the west I dropped Loofah down to his stalling speed, which was a mere 25 miles per hour, and touched down on his oversized rubber wheels. The landing impressed even me. I taxied the microlight about 100 metres, stopping under a large thickly leafed tree. The goats were nowhere to be seen, and when I turned the engine off there was a blissful silence, interrupted only twice by the distant bleating of those swiftly retreating ungulates.

The first thing I wanted to do was to get some of those extra bits of kit out. I had seen that there was no nearby habitation, so I started by unpacking the shotgun, and checking it was loaded with the 'bean bag' shot. I also put a can of CS gas in my pocket and a 'thunder-flash'. Leaving the shotgun within arm's reach, I moved the bags from one of the purple topped runner boards that ran along both sides of the cockpit. These boards, when loaded, where what looked like the thighs of the dragon, giving it the appearance of a bird in flight. They were where my equipment was strapped into place during air travel. They were both about one and a half metres long, and three quarters of a metre wide. At a thickness of about four centimetres they were supposed to have a honeycombed internal structure to give them rigidity and strength without being too heavy, but the left hand one now secretly contained about 40 litres of something similar to napalm. Thanks to Harry the tubular frame of the microlight had an interesting bit of alternative construction in the two main supports that ran down to the nose of the craft. Both had thick plastic plugs that could be removed from what were effectively the barrels of my secret weapon. At the pilot's end of both of these supports there was a long thin chamber that could hold about a half a litre of this strange napalm-like liquid, and both could be pressurised with a small pump to about six atmospheres. At that pressure, when a tube was opened, the liquid would squirt out in front of and below the craft, and ignite into an impressive ball of flame. I had to be flying quite slowly when I did this to avoid ending up engulfed in the fireball myself. I had even managed to cause some 'difficult to explain' damage to parts of my dragon (Loofah 2) during practice runs a couple of months ago in one of the valleys of the Pyrenees. This liquid was very dangerous stuff. If I was stupid enough to crash Loofah 3 in 831, and in doing so manage to crack that running board, I would turn myself, my kit and the microlight, into a very expensive kamikaze fireball. Still the 'Harry Gill' running board had been re-designed of some other tough stuff, and although now almost completely hollow, it was compartmentalised but still very strong indeed.

The liquid was fashioned to ignite on contact with the air. If it was poured into an open pot it would burn like a lit can of petrol, but would not explode. By blowing it out of the front of the microlight the whole ball of spray would ignite like a fire-eater's display. It wasn't napalm, which sticks to anything and slowly burns through flesh, as we just wanted to frighten and amaze the populace, not exterminate it. We had tried experimenting with a liquid that needed to be lit on the way out, like a flame thrower, but it was hard to fit the pipe work for the trigger flame without causing suspicion. It was also difficult to use the whole tubular frame as a sort of continuous tank for the liquid, and hence I was obliged to fill those two tubular chambers before every dragon 'burn'. All that said, and despite how dangerous the liquid was, I was well pleased with the results. The ethics committee had only allowed me to use a pyrotechnic type of smoke canisters with ring-pull ignition to give the impression of fire from Loofah the dragon's mouth. To me it seemed not only naff, but a bit Heath Robinson to have four lengths of cord leading from the canisters in their four sets of clips at the front left side of Loofah's mouth. These ran through simple wire eyelets into the floor of the cockpit. The smoke only squirted a couple of feet out, and down, making it look as if I was flying a dragon with a bad smoking habit. I had decided 'bollocks to that' and now, thanks to Harry, had a beast that really did breathe fire.

This left hand running board had five hidden nozzles, for five separate compartments. Each compartment contained about eight litres of the fluid. Two of the cans of spare diesel fuel I was carrying were designed very differently from all the others. Although they looked like smaller versions of the rest, they could also be used to carry the 'fire liquid', and had tubes that could be attached to enable me to safely drain it off a compartment at a time. I took one of these, and emptied the diesel it contained into Loofah's 120 litre tank. I then attached the can up to the middle of the five compartments and drained out the first eight litres of Loofah's fiery breath. 10 minutes later both of the fire chambers were full, and pumped up to pressure. The 'fire liquid' container, with seven litres still in it, was packed back onto the left runner board with a piece of red cloth tied through the handle, and a big cross scratched into the paint each side. If I was stupid enough to try to put that stuff in Loofah's tank by mistake, I would almost certainly remain in 831, or at least my ashes would.

I then went to work on the other running board. This one had to be completely unloaded. I was briefly interrupted by one of the goats returning, but it bleated and ran when I threw a stick in its direction. This running board contained my pride and joy. I had only been allowed to bring the shotgun, with a range of pretty non lethal ammunition, for personal protection. After all, I did not really count stuff like the CS gas. But in the running board I had a high quality rifle! The weapon was a semi automatic 762 FN rifle. They used to be the standard weapon of the British army before they made the mistake of changing it to the smaller 556 to please the Americans. The 556 was supposed to be just as good, but it was nothing like the 'man stopper' that the 762 was. In fact the army retained the General Purpose Machine Gun (GPMG) which fired the 762 round, as it gave them a weapon that could still be used at a range of 3,000 metres, which was something the 556 simply could not do.

My FN rifle was brand new, with a lightweight plastic stock. The weapon, with 200 rounds of 762 ammunition, filled nearly one third of the space in the right running board. It would enable me to take on any threat, and also do a bit of real hunting. I had fantasized about finding an Auroch, an ancient giant wild ox. There were supposed to be such beasts still around in Britain in the ninth century. At over two metres tall and a ton in weight, it would be a real challenge, and I would be the only modern man ever to hunt one. The last Auroch died out somewhere in Eastern Europe some 400 years ago. (Or in 800 years in the future from now, if you want to be pedantic).

So you can have some idea of how pissed off I was when I opened the cunningly hidden lid of the right running board, and my bloody rifle was not there! That's right, not fucking there!!!!!!!

Someone had put some other items of kit in the moulded spaces for the rifle and ammo, including a sawn-off shotgun that looked surprisingly like the remains of one of my double barrelled Remingtons. On top of this extra unwanted crap was a small square envelope with nothing on the outside, and it was not even sealed down. The card inside had a picture of a lover's heart on the outside, presumably supposed to be a human heart, and not that of a BLOODY AUROCH. It read;

My darling Bill, (Dick Dastardly)

I have grown to love you so dearly over the last few months. In fact it would be fair to say that the time I have been with you has been the best ever for me. I do not want to lose you, and even if you come back and decide you do not want to be with me, I will still love you forever.

Because of this I have done a terrible thing. I have taken the gun, and replaced it with a few things that might be useful. I know that the gun greatly increased the risk that you would change the future too much. To prevent that, 'time' (or whatever it is), would probably solve this conundrum by stopping you, which means killing you. I would do anything to prevent that.

I know you will be cross with me, please don't be. I hope you will forgive me.

Please come back safe.

I love you,

Monty (Penelope Pitstop) xxxxx

Well, she was right, I was bloody angry. There were only a couple of other people who had any idea about the rifle, and none of them had anything to do with the overall plans for the trip. They had provided the weapon, or ammunition, or built the customised running board. But the only person who knew everything about my intentions was Monty. She had been the only one I had fully trusted, and look what she had done to me. I stood, and shouted, and then kicked the side of Loofah so hard that the nose moved sideways. It also twisted my ankle. Fucking idiot! Fucking women! Fuck, fuck, fuck!

It took me a good five minutes to calm down. The fact that she had done this because she loved me was slowly seeping through my somewhat impervious cranium.

There were various items Monty had added to fill the spaces in the running board. Everything from additions to my already complete first aid kit, to extra ammo for the shotguns, a number of CDs and a spare Verey pistol with magnesium flares. I suppose I was just still very annoyed at losing the rifle, but I packed some of the bits of kit I would not need, including the collapsible wheel barrow, into one of the smaller kit bags. I tossed them onto the ground some distance away and set up the simple defence perimeter around Loofah ... I was still fuming ... what about the bloody Aurochs!

The defence perimeter was something I had worked on quite hard over the last few months, and had a few arguments with the ethics committee over it. I was not allowed to protect myself, or Loofah in my absence, with anything deadly, so the use of something like a Claymore mine was out of the question. A Claymore weighs in at one and a half kilos, and sprays 700 small pieces of lethal shot a couple of hundred metres. Sadly my suggestion for a much smaller version still seemed to upset them, but what the eye does not see the heart does not grieve, eh! We settled on a number of (official) layers of defence. On the sides on the microlight were small movement sensors, a bit like the alarm sensors in a house. They covered the area around Loofah with two separate systems, one ranging out about 50 metres, the other about 10 metres. When a large object/animal came within 50 metres there were bright lights that would come on as if the craft was waking up, and a deep voice would warn anyone approaching to go away or they would be attacked. (The voice spoke in ancient Saxon, as well as Celtic Welsh of course.) This voice became louder as anything moved closer, or stopped if they moved outside of the 50 meter range. If anyone came within 10 metres the second system cut in and there was a shrill screaming siren device triggered. This was so loud as to be very painful to the ears, and really was quite unbelievably terrifying. The cockpit could also be locked. I had a secret extra system which could deliver a very serious electric shock to anyone touching the craft's frame, but I did not bother to set that one. All of these systems were battery operated, and were re-charged when Loofah's engine was running. As well as these I had over a dozen extendable trip wire devices that could be set up to trigger thunder-flashes or other, non lethal pyrotechnical devices I had been permitted to bring. I had, of course, a number of those more lethal items, which I should not have had with me, hidden in the running board alongside WHERE MY BLOODY RIFLE SHOULD BE! which could be set off by these trip wires as well.

I did not think the trip wires or electric shock options were needed. So with a map and compass in my hand, I pointed the small device, like the ones used to lock a car with, at Loofah. I pressed the three buttons in succession to lock the cage, and set two of the onboard systems and a small red light winked at me to tell me everything was set. I picked up the shotgun, shouldered the kitbag, and set off northwards.

I reckoned that I was about a mile from the departure site, but it turned out to be closer to two. There were animal pathways through the woodland, and I saw the remains of a small fire at one point. It was not until I got quite close to the Roman road that I saw real evidence of human habitation. I remember Privet Hedge telling me how sparse the population was when you were travelling across country. I heard a horse and cart in the distance, and saw an item of clothing, probably some sort of child's smock hanging over the lowest branch of a tree. I reached the road, and taking a bearing from the escarpment above, I set off west towards Gloucester. The cart came into view pulled by a barrel bellied, shaggy haired pony. Walking alongside the beast was a short and dirty looking man with bow legs and a rolling gait. We met just before I reached the point where the lane, leading to the old Roman villa, intersected with the road. He clearly thought I was both very strange, and a threat. We had taken great lengths to make sure my clothing was suitable for the time. But I suppose I was bigger than most, healthier than most, and obviously cleaner than probably anyone he had ever seen. I also had what he probably saw as a very weird looking, partly metallic, club-like stick hanging over one shoulder. With information from the previous travellers I knew the accent I had was at least understandable – if a little strange to their ears – so I greeted him with a friendly smile and a few words about his magnificent beast. He responded with a nod and a smile, and a comment about the hill he was about to climb. I wished him well and turned into the villa, waiting there until he had walked out of sight. It suddenly struck me ... I had just had my first interaction with someone from 831. I had just spoken to someone who died over a thousand years before I was born!

The lane to the villa gave me a very good reference point, and at last I could see the overlay of the present and past at the same location. The trees would go, the road would change, but the shape was still there.

I attached a small device to a tree on the corner by the villa entrance, and set off with the compass. Stepping over a shallow ditch at the south side of the road I started pacing out the same distance that I had done a dozen times in 2006. There were some small trees in the way, but none of the fences and stone walls that would eventually be there. I paced out the right distance, and then dropped the kit bag and started using a device that could tell me exactly how far I was from the villa entrance. At 407.5 metres from the entrance I walked east and then west looking at another small device that was trying to locate a large piece of iron-rich sedimentary rock that was probably part of the terminal moraine from the last but one ice age. This stone block was about 20 metres across and a metre deep under the soil. In fact I could see a small area of bare rock in the centre of the clearing. I had stood here nearly 1200 years in the future, and knew that by then the sandstone would be under about three foot of soil. This was my last marker. I had found it within a few minutes. The worm hole would be opened directly above this rock. I went back and collected the kit bag, and stood on what was, as far as I could tell, the exact spot, within a couple of paces, of where I would, in three and a half weeks, jump back into the future.

It was a relief! It had been as easy as I could possibly have hoped for. I took a small axe from the bag and cut a small piece of bark from the three trees that effectively surrounded the clearing that was the return point. I also took another small electrical device with a spike on it and tapped it gently, with the back of the head of the axe, into the nearest tree as high as I could reach. It looked like a small knob of wood, and therefore part of the tree. The second button on my range marker gave me distance and direction to that tree from over a mile away. I could find the right spot for my departure in thick fog, complete darkness, or driving snow. Having done this I felt a bit better, and set off south. I soon found an old oak with a massive branch that had been broken off in a storm. The enormous limb was almost a third of the tree itself, and now lay amongst thick brambles as its twigs and smaller branches started to succumb to rot. The ragged stump of the limb still stuck out from the tree some 12 feet above the ground creating a hollow between it and the two other main stems. I clambered up using a small bough which stuck out horizontally some eight feet from the ground and stashed the kit bag in the hollow. The bag contained most of the excess equipment I would not need, as well as a small set of emergency gear to cater for all possible eventualities at departure time. Along with the bag there was also the redundant folding wheelbarrow. I had wrapped the kit bag in a green plastic sheet so that it fitted snugly into the hole, and would stay dry. I left the ranging device on the tree by the villa, as it was as innocuous as the second one and would probably never be noticed, and if it did, no one would have any idea what the hell it was. It was, of course, also a useful back up in case something happened to the tracker sited at the departure point.

I got back to the microlight in a good mood, and was suddenly reminded that my bloody rifle was not there. In fact it was not anywhere! It was 1200 years in the bloody future! I set off the alarm system before I realised I had got too close to Loofah, probably because I was getting pissed off again just thinking about my gun. I turned off the growling voice telling me to go away in Saxon. I remember saying "Fuck off! You are only a machine ... and a machine without my fucking rifle on board."

I took the time to eat the last of my modern day sandwiches from their Tupperware box and drink the best part of a litre of mineral water. Then, with Loofah fully loaded, I was preparing to stash the shotgun down beside the pilot seat when one of the goats made a noise behind me. I turned, startled, gun raised, and then after a moment of deliberation I fired the shotgun at it anyway. Just out of spite. Not a nice thing to do, and the poor creature was bowled over as the bean bag struck it on the rump with a 'smack' sound that mingled with the noise of the discharge. The poor beast scrambled to its feet and set off at a hobbling run, making a plaintive bleating sound. As I said, this was not a nice thing to do. My only mitigation, other than the general one of me being a bit of a shit in those days, was that I was still thinking about that bloody rifle!

I had flown a little west of south, keeping the river Severn below me as my guide. I needed to find somewhere to sleep, and although I would have been happy enough hiding out, and camping in woodland, I saw no reason why I should not take advantage of the comfort of human habitation. Besides I needed to start taking some of that valuable video footage to go with my public speaking opportunities.

From the widening estuary of the Severn I was probably somewhere over Bristol when I remembered that I should have buried one of those historical evidence things at the recovery point. It was a piece of impregnated oak, with a number of items imbedded in it, all sealed inside with epoxy resin. One of them was something to do with an experiment on long term decay rates for the building industry, if I remember rightly. Still, the piece of oak was in the kit bag in the tree, so as long as I got there with an hour or so to spare I could still bury it as I was supposed to have done.

Chapter Six;   Kadbury.

I have spent all my adult life with an excess of confidence, and a complete belief in my own abilities. I was advised, in no uncertain terms, to steer clear of anyone seeing me with the microlight on the ground. Although caution in this and many other things had been drummed into me, and I was supposed to avoid confrontational contact at all costs, I had decided that I would probably be as scary to most people as I had been to the man with the cart. I wanted to get down near to Cornwall before I started to buzz villages, so when, after about 40 minutes, the coast started to angle away westwards, I stayed inland, and continued on the same bearing, heading for the south coast somewhere near Exeter. After about another 20 minutes, with the coast visible in the distance, I started to lose height, looking for habitation and somewhere to land.

I decided not to buzz the village I saw below me, as I did not want to be attacked by terrified locals who might decide not to run away. So I dropped down close to a river, which I later found out to be the River Exe some eight miles north of Exeter, which in those days was called something like 'Exanton'. I was about a mile and a half east from the village I had seen, and below me was the wide, flat flood plain of the Exe with the river meandering back and forth across it. Marshland with startled birds rising off it in every direction rushed by as I headed up the steep western slope towards the top of a hill that must have stood 700 feet above the river valley. Ahead of me was another hill with a flat open top surrounded by an embankment and woodland, so I hugged the canopy as I dipped down to my left towards the village.

The village was visible beyond a wooden building that looked different from the rest. I bought Loofah down into a shallow dive, taking him behind a coppice of trees, the other side of a narrow valley and out of sight of the village. Selecting an open piece of ground, that looked as if it had sheaves of harvested grass sitting neatly on it, I started to land. I suddenly decided that I needed to test the flame liquid, and scare anyone seeing me touching down into running away. Besides it seemed like a good idea at the time. I pulled up away from the ground and selecting a sheaf of grass near the edge of the field, I tried to hit it with the ball of flame from the right hand tube. I missed because I was higher than I thought, and having not tried to fire the flame at a target I got the timing wrong. Still, I was well pleased with how the fireball hit the ground and sort of spread out to a doughnut of flame thirty feet across. The flame went out in barely a second, but firing it onto the ground worked surprisingly well. I circled to see the effect, but could only see faint whispers of smoke from the slightly charred grass and leaves.

I landed near the top of the field and rolled Loofah under the overhanging branches. I positioned the craft in a small clearing so that I could set out four short wooden posts with steel spikes on the bottom. I positioned these about 20 feet away from Loofah so my dragon was surrounded. I then fitted on these posts four of the unauthorised devices I had bought with me. These would provide a real deterrent for even a determined dragon slayer. I put the three bags containing the most valuable and vulnerable kit into the cockpit and closed the lid. I put the portable video system in my backpack, attaching the shoulder camera to the clip on the top of my right shoulder strap. I then picked up the cartridge belt for the shotgun, and tied it round my waist below my woollen tunic, and over the linen one. We had discussed the untimely use of cotton in a country clothed in wool and leather, but in my view I had paid handsomely for the right to wear something a little more comfortable.

I was wearing woollen trousers that felt rather warm now that I had landed. I had already removed the thick pilot's coat, hat and gloves. These had been essential for the high flying, but were too out of place, and too hot, down on the ground. The backpack was hessian on a wooden frame, and apart from the tiny camera on the shoulder strap, was supposed to look quite normal for 831. I slid the shotgun into a leather bag that was designed so that I could hold it in my hands with the barrel just out of sight at the open end, whilst I could keep a finger on the trigger through a hole in the side of the bag. The shotgun was a pump, rather than semi auto, to reduce the risk of 'stoppages', but I was able to work the action with my other hand just by gripping the forend over the leather and pulling backwards on the weapon's slide bar. This would briefly expose the end of the barrel through the open end of the bag. If I worked a cartridge into the chamber I had a capacity of six shots, more than enough for my needs.

I walked down the hill and into some woods that hid a stream at the bottom of the valley. A couple of large stones provided a way to cross without getting my feet wet, and I set off up the steep hill towards the village. I saw a man hiding above me, near the wooden building, so I turned on the video, and carrying the shotgun nonchalantly in one hand, I sauntered up to edge of another small field, and towards my first proper interaction with a resident of the year 831.

As I approached the man remained cowering behind a large piece of a tree that was set above the ground on logs. I called out to him, saying there was no need to be scared. He replied in understandable, but accented Saxon –
"You must be a great lord, great enough to know that we are but a poor village. Please do not harm us, we are simple folk. We have little money, and nothing worthy of food for your flying beast."
"The flying beast is called a 'dragon'," I said, "but if you leave it alone it will do you no harm. Tell no one that it is there, you must keep his sleeping place a secret, or it will eat you alive."
He then sort of whimpered and turned to run away. I said
"No, wait! I will do you no harm. I only need shelter and food. I can pay for it."
He stopped and tuned again, clearly terrified. I said, "My name is Bill, Bill Marlin." I then paused, not knowing what to say next, but eventually came out with the somewhat lame "so what is your name?"
With a stammering voice he replied "I am called Eathelwold. I am now a monk, and I have taken the Christian name of James. I look after the souls of the people of this village. Please do not harm us."
"I have no intention of harming you, or anyone else. I am just a computer wizard who is a very long way from home. In the place where I live there are many beasts that fly in the air. My dragon will not harm you."
He gradually recovered some courage, and eventually said
"Greeting then, Lord Maerlin of Pewter, I will take you to the head of our village." I corrected him, saying "'Computer wizard' is a better description, but it is not important... perhaps you should just introduce me as the 'Dragon Lord'."
Yes, I know, arrogant twat or what! But in a mitigating afterthought I

decided this would be a good way to prevent anyone challenging me, as well as it possibly triggering future stories about dragons. Besides, I have always rather liked people to be a bit in awe of me!

"Tell them that I am the one who can make the dragons fly. Who but a great wizard could do that for them, eh!"

We walked up the hill, to the village. There were about ten buildings I would describe as houses, with roofs of dried grass or reeds, and solid wooden walls. Some had panels of mud plastered over a lattice of wood. There were places where stout wooden uprights showed through at the corners of the buildings, and others where dried mud had crumbled off so that the wattle of the wooden lattice panels became evident. On the far side of the brown patch of earth in the middle of the huts were two slightly larger buildings. One of them had a visible glowing fire showing through a wide barn doorway. There was a silence in the village that suggested that someone had seen my arrival, and that everyone had now run away.

It took a good half an hour to get most of them back again. James had to stand beside me in the middle of the village, calling out again and again that all was well, and that they would come to no harm. Eventually there were more than thirty people who had returned to what could best be described as a hamlet. Many were standing around us as I was formally introduced to the head of the community. He was called Smith and was the man who worked iron for the other villages in the area. It was his smithy that stood at the far side of the muddy community plaza, and the stack of charcoal at the side of the building was covered with animal hides and weighed down with stones. He was about my age, but possessed rather fewer teeth. His work had given him a muscular wiry look, and his short beard was prematurely grey. His son was a tall, broad faced blond boy, of about 17 years. He was already developing his father's physique, and stood a good six inches taller. His blond hair made him look different from the rest of them, but I later found out that this was due to his mother being a Danish woman purchased by his father 20 years earlier. Eric Smithson had a broad, high cheek-boned face, with the first growth of hair light on his heavy jaw. He looked intelligent and capable beyond his years. He was someone who I took an instant liking to, and when I took his hand I had no idea that the future had such strange plans for us.

I spent that evening in the other larger building in the village. It was the house of the Smith and his son. It was one big room, or hall, which was also occupied by the three younger daughters of Smith, a female slave (who apparently provided Smith with his night-time 'entertainment') two dogs, one horse, and an unknown number of farmyard fowl. The fire in the centre of the room filled the rafters with smoke that seeped out through the thatch into the cool night air. From the moment had I walked into the centre of the village with James the monk, the all pervading sensory issue for me was that of smell. The farmyard smell of stale urine was everywhere, and inside Smith's home was no different. The only thing was that, by the time I went to sleep on a bed of hay, covered in slightly mouldy animal skins, my nose had just got sort of used to it. Well, if I was going to experience 831 properly I had no choice but to get used to it. There was an ameliorating effect from the fire in the centre of the hall, which seemed to reduce the power of those other smells. Perhaps the smoke actually took some of the adverse odours with it as it rose to the roof before making its surreptitious exit. It did occur to me that in bad weather, if they had had any sort of chimney hole, it would have been a bit of a problem.

I had spent the hours since landing turning the video on and off at appropriate times in attempt to skip the boring bits and save both recording capacity and battery. I had probably got some good footage from the introductions when villagers had returned after their initial scattering, and my imperfect Saxon seemed to be understood well enough. I had been invited by the Smith into his home for the night. He was the head of the community as he was the only real skilled artisan. During the evening I had seen three older women working leather at the corner of one of the houses. They were making items of clothing, sewing the skins together with a waxy thread. I asked them what they were making, and they said coats for the coming winter. I could see all of them were holding their sewing at almost arm's length, trying to see as well as they could, despite the fading light.

My eyes were starting to go a bit themselves, so I could empathise with these 'crumblies'. There was a compact set of cheap spectacles in every bag I had with me, as well as two, very expensive, pairs of prescription spectacles for reading. I had no intention of being caught without being able to see things close up on my travels. I suppose all those years reading computer screens were not the best thing for my eyes. But for the sake of posterity, this interaction was fully recorded, and the camera was still rolling as I gave them a set of my cheap x2 folding glasses in a tube about the size of a cigar case. I showed them how to get them out of the case, open the arms, and then I gently placed them over the ears of a woman called Eowen, who was the one nearest to me. Sliding the arms of the spectacles under the lank grey hair that was tied back with a simple piece of cord, I explained as well as I could that they would help her to see. Eric Smithson, who was showing me around the village, added an explanation that I did not fully understand, but it was something to do with 'magic eyes'. The delight on the face of the old woman as she realised how they improved her vision made me smile. The villagers had become used to me now, and her two friends clamoured to try them on. I had to step forward and prevent them from grabbing them from Eowen's face so as to avoid the spectacles being torn apart. I understood them to be saying "Pass the eyes, pass the eyes," and it occurred to me that there would be an interesting analogy with something in one of a future famous bard's plays. So I made some suitably smart arsed comment, in modern English, for the sake of the camera, to entertain my future audiences. On hearing a strange tongue all three looked up at me, suddenly remembering that they were in the presence of a self confessed wizard, albeit a friendly one, and they subsequently went into a display of genuflective appreciation for the magic gift from 'Marlin the Great Wizard'... I was getting to like this stuff.

The meal that evening was a simple one, mainly of goat meat that I had watched them slaughter at the back of one of the houses. The goat had been strung up by its heels, and its throat was cut. The blood was collected in a pottery bowl, and I presume was used in some local recipe. Nothing was wasted. By the time I went to bed at the side of the hall I had a considerable amount of good video footage 'in the can'. I had been asked by them to tell stories of the land I came from, and it had been with considerable difficulty, especially considering the ale I was drinking, that I managed to concoct something that was a mixture of the truth, and believable fiction, which seemed to satisfy everyone. I told them tales of how I hunted dragons, and explained that only a great wizard could control them. I had very few things in my pack or pockets to amaze them with, other than the shotgun. But that was one secret I wanted to keep to myself. I did show them that I could produce fire in my hands at will, without burning myself, and without the use of flint and tinder. So a small plastic cigarette lighter, costing about 50 pence, became the key proof of my wizard's magic powers. I also had a small but powerful 'headlight' LED torch that I ceremoniously strapped around my forehead. I declared myself as having a magic third eye for hunting dragons in darkness, and in splendid theatrical style, I turned it on and lit up the crowded hall. There were at least twenty people in Smith's hall for the meal, and their startled, scared faces made great video.

By the end of the evening I still had about half an hour of recording time left, which I planned to use up in the morning before I flew on. I had had no intention of returning to Loofah for more tapes when it was not absolutely essential. I did not want anyone else knowing where my one and only means of transport was until I was good and ready to take off again.

I awoke about an hour after dawn. My later guess was that what the occupants of the village suffered that morning had been even worse for those villages closer to the river. Because the first thing I heard when I woke was screaming from outside the house and dogs barking wildly. There was a solid wooden door that had stood open all night, and the opening had been partly closed on that warm evening with a wooden frame stretched with an animal skin. This frame was flung aside and blonde Eric Smithson was there in the doorway shouting "NORTH MEN. NORTH MEN ARE HERE. RUN!"

I had slept in my under-tunic, and hurriedly started to throw the woollen one over my head when through the wall at the back of the house crashed a man. Well I assume he was a man. He looked massive, covered in chain mail and surrounded by a cloud of dust from the wall he had just barged through. The wattle frame had partly held together and fell away in front of him like a cardboard box being kicked to one side. He held a large round shield on his left arm, which caught momentarily on the side of the opening he had made before he was fully within the hall. A split second later a second of these monsters stepped into the frame of the doorway recently vacated by Smithson.

In a strange way time seemed to slow down and speed up all at once. Even now I struggle to piece the events together as well as I should. I started by thinking of running to the back of the hall, and moved two paces before I realised how stupid that would be. I turned and took those two paces back towards the bedding intending to pick up the shotgun that lay beside my discarded covers. Some sort of clock or measuring device was going on in my head, and I knew I did not have time to pick it up before I was struck by the Viking who had come through the back wall. Two of the Smith's three daughters were still in the room, but one had been caught by the wrist by the man at the doorway, and the other had disappeared behind a table covered in the bowls we had eaten from the night before.

I dived forward and rolled across the bedding area. The man behind me missed with his swinging blade and the one in front of me was holding the smock of the elf-like Eored, the youngest, in the balled fist of his shield hand. He had an axe with a head the size of a bloody dinner plate in the other one, which was now being raised. I was both terrified and calm at the same time. Just my bloody luck! Travelling back 1200 years to get killed after only one fucking day here!

The man in the doorway had long plaited hair that hung across his shoulder, and down his massive chest. He pulled Eored across in front of him in his left hand as he raised his shield awkwardly on his left forearm. I changed direction to my right and his raised axe could not be used as the edge of his shield, and the skin covered wooden frame, hanging lopsidedly from the edge of the doorway, were between us. I took hold of a large basket containing a goose-like bird and turning quickly I threw it at the man who was following me across the room after his entrance through the back wall. The basket seemed to explode in feathers and fell down in front of him still miraculously intact. By the time he had stepped round the basket I had grabbed the can of CS gas that I still had in my tunic pocket and knocked the top off with my thumb. I raised the can in front of me, pointing it threateningly. I could see the teeth of the dust covered giant as he grinned in a battle rictus of delight. He obviously saw me as no threat, and was going to enjoy taking my life. I was glad of those few moments, which seemed like whole minutes, as he slowly walked those few steps towards me, because I realised that I had originally raised the can with the nozzle facing off to my left. With my slightly trembling hands I adjusted the direction and then with my right forefinger held the button down.

The effect was not instantaneous, probably because my internal time appreciation system was still working at a completely different speed to the rest of the planet. The smile collapsed into a grimace with his whole face scrunched up behind the nose plate of his helmet. His sword fell from his right fist, then both his hands came up to his face, scrabbling and clawing at his helmet and eyes. As he dropped to his knees, his head down still pawing at his face, his helmet came off, and I realised that I was still spraying the can directly at the top of his head, so I swung it towards the man in the doorway. Luckily he was staring, wide eyed, over the top of his round shield, so as I turned the spray ran diagonally across it and into his eyes. This time I stopped spraying as soon as he started to collapse. Eored the Smithy's nine year old child, who had fallen to her knees under his shield when I had crossed in front of them, was suddenly released. I stood rooted to the spot for a few moments before she grabbed my tunic and started to pull me out of the doorway. From the entrance I could see two bodies on the ground in the middle of the village, and a number of people moving into the trees. I could hear shouts and screams, and suddenly remembered the shotgun. Dragging the girl, because she was still holding my tunic, back with me, I headed to the bed. I grabbed my pack and shotgun and set off out through the hole in the rear wall of the house without looking round. It occurred to me that I still only had socks on. It was not until I was outside, and 50 yards into the woods, that I realised that both girls had followed me, and my feet were hurting. We ran on anyway.

The woodland behind the house was very steep, shrouding the hillside above us below its open top which I had seen from the air. After getting well above the houses I set off to the left, north east, parallel to the hillside and, I hoped, away from danger. My guess is that we were less than a quarter of a mile from the village before we stopped. I was blowing hard, the extra weight of the bag and shotgun, and trying to run quickly with them in my hands, made my gait awkward. I had also had to be very careful where I trod, as branches and thorns were everywhere amongst the leaf litter under the trees. We had avoided the denser undergrowth, but by the time we stopped I knew I had injured my feet quite a bit. I sat down and pulled a couple of large thorns from my right foot. There were visible patches of blood showing through the wool. Rossanna, the older girl, who was about 12, got to her knees and started to tear the bottom off of her smock. She was saying something about me saving them. Like hell I did! But considering she was using half of her already meagre clothing to bind my feet, I kept quiet.

I needed something substantial on my feet, like boots, and there was now an overpowering urge to get back to Loofah and make sure that I could still fly out of here. Walking quietly and breathing heavily I headed north, down towards the roadway, if that is the right description of a wide muddy path that led back towards the village. I later discovered this was the main route between Crediton and Twyfyrde (two fords) and it ran along the north side of that open topped hill I had crossed when I had first arrived. The village lay along a muddy lane that ran from a T-junction with this Crediton road back towards the river estuary. I was on the side of the hill above this main road, and I needed to cross this thoroughfare twice to get back to the microlight. Telling the girls to keep quiet, something that was completely unnecessary as I was the clumsy loud one out of the three of us, we set off downhill to this path. With the pack now on my back and the cartridge belt on the outside of my woollen tunic, I hobbled down through the trees. From the safety of a large bush of thick foliage but unknown genus, we watched the path for a minute before trying to cross it. I was pleased we had done this, as after a few moments along the trail came two warriors mounted on horses and another on foot. The man on foot was holding the end of a piece of rope that was tied round the neck of the eldest of Smith's daughters who was about 14, and another woman of about thirty years of age. They were both dirty, and the older woman had a bruised and swollen face, so swollen on the left side that her left eye was completely closed. She had caked blood smeared across her chin and neck, and was walking with a pronounced limp. The oldest Smith girl, Esthelwan, had a long pigtail down to the small of her back and was walking oblivious to everything around her. She was just looking at the path at her feet and crying.

I felt a dig in the side of my ribs, and Rossanna 'Short Skirt' was beside me pointing at her sister as she was being led back to the village. She clearly wanted me to do something. But what the fuck was I supposed to do?! All

I had was a shotgun which fired bean bags, half a can of CS gas, a pocket knife and a thunder-flash. In my cartridge belt I did not have any of the real shot cartridges I had smuggled onto Loofah. I had a whole box full of real man stoppers in the rifle compartment on the microlight, but they were half a mile from where I needed them to be right now. Apart from eight bean bag cartridges, all I had in the belt were four rock salt and four CS cartridges. These were going to be fuck all use against someone wearing bloody armour! What was I supposed to bloody do? This was not supposed to be happening, fuck, fuck, FUCK!

I raised the shotgun – I knew I had five shots in the magazine, but for safety reasons did not have one 'up the spout'. I also knew that they were all bean bag shot, which would bounce off armour, and would probably not even knock a man over. I worked the action, and then in quick succession I fired a round at each horse's rump. The animals were twenty metres away, and the noise combined with the 'thwack' they each received had a dramatic effect on both of them. The one in front I hit first, and it set off at a gallop so fast that the rider dropped his shield and swayed back almost falling off as he disappeared in an explosion of hooves. The second reared up initially, before he followed his equine companion in equally impressive haste. During that process he lost his rider in a cascade of chain mail, leather, metal and flesh. The departure from his steed was clearly unexpected, and the fall was fully onto his back and left shoulder. I did not have time to see if he got up because I was aiming the gun at the man standing a mere ten paces from me, who seemed rooted to the spot. I fired at his face in the hope I would do some real damage. I must have been a few inches high as his helmet literally flew off his head and he staggered backwards, arms flailing as he tried to regain his balance, into a bush at the far side of the path. When he hit the bush he sort of bounced forwards back onto the trail. He had dropped the rope and his shield arm when I had fired, but I was watching him rather than reacting quickly enough, so he had his sword out of its scabbard and had recovered his shield before I worked the action and was ready to fire again.

I fired again at his head, but this time he seemed to expect it, and his head ducked behind his shield as I fired. I suppose, despite the noise and fear and surprise, he was a warrior used to defending himself instinctively. For most people in the ninth century I would have hoped the very noise of a shotgun would make them run for their lives. But this one didn't!

The bean bag is moving at the speed of a driven golf ball. The shot I was using was the most powerful that the ethics committee would allow me to get away with, but when the bean bag hit the edge of his shield, all it did was audibly bump the shield against his head and make him step back a pace. He did not seem to know what to do next, and stood rooted to the spot. By this time the two girls had rushed forward and were running with their sister, and the older woman, up the trail off to my right. They then dived left into the undergrowth on the far side of the track as I worked the action once again. I heard a groan from nearby as the man who had suffered such a messy dismount started to stir. The raised shield gave me an opportunity with the other raider from this distance, which I probably would not have had from closer in. I fired the last cartridge below that elevated shield, directly into his groin. The chain mail must have slowed the shot down quite a bit, but the effect was still very satisfying. He doubled forward, and then clutching at his bruised plums with one hand he sort of crawled under his shield with the other. I left him there trying to kneel behind the protection of his shield while his gut wrenching pain subsided. Despite my injured feet I set off after the women at a fine speed. A speed which I hope was sufficient to deter the two men behind me from bothering even to try to follow.

The other side of the pathway was almost as steep as the one we had just come down. Within a few paces I could hear the women in front of me. I caught up with them as they were trying to remove the ropes from their hands. They had already managed to get the rope off the neck of 'Pigtail' and both 'Elf' and 'Short Skirt' were desperately trying to release her hands. I grabbed the rope that was still around the neck of the older woman, 'One Eye', and set off down the hill as she was still trying the get her hands free. I kept going, splashing through a stream that was heading down the same hill as us, feeling the blessed cold sensation in my feet as I ran through the shallow water. We headed left along the slope and then across a narrow pathway, until I was sure we were not being followed, before I stopped and pulled the whole group into a small hollow on the hillside. There, as we recovered our panting breath, I used my knife to cut the rope from both Pigtail and One Eye. My feet were cold but hurting again.

When I had finished with the ropes, I reloaded the shotgun from the cartridge belt. For some reason I decided to put a CS one in first, followed by two rock salt. I then loaded three bean-bag cartridges, with one of them ready in the chamber. The women were whispering and crying, but they had a determination that impressed me. I told them that I was going to leave them, but they insisted on staying with me. So I set off at a hobble uphill with the intention of re-crossing the Crediton road to the west of the village. We managed to do this without being seen, although we heard a loud screaming in the distance that went on for a good 30 seconds before being cut off. I headed south, down through the woods and then skirted the fields on the slopes below and to the west of the village. I was heading back south east to the corner of the fields on the other side of their little community. A couple of times I walked down to the edge of the undergrowth to get my bearings. In places I could see across the valley to the houses above the chapel, but there was nothing, and no one, to be seen. From the hillside opposite, at this angle I could not even see those distant bodies which I assumed were still lying there in the middle of the village. Short Skirt and Elf suddenly ran off to our right, and returned with the priest and five villagers who had been hiding in the thicker vegetation above us. It was getting a bit crowded for me now, and I was becoming desperate to check if my microlight was still OK. I managed to persuade all of them to stay together while I went ahead. I pulled the priest to me and said to him. "I must check on the dragon, Loofah. It will sleep forever unless I awaken it. Just keep them here, and do not tell them it is my steed." He just nodded and continued to look terrified.

I crossed another stream and circled around to where I knew Loofah should be, working my way down towards it. From a hundred metres I could see the microlight sitting undisturbed in the clearing under the trees. The relief was almost overwhelming! I was alive, the means of getting back to my own life was here, and I would be safe. I had survived two genuine encounters with death although I suddenly realised that the video camera had been off all the time, so no-one in the 'future' would ever believe me. Fuck it! Who cares!

It took me less than five minutes to take down the perimeter equipment, clamber into the cockpit, and get airborne. I did not even take the time to find any footwear from the kit bags, so I flew with my cold feet wrapped in rags. I flew eastwards down the valley, and then left up to the main trail heading towards the river. Below me I could see groups of men on foot or horseback heading east, some were carrying things, others were leading prisoners. All of them scattered off the trail as I flew past. When I reached the river their two boats were moored against the bank. I swung south buzzing the boats, causing men to hide and run. I then turned the microlight round, and flew upriver, a mere 50 feet above the water, towards the vessels. I released the second fireball into the rigging of the nearest one with a satisfying roar as I climbed upwards. Turning left and westwards I looked down. The rigging and sail were smoking, but I could not see flames. I had hoped the bastards would have to row all the way home.

The Chronicles of Eathelwold 'James' Trefell; Monk.

Book 1 Chapter 1.

And it came to pass in the year of our Lord, eight hundred and thirty one, there was delivered unto us a great wizard. He was a most powerful wizard who travelled on the back of a dragon. He claimed that he was the guiding power, the brain of the dragon. He was therefore the head of the dragon, he was 'Pendragon'. Verily I say unto thee that this be the truth of my own eyes. I am a man of the cloth, devoted to the church, and have spent all my long years in the service of God. In the presence of him the great power over all, and as he is my witness, all that I say in this record of what took place is true. I beseech thee to listen and wonder.

I can only assume that as our Lord works in mysterious ways, it was he who hath sent the wizard unto us in the time of our need. The sorcerer was called Maerlin and in truth he came to us on the back of a great dragon. I witnessed the beast in flight myself, and I was in great fear. The dragon was a huge monster with flame for breath. The width of its wings was ten or twelve paces, its hide was so hard that no blade could penetrate, and when the wizard put it to sleep it slept so soundly that no man could waketh it, yet it slept with its eyes wide open, watching all. The dragon was named L'uther. I did not know of this at that time, but later heard the wizard speak of the creature by its name. I am the only person in the village that has the skill of the Frankish tongue and I believe that is whence it came, and why the creature's name is so. It must be known, so that if any person ever travels to the far land of dragons, that it was L'uther that carried Maerlin the wizard to us, and although L'uther was lost to us, we continued to be blessed with the Pendragon of L'uther. Does not the Lord work in ways of great wonder and mystery!

I had been in the crypt below our wooden church on the hillside above Caardbury when I heard the noise. It was a terrifying howl, more like the wolves that used to roam these parts but are now hard to find. I stepped into the sunlight to see the dragon throwing fire down at our crops. It was a terrible sight to my gaze. The beast travelleth through the sky slowly without even needing to flap his mighty wings, it was like a giant eagle, I could hear a child screaming. Then it turneth toward me. I stood rooted unto the spot. I was in the grip of fear. The beast growled with each breath it took, and reminded me that our Lord warns us of beasts that live in the underworld, where the unrepentant sinners will spend their eternity.

The creature landed on the pasture furthest from the village, only some two or three hundred paces from my church. It moved to the edge of some woodland bordering on the stream before it stopped growling and howling like the beast it was. I was greatly afraid, and dare not approach, but had remained close to the church near the pagan Yew we had downed. The quartered body of the tree, on the weathering logs, stood to a man's height above the ground and gave me good protection from the beast's breath. The wizard had climbed from the back of the beast, and strode toward me. I realised that the Lord had put me in that place at that time, and it was my responsibility to speak to the Dragon Rider. I need to find out what he wanted, and how I could preserve my reluctant flock.

I challenged him as he drew close. In truth I was still wary, and made my challenge from the safety of the quartered Yew. I asked him what he wanted from the poor folk of my village, and declared unto him that there was no gold here to feed his dragon. He responded by telling me his name, which was Maerlin. He said he was a 'Pewter Wizard', and just to behold him, I knew that he speaketh the truth. Why he said claim to be a wizard of the ancients metal I do not know, and have never truly found out. Verily I say unto thee that just to see this stranger, his clothing and his devilish steed spoke of this truth. Yet in the years since, I have seen such miracles of his magic as to convince all men, for all time, that Maerlin was truly the greatest of all wizards. I hope that I will not be judged as wanting in such matters, as a man of the cloth. But the Dragon Rider did not need to make that claim, for verily he hath proved to be the greatest of all wizards. He alone has shown me that the truth of our God is mixed with the truth of magic and the old Gods, and through my belief and love of God I have concluded that Maerlin was sent to us by the one true God for his own purpose. I also believe that Maerlin's denial of our Lord's intervention is merely a test, and that his heathen powers showeth us that our God controls both the old religion, and that of the true Christian faith. Amen.

The morning of the raid of the North Men was a time of terror, a time of judgement from our Lord. Many of the men in the village had taken more than one wife, and the Lord punished the men of the village by allowing the North Men to take two of their lives. He also punished women for their part in this heresy by taking three of their weaker sex from us. I do question his wisdom in taking two such young girls, but the Lord does work in mysterious ways, the Lord gave us Maerlin. It was his intervention, clearly driven by our Lord that prevented many more being taken. It was even he that blinded two of these Satan worshiping monsters from the cold lands, such that 'our Thor', a name I only use in jest, could take their blaspheming lives with merely the use of his hammer. How could this have happened without the Good Lord's intervention? There is no doubt in my mind that Maerlin was sent to us for this reason, to show us the way. It is my belief that Maerlin has no idea that he is God's instrument. It is also my belief that I was placed here in this small village for the Lord's purpose, not as the Abbott suggested, because of my behaviour, and my failure to cherish the words of the venerated Bede. It is my belief I had copied his work with great accuracy, and that the drawings I used to enhance his text were factual, from my own observations, rather than salacious.

Maerlin left our village on the morning of the raid. He left to chase the North Men away. It took him many days to chase them all the way back to their frozen lair in a far land. He left us upon his Dragon Steed named L'uther. Maerlin was truly the head, the master of the Dragon. He was Pendragon. It is my belief he named his Dragon L'uther because there is a meaning of a similar name in an old Frankish tongue which is 'fearsome'. There can be no truer name for such a beast. Yet when I spoke of these matters with the wizard he just smiled and said the name was given to the beast by his one true love, and he claims it is a name given to the beast when he was in a place of bubbling water, which will lack meaning unto others. But I do understand. They must have been baptising the beast in a river. Forsooth, in so naming his steed he was showing that the good Lord had a purpose for the beast, and that purpose was to place fear in the hearts of our enemies, to make them change from the old ways. The wizard may not have known this fully, yet we can but wonder at the power of our Lord.

I know the Lord wished us to defeat the old ways, and strike down the heathens. The signs of the pagan religion must be cast down, and it was I myself was the one that tamed the old Yew tree in the village, the one beside the chapel. I had been instructed to build the chapel by the tree to show we could live alongside the old ways. But I was eventually allowed to cut the tree down, despite the rituals they still wished to use it for. The leaves of the tree had killed three cattle when a branch had mysteriously fallen far from the tree and over the wall, into their enclosure. The Lord moves in those wonderful ways, and that tree, even in death, eventually saved our people from further ravages by the men from the north.

Chapter Seven;   The Return.

What happened over the next three weeks may be recorded at some time in the future. But for the present I will stick to the main, and what now appears to be relevant, detail.

In glossing over that time I feel obliged to say that I enjoyed myself considerably. Given the horrendous experience at the village I now know as Kaardbury, from then onwards I always carried a number of items for self protection when I left Loofah. I found a place high up on the moors, where no one seemed to go, and stayed there for over a week whilst terrorising village after village with my fire breathing monster. I was sure as hell going to make the legend work for me. Then I would travel on foot claiming to be a dragon slaying wizard. A couple of times I even flew low over a village standing in the cockpit so that I could be seen, waving a sword or axe about, trying to give the impression I had climbed onto the back of the monster and was fighting it in the air.

Then I would walk down and meet my admirers who would marvel at my bravery and shower food and gifts on me for ridding them of the monster. My feet recovered quickly with the precautionary use of antibiotics and my spare boots stayed on all night when I was sleeping under the hospitality of locals. There were a number of occasions I was offered the company of a young woman to warm my bed, but despite their charms, and my predilection for the activity they offered, I felt surprisingly constrained. I could excuse my failure to partake of these delights on the limited effort they had applied to improving their appearance and odour. I could even suggest that I felt constrained by my position of power rendering such union as inappropriate; just as a teacher shagging one of their pupils is extremely 'bad form'. But the truth of it is simpler, and even to those that knew me in my younger days, laughable. When I tried to hold one of these nymphs in my arms I could only think of Monty. I found I could not partake, because I had fallen completely and hopelessly in love with someone who would not be born for more than a thousand years.

But I did have great fun.... At one place I even challenged the local hard man to a fight. I insisted that we strip to the waist, and that we had one non-bladed weapon each. He had a fearsome looking club, and I had a Taser. I had imbibed quite a few drinks, and in retrospect this was a foolish risk to my own health. But he was very drunk and very obnoxious, so I felt justified. I was lucky. He felt so over confident due to the small size of my equipment (no surprise there then) that he walked up to me with arms spread wide, laughing. The Taser was so effective that he actually shit himself as he lay on his back performing a good impression of an electrically induced epileptic fit. My status went even higher, as he slunk off never to be seen by me again. I got so drunk that night I could not have induced the relocation of blood required to have achieved penetration of either the two women who tried to clamber on top of me, even if I had wanted to. And I definitely did not want to.

By the time I had only four days left before the worm-hole opened, I had used up three quarters of the fireball juice, and all but seven of the bean bag cartridges. I have to admit to a significant level of misbehaviour with the shotgun, taking delight in knocking over goats to impress kids, (sorry) or to induce significant bruising to the occasional peasant's posterior to the drunken delight of local dignitaries. By that time I had decided that I would return to Kaardbury before I went north to Gloucester. The dramatic events of that first morning still ran around in my head. I felt a strange guilt at leaving so suddenly without doing what I could to help. I felt that I had let them down, and that by going back I could pretend that I had had to leave to chase off dragons, or Vikings, or something. I did not want them to feel as if I had just run away. Anyway, I wanted to know how they were doing, and if Smithson and his father were still alive. I had plenty of fuel to get to the time-gate, and assuming the Vikings would not attack the same villages twice in a month, what was the risk?

I landed in the same place as I had done on that first day. This time I did not bother with any theatricals, and flew in to the top corner of the field as unobtrusively as possible. To my astonishment there were garlands of flowers hanging in the trees around where I had left Loofah last time. I got out and set up the usual defence systems, and could see that some of the garlands were withered, and some were very fresh. Did they think I was dead? Did they think that the dragon had carried me off?

90

I walked up into the village and was virtually mobbed! Eric Smithson and his sisters led what appeared to be everyone in the whole community as they embraced me. Some of the children ran up to me and touched my clothing, as if for good luck, before they ran off giggling. Elf, Pigtail and Short Skirt (now wearing a long one), seemed to think I was their possession, and stayed with me throughout the day. One of the first things I was shown was their father who was lying in the shade of a latticed awning beside his hall. He had been seriously injured in the attack, and a sword thrust had badly damaged his left thigh. He looked wasted and very ill, and on being shown the wound he was clearly now suffering from a significant infection. The wound was covered in cloth, which when removed caused a low moan from the subdued onlookers. The wound itself seemed innocuous enough. It was about four inches across and had been neatly stitched closed. But the whole thigh was the diameter of a basket ball, and had a horrible mottled purple colour with a pale fluid which seeped from between the stitches, sticking to the covering.

I had great difficulty in getting everyone to wait in the village while I went back for the first aid kit. The only way I got away was by allowing Father James to come with me. He was the one person who knew I had arrived on the back of Loofah on that first day, and I suppose I thought that as a man of the cloth I could expect him to keep his promise of secrecy. I left my backpack with the three girls and actually ran back down the hill through the woods and up to the microlight. I set off the alarm deliberately to scare the priest, before grabbing the first aid kit and returning to the others. Father James kept pace with me well enough, with his skirts flying round his knees. I have to admit to slowing to a walk for the last couple of hundred yards. I was reasonably fit, but it was a steep slope, and I had to wait for the priest, of course.

My knowledge of medicine is limited, but I gave the Smithy an injection of broad spectrum antibiotics as per the instruction I had been given during the short paramedics course I had been obliged to take before the trip. I left two of the villagers looking after him and sat down to eat some of the food that had been rustled up for me. During the meal, which I ate under the gaze of at least a dozen people, I found out what had happened during the raid.

91

Two of the villagers had died, and three were taken prisoner. There would have been at least two more if I had not intervened on behalf of One Eye and Pigtail. One Eye was demurely grateful, and despite significant blue and yellow colouring around one of them, clearly now had the requisite two eyes. Another prisoner had escaped where the Vikings had abandoned the trail when I had buzzed them after the attack. There had even been a report from one of the other communities, closer to the river, that the dragon had been seen trying to set fire to one of the Viking longships.

There were about ten small settlements in the hills to the west of the river, and the Vikings had rampaged though most of them that morning. Eight had died and fourteen were taken prisoner, many of them children. For the Vikings, as far as profit goes, it had probably been seen as a successful raid, as slavery was apparently their main money making business. Rape and pillage was more of a diversionary bonus. Having anyone fighting back was unusual. They had attacked up the river three times in the last five years, and with communities that just ran and hid, they had little to fear. This time, for probably the first time, they had had some actual losses. The two men I had sprayed in the Smith's hall had been killed by Eric Smithson with a forge hammer. His achievement was seen as something very special. These were hardened warriors wearing chain mail, and he had dispatched the pair of them single handed. He had tried to explain that he had attacked them in a fit of rage over the disappearance of his sisters, and the men he had slain were helpless on their knees at the time, but that was brushed aside by his admirers, and they had started to give him the nickname of 'Thor'. In one of the other settlements there had been another killing by a woodsman with his bow. Apparently he had killed one outright, and wounded two others before he had been obliged to flee.

That evening I stayed once again in the Smith's hall. This time I kept my boots on. The following morning one of the villagers bought my original footwear back to me. They had obviously been worn by someone with smelly, and dirty, feet. So I gave them back to him saying he could keep them with my blessing. Two other things happened that morning that were of considerable significance. One was that Smithy appeared to be improving already. The swelling was down and he was more lucid, so I started him on a course of oral antibiotics. I was questioned by the priest who claimed to be skilled at healing, although I was aware that the majority of such work was usually done by one of the older women. I tried to explain that in my country these pills were the 'holy grail' of medicine, and that so long as he took one of these pills three times a day for the next seven days, he would probably live. He promised me faithfully that he would administer the pills with his own hand – I was starting to like Father James.

The second thing that happened was that three people arrived from other settlements. They had heard of my return, and their distorted interpretation of my involvement the morning of the raid had given me celebrity status. They arrived to the excited yapping of the dogs that lived with the community. Whose dog was which was often not easy to ascertain, but the noise they made was an essential part of the village's early warning system. Interestingly, when I referred to them as dogs (or dogge) I was greeted with blank looks. There was apparently no word in Saxon that properly fitted this use. The word they called them back then was 'hound' or 'hund'.

These new arrivals wanted to thank me, and ask what I could do to protect them in the future. They came from communities north of the town of the Exe, and from west of the river of that name. I listened to them in grave silence, trying hard to avoid the questions about whether I would stay and help them. They wanted to know what to do about these raids, but I suppose telling them that they would have to wait for someone called 'Alfred the Great' to be born, which would be in about 20 years from now, would not be what they wanted to hear.

That evening four people were bought to the village from outlying communities. Two had injuries inflicted during the raid, and for one of them a course of antibiotics for a wound in his back was probably the only way he was going to live. I prescribed another course of the pills, using Father James as the person to best explain how they should be taken. I took the liberty to say that the pills were magical, but overheard the priest applying his own interpretation that gave his God all the kudos. Whatever ... perhaps I would accidentally improve the proliferation of Christianity as a by-product of my time in the ninth century. After some discussion it was decided that the best course of action was for the 'Injured Back' man to stay in our village so that the priest could administer the pills personally. The other man appeared to have had a crippling wound in the back of his left leg. The tendons and muscle had been cut to the bone, so that his foot hung limp. He would never run again, but I suggested someone make a brace for his leg, and used a piece of paper from my note book to sketch out a design I had once seen on a friend of mine who had had a bad skiing injury. The man left clutching the sketch, saying he had a brother who was a wood worker, and a friend who could make the leather strapping.

The other two people had obviously been suffering from their ailments for some time. I could do nothing for them, other than try to give them a belief that they would get well. It has long been established in the modern world that 'faith' or 'belief' is of huge benefit to someone's well-being. This can be faith in a god, faith in a treatment, faith in a doctor, faith in science, etc. They did some research on acupuncture (which I am not knocking as there has been other research showing that for some ailments it is a genuine treatment), one of the best known alternative medicines. They compared a control group for whom nothing was done, to a properly administered acupuncture group, and a third group who were given pretend acupuncture with the pins in all the wrong places. The genuine acupuncture group gained significant benefit from their treatment compared to the control group. But interestingly the benefit from the real acupuncture was almost exactly the same as the benefit experienced by the pretend acupuncture group. This suggests why the placebo effect works, and why doctors, who are often not sure what is wrong with you, will go to great pains to assure you they know exactly what they are doing. Faith really does move mountains. What they don't tell you is that this is an internal process, and whatever you believe in will do you good. Hence I did a bit of theatrical magic for those two plaintive in Kaardbury. This involved creating a harmless potion in a cooking pot and a handful of contents from one of the remaining rock salt cartridges thrown dramatically into the flames. (I really did enjoy the response to that one.) Believe it or not they both improved considerably over the following months, but it was actually nothing to do with me, and the fact that I know this is why this story continues.

So it was that with less than two days left I started to say my farewells. I wanted to get to the portal in plenty of time, and planned to spend the last day in 831 in, or near, the town of Gloucester. I had a mere 85 miles as the crow (or dragon) flies, and would be there in about an hour. Still, better safe than sorry eh!

I was saying goodbye to Eowen, the old lady I had given the spectacles to, when I heard the noise. It took me a few moments to realise what the sound was ... it was the warning siren from Loofah, the final alarm in the system. The shriek from the horns on the microlight had been designed to be almost life threatening if you were close enough to the cockpit cage to try to open it. The wail from the beast was terrifying, almost animal. It was a wailing shrill death cry, as I set off at a flat run down the hill, which was so steep that I tumbled twice. I took no notice of the footsteps that were following me, although it transpired that almost half of the village tagged along to see what was going on.

Not bothering with the stepping stones, I headed to the top corner of the field with soaked boots, oblivious to the animal droppings. There were now no livestock anywhere near, which was not surprising. I wondered if I had set the systems properly. Perhaps the other systems had not been functioning, and perhaps an animal had blundered into the chassis, setting it off. I ran hoping that it would be OK. I ran thinking of Monty and seeing her in two days. I ran with my heart in my throat. I ran hoping, and hoping, and hoping.

FUCK!!!

Loofah was exactly where I had left him ... only now there was at least a ton of oak tree on top of my only means of getting home!!!

The tree was only about two feet across, and it had been standing about 20 feet from Loofah. The wood chips from a felling axe lay on the ground at the base of the tree, which had fallen towards the field. Due to the competition for space in the tree canopy the oak had grown tall and had only one significant branch on the length of the trunk. The branch was at about 25 feet from the ground, so when the tree was felled the section of trunk where the branch joined it had landed on top of the wings of my craft. It was clear that for Loofah to ever fly again, it would take weeks of work by expert engineers using the right repair equipment to rebuild it. I had only two days, no experts, and apart from a few spare parts, NO FUCKING EQUIPMENT!!! FUCK FUCK FUCK FUCK FUCK!!

I knew I had to do something quickly. But despite the urgency I turned off the siren and simply sat on the ground with my head in my hands.

It may have been five minutes, it may have been thirty, before I stirred. I got up and went to the machine. I had to fight my way under some of the foliage of the smaller branches to get to the kit strapped onto the sides. I took a few items and then turned to the onlookers. I wanted a horse, and someone to show me the way to Gloucester. I also wanted no one to touch the carcass of the dragon. Some possessive, protective, logical part of me still wanted it to be guarded day and night. But if I was to have any chance of getting to the portal in time I had to set off as soon as I could.

Eric offered to travel with me, and somehow we managed to get hold of two reasonable horses in less than an hour. By now it was gone 10.30am, and I had to be at the portal at 13.47pm the following afternoon. Eric convinced me that the only way of getting there was the old Roman road from Exanton, through Bath Town, to Cirencester. He did not think we could make it, but we set off anyway.

We set off with bags of food and water, my shotgun and a few other useful items. It took us two hours to get to Exanton, modern day Exeter. Eric had explained that the ford across the river Exe was at Twyfyrde (two fords) to the north, but once across the river the journey was so convoluted that by far the quicker route was the 'old road' north which could only be reached quickly by first going south to Exanton. I was dismayed at the extra mileage but had no choice. We could never have crossed the river north of Exeter with the horses, even if we had been able to get a boat to carry the two of us across. This detour meant that the whole journey was now about 100 miles, so in frustration we struggled through the narrow smelly streets, with their strange mixture of decaying Roman stone walls, and wooden huts and halls of all different sizes. The mud and filth in the town was a stark contrast to the cleaner environments of the villages and hamlets I had seen in my travels. We pushed and bullied our way through, twice having to lead the horses who were becoming spooked by the stressful activity all around them. It was early afternoon before we were on the old Roman road and heading north eastwards. We managed to canter for a few miles. The traffic on the roadway was light, and the surface underfoot quite firm. There were sections where what appeared to be the old Roman road surface was visible, and on which our horses' hooves clattered loudly.

By nightfall we were at a place called Sommertown, and from questioning a local discovered we had travelled 40 miles from Exanton. He reckoned it was two days travel to Gloucester, and that was only if the weather stayed good. We had to walk the weary horses for much of the night, arriving in Bath Town well after daybreak and in a very sorry state indeed. I vaguely remember almost falling a number of times with only the rope that purported to be the horses bridle preventing me from dropping onto my knees. The horses by then were all but finished. We wasted a bleary half hour trying to rouse someone to give us fresh mounts before we simply stole two we found tethered in a barn near the road. I question why they were tethered, because neither beast turned out to have the capacity to have escaped. They were unable to carry us more than a few miles before all the goading in the world could not encourage them to even raise to a trot. It must have been gone 11am, with only two and a half hours to go, that I finally gave up.

I had had no sleep for over 24 hours, and had already walked or ridden at least 75 miles. By my calculation we had a bit over 30 miles to go, and needed to travel at a steady canter all the way to stand a chance of getting there in time. A steady canter on horseback, which required at least two changes of horse during the journey to maintain anything like that speed. But we could now barely walk, and the horses we had were useless. Every inch of me hurt, my feet were raw and bleeding into my boots ... boots which I had not dared take off last night in case I was unable to get them back on again. Eric looked awful, but said he was happy to carry on, despite the pain he was clearly in. I started to cry....

Pathetic I know, but everything ran through my head, all the aspirations and hopes for my life. These had been going round and round inside my skull as I had ridden and trudged, and ridden again, through the night, so now they all came back to me ... my good, happy, fun life, my baby girl, my money, my status, my gadgets, and most of all, absolutely most of all, my Monty, all gone ... all gone forever.... So I sat down and cried. If I had been less exhausted, if I had hurt less, if I had anything left in me at all, I probably would have found someone, or something to hit, very hard. Or at least I would have shouted at someone ... something ... anything ... but I had nothing left ... so I cried.

I slowly came to my senses. Eric was worried about me and eventually helped me to my feet. In some strange way after the energy, the drive, the pain of the journey over the last day and night, the realisation that there was nothing I could do was almost a relief. We staggered into a hut belonging to an elderly couple who lived by the road, who made what little money they could selling fresh water from their well to travellers. I paid them handsomely in the fake coins in my pouch for somewhere to rest. They gave us meat stew and dry bread and sweet cold water, and at just about the time I should have been cantering down the hill from Cirencester to the time-gate, and back to my modern life, I was fast asleep in the corner of a hut about four miles north of Bath Town. I know that was the time, as although I had turned the 'one hour to go' and 'ten minutes left' alarms off in my pack, the ones in my wrist watch and pendant I had forgotten about chimed loudly, and woke me up anyway. I turned them off and went back to sleep.

I had not spoken with Eric much on the journey north. He was a nice young man, keen to listen, keen to help, and keen to learn. We returned on our route, but took five days to do it. For most of the first two days we rested and dressed our torn feet. On day three, after returning the stolen horses, we started south from Bath. We even managed to recover one of our original mounts from the field we had left him in. The other had gone, never to be seen again.

As we travelled we talked, and I found out quite a bit about Eric, his family and his life. His tall figure beside me was comforting. But despite his angular wide features and broad shoulders, he had yet to reach that depth of chest, and facial strength that would mark him as the hardened warrior he was to become. His voice was deep and softly spoken as he commiserated with me over my loss. On a number of occasions, when the emotions became too much for me, his heavily muscled arm would rest across my shoulders, or his broad palmed hand would grip the back of mine as tears flowed. Apart from the desolation of losing Monty, it was a bit difficult talking about myself, and about my real life. But I managed to build what was mostly the truth around the idea that I had come from a very distant land, and had travelled on the back of the dragon that had been killed at Kaardbury. I explained that I had been a Computer Wizard, but had sold my magic to another man, as I wanted to live as a normal person with my daughter and a lady I had come to love. I explained that the only way I could have caught another dragon, and returned home, was to have been at Gloucester on time. We both walked, and talked, all the way. We led our one horse, and stopped each night in a wayside eating house. To call them pubs or taverns would be over-selling the venues. But we had straw to sleep on, and warm food in our bellies every night, and I paid in simple coin slightly over the price Eric said was right. I avoided performing any magic tricks. Our only real problem came in Exeter on the evening of the fifth day.

As we were leaving the town two big men, one with an axe and the other with a stout quarter-staff, barred our way. They said that they liked our horse, and wanted it. They also said they had seen us with money and they wanted that as well. Eric was taller than either of the men, but not as heavily built. I was about the same size as the smaller one was, but nowhere near as ugly (well at least I thought so). Despite my position of having had my whole future taken from me, I did not want to die, or receive a nasty injury. I did not want Eric to be hurt either. Besides, I was very pissed off, and was in no mood to be mugged by these two assholes. The axe looked heavy and sharp, and the staff was six foot long and nearly two inches thick. My hands went into my pockets as if to find money, but in reality I was searching for inspiration.... The first thing that came to hand was one of the thunder-flashes. It was in the side pocket of my jerkin. I had used a few of these, and a couple of the 'nine-bangs' in scaring villagers during the last few weeks. But Eric had never seen one. With renewed confidence I informed the men that the horse was not going to be given to them, and as I was a famous wizard and dragon rider, I was going to give them a sample of dragon breath for free. I took the thunder-flash from my pocket, twisted to top off, and struck the fuse against the friction pad inside the cap. I pointed the fizzing, smoking tube straight at the one who was leading the conversation, who then glanced at his companion and stepped backwards. I said "I will make the dragon roar, I will set you on fire ..." and tossed the thunder-flash to his feet. They had danced backwards, but then decided that the smoking tube was not a threat, and stepped forwards again just as it went off, literally, under their noses (or ears). The noise from close up is deafening, and there was a spectacular eruption of smoke which momentarily engulfed the pair of them. They dropped their weapons and ran. One dived over a roadside hedge, and scampered away across the field to our left. The other kept running until he was out of sight, round a bend in the road, a hundred yards away.

Luckily I had held firmly on to the horse, which almost lifted me off my feet. Eric, who had not been expecting the noise, was twenty yards back up the road behind me, giving an impression of someone holding their head on, while at the same time trying to dance backwards, badly. I shouted to him to stop, and that everything was OK, but my words were muffled and distant. My ears were literally ringing with the clap of sharp sound they had just suffered. The horse dragged me backwards down the road until I was level with Eric, who just sat down in front of me, and started laughing. Perhaps it was relief at realising it was just another trick by me, the computer wizard, or perhaps it was just stress release after our ordeals.

I hooked the axe into the bedding strapped onto the horse, and Eric took the quarter-staff to walk with, and we resumed our journey still chuckling. We saw nothing of the two men, although we heard cracking and rustling sounds in distant woodland off to our left, which was probably the hedge jumper trying to put more distance between him and us. Eric, still with the occasional chuckle, asked if what I had thrown was really dragon's breath, and if so how did I capture the breath in that tube. I decided there and then that the ability to do magic was going to be very useful for my future wellbeing. Perhaps I could have some sort of life here if I retained the status of being a warlock, or a wizard. So I came up with some suitable bullshit about capturing dragon breath, and started to think through what I still had left of my equipment that I could possibly use to amaze the inhabitants of the year 831.

Chapter Eight;   A New Direction.

My return to the village was a mixture of subdued shame about the death of my dragon, and quiet enthusiasm at having someone with magic power amongst them. The Smith recovered fully, and returned to his role of village leader and head man. Eric led a team of villagers in building me a home, well, half a home. He had wanted me to live with his family, but I felt quite depressed, and needed to be more alone. I told him that I needed to take stock of my life, and decide what I would do now given I had no option other than to remain in the land of the Anglo-Saxons in the ninth century. He tried to persuade me that I still might be able to travel back to my own land by sea, but I told him it was far too far to travel, and that no man had ever made the journey other than on a dragon. I also said that we had a law in our land that prohibits any attempt to rescue a dragon wizard who was lost. To do so would make all the dragons die.

I attempted to find out who the hell had felled the tree onto Loofah. Father James said he had seen two men who claimed they were from near Kirton, and who were asking about the raid during the time I was dealing with the sick and injured from the other villages, when I was busy creating my placebo healing potion. They had asked if it was true that a man riding a dragon had tried to set fire to the longships. Father James denied telling them anything about the beast, but from his demeanour I could see that the priest was being evasive and had almost certainly been far too forthcoming with information. And even if he had not divulged the exact location of the slumbering Loofah, my guess is that he must at least have hinted as to its whereabouts.

I spent some weeks touring the nearby villages, looking for these men, with Elf as my constant companion. I was well tooled up with protection kit, and had a few of my precious proper cartridges in my shotgun, so we were pretty safe. If I had found the culprits I would probably have killed the pair of them ... perhaps.

After a couple of months I set up home in the hut they had extended for me, on the slope above and east of the centre of the village. The hut had belonged to one of the men killed by the Vikings. His wife and small child had abandoned the structure and gone back to the community where her parents lived. I had asked for a significant extension built to the property and, as I have said, it was built mainly by grateful villagers, led by Eric. I got them to clear the woodland around the hut, and used the logs to erect a cabin set into the hillside behind the original structure, partly built into a deep cutting. The new cabin was constructed with very thick walls, and slit windows too narrow to climb through. With a turf roof over thick logs above, this small but very substantial structure was only accessible through a narrow heavy doorway set in the rear wall of the old hut. I explained that for me to practice magic I needed thick walls to keep the villagers protected. In reality this was my safe sleeping and storage place, and the old front part of the hut would furnish me with somewhere to live peacefully in reasonable comfort.

One Eye became my sort of house keeper, helping me sort the place out, showing me how to do things, and keeping me supplied with at least one hot meal a day. Her husband had been the other man killed during the raid, and because I had saved her from the raiders she sort of adopted me.

Since my return from the aborted journey to Gloucester, I had asked the village to keep vigil over Loofah, and they had done so, albeit often posting guards who were mere children of 13 or 14 years of age. Early on I recovered all the moveable kit, and stored it initially with Eric Smithson. They had treated it with great reverence, and I was later able to move all of it, intact, to the sleeping room of my new abode. After getting the offending oak tree cut up and removed, leaving the sadly disfigured Loofah looking like a broken-backed butterfly, I set about dismantling the whole craft. Then with assistance from Eric and his two best friends, we got the entire machine carried, piece by piece, up to my hut. The cockpit and engine were virtually undamaged and the distorted wings were quite easy to take to pieces. In reality the craft is not designed to be that heavy, and the task was not a difficult one. Eric's friends were both young men with dark hair. One had a proliferation of acne on his face and a cheery smile, the other had one his little fingers missing due to a careless encounter trying to feed a goat as a child. I got the three of them to swear a great oath of secrecy, and then required them all to drink a harmless potion that I said would make them fall ill and die if they broke their oath (not a nice thing to do, but perhaps a good idea anyway).

At this potion drinking demand 'Spots' was, for the first time, very quiet and unhappy, and 'Little Finger', with tears in his eyes, wanted to refuse to take the potion. So I relented, and got the three of them to stand holding hands in a circle in front of my hut with their eyes shut. Somewhat theatrical I know, but I was starting to see the value of this sort of ritual in creating an essential mystique. A quick visit to my back room resulted in my returning with a small finger bar of chocolate which I broke into three pieces. I said that if they ate this magic brown substance, which I would place on each of their tongues, they would not have to drink the potion, and would not fall ill or die. If the brown substance tasted sweet to them they would certainly be very virile all their lives and each would have many strong children. But, I added, as only a great favour to me I asked that they keep the new location of the dragon's body a secret. They all perked up at that, especially after the sensation of eating the chocolate, which must have been an unforgettable experience for anyone who had not tasted it before. With delighted smiles, all three claimed they were bound not only by an oath of secrecy, but that I could call on any of them, at any time, for any help, in anything.

When they had left me alone I made a point of hanging a red shirt on a tree on the path from my hut to the village, which I had told them was a sign that I was practicing my magic, and therefore no one should come close. I then took the folding shovel from my kit and dug the hole for Loofah. I had begun carefully wrapping each piece in tarpaulin, and bagging pieces up in the heavy duty plastic bags every traveller has with them, when I started to have a change of mind. I eventually only buried the wings and frame of the craft. I had some ideas about uses for the rest of the carcass of my dragon.

It took me two days to set up the engine in the corner of my sleeping room so that I could use it to charge up all the batteries, and run all the floodlights. I reckoned I had about 10 hours flight time left, so run at low speed perhaps 20 hours of run time in terms of fuel. I fitted the exhaust pipe so that it led out through the side-wall of the safe room, and into a dense bush on the bank outside. I cut out the two 'fire breath' tubes from the chassis, so I had two five foot lengths of silver tube, each with a 500ml chamber at one end that could be pressurised by the foot pump from the kit bags. I could fire them by hand as I fitted a loop of wire into the trigger mechanism to replace the cable pull that had been there originally. With 10 litres left of the fire juice, I really did have something I could used like a wizard. I had to discharge the tubes horizontally, or by pointing them slightly downwards, but they would work really well. I decided to save them for very special occasions.

The covering of Loofah, the Kevlar woven material, was a bit like a jacket for a good sized settee. It had that strange scaly pattern, and of course my carefully selected dragon colouring. My guess is that it weighed about 8 to 10 kilograms (about 20 lb in old money). It was almost impossible to cut to fit anything, but I found that if I put one end of it over my shoulders, and clipped the bottom edge up, it worked reasonably well as a heavy cloak. If I then clipped the edges together on both sides, and put my hands through the resultant loops, I had a lumpy sort of protective cape, which I knew would stop any arrow, or sword thrust. The only part of me still at risk was my head, and that was partly protected by the ruckled material on the top of my shoulders, caused when I pulled the cloak around me. I was also aware that I could be hit by something heavy, like a hammer, or axe, but I was pleased with the conversion anyway. This would have to be another item that I would use sparingly. Anyway, it was too fucking heavy to wear just for fun!!!

On the undercarriage of the microlight there had been four lengthy steel springs, each about three and a half feet long. They worked in pairs to provide the suspension for Loofah on landing. They were quite heavy, and a good quarter of an inch thick. You will have to forgive me for flitting from the old forms of measurement to metric and back again. For the uninitiated a metre is about a hands width longer than a yard. So one mile approximately equals 1.6 kilometres. A litre is about 1.76 pints, and a kilogram is about 2.2 pounds. Oh, and an inch is 2.54 centimetres. Sadly I still have those conversions ratios in my head to a great deal more accuracy that would ever be needed. For instance a mile is 1,609.344 metres, but that is because I was, and perhaps still am, a bit of a nerd.

So the springs, or callipers, from Loofah were just over a metre long, and about 0.7 centimetres thick. They were also some two inches, or five centimetres, wide. I have done quite a lot of reading in my time. I have also had some fascinating contacts with some very interesting people during my life. My grandfather recovered a 'Kukri', or 'Gurkha Knife' from a First World War battlefield. To me as a child this was a monstrous weapon, and although the later versions were considerably smaller, I found out that they were now made from the springs of scrapped Landrovers. It turned out that the requirements for the steel for the suspension springs on vehicles were exactly the same as the best quality steel for knives. They gave good flexibility of blade with an excellent cutting edge.

I took one of these springs down to Eric, and asked him to make a sword for me in secret. I told him it was a magic steel calliper from the leg of my dragon. I was aware that good quality swords were difficult to make because of the indifferent qualities of the metal available at that time. The method I understood to be used by the best craftsmen involved taking a number of lengths the softer wrought iron interspersed with rods of their brittle steel (or cast iron), then forging and welding them together in a multi-layered sandwich. They then twisted this rod a number of times before flattening it out to make the centre of a blade. Then harder, more brittle steel was added to the edges. When repeatedly heated and hammered, they fused all this into one blade. Etching the surface with acid shows the woven pattern of the mixed and twisted metal core, which is visible down the middle. These swords were carefully heated and quenched to fix the right properties into the metal. The final stages were hafting the blade, then sharpening and polishing. These swords took a great deal of time to make and when suitably sheathed were valuable and rare weapons for only war lords and the greatest of warriors. Two Viking swords had been recovered by Eric from the men he had killed. Both were shorter than the blades used by Saxons and one of these swords had been given by Eric to his father on his recovery. The other had been sent to the local Lord of the land who lived in his hall at Kirtun (Crediton), some four miles to the south west. He was a Lord, or 'Thane', who seemed to be no use at all when it came to protecting his people. When the Vikings came he simply hid within the walls of his personal stronghold. Eric had kept the axe for himself.

Beouf Eglind was Thane, and Lord of the manor in Crediton. The whole kingdom was broken up into areas under the control of these local lords. Discussions with villagers revealed that at the time the ruler of all the Angles and Saxons was King Egbert, who had taken over when King Wiglaf had been defeated somewhere far to the north east two years before. The only person in the village who had ever actually met Egbert was the Smithy. But travelling was not uncommon, and quite a number of people came and went from the village. There was the more heavily used road just to the north west of our community, linking Twyfyrde or (two fords) Tiverton with Crediton. I had crossed this road twice on our flight from the raiders, and the two horsemen and the warrior on foot had been on that road when our second confrontation happened that morning of the raid.

I digress ... I asked Eric to make a sword from the spring. I wanted to see what qualities it would have, and perhaps use it myself. I was aware that the protection kit I had with me would not last forever, and that I would need to plan long term ... very long term.

I was able to research the type of metal suitable for knives and springs as I had those CDs Monty had included, which were crammed with what I had thought was useless information. It transpired that the type of steel from the springs had a precise carbon content of about 1 percent, which was exactly what was needed to make a good blade. Steel was very difficult to manufacture with the colder forges prior to the advent of coke production. It was not until the Bessemer process in the mid 19th century that steel was mass produced. A carbon content of much over 2 percent resulted in the brittle cast iron, and much less than 1 percent carbon resulted in a metal that was too soft. With the colder forges all a smithy could do was to hammer a glowing piece of iron out, then fold it again and again. Many layers of metal meant that much of the carbon from the cast iron was bought to the surface and burned off in the flames. By this laborious process the carbon content could be bought down to near 1 percent. But there was a great deal of guess work in this, and almost always pockets of carbon that gave the metal a weakness remained. With this spring metal from Loofah, and with Eric's feel for how to play with the quenching and heating process, I thought he should be able to make a blade that cut well, but did not shatter. I even suggested the Japanese method of painting layers of clay onto the blade before the final heating and quenching process, as this was how they slowed the cooling of the body of a blade to retain ductility but speeded up the cooling of the cutting edge to promote hardness.

Keeping the sword a secret resulted in the making of it becoming a slow process. Eric was only able to work on it when his father was away from the village. During the weeks that I waited I did a number of things. I did some of the things One Eye wanted me to do, such as cutting and stockpiling wood for the winter, and smoking meat to be stored. I was pleased to do this, as I did not want my wizard status to mean that I could do nothing normal for myself. I learned some skills that must have been almost forgotten with the passage of time, such as plaiting cordage from tree bark, and collecting and storing roots and berries. Actually they didn't plait cordage, they more or less wove it, rolling the fibres on their thighs to create the twist in the braids, and overlaying them so that they sort of wrapped around each other. The end result was a somewhat uneven, furry rope, which was surprisingly good.

I made a full inventory of what I had bought from the 21st century, and discovered one or two bits I had nigh on forgotten. Items such as a 150 foot climbing rope with a harness, karabiners, and a few bits of climbing protection such as nuts, cams and slings. It wasn't much, but I had intended to climb a few Cornish cliffs at some stage in my travels. It was a strange contrast to the rope I had painstakingly made myself by hand.

As the weeks drew into months I slowly came to a decision about the future. My future. I was going to try to help these people live safer lives. I had to find a way to help them to protect themselves against the Viking raids. How the hell was I going to do that? I considered that I could perhaps scare all the villagers with magic, so they were so terrified that they obeyed me in what I told them to do. But after some deliberation I decided that this would not work. I would soon run out of the magic tricks I had available to frighten them with, especially as I would almost certainly have to engage many more people than just the occupants of Kaardbury. I needed a more strategic approach, and that would take time, and leadership, and knowledge.

On the knowledge bit I had some ideas bubbling around already – some sort of early warning system was one of them. I also had access to some useful information about successful tactics from history (my history of course, the one that looks back from the 21st century). I had two laptop computers with me and a fistful of CDs crammed with information, much of which I had originally thought would be irrelevant and had never even left my bags. But now I started researching.

The laptops could be run using the big batteries from Loofah, but one of them also had a solar panel built into its lid. I could leave it on the roof of the safe house when the sun was out, and fully recharge its internal battery in only a few hours. In addition I had a small dynamo charger, which required about 15 minutes of hard work from me to do the same thing (I wonder what the villagers thought was the cause of the sudden improvement of the muscular development of my forearms?). To cut a long story short I had some interesting stuff on the Romans that I thought would be ideal.

It was a mist shrouded morning when Eric arrived at my hut alone, carrying a long, cloth wrapped item in his hands. He walked through the doorway, stooping to avoid cranial contact with the lintel. There was one of his irrepressible grins spread across his young, happy, face. He placed the hessian covered item on my table, and proceeded to unwrap it.

There on the table was something of wonder. The sheath was of wood, polished and stained with bees wax to a deep amber colour. The sword had a purple coloured handle of leather cord frapping with a pommel shaped like a closed fist. The guard was much wider than those usually found on a Saxon sword, and these were shaped much like Loofah's wings. The blade was over three feet long and wider towards the fore end, before it tapered to a wicked point. The texture and colour of the steel was nothing like any Saxon blade I had ever seen, and it was finely burnished, with a thin sheen of oil. Along both sides of the blade there was a diamond like decoration of overlapping elongated lozenges or rhombi, etched into the steel, giving the impression of there being a crystal core running down the centre of the blade from guard to tip. This was a pattern apparently inspired by the lattice of cockpit cage on the microlight. I picked up the sword with great reverence, and could tell at once that the balance of the weapon was perfect. I could almost smell how sharp the blade was in that confined space. I looked at Eric and saw pure joy in his face.

"It is my best ever work – the metal is a true wonder! The edge is so sharp, the blade so strong! I have never seen the like of this! This 'ex-spring' is a sword fit for a king!"

We took the sword into the clearing in front of my hut and each of us swung it as if in battle. Eric showed me how he could cut through a four inch sapling with a single stroke, before he lovingly returned it to its sheath, and wrapped it again in the cloth. He then held out the weapon to me, saying "Marlin, my friend and great wizard, I made this with your dragon steel, it must remain in your possession, it must remain with you the dragon rider, the Pendragon." I had a sudden idea ....

I spent some time that morning with Eric, whom I had often heard being called our 'Thor' since his success at dispatching the two Norse warriors in his father's hall. I discussed with him how the people responded to the Viking raids, and how the communities thereabouts could be bought together to resist those attacks. I understood that an outsider like me could not take control over the Saxon peoples of the district, but he agreed that his father could, if he was well enough supported, and as long as the local war lord could be persuaded to stay out of it. I suggested that the Lord Beouf may be bought off with a gift of the sword, but it was a suggestion the Eric baulked at. Beouf was despised, and already the sword was clearly much loved by Eric. Eventually we decided that we would have to discuss this with the Smithy, but that we could have some magical event to give the sword high status, and by the sword choosing a leader for the people, we could sideline Beouf back into his safe little fortified enclave.

Chapter Nine;   The Lake.

The Saxons laid great store in the mystical, and the afterlife. Lakes, ponds and still-water were considered to be places of reverence and gateways to the Gods, and every year there were a number of Pagan religious ceremonies that the village participated in. About two miles from Kaardbury, in the eastern valley below, there was a large oxbow lake – one of those classic lakes from every schoolchild's first year of geography. It was the location of certain pagan ceremonies that could be very useful to someone who was intent on influencing the easily mystified.

We were two weeks away from the Saxon equivalent of a blessing of the harvest festival, which would include the offering of some items from the harvest to the Gods. This was explained in detail to me by Eric who, at my request, took me down to the lake to see where the event took place.

The lake was a beautiful spot – quiet and tranquil, apart from the faint distant noise of the main river a quarter of a mile away. The lake was surrounded by woodland, and there was an overgrown pathway that led to a little rough built wooden jetty which jutted out to the deepest part of the lake. The jetty had lost some of its length, as I could see two sets of uprights beyond the end of the jetty, standing clear of the water. Eric explained that when they built the jetty they had almost completed it, and were adding the last few feet of boards, when there had been a sudden storm, and lightening had struck a tree beside the lake and the top of the tree had caught fire. He pointed across the lake to a tall tree that had clearly lost an upper branch some years ago. The blackened split stump of the branch could just still be seen through the foliage. He explained, "My father was a younger man then, and he was working on the walkway with three men from the village. After the storm they carried a piece of the burnt tree back to our community and consulted with old Martha – the crone. She is dead now, but when she read the signs she said the Gods did not want them to build the walkway any further into their lake, as it would block their passageway, their access to earth. So it was left as it is, and the offerings are now thrown off the end of the walkway, we hope through the "doorway of the Gods."

The walkway, or jetty, was well constructed, and only wide enough for a single man to walk along. I went to the end of it and looked down into the lake. There was some discolouration, but I could see down through the water, at least two or three feet, where small fish were twisting and turning amongst the tops of the weeds below. Looking forward there were the unused four posts, sticking up from the water where the construction had been stopped, two each side, with their shafts visible well below the surface. Eric told me that his father had said that before they were hammered into the lake bottom, they were at least 25 feet long. As some five foot had been driven into the mud, the depth of water would be about 15 foot. Also evident about one foot below the surface there were two struts that reached out on either side of the jetty below me and beyond the end of the walkway. These struts stretched approximately seven feet to the first two posts. This had clearly been the last part of the structure that had been completed before the lightening strike. Moss and lichen could be seen blurring the dark edges of the wood below the surface. I was so deeply in thought I almost fell in … almost ….

I wanted the sword to appear from the lake, as if the Gods had given it to someone chosen to lead. This would give that person a status that should enable them (with my guidance) to coordinate the efforts of all the communities in the area, to defend themselves – ourselves. That was the plan anyway.

I secretly devoted some time to trying out and testing various methods of arranging the sudden appearance of the sword in a suitably spectacular fashion. I became exasperated for a while and wondered if a simple bit of theatrics would work – perhaps I could just produce the bloody thing from under my cloak. But I persevered, and two days before the big event I was all ready. I asked Eric, Little Finger and Spots to ask someone of importance from each of the nearby communities to come and watch the Thankful Harvest ceremony at the lake. I told them to say that Marlin the wizard was going to speak to the Gods, and was going to ask the Gods what we should do about the Viking raids.

The big day came…. I will not bore you with all the build up. I certainly will not bore you with details of the secret testing on how I should get the sword to appear. Nor about the time I spent down at the lake and other watery locations on those days before the ceremony. Suffice it to say there were some surprised fishermen who found dozens of stunned and dead fish floating downstream in the river Exe a week beforehand. They were even more surprised to find the fish were fresh, healthy and edible, so long as they got them out of the water that day. A small round coracle belonging to one of the men who fished the river went missing for three days, and a supposed wizard who had all these wonderful skills and magic still managed to get himself soaked to the skin on two occasions, despite how dry and warm the weather was.

I made a big show of the theatrics as we went down towards the river that afternoon. All the villagers were there, along with a surprising number of others from near and far. Father James kept a low profile, but he did talk to anyone close enough to listen. I overheard him explaining that his God was in fact in charge of all the other Gods, so whatever happened today would really be his work. I wonder if he had a premonition, or perhaps he was just banking on me coming up with something special for the occasion. I had talked at length with Smithy about the need to have a leader, one who could coordinate the efforts of all the villages, and he agreed eventually and reluctantly that it was the only solution. He initially refused to take the job, despite me claiming he had been already chosen, as I spoke to the Gods personally. (I wonder how many men in history have claimed that load of bollocks eh! Quite a few apparently ... I wonder how anyone was supposed to tell which of these supposedly 'chosen people' were in reality just ordinary folk with schizophrenia or just some con artist/priest pretending to hear God's voice so they can have an easy life of power and luxury?) I decided not to tell him about any of my plans, and I swore Eric to secrecy about the making of the spring sword, which I now called 'Dragon Leg', saying that I needed his father to believe that the sword came from the Gods. I also needed Eric to believe in the magic, so I told him that the sword had already been given up to the Gods by me in the dead of night, and that I had sent it into the sky, fired with dragon's breath. I told him that only if the Gods returned the sword to us with proof that they had chosen a leader would we see it again. Eric seemed happy with this explanation, but was clearly miffed that I had not allowed him to witness the passage of his sword to the Gods.

To console him I told him that I sometimes have to send messages and offerings to the Gods. To this end I got hold of one of my last two small firework rockets. The ones attached to wooden rods you stick in a bottle. They were not the only pyrotechnics I had with me, but I only needed a little show for this occasion. So I took Eric and his two mates, Spots and Little Finger into the woodland well away from the village late one night. Here I made a big deal about sending an offering of a golden ring to the Gods. I attached the ring to the rocket with a piece of thread, and fired the thing from a small clearing, up through the canopy, and supposedly to the place of the Gods. I tried to ensure we were unable to see the end of the rockets flight too clearly but we could just make out the sparkly cascade at as the firework burnt out. I explained that that was the moment the offering had entered the domain of the Gods. They all seemed suitably convinced.

The ceremonial procession wended its way down towards the lake – to the gateway of the Immortals, the portal to another world. I was chanting and calling out to the Gods to bless the harvest and to speak to us in their wisdom. I was calling on them to show us a sign. I was demanding they tell us what to do to save ourselves from the northern raiders (I was laying it on a bit thick, but what the hell eh!).

When we reached the lake I walked to the end of the jetty right behind the Smithy. His broad back blocked my view of the end of our little pier. Following us were the villagers chosen to carry the offerings to the Gods. We went through what was apparently their normal routine with me being the last person in the line along the jetty, who passed each item to Smithy, who raised each one in turn, for all to see. He then cast each of them into the lake, one by one, throwing them beyond the last two isolated posts still standing in deep water some fourteen feet from the end of the walkway. With each offering he chanted the name of one of the Gods followed by "Take this fruit of our land. Take this gift from my people. Bless us with food and warmth in the coming year."

Most of our offerings just bobbed back to the surface and floated away. Some of the items, such as preserves in pottery jars, and pieces of jewellery, disappeared with a plop! The pottery items caused me a great deal of concern, but to my relief nothing stirred from below, and the ceremony continued.

The offerings took 20 minutes to all be blessed and cast into the water. No one seemed to be the slightest concerned that much of what was offered appeared to have been discarded by the Gods, and was to be left floating amongst the reeds at the far side of the lake. Still, who am I to argue?

When Smithy had finished he gave me the signal that his part was over, and I then stepped past him onto centre stage. I loved this bit!!!

I started with a bit of calling and ranting. I was beseeching the Gods to give us a sign. I was asking them to show us how to deal with the Viking raids. After a suitable over-the-top bit of pretend emotional turmoil, I claimed the Gods wanted me to go to their portal to hear them better. So I gingerly stepped down onto the submerged right hand wooden rod connecting the walkway to the closest post standing in the water on the right side. I was making my way out onto the unfinished section of the pier (I had tested that a number of times in the last week. I had even added some new binding so that the damn thing was definitely not going to let me down – again!). Anyway, holding onto Smithy's hand I retained my balance well enough to stretch out and take hold of the post which stood a metre above the surface of the water in front of me. Balancing there on one foot I leaned out to my left and took hold of the left hand post, and then made a big show of stepping carefully out into the gap between them. I stood there for a few moments, before letting go of both posts and slowly turning round to face my audience. There were gasps a-plenty. Some of the women put their hands to their mouths, and everyone craned their necks to see the wonder. Marlin the wizard was standing on water…. With the first two posts from the unfinished section of the jetty on either side of me it could be clearly seen that I was standing on the water. Well almost. My feet and ankles were under water, but the water below them was clearly visible, there was nothing apparently holding me up, and it was as if I had walked onto the water, and it had turned solid below me.

I had found an unexpected use for the Perspex visor of Loofah. Braced across the end of the two wooden rods that ran out to the first two posts beyond the jetty, it provided a two and a half foot wide platform for me to stand on, which was virtually invisible. If the water had been crystal clear someone may have seen the outline of the microlight visor. But the water was not crystal clear, and my status had just jumped a few notches.

Before the ceremony I had pinned my cape up a bit higher than usual, and the lower edge of it hung a few inches above the surface of the lake. I started some sort of incantation – I was using the tune of an old Beatles song with a few practiced lines of suitable lyrics. I had already checked that the stout fishing line I had tied to the posts just above the water surface were still attached. We were all ready for the big finale….

The chord that ran down my left sleeve was much more difficult to pull than I had expected, so I spent a few worrying moments with my right hand up my left sleeve giving the appearance of someone trying to deal with a particularly nasty insect bite, when suddenly I was engulfed in smoke. In the turned up skirt of my cape there was one of the unused smoke canisters that had been the original method of providing Loofah with breath like a dragon. This was the second of these canisters I had ever used, as the fire breathing effect had always been my preferred pyrotechnical option. The first canister had been used simply as a test run eight days ago, early in the morning at very first light, outside my habitation. The smoke canister burnt with very little heat, and lasted about 45 seconds or so. The volume of smoke it gave out was amazing, and I had visions of half the village rushing up to my hut in an attempt to rescue me from certain death, as it must have looked as if my hut was ablaze ... but no one came, and the cockerels had crowed as usual.

In the turned up hem of my cloak there were two of these canisters. One was a back-up in case of problems. They were both wrapped in tubes of green wood bark, to insulate my precious cape against possible damage. When the canister went off the smoke came out of the loosely pinned, turned up hem, all around me. I could not see very well, as much of the deluge came out at the back of my head and around my chest, but I have been told the effect was quite extraordinary. I had instantaneously turned myself into a column of smoke. Well, I was the base of the column, and from me it poured out into the air around and above my head. By the end of three quarters of a minute of the intense emissions from the canister, most of the lake was covered by a thick layer that drifted away as it slowly rose into the air. I had held my breath for the majority of that time, but the effort of getting out into the 'walking on water' position made holding my breath somewhat harder than I expected. My first gulp of air included a fair quantity of the supposedly non-toxic fumes, and I spent a good thirty seconds coughing it out again with my eyes watering like buggery. Still, no one seemed to mind, and perhaps they were just amazed that I was still alive. Perhaps, for them, there was always some sort of fire with smoke.

This put my meticulously choreographed schedule out a bit, but by then I had got the carefully weighted thunder-flash out of my pocket, and was holding it in my folded hands, unseen, up my sleeve. I said a few more words about giving us a sign, and said "Take this last offering from the good people of Kaardbury. It is a wizard's candle to represent the flames of our cooking fires when we are hungry, the lighting of our homes on dark nights and the warmth of our hearths in winter. If this final offering satisfies you, please give us a sign. I, Marlin the wizard of Kaadbury, call upon you to give us a sign...."

I had already twisted off the cap off the thunder-flash, so I struck the head across the rough surface inside the cap, and tossed it into the water to the side of the jetty, as this was the area most visible to the people thronging the bank of the lake. It disappeared beneath the surface with barely a ripple, the smoke from the fuse leaving a momentary arc in the air. The surface of the lake bubbled frantically. There were some gasps of breath, and one or two of the village folk stepped back from the water's edge, as if some divine premonition was warning them.

To me it seemed forever, well ages anyway, although I am fully aware that it was almost certainly only the expected seven seconds before the surface of the lake literally erupted....

The bubble of gasses as the thunder-flash went off at the bottom of the lake must have been at least six feet across. I had once seen a demonstration of the power of these things at an army barracks in the south of England. They contain one and a half ounces of powder, and because they are constrained by the compressed cardboard casing of the device they really do explode with one hell of a wallop. That

116

demonstration involved putting one under an army tin helmet. It blew the helmet over 100 feet into the air. So despite the noise being muffled by the water of the lake, the explosion of gas was spectacular. I knew this is exactly what would happen, because it was one of the aspects of these theatrics I had had great fun in trying already.

The water showered those along the edge of the shore and some fell over as people jumped backwards out of the way. I had a smattering myself. Then to my delight an unexpected bonus happened. Up into the centre of the still churning water there appeared the handle of a sword. It was clearly the handle of a sword, as it had risen so swiftly that when it first reached the surface a good foot of the blade was momentarily visible, before is dropped back, bobbing up and down a few times. When the waters had calmed, the haft of the sword settled above the surface and started to drift across the lake as the villagers began to point and call out. Each side of the handle of the sword was a hand, a pale-skinned, rather puffy hand, appearing to be holding the handle of the sword above the water, as it floated further from the bank. The reason the hands were there was simple. The floats I had used on the blade were a couple of empty plastic tonic water bottles (with added lemon, of course). But over these bottles I had stretched some inflated rubber medical gloves from my First Aid kit. Inflated they added a little buoyancy, but most importantly they gave the desired effect of making it appear as if the hands of a God were passing the sword though the portal into the world of mortal men. Good eh!!

The sword had been attached, by me, to a stake pushed deep into the mud at the bottom of the lake. I had added a good sized lump of rock as well, although dropping that rock over the side of the coracle had made me fall out for the second time. I had tied a flat piece of wood to the stake, so that it held the sword upright, trapping the sword between them. The binding was done with that stout fishing line and using a slip knot. A sharp tug on either of the ends attached to the unused jetty posts would have released the sword to the surface. It was a lucky bonus that the vibration of the detonating thunder-flash did the job for me.

The trouble with this exciting, successful piece of theatrics is that it rather takes one's concentration away from other things. As people on the bank were recovering, talking excitedly, and pointing at not only the sword, but also the other magnanimous gifts of the Gods (in this case the dozens of stunned fish coming to the surface), … I neglected to keep my balance.

I fell, almost unnoticed, backwards into the lake. I tried to keep my footing, but one of the interesting qualities of a sheet of Perspex under water is that it is bloody slippery. I not only fell backwards, but in trying to keep my balance I kicked the transparent visor off the wooden rails and down into the depths below.

The following few moments were both wet and confused. I shouted to Smithy to stop anyone getting into the water. I had the presence of mind to yell something about the portal to the Gods was still open, and there was great danger in getting into the water before it closed. I discarded my cloak, and hung it over one of the poles sticking above the surface. I told everyone to stay on this side of the lake, and set off to swim to the sword. I had arranged to have the coracle nearby, and Eric had been primed to come forward with it when I called for him. Instead, I swam to the bobbing sword, and then swam on to the far side of the lake. The total distance was no more than 100 metres, but I was fully clothed, and with boots on. By the time I struggled to the shore, through the reeds and cloying mud, I was blowing badly. By the time I walked back round the lake, wet, muddy and bedraggled, I had removed and pocketed the bottles, gloves and bindings from the sword.

I must have looked a sight. But no one had the affront to laugh at someone who had just summoned the Gods to give such a sign. Squelching with each step I walked back to the jetty. By the time I got there Smith was just reaching dry land and the pier had been emptied of villagers. A strange silence fell over everyone, and a wide circle of people gathered around me as I approached the Smith with the sword held out at arm's length.

"Smith, the Gods have spoken to me. You saw how they passed this sword though the portal. They said that the one who works with iron is to lead the mortals. The one who works with iron is to show the people how to defend themselves against the fair haired raiders. The one who works with iron is to be obeyed by all the people who live hereabouts on pain of angering the Gods."

Then to my surprise he went and buggered it all up. He was obviously as shaken as everyone else, and also clearly somewhat fearful. He took the sword in his trembling hands and said. "I take this sword of the Gods. The sword given to us by the woman in the lake.... But as we all know many people work with iron, especially our warriors and War Lord. I am no soldier, and this sword has to be taken by a worthy warrior, and he will then lead us in our defence against the Vikings."

Fuck, fuck, fuck. Despite my brilliant performance, the cowardly bugger had not wanted the job in the first place!!

The Chronicles of Eathelwold 'James' Trefell; Monk.

Book 1 Chapter 5.

When Maerlin came back to us we all rejoiced. He came back unto us tired from his journey to the cold lands, yet he showed the healing power of our Lord by allowing me to give tiny pieces of holy food, smaller than a single goat's dropping, and as hard as a piece of dried clay. These tiny white morsels of 'the body of Christ' must truly have come from the holy chalice as they summoned a man all but dead from profound purification, and deep with infection, back from the very brink of the abyss. I confess to eating one of these blessed offerings myself because as a holy man I must not allow my flock to suffer when I do not. The effect on me was not great as I only ate one. But to show how the Lord does not wish us to take strong drink his holy food made me most unwell that evening when I was obliged to share mead with the rest of our community. Maerlin saved the lives of many who came to him, not unlike our Lord's wonderful miracles saving the lives of simple folk in the holy land so many years ago. Yet Maerlin was blissfully unaware of being the Lord's instrument. He confided in me that despite his heretical doctrine the white nuggets were truly from the holy grail, the cup of Christ himself. No wonder that the Smithy lives, and that we all stand in awe at the ways of our Lord.

It was hence our Lord's work that kept Maerlin with us. He pinned down the dragon so that Maerlin could not leave us. The beast wailed like the monster from hell that it was, but Maerlin silenced his pain and sent his spirit back to the dark world it came from. Maerlin tried to return to his home land and I was most distressed, but he was returned to us by God's will to carry on the work of his true destiny.

Book 1 Chapter 7.

Maerlin made preparations for the Pagan thanksgiving which I have been obliged to attend over the years. I have since written to the Abbott suggesting that we create a similar Christian ceremony to celebrate the harvest. If Pope Julius could decide to give our Lord a day of birth that coincided with a pagan ritual of solstice at the low point of the winter sun, why should we not try to take unto us their festival of Yule?

At the ceremony, which started much as they have done every year since I took up office in Caardbury, events took place that few would believe. I can only assure you that I would willingly swear on the holy book, and prostrate myself upon the holy alter in the presence of the Pope himself, to be testament to the truth of what I now record on these pages.

I stood behind a shapely woman and her young son, only a few feet from the old river lake by the Exe. From this vantage I had a good view of the proceedings, and happily saw, yet again, no response from the Old Gods as the offerings were cast into the waters. Yet when Maerlin spoke all things changed. He was clearly possessed by the Holy Spirit. I have never seen such a spectacle. He stood upon the water itself, just as our Lord had done, although with his lesser powers he was not able to stand fully out of the water, and at the end of the ceremony the water ceased to hold him upward and claimed him, as if in baptism. Yet when standing on that water the Holy Ghost literally opened the upper portal from hell and allowed the smoke from the fires below to be seen by the world of men. Then at his request our good Lord gave us a sword of vengeance. "Vengeance is mine" said the Lord, but we are the Lord's instruments and do his bidding, so if the Lord bids it we can be the instruments of his vengeance. He gave us 'Ex-Calliper,' a wonderful blade forged from a single piece of steel, such as I have never seen before. (Many weeks later I was allowed to inspect the weapon and I can honestly say that I have never seen the like, before or since. No mortal craftsman could create such a blade. I have also seen this holy weapon used in combat, and seen the blades of the North Men shatter when they are struck by this holiest of Christian wonders.)

It was the arrival of this blade into the world of mortal men that astounded us all. It came from the deep water, and was in the hands of a fair maiden. It was the lady of the lake, an angel doing our Lord's bidding, and she held the haft of the weapon above the surface for all to see. After lowering Maerlin into the waters of the lake, to show him that as a wizard he was only the instrument of our Lord, Maerlin was allowed to collect the Ex-Calliper sword and bring it unto us.

This holy weapon is a weapon only fit for a king among men. Maerlin said that he had been spoken to by God, and that the weapon must be held by a leader of men. A leader who would stand against the heathens from the north and drive them back into the dark waters of the sea. A king amongst men.

Maerlin said that God had told him that the weapon must be carried by a man of steel. But then, in error that I knew would fail, he offered it to the Smithy who, although a leader in our community, is no king.

Chapter Ten;   The Test.

I recovered the sword from the Smith. Perhaps I had done the theatrics a bit too well, and scared him out of it. Perhaps the responsibility had just got to him. Either way I was back to square one. Well almost. At least we had a sword that had the required status. All we needed was someone to wield it, someone who would bloody well listen to little old Bill Marlin, the computer wizard. Because I was the one with the bloody CDs crammed full of the best bloody battle tactics in history!!!

Surprise, surprise, the following day Kaardbury was blessed with a visit from Lord Beouf. He turned up on a very large horse with a dozen mounted men. Where were you lot, I thought, when the Vikings attacked the villages? He demanded to speak with the Smith, and this brief conversation resulted in him demanding to speak with me, Marlin the wizard. I had been in the village when he had arrived, sitting eating a breakfast at a table next to the house where the three old ladies did their leather work.

I had been a little scared a few times since my return to Kaardbury, although none had come close to the terror of the Viking raid. Beouf was a corpulent man with a chubby, but hard looking, face. He would have made an excellent east end villain in a '60s gangster movie. His sweating red face turned to me and he glared as he looked down. "Where is my sword?" was the demand.
"It is the sword of the Gods" was my reply. A large man got off his horse from behind Beouf and walked to the table I was sitting at. His weapons chinked as he approached me. His sword gave a sickening scraping noise as it was removed from its scabbard, and I genuinely thought I was, in all probability, going to die. I stood up and backed off. Beouf said "None of your bloody conjuring tricks. Where is my sword?" I swallowed hard, the man in front of me took hold of the front of the smock I was wearing and backed me against the wooden wall of the hut behind me. We stood nose to nose. My shirt front was balled in his fist against my throat. His breath smelled of rotting meat. "I will get the sword for you."
"Too right you fucking will!" was his foul mouthed reply. I have to admit I was more than a bit scared.

Beouf insisted that 'Bad Breath' accompany me to my hut to retrieve the sword. Beouf stayed in the village to swagger around a bit, and drink some free ale, and we walked up the hill to my home. I wanted Bad Breath him to stay outside, but he refused to do so. I had spent the five minute walk thinking hard and, despite his refusal, I had what I thought was a good plan.

From when I first moved into my new home I had rigged my hut for defence. When the reassigned alarm systems I had removed from Loofah were set, I could walk away knowing that no human would dare to enter my inner safe room. But I did not intend Bad Breath to get as far as that. I wanted them all to leave here truly frightened of me. I had no intention of opening the door to my inner sanctum, so when the two of us were inside my hut I unwrapped the hand held electric stun device I kept by the door. It was about the size of a cigarette packet, and had two blunt electrical contacts sticking out from the business end. I also picked up the pair of rigid bar hand cuffs I kept with them. I held the electrical device in my right hand behind me as I lifted the cuffs in my left hand as if to show them to the man. I was close to his left side and he was looking down at the cuffs and even managed to demanded "What are they for?" as I thrust the electrical contacts into the back of his exposed neck. The effect was very satisfying ... Bad Breath went into a convulsive rictus and dropped forward onto his knees, and then his belly, striking his forehead with a satisfying 'clump,' against the edge of my table on his way down. His hands were partly trapped underneath him, but I had maintained the pressure on the electrodes all the way to the deck. I lifted the device and he sort of relaxed and sagged at the same time. I dragged his left arm from under him and applied the cuffs. Pulling his right shoulder back I was able to release the other arm and cuff both hands behind him. There was no resistance whilst I did this other than him being bloody heavy. After a minute or so he seemed to be back in the world of the living and by grabbing the scruff of his jerkin I was able to pull him up to his knees. I told him to stand up but he shook his head and said "Fuckin bastard wizard." He hit his head a second time when I pressed the Taser into the back of his neck once again. The next time I told him to get to his feet, he did. By now he was visibly shaking. I had stepped over the Rubicon; I had now made some serious enemies, but I had had no choice. I was obliged to try to act in a way that would make Beouf and his men go away for good. They had to be very scared of me. If I got this wrong I would almost certainly be dead, and I would put the whole village at risk. I now had much to do before the rest of them turned up to find out what was happening.

By the time Beouf and his remaining entourage arrived at my humble little abode, the sword was safely hidden and I was sitting on my favourite log by a rough wooden table in front of my property. I had had plenty of time to arm myself with a number of goodies to make a very reasonable attempt at sorting this business out. Despite the weaponry I was genuinely scared! A dozen big fellows wearing chain mail and carrying long swords can do that sort of thing to a computer nerd.

The riders spread out as the pathway led into the clearing in front of my ninth century home. I had tied my hand-made rope between the trees, blocking the path from the village. In the centre of the rope was my red shirt, the flag was to keep others away when I was practicing my magic. Bad Breath was cuffed, and bare-chested, with his arms around a tree near the hut. I stood up, using my silver staff to get to my feet. I un-slung the shotgun from my shoulder and pointed it at Beouf. He looked a little less certain. "You will die for this. I am Thane of this land and you have struck one of my men." He was clearly pissed off. My reply was "If you are lord of these people you should protect them, not hide in your little fort. The sword must be wielded by a true leader. If the sword chooses you we will all follow you."
"You talk in riddles, you foreign bastard" he replied. But I went on, "There will be a test that any man can take, but the sword will only chose the right one to lead us. If you pass the test you will be the one to lead us." He replied "Nonsense, kill him" and indicated to the man on his right to cut the rope.

As the man drew his sword I raised the shotgun to my shoulder and fired a solid bear cartridge into the chest of his horse. I hated doing it but I had no choice. A bear cartridge is a single plug of lead the width of a shotgun barrel, with flanges on the sides to give it spin and some stability in flight. Not a particularly accurate weapon, but at this range I could not miss. Being designed to kill a fully grown bear and with what is, in effect, a bullet the size of your thumb, the impact is devastating. The deep barking bang of the gun startled everyone. Smithy, Eric and some of the villagers had followed and were behind the horsemen. One of the villagers had a man in chain mail land on top of him as other horses reared up, two or three of which set off out of control through the woods and downhill towards the pathway below. Beouf managed to pull his rearing horse down, as the horse I had shot was next to him and it literally toppled over. The slug had entered the centre of the animal's chest, spreading as it hit the ribcage, before tearing through heart and lungs and ending up on the far side of the chest cavity. I know this detail because I was involved in cutting the horse up for meat later that day. It was dead before it hit the ground. The poor beast's life was the price for showing these bastards I meant business.

I pointed the shotgun straight at Beouf and waited for those who were still there to get their horses under control. The man on the dead horse had his left leg trapped under the carcass and was flopping about trying to get free. Beouf circled his mount in front of the small crowd of villagers before coming back to the rope. "What have you done, wizard? I am a Thane lord appointed by the king!"
I was angry that I had been forced to kill the horse. So was virtually shouting now, "If you do not protect your people perhaps we need a new king, and a new lord. Get off your bloody horse and we will talk about the sword. The sword will choose a new leader. Perhaps the sword will even choose a king for the people. If you are not chosen you can go back to fucking Crediton, hide in your fort and leave us alone. If you are chosen, you get the sword and you can then lead these people against the raiders. JUST AS YOU SHOULD BE FUCKING DOING ANYWAY!!!"
Beouf had dismounted but would not approach beyond the rope. Behind him two more of his men got off their horses and walked to his side. I must have looked rather puny all alone in the clearing in front of my hut, despite everyone knowing I was able to strike a horse dead by some sort of very loud wizardry.

"It will be a fair test" I said, "all men, you, and all of your warriors can try to claim the sword. But the sword will choose who will lead us. If the sword chooses you, we will follow you. If the sword chooses another then we must follow that man, whoever is chosen must lead us. For, if we do not, the Gods will be very angry."

Beouf was clearly not happy with that. He glowered at me. Perhaps the single loud noise, and a horse dropping dead was not enough to convince him that he was up against a superior force. I certainly wasn't convinced, so why should he be. He jerked his head to the two men beside him who lifted the rope over their heads and started towards me. Perhaps Beouf now felt safe as he was not on horseback. I put the shotgun on the table and picked up one of the metal rods.

The slower of his two heavies was under the rope by the time I had lifted my silver staff, and turned the flame tube towards them. There were anxious glances between the men gathered beyond the red shirt on the edge of the clearing. The two warriors on foot, having cleared the rope, started towards me, and I could see Eric and the other villagers who had come to watch begin to wisely move away further down the path. My last words were "Come no closer," but they were under orders and I was just an unarmed man in a silly cloak, holding a thin metal rod, who didn't even speak particularly good Saxon. They were 10 yards from me when I released the flame.

Loofah's fiery breath was designed to come out very fast to compensate for the speed of the microlight. If it had been too slow the craft would have been engulfed in flame every time it was used. The high pressure created in the chamber, combined with the cleverly designed nozzle, ensured that the flame was thrown forward with great force. The half litre of flame juice became an instant fireball, but the two heavies were so close to me that the narrow shaft of flame coming out of the tube passed between them before blossoming into a 30 foot wide ball directly behind them and, as it happened, in the faces of Beouf and his remaining mounted men. I had only tried the fire tubes once by hand, and then I had braced a tube under my arm, and against a tree. The force of the discharge now threw the nozzle upwards as I staggered back, allowing the air pressure to partly escape, so by the time I pulled it down again and the last half cupful literally just splattered out of the tube, where it engulfed the two terrified men on foot, who were now only five paces in front of me, and now in their own little piece of hell.

My understanding is that no one was killed, but Beouf and four of the mounted men had severe blistering on their faces and arms. Another broke his wrist badly when he was thrown from his horse, and one of the two who had approached me actually crapped himself. We know this because both of them ran into the woods, and one was found still hiding in a thicket in the valley below Kaardbury that lunchtime. Beouf, I understand, ran back to the village, where he grabbed a horse from one of his men, and rode off to Crediton. We released the man from his cuffs, and helped the one trapped under his horse. The villagers tended the injured men as best they could, and rounded up the horses that had bolted.

I sat the two men, Bad Breath and Dead Horse, down at a table in the centre of the village. I apologised for what had happened, but explained that I was only doing what the Gods had told me to do. I was a mere wizard who obeyed the Gods. I told them that within a week there would be a test that all of Beouf's men could take. It would be a test of strength or skill, and that whoever the sword chose would lead us. I even gave them both one of my few remaining favourite boiled sweets saying that they were treats given by the Gods that would give them a pleasure no mortal man had experienced. They left sharing a mount, each sucking a butterscotch sweet that would not be invented for another thousand years.

Three days later the night alarm I set outside my hut went off at about three in the morning. It might have been a stray deer, but I suspected not. The piercing wail bought four men from the village who arrived at a flat run carrying blades and axes. No one was found. The following night I had set a number of quite nasty devices, and one of them went off just before dawn with a loud 'CRUMP'. I turned on the floodlights and went out to find a semi-conscious man covered in blood, and could hear another thrashing through the undergrowth to the east. The man on the ground was thin faced, scarred, and well armed. I kicked a long wicked looking sword away from his hand, into the leaves. I removed both his knife and cudgel and threw them in the same direction. He had taken much of the blast of a customized mini claymore mine, a small version of the army weapon I had described that contains 700 ball-bearings. My smaller version was the size of a mobile phone, and only contained a tablespoonful of number 6 shot, but at very close range this could still prove to be lethal. I had not intended to kill anyone, but having suspected that my life was in danger from Beouf, I was now playing deliberately dirty. I had no idea how they had got past the first trip wires which should have set off the alarm again, but there were other dangers for any would-be intruder had they managed to get even closer. Most of the shot appeared to have gone into his upper arm, but the right side of his face was oozing blood from half a dozen small holes, and it appeared as if one had gone into his right eye ball. He was starting to groan as I applied the cuffs.

I cuffed him to a tree and armed with the shotgun went into the village to get some help. By the time I came back with Eric, Smithy and five others, all carrying weapons, someone had slit the throat of the man whom I had definitely left alive (I have a good memory for this sort of thing). I assume the other assassin had returned, and unable to remove the cuffs they had chosen to prevent my captive from naming his employer. His throat was cut so deeply that his head was sagging backwards at an impossible angle, and the white bone of the spinal column was visible at the back of the wound. We made a search in the gathering light, and even went back to the village to get two dogs which were used by the woodsmen to try to find the killer. By lunchtime we gave up, the murderer could have been in Exeter by then.

The person who was responsible for reporting such matters to the local lord was the head villager, Smithy. He made the decision that unless someone came looking for the dead man we would say nothing. It was quite likely that the other assassin would not want to report what had happened, and to keep his own throat intact he would just disappear. By keeping quiet we would be able to keep the opposition guessing. So the body was buried, and no one ever came to ask of his whereabouts. He had not been recognised by anyone, and no one had the affront to suggest that I had been the one to end his life. From that evening onwards the villagers kept an all night vigil outside my hut. I did not want them to be attacked themselves, and I did not want them blundering into my protective devices. But after much discussion I allowed them to keep sentries posted on the path from my hut into the village, and on the road that ran 100 yards (or 91.44 metres for any pedants out there) below my hut. It was the road to the village of Thorverton, a community two miles (or three kilometres, 218 metres and 68.8 centimetres) away to the south east. (I will quit all this conversions stuff ... they are only approximations you know, so from now on work it out for yourselves.)

Nothing else of note happened before the day of the sword test was upon us.

Over the week leading up to the day of the test I got Eric, Spots and Little Finger, along with three others, to make two trips with an ox cart to a hillside quarry some four miles away to the west. They collected the best part of two tons of rock and built a waist high pile of it in the centre of Kaardbury. For my part I loaded the lockable cockpit of Loofah onto the cart, and took it down to the rock-pile. With the help of the young men I built a test of strength that would defeat all but 'the chosen'.

I selected the day for the test as Sunday, the holy day. This suited me fine as fewer people would be in the fields, and I wanted witnesses. I had sent out the word that all-comers could attend Kaardbury to be tested. I was questioned about the original demand made by the Gods that the chosen would have to be someone who worked with iron. This had initially just been a load of bollocks that I had been intended as an identifying aspect of Smithy that would ensure he was 'the one'. But, as was pointed out, any warrior, farmer or huntsman would qualify just as easily. So, as I said, all could come.

By lunchtime, and the closing time for entry, we had 108 applicants. Many were big strong men, but there was an unexpectedly wide range of people who fancied their chances. I had briefed Eric, and had given him a leather gauntlet to wear during the test. He was the youngest applicant, and appeared to be a bit overawed by the clamour of the horses, chain mail and weaponry of the attending throng. I was only worried about another confrontation with Beouf.

Beouf had turned up with his men only half an hour before the closing time for entry, sporting a blistered face and bandaged arm. I had been prepared for him, and despite sweating like a pig, I had the shotgun slung under my cape, and both fire tubes primed and bound together as my staff. By the time they arrived the Dragon Leg sword was on display in the cockpit cage. I had experimented quite a bit on how to set up the cage, as

I wanted the test to be uncomplicated and to avoid anyone rattling it about so much that the battery maintaining the locking mechanism became disconnected. In the end I kept it simple. I had the cage laid on its side on a wide flat piece of rock at the roadside, where some cutting into the hillside had been necessary for the wagons to pass along the road to Thorverton. The rocks had then been piled onto and around it. We ended up with having to dig down about a foot into the roadway to build a stance where a man could grip the handle of the door of the microlight cage at chest height, and then to try to pull it towards himself to open it. The cage had to be opened one handed and, after the first two attempts, I also introduced a time limit of one minute counted out by one of the old ladies from Crediton. After some further argument the old lady was made to face away from the cage so that she could not favour anyone from her home town. There was a great deal of rattling of the handle, but it was well made, and there could not have been a man alive who would have been able to move the cage with well over a ton of stone on top of it, or to open a magnetic lock with a holding force in excess of 1,200 pounds with one hand. (You work it out.)

The sword was clearly visible in the cage. Tantalizingly close for Beouf as he took his turn. He even used both hands, and despite my protests fought with the handle for almost two minutes before storming off to stand with the rest of his men. Time wore on, and it became a bit monotonous watching man mountain after man mountain try his hand, literally. The crowd were becoming restless, so I called Eric forward to take his turn. He was wearing the gloves as instructed, but seemed unsure in front of so many. I urged him forward. He took hold of the handle and pulled. The cage opened so easily that he fell backwards and sat on the roadway quite shocked. There was a gasp that went round the onlookers. They had all expected the Smithy to be the chosen one, but after his dismal failure by the lake I was not going to go through that again.

Eric got slowly to his feet and gingerly put his hands into the cage to take the sword. A shout went up, and Beouf strode forward. "This boy cannot lead you! I am the lord of this land." Instead of taking the sword Eric stepped back and closed the cage again. He turned to Beouf saying, "Yes lord, I am not worthy, please take the sword," and while Beouf fought with the handle again Eric came to me and removed the gloves. He looked me straight in the eye and handed them to me. "Maerlin, if I am truly the chosen one, I should be able to take the sword from the stones without the aid of magic gloves. I could feel the electronic key card in the back on the gauntlet as I took it from him. Fuck, Fuck, Fuck!!! .... Oh well, plan B then!

After Beouf initially refused to move away from the cage again, the crowd started to jeer at him. He was losing his bandage as well as his credibility amongst his own people, very quickly. So after I lowered the tip of my staff towards him in subtle menace, he stormed off to the side once again. I moved closer to the rock covered cage, standing only a few feet from Eric as he stepped again into the shallow hole in front of the sword. As he took the handle I held my arms wide and shouted out, "Behold the Gods choose your leader from amongst the believers!" Thankfully in doing so I was able to get the battery operated remote in my left hand close enough for the signal to be picked up by the cage. I had tested this before, but with the rocks around it I needed to be less than six feet away for it to work. There was a faint click. Eric, displaying a calm serenity I had never seen in him before, slowly opened the door and lifted Ex Spring out from the stones. Eric raised the sword above his head as the crowd roared, "Thor, Thor, Thor!!!!!" Beouf simply took hold of his horse reigns, turned, and with his entourage, just walked away.

The Chronicles of Eathelwold 'James' Trefell; Monk.

Book 1 Chapter 12

The sacred sword was the talk of our community. It was wondrous to see what the Our Almighty God was able to do, but we were not sure what would happen next. The War Lord Beouf came to us for the weapon, but could not wrest it from the trial made by Maerlin, who used his magic to keep that corpulent beast in his place. There was a promise that all could be tested to see who the sword would chose to lead us against the North Men, and it was Maerlin who oversaw the preparations for that test. As you can imagine I had no intention of taking the test myself. As a man of the cloth it would be inappropriate for me to take the test as I would surely have passed it. As the only person in the community with any real claim to a connection with our Lord, I was the obvious choice. But in deciding not to partake in such a test I considered it to be of interest as to whom our lord would choose in substitution for myself.

Maerlin, guided by God, chose a test of strength, and the

sword Ex-Calliper was encased in stones. I watched with my own eyes as warrior after warrior, man after man, tried to wrest the blade from the clutches of the stone, but all failed. Then to my amazement 'Our Thor' (Lord forgive me) stepped forward, and opened the doorway to the sword so easily that he fell to the ground in the praise of our Lord. Then, after showing again that the door still would not open to others, Our Thor ('Eric' seems unsuitable for one so chosen), with great calmness, walked forward and took the sword from the stones, as if that had always been his destiny. I was greatly pleased that I had elected to stand back and that I had permitted him take the test, for he is a good man, albeit tender in years, and I will happily step on one side to sanction him to lead our peoples in this time of need.

In truth I had expected Wulfgar, a great warrior who to my understanding uses a lance a lot in battle, to be the one to take the sword from the stones. He was a friend of the village and his twin brother, Holt the woodsman, had been the only other wielder of a holy instrument of death to the pagans — his mighty longbow. The good Lord tells us many things, and although the meek shall inherit the earth, I believe that he

expects me to look after his people until that time. I am the
one who blessed Holt's strong arms and powerful weapon at
ceremonies in Caardbury. Holt may have thought that it
was one of the old Gods who gave him the strength to kill a
North Man, but in truth it was the one Lord our God, and
his blessing was given quietly and unseen.

Chapter Eleven;   The Shield Table.

The celebrations went on for the whole evening, and much of the following day. I was at great pains to get certain things done as soon as possible. Firstly I wanted the cage from the microlight to be left alone or removed. The chances of it being left alone, if all these people were still around, were minimal. So I struck upon an idea. There were hundreds of people there, and over a hundred rocks in the pile. Each stone weighed between 20 and 50 pounds. So I made an announcement saying that each family could take away one stone to keep in their household. These stones were to remind them of this day, to remind them of the power of working together, and building together, and most of all they would bring any household with a 'sword stone' as a hearth stone in it, great good fortune. I got Little Finger and Spots to oversee the dismantling of the test site, and to protect the cage, which on my instruction they carried to my hut while I got hold of James the priest, and some writing materials.

During the following celebrations I got James to speak to everyone present, record where they were from, who was in their household, their community, and so on. I especially wanted to know if, having seen what they had seen, they were willing to pledge their support to Eric. It occurred to me that although this sword test had been a pain to arrange after Smithy had failed to take the plunge, I would probably have had much greater difficulty winning over so many followers so quickly. Some were from villages that were just too far away, and with regret I explained that we could not include those communities that had too far to travel. This was because the key to our plans was to create a place where all could come together to defend ourselves against the North Men. This process of gathering everyone into a safe place was limited by the amount of warning we would get. There was no point in making agreements with communities who simply lived too far away. But I did have plans, lots of them....

The following days were filled with actions, decisions and the start of a new direction. Our first step was to decide who would be included in our miniature kingdom. The constraint had to be the time it would take for the Vikings to get to attack the safe place chosen as the stronghold – the stronghold that I had decided needed to be built. During the previous few months I had wandered the outlying area quite a bit, and had considered and discussed options at length already. Yet the best choice by far was right on our doorstep. Well, not so much our doorstep as on our roof....

At the top of the hill, high above Kaardbury, there was an old large earthwork circle which, from looking at some of the data I had on my laptop, was clearly an Iron Age fort. This is a fort that had remained as a significant structure even in the 21st century. I had seen the earthworks from Loofah when I had first arrived at the village, in what now seemed a lifetime ago, and I had had the opportunity to explore it extensively since.

At each stage I had to get the general agreement of Eric and the village leaders, but given this location for our place of defence we were able to decide on which communities could be included in our little kingdom, clearly limited to those who could reach this 'safe place for all' in times of attack. The furthest up-river that a boat of the size of a Viking longship could travel was to just below Thorverton, where shallows and low rapids made voyaging beyond that point very difficult. Previous raids had beached at that place, so we worked back from there. Four miles of uphill travel on foot, carrying weapons and armour, would take an hour at least. They had horses, but these always stayed with the men on foot until the last moment of attack, as they were too few to ride on alone. Any community within a one hour of easy journey time could be included in our catchment area. So we set our limit of a three mile journey from north, west and south, and all the way to the river to the east. On my modern day map of Devon and Cornwall this included villages that were eventually named Well Town and Bickleigh to the north and north east. Upham to the north west, Cheriton Fitzpaine and Stockleigh Pomeroy to the west and south west, and of course Thorverton to the south east. Within this catchment area there were eleven identifiable communities and villages. We had also included anyone living on farms and homesteads, or working on the land such as shepherds or woodsmen.

The strangest thing for me was that there was little idea of exactly what distance a mile was, or how long an hour took. In those days it seems as if everything was very approximate. I did not realise that supposedly official measurements had been altered again and again by different rulers wanting different parts of their body to be the standard foot, or cubit. Or that time was a strangely flexible thing because the best measurement was that the daylight, and night time, were both divided into twelve hours, which varied considerably in duration with the change of seasons. There would be no real need for accurate timekeeping until navigation across oceans required it to enable longitude to be calculated in the 1700s, almost 1000 years from now. When you think about it the planet is just over 24,000 miles (40,000 kilometres) in circumference, so for every 1000 miles further west you go, midday is an hour later. Hence genuine midday, when the sun is directly overhead, is 7 minutes later in Bristol than it is in London. The choice of twelve hours was apparently, according to one of my history CDs, due to the numbers 12 and 60 being the best numbers for sub-dividing into smaller whole numbers, back in Egypt about 4000 years ago. Consequently there are 24 hours in a day and 60 minutes in an hour. So eventually it was down to me, with the discreet assistance of my modern day timepieces, and a sketch of the map copied from my laptop, to establish the boundaries of our little kingdom by literally pacing them out!

In total we calculated we could bring together about 300 people within the travel time available. Of these we decided we probably had about 70 able men of ages between 16 and 50. As a fighting force out in the open we would all be slaughtered in minutes by the crew of a single longship, but with the right defences we were more than enough to hold a fort. Harlech Castle in Wales had survived a seven year siege with a small garrison, and although we would not be building 30 foot stone walls, the Vikings would not be attempting a protracted siege. Through all the historical data I had it was clear that good defences were everything. Even the Roman soldiers used trenches and palisades every night when they camped. On average a defending force lost one warrior to the attackers' seven, if there were proper fortifications in place. I hoped to do even better than that.

The communities who we could not include were thanked and told that they could either look to Beouf, or to try to copy what we were doing for themselves. What did happen was that a number of families deliberately relocated to within our catchment area (but who could blame them?).

I persuaded Eric, who had started to believe in himself a bit too much, that we need to give the appearance of taking heed of the advice of others.

We needed the head men of these communities to be involved in decision making from the start. So I got a local carpenter to take one of the captured Viking shields and turn it into a table. It was about the right size for four or five men to sit around, and gave us a suitable focal point for discussions. If nothing else it was a great reminder of why the hell we were doing this in the first place. Anything said at that table had to be honest and true, and every village representative had to swear an oath with his hand placed in the middle of that round shield table. Given that Eric was 'the chosen one', they all had to swear an oath the follow him, and work together. Even his father, Smith, who for the first time offered up his given name of Hector, swore the oath on the table. His father seemed somewhat abashed by this nominal revelation and excused himself by claiming that he had been named by a priest that had once read an old Grecian book about a famous siege. Our meetings took place in the evenings as each daylight hour was filled with toil. So it tended to be that these leaders from the villages travelled in the darkness to sit at the table with Eric and to plan for the future.

I had been aware that many of the occupants of Kaardbury were related, and that kinship was the key to holding these communities together, but I was surprised at how many connections with their extended family there were in our catchment area. In the 21st century we sometimes joked about suspected interbreeding amongst families in some parts of the globe. In fact before I left the modern world scientists had identified serious genetic diseases caused by inbreeding in UK families from Pakistan, many of whom were required to marry their own cousins. But I saw little to suggest that this practice had much affect in the ninth century. My guess is that whereas in the 21st century we would keep the affected children alive at great cost to the state, here in 831 they just died.

Then we got on to the heavy stuff. We needed an early warning system that would alert everyone of the arrival of any North Men. We needed to build our defences, and not only get the men together to do it, but find some way to help those men continue to tend their livestock, and plough and sow and reap their harvests. It would be no good saving everyone's life if they would just starve in the winter anyway. We also had to find the best way of arming these people. These were hard working farming people. We could not afford to buy in mercenaries to fight for us, and we could not train a fighting force capable of matching Viking warriors in ordinary combat. But we could build a fort, or defensive compound, that would be difficult for the enemy to get into. It would also be much more effective, in the long term, if any attack on our defences cost them dearly. If we could make that happen, it would be the one sure way of making them go away and leave us alone for good ... I hoped.

For the early warning system we decided on bells. None of them had seen a bell, although a number had heard their chimes on their travels. One of the older members of our circle of 12 had travelled all the way to Aquitaine in southern France in his youth, and had heard bells in churches there. He even claimed to have been inside one of Charles the Great's palaces. It took me a visit to my laptop to realise he was talking about Charlemagne who had died less than twenty years ago.

I had got Eric to make a decent sized bell about the dimensions of a policeman's helmet. Suspended from a pole, it made a surprisingly loud peal when struck, causing a number of the villagers to run into the smithy to see what had made such a noise. It had turned out that the trick was to avoid using iron as, unless it was made of good quality steel, it would not ring. And without a blast furnace to produce the steel it would take forever to fold and beat enough iron to get all the carbon out of it. In the end we tried making it out of bronze, an alloy of copper and tin. Fifteen hundred years earlier bronze had been the currency of the age, and a great symbol of wealth, but now it was just another metal. Not as common as iron, but easier to melt and cast, and much easier to produce at a high level of purity.

After quenching, the bell had been re-heated and hammered out to a smoother shaped dome. The result was not perfect, but it had a loud resonating peal of sound. Amongst the 12 communities there were four smithies, and the secret of making bells, and the responsibility for producing them would be shared. We calculated 40 bells would cover the whole area with some extras for riverside listening posts. The area of our little kingdom was about 30 square miles, and no one would be more than one mile from a bell. We tested them and a single bell could be easily heard over two or three miles, even more if the wind was right. Even in bad weather it was quite easy to hear the bells a mile upwind. So, short of

142

a hurricane, or an excess of intoxicants, we would all hear the warning.

We set up one bell in each village, and four along the river at fishermen's cottages. The rest were spread out amongst the isolated farms to make sure the distribution was evenly spread across our little realm, and that we kept to our planned one mile limit so that everyone in the catchment area would be in earshot of the bells. There was, of course, a danger of someone being too deeply asleep, or making too much noise, so that they could not hear the warning. But we could not cater for every contingency, and we hoped that even in the event of an early morning raid there would be someone wide enough awake in each village to set off the alarm locally.

We had a test day which was to be every Sunday, or Sabbath day, the day of rest. At this time the original pagan seventh day celebrated on a Saturday had been moved by the new religion of Christianity to Sunday. So, from then on, every Sunday at midday we tested the bells. We also had more than one signal using the bells. For the main alarm, the bells were rung at least five times in succession, and if it was safe to do so, presumably because the attackers had not reached the bell ringer, they were to be rung continuously for at least two minutes. This was the warning signal for a Viking attack. If the bells were struck once and this was repeated a number of times with an interval of at least 10 seconds between each strike, this was the 'all clear'. The third signal we used the bells for was to call an emergency meeting of our council of elders. The 11 spokesmen for the villages would meet at Kaardbury every Sabbath, or in an emergency at the call of the bells, when there was a need for a joint decision on any issue of great importance. With Smith (Hector) who was the head of our community, and with Eric (who was now answering to 'Thor'), we had 12 to seat in Smith's hall. I made a point of remaining as just Eric's adviser, and making sure he knew what to say each time they met. I always sat behind Eric, and to one side. There was a great respect for me and the powers I had, but I was still an outsider, and I still spoke with a strange accent. The only person at those meetings who fully trusted me was Eric, but that was enough to make things work ... just. However, there were some heavy arguments.

Our key observation-post over the Exe was on a steep hill just to the south east of Thorverton. The hill had a precipitous escarpment down to the watercourse some 200 feet below, and there is a good view of the river floodplain southwards towards Exeter. From that vantage point a watchman could see over three miles downriver to where the Exe is joined by the river Culm and they head west into the northern outskirts of the town. After some discussion we allocated the task of manning the viewpoint with youngsters from amongst us. All children between the ages of 10 and 13 were to be on a rota. The total number of children involved was 23, and the number would change with each child's birthday. There had to be two on duty at any one time, and they only worked about one four hour shift every two days. It may seem a little odd to us now, but a four mile walk for a 10 year old was no big deal then. The five village priests managed the rota, and occasionally filled in when a child was unwell. What they did also undertake was teaching the children to read and write while they were on their daytime watches. A priest would spend about a week at a time in Thorverton, sleeping in the village and tutoring during the daylight hours. Most children of any era need to be nailed to the floor to keep them still enough to enable any teaching to take place. So here, at last, the priests found their captive audience. My only caveat was that they were not allowed to preach to the kids. They balked at this, but by using their bibles as one of their main reading books, they still felt they were spreading their word.

The biggest problem was getting able-bodied men away from their continual grind of everyday work, the work they needed to do to feed their families, because this was the manpower essential for building our fort. We came to some compromises. I took the four blades from Loofah's propeller and had Eric weld them into ploughs that would not have been out of place in the 1800s let alone the 800s. With two blades on each of our two newly design ploughs, we were able to cut in half the time it took to till the soil on each farm or smallholding. Restricting the use of these ploughs rigorously, to only those who were contributing work towards the fort, enabled us to get started. We were also able to take on the labour of four woodsmen who were willing to work a whole year for three gold coins from my emergency hoard each. I had over a kilo of silver pennies I had barely touched that were the usual currency of the time, but the gold was a much rarer and more valuable currency. I appreciated that I was giving them about two years' pay, but we had to get the fort built quickly. After realising my unintentional generosity I managed to persuade one of them to bring along his 16 year old son, another to bring his twin brother who had been in Beouf's service, and the other two to commit their wives to providing cooking for our workers.

The hill fort above us stood the best part of 300 feet higher than the village, and probably 700 feet above sea level, so it would be a climb for any Vikings trekking up from the river at Thorverton. The top of the hill had steep slopes on all sides except to the south, where a half mile long slope ran downhill to the Thorverton road. The pathway leading up the ridge from the Thorverton road was about three quarters of a mile south east of the main junction in Kaardbury where it met the Crediton road, and was only a few hundred yards south east from my hut. Walking up this pathway towards the fort there were a number of small cultivated fields, and some large areas of woodland. The centre of the fort, which was some 100 yards across, was being used for grazing animals, and surrounding the fort were mature, mainly deciduous woods.

The first task was to clear this woodland so that the fort had a clear view of fire in every direction. Some of the trees were very large, and the two saving graces were that much of the wood could be split into posts for building our palisade, and that this land could be used in the future for more grazing, which would be of benefit to the village. Eight of the big trees and 17 of the larger saplings were growing more or less directly out of the earth bank of the fort. These we kept, only taking off the lower branches to incorporate the trunks into, or just behind, the palisade itself. I was pleased with this idea as they provided significant extra support to the structure. The felling of the trees was assisted very little by the two axes I had with me. One was a high quality felling axe, the other a hand axe. Despite their superior quality they were not significantly better than the axes produced by the Smithy for general use. More valuable were the two saw blades I had carried. The bow saw handles had not been included in my equipment to save space, but the blades were flexible enough to be coiled into a billy can, and this trick is a must for any serious backpacker in the 21st century. These modern-day saw blades, when fitted into wooden handles, cut far better than the brittle locally produced tools.

The earthworks of the Iron Age fort were actually very impressive. The volume of material they had shifted was huge. The southern part of the fort was almost exactly circular, and the north eastern and north western sides were straighter, making the whole thing sort of fan, or scallop, shaped. The earth wall was surprisingly high, with a drop of about twenty feet from the top to the outside ground in most places. On the inside of the fort the drop was much less, but the slippery footing of the encroaching winter months meant they were still very treacherous. We completed the wood clearance by mid winter, but had to wait until the frozen ground had softened again before we could complete the wall of the fort. This palisade was of stout poles about 8–9 inches in diameter, or of square wooden posts made from splitting the lumber from the bigger trees. By the end of the spring we had over 1000 nine foot long posts set in our earth bank to a depth of four feet. Where the trees did not support the wall we used bracers. The whole wall was pinned together at ground level with 12 inch squared tree trunks, and again a foot from the rim with a six inch by three inch planking. Much of the wood had been from the surrounding forest, but during the winter months many of the nine foot posts were manufactured in the villages and on the farms, which we collected by cart in late February.

Our fort where 'all could come' was very impressive, although the grazing land in the centre of the structure, which in total was about two acres, had given way to cloying mud, churned by our workers' boots. Outside the walls the rough ground and numerous visible tree stumps had that First World War no-man's-land look about it. But now we had good visibility, and there was no hiding place within a hundred yards of the wall. I had left the construction of a suitable gate in the southern face of the palisade in the hands of those with greater carpentry skills than me. The wooden wall either side of the gate was higher, as this was the one place where the earth bank was at its lowest, and presumably where the original entrance had been. Here, with the help of two of the retained trees, the wall was 15 foot high with the gate only just over one third of that from ground to lintel, and with a width of a mere four feet. I did not want anyone rushing through that gate in great numbers. It was exactly the right size to lead horses through, or take an ox and small cart through. The best that any attacker could do was to enter the gate in pairs, and on foot. This suited me just fine. So the gateway was more like a door in the middle of a large wall. The palisade wall, into which this doorway had been built, was deliberately solid on both sides of the door and all the way to the top of the wall. If they attacked the door the only way into the fort compound was actually through it. To make it particularly difficult to set fire to the big wall I got them to ship in some slabs of slate from a nearby rock outcrop. I had them cut and split 18 sheets from the rock. Each piece was about eight feet long, three feet wide and three inches thick. Each weighed the best part of a ton, but sunk three feet into the ground along the front edge of the wall they made it almost impossible the set fire to any part of that fortification apart from the doorway itself.

There was logic to this as I eventually needed to build into the construction of our fort a 'killing ground'. That was going to be the only way these unskilled farmers would be able to make Viking warriors pay heavily for their raids. As spring turned to summer the construction continued. I was greatly worried that we would be attacked again before the fort was completed. As it turned out that is exactly what happened.

The Chronicles of Eathelwold 'James' Trefell; Monk.

Book 1 Chapter 15.

After the sword was taken from the stones by 'Our Thor', our new king, I was given the task to speak to all those gathered, such that my mighty pen could enable great works to be done by our peoples. It was my pen, and the writing skills I am blessed with, that made possible what followed, just as our Lord would have wished.

There were twelve chosen. Twelve leaders of the people came forward, who had each stepped out from the darkness and out of the night, to swear allegiance to our king. Each of these men from the night sat at the round shield table to swear their oath, and in so doing created a new direction for us all. So it transpired that it was my pen that became the greatest weapon of this new age, greater even that the sword.

Verily it was through these meetings at the round table that the will of our Lord came to pass. These men from the night shared their thoughts with 'Our Thor', and despite the

mutterings of the wizard Maerlin, we decided that it would
be most frugal, as befits a Christian community, to make use
of a fortress from the old times. This fortress which was built
with pagan blood, but became blessed by the transformation
planned under my pen, into the 'come a lot' place that must
surely sanctify that heathen ground for the Almighty's
purpose. So with our one true God's blessing we set about
transforming that heathen topped hill into a place for
Christian people to gather and be safe.

Chapter Twelve;   The Bells

The bells started just after dawn on the 28th of May 832. This was early in the season for a Viking raid, but they were attacking more frequently now and it was no surprise that they wanted to hit us again, given their losses in 831. It turned out later that it had been one of the fishermen setting out early on the river who had seen the longship first. He had been readying his boat for a day of fishing, and had rushed to the bell and started the alarm, before grabbing his possession bags, wife and kids, and setting off for what came to be known as the 'come a lot of people' fort. A name which had stuck after my early description of 'a place where all could come' had been taken up by others, but which failed to translate easily into the ancient Saxon/early English tongue. The community that would always get to the fort first would be the occupants of Kaardbury. This meant that our villagers had special tasks that had to be completed. We had not yet finished the fort, but the outer palisade was complete, and everyone had been well briefed. When we heard the bells everyone was awoken. Each person now always kept their most valuable possessions in a bag in their homes, so that no time would be wasted and these prized belongings could be carried to the fort. The larger livestock were either deliberately released into the fields or taken to the fort as well. From Kaardbury there were three narrow carts built to pass through the gate that contained flagons for water. The filling of the flagons took some 20 minutes and many hands, but within half an hour there was in excess of 2,000 litres (3,520 pints) in stout three gallon jars, weighing about 40 pounds each, on their way up the hill in those carts pulled by oxen and horses. With around 300 souls in 'Come a Lot' I calculated we had at least three days of water. There was also a large ground tank built of sunken logs and clay, that we kept topped up within the compound of the fort, for the livestock. There was about three foot of water in it. Not enough for a proper siege, but more than enough for the time the Vikings would stay.

There were other tasks to do. One of them was to set up the ladders. With such a small gate we ran the risk of large numbers of people arriving at the last minute, with Vikings hot on their heels. To speed up access to the fort there were five long ladders that had to be set up around the fort so that people could climb into 'Come a Lot' from any direction. These ladders were pine trees selected for their suitability, and braced with longer branches at right angles at the bottom so they would not rotate when they were being used. The rest of the branches of the pine trees had been cut short for the steps, and these trees were light enough to be hauled over the palisade by ropes that remained attached to them. The edge of the palisade was protected by thick hessian mats to minimise wear and tear on both the ladders and the top edge of the wall. The earth rampart below the palisade was very steep, and in dry weather it was difficult to crawl up it on hands and knees. In wet weather it was simply impossible to scale. We went to great lengths to prevent the children playing on this embankment. We wanted there to be a good layer of short grass that gave little purchase, but prevented erosion. Given that these ladders could be climbed by all the children and younger adults, we calculated that only about 100 elders and nursing mothers would need to enter through the gate along with the livestock.

That morning with the sun still barely above the hills the other side of the Exe, the people started to arrive in groups of five or 10. Within the expected hour we had almost a full compliment. Each of our village leaders had a list of people in their community to check as a sort of roll call. Five of these men could not read and were assisted by the priests, or by others from their area who were literate. Six were still missing, but none of these were from the direction of the river, and Eric felt sure that they had not been captured already.

It took a great deal longer than expected for any of the raiders to be seen. I had a good pair of binoculars, a small monocular, and a decent sized telescope in my kit. The telescope was more powerful than was needed, but I lent my 'magic eye' x8 monocular to Eric to enable him to scan north and west, while I retained my x12 binoculars for the south and east. As it was, it was one of the kids who shouted out first from his viewpoint in the lower canopy of one of the trees towering above the gate. I trained my glasses on the main path toward Thorverton, and there walking up the hill were about fifteen warriors. A few moments later another group of six or seven appeared out of the woods to their right, and a few moments later another half dozen appeared further west as if these had come up the hill directly from Kaardbury.

It was surprisingly quiet. I suppose this situation was one I had not played through in my imagination, but after about 20 minutes there appeared to be the whole of a ship's crew, about 50 men, in ragged groups on the hillside below us. Four were on horseback. No one from within the fort shouted out or taunted them. This I later decided was a wise move, and had I thought of it before I would have got Eric to issue an order that everyone was to remain quiet. The Vikings must have been able to see our many heads above the palisade, watching and waiting. A baby started crying, and there was a muttering amongst the people around me. I was standing at the wall facing south, opposite the raiders. Eric had joined me from where he had been on the far side of the compound, although he assured me that there were still sentries facing out north, east and west, in case the fort was attacked from any another direction.

Two of the mounted men rode half way to the wall, stopping some 50 metres away. They were clearly having a good look at the structure. They had both kept their round shields in front of them preventing any expected missile from striking their body. Chain mail is a good protection against a sword blow, but less so against an arrow or spear with a narrow point. They were being careful. One of them shouted out something in what was presumably the Nordic language. There was a shouted reply from near me on the wall in what sounded like the same tongue. I called out for the person who spoke Norse, and who understood what had been said, to come and stand with me and Eric.

There was something else shouted in Anglo-Saxon as a man known as 'Percy of the Vale' came to my side. "My Lord, I speak their tongue" he said as he spoke to Eric (a bit over-the-top I thought, but did not have time to take issue). "What did he say?" I demanded. Percy Vale replied, "He is saying we are hiding in a pathetic little fort. He says that we had best send out our women and children so they can be with real men, or they will come in and slaughter us all." He continued "I took the liberty of responding by telling them that they all had cocks that had become so shrunken with the cold in the north lands, that they could not achieve penetration of a woman, let alone enter our Come a Lot fort." Eric smiled at the taunt, and I said to Percy, "Tell them that there is nothing here for them. Tell them to go away for there will be no honour for them to have their lives taken here." He shouted out again with the strange Norse words, and the reply he translated was, "Come out and fight you cowards, or must we enter this little camp and rape your women before your eyes."

I did not reply but called over Holt the woodsman who carried a huge longbow. His twin brother came with him. Their grim faces and dark looks reminded me of the Krays, Reggie and Ronnie, the London gangster twins from the 1960s. Our Saxon version of Reggie and Ronnie had been great assets in the building of the fort. I was also aware that our Reggie was the best bowman in the district and had been the only other man to kill a Viking on the last raid. I said to him, "Can you hit that man with an arrow?" His reply was, "Of course, but it will be only luck if I get beyond his shield." So I said to Percy, "Tell them that we have many bowmen who will make them pay a greater price than their wives would wish." I then turned to Reggie and said, "Try to hit him now."

Without a moment's hesitation his bow was raised, and the arrow left us with a thud-twang sound as the bowstring struck against the leather strapping covering his left forearm. I watched from the wall and the arrow travelled the 50 yards in a blink of the eye, striking the top of the shield a moment before the noise of the hit reached us. The horsemen pirouetted and sped away towards the rest of their men, the shield still spouting Reggie's arrow, held one handed over his shoulder protecting his back. All their Viking shields came up, and they gathered again at the forest edge. Briefly there was silence once again, which was followed by some sort of shouted argument that could be clearly heard across the tree-devoid gap. Percy Vale translated bits about "more men ... kill them now ... take the risk ... search the villages...." and so on. But, after a few minutes, they all nonchalantly lowered their shields and just walked away.

Everyone at 'Come All Place' had been required to bring some food. Most had grabbed whatever they had to hand, so there was a quantity of bread and cheese, and cold meats. An old ox from one of the nearby villages had been purchased by me for a half gold piece some weeks before on the understanding it would be bought to Come a Lot in the event of an attack. When the Vikings disappeared into the forest we set about starting the fire we needed to roast the whole beast. It was a good way to distract everyone. Feasting was a way of cementing relationships between communities. It was a way of showing power.

One of the preparations had been to stockpile fuel, and have some equipment available to support so many people during a short siege. These were stored in a crude but substantial barn we had built in the middle of the compound. We knew that the Vikings would not stay for long at any unsafe place. Their ships were vulnerable when they were raiding. The last thing they would want is for there to be a successful attack by the locals, on their one means of escape, while they were otherwise occupied.

It took almost the whole day to cook the beast properly and you would be surprised at the number of ox roasting experts there were to give sage advice on the cooking process. There was a bubbling excitement amongst those in the compound. They were not sure they were safe yet, but no one had been hurt, no one had been taken and so, despite worries about what was happening in their undefended villages, most of the throng were happy. Four of the missing arrived at lunchtime. They were a couple, with two children, who had been away for the night at a market in Exeter. Their arrival was greeted with delight from those who knew them, and they tucked into the food they were offered quite happily. The last two missing people arrived just after the ox was dismembered for consumption. The first sizzling pieces of meat were being distributed when a shout went up from the north wall. They were a young couple who had slept through the early warning, and the shouted alarm from passing neighbours had not penetrated their slumber. Young Egbert was the subject of derisory and ribald comments suggesting he was too deeply engrossed in satisfying his young wife's needs to worry about such a trifling issue as a band of marauding Vikings. We were again subjected to a range of advice on how to successfully complete such an intimate and demanding task. It occurred to me that there was little these simple folk had to learn from the supposed sophistication of sexual prowess in the 21st century. Egbert went a bright red. He tried to explain that he had only realised what had happened after spending the whole morning ploughing, which caused side splitting merriment for many, and then made the mistake of telling us that he had even travelled to Upham in the afternoon in the hope of bartering for some grease for the axle of his cart.... After that comment I was a little surprised that no one actually died from truly hysterical mirth.

During the day we saw, or thought we saw, Vikings on three separate occasions. A couple of them came to the edge of the woods to gaze at our palisade, once from the west, and twice again from the south. The last time we saw them was just before midday. They came no closer than the far side of the clearing, and then turned and left each time. As darkness fell we lit large wax candles we had stored for this purpose. They were in glass fronted cages to stop them being blown out by the wind, and hung on the outside of the wall they gave a pale light to enable the watchmen to see thirty or forty yards from the palisade in the moonless dark. The crude glass was made from melting the broken pieces recovered from an old Roman villa, and had been intended for use in James's church.

On one occasion a shout from the wall caused a flurry, and torches were hurriedly lit to improve the visibility. Three deer scampered away from the light and disappeared into the deeper obscurity of the woodland behind them. We had quizzed our late arrivals, and they had seen nothing apart from a few distant palls of smoke from burning buildings.

At about 10pm I asked Eric to convene a meeting of the twelve head men. They sat in a circle away from the others and discussed how we should check on the Vikings. We needed to know if the raiders had gone. Horses were considered as they would take the rider away from danger quickly, but there was the risk of a horse stumbling in the dark, or of noisy riders being ambushed. Horses were noisy. It was decided that the Kray brothers, the fisherman who knew where the boat was moored, and me, Marlin the wizard, should go. Ronnie was a real soldier, who was good with sword and shield, and even better with a lance. Reggie was our bowman, Bertrand was the fisherman, and I was voted in presumably as the secret weapon. I was OK with this, so long as I could get some more stuff from my personal store.

Just before midnight we set off towards my hut. The direct route down the hill got us there in less than 15 minutes. I had tried to make the pathway to my home less obvious over the winter months, so that any outsider would only find it by accident. I was also conscious of the need to keep my valuable 21st century stuff safe. I had enlisted the help of Spots and Little Finger to dig out the back wall of the safe room to create a cave.

155

The cave was supported with joists, and the entrance was disguised with a slab of slate that looked as if the lower half of the back wall of the safe room was made of solid rock. The slab was nine feet across and three feet high, and on carful inspection in bright light it could be seen that it was in fact in three pieces. There was a three foot section at the left side, then a two foot wide section held in place by overlapping joints on both sides, then a four foot section to the right. The two outer pieces were set a foot into the floor, and pinned against the back wall by the corner pillars of the room. The middle section weighed about 50 kilograms, about one hundredweight in old money (112 pounds), and was my hidden doorway. There were two sturdy hooks hidden on the rear of the roof joist nearest the back wall directly above the sides of this centre piece of slate. There were two narrow slots in the top of this piece of mud-rock that were usually covered by innocuous items of no value, a small animal scull, and a clay cup. Into these holes fitted two pins with large eyelets on the top, and a short T bars on the bottom. When these were inserted into the slots and turned at right angles they provided two rings by which the slab could be lifted upwards. Two stout chords tied to these rings strung over the hooks on the roof joist enabled a reasonably strong man to lift the slab up the wall. Two pins on the second joist out from the back wall enabled loops on the ends of these two chords to be fitted over them to hold the centre slab three foot above the floor. The resultant narrow entrance gave access to the cave, cut a further four foot into the hillside. With rock and soil all around, this cave was not at risk of fire even if my hut and the safe room burnt to the ground, and this was where I now kept my most valuable equipment.

I reached the hut in deep darkness. I left the Krays and Bertie outside and disarmed the security devices I had left in place. I lit a lantern.... Everything was in its place. Nothing had been touched. I lifted the screen in the back wall of my safe room, and within moments I was able to select what was needed for the night trek. I already had one of Loofah's headlamps fitted to a portable battery slung over my shoulder. A million candle power of light in un-expecting eyes can be a useful weapon, but I had not used it up at the fort. I also carried a Verey pistol and the shotgun. I had now collected a set of night vision glasses, and a small device that fitted onto one of the cameras that showed up heat sources by reading the infra red part of the spectrum. I put both of these into my shoulder bag along with three extra nine-bangs and returned to the men outside.

Our journey down to Thorverton was slow and cautious. I used the night vision goggles and the heat sensitive camera again and again on the way to the river. It took us over three hours, much longer than the slowest of walking paces. But with only half a dozen heart-leaping events, involving animals of both the domestic and wild variety, we reached the river unmolested. Bertie showed us his hut, now a smouldering pile of ash with protruding stumps of blackened wood, and then he showed us where the longship had been moored. It was, if you can tolerate the pun, long gone.

There was a growing light on the horizon behind us as we approached our 'Come All' fortress. Excited sentries of very tender years 'halooed' us from a distance as were seen leaving the tree line to the south of the camp, heading uphill towards the gate. There must have been some very obvious non verbal signals from the men behind me, because the words I tried to say to Eric whilst surrounded by an initially whispering throng inside the gate, became obscured as the shout went up, "They have gone, the North Men have gone. Our Thor, our Thor, our Thor!!!" I gave up trying to speak clearly above the din, and waited for Eric to draw me to one side while the rest of the camp was roused by our small group of excited news givers.

I was tired and wanted to sleep. As the dawn grew into day the good people from 'Come All' set off in their varied directions to investigate the damage done by the raiders. There was some concern, but the overall feeling was of great success. There was joy that no one had been taken, that no one had been killed or even injured. One of the comments I heard as my heavy lidded eyes started to lead me down to my little hut was a loud whispering between a small group that were heading to Thorverton. "De Wizard as an eye dat can see in de dark, it is the metal eye of a dragon, I seen it meself, it showed up two sheep stannin in a ditch one undred paces away, like glowin balls o light them was. Ee said it was an 'eat sigmature'. I fink dat shows ow dems dragons get to eat so easy at night aint it."...The fisherman had an unusually broad local accent.

I could not have kept all my kit hidden from the fisherman or the Krays. What the hell, it just meant a little more mystique for Marlin the computer wizard. I made it to my hut, just about managed to remember to turn off the alarms on my arrival, and fell into bed. I was vaguely awoken by the quiet opening of the door which I had foolishly not locked, nor set the alarms for. It was thankfully no assassin, only One Eye, my friendly house cleaner and part-time cook. I had always been very civil to her, and despite my desperate exhaustion could not bring myself the berate her. I was falling asleep again as her naked body slid into my bed for the first time, her naked backside nestling into my partially clothed lap, and her head resting on my right forearm. I fell asleep with the smell of her hair in my nostrils and a faint twitch in my groin that I chose to ignore.

The Chronicles of Eathelwold 'James' Trefell; Monk.

Book 1 Chapter 23

So it came to pass that the invaders from the North, those who would spread death and destruction and the praise of false Gods, came again to our land. Yet it was a day for our Lords blessing, a day in which the power of a Christian community overcame the evil driven by other Gods. A day in which the 'come a lot' fortress, our safe castle, saved many lives.

The heathen invaders sailed up our river and came into our land to pillage and rape, to kill and steal and abduct our women and children. But the 'Come a Lot' place held them back. They came to its great walls and saw that they were defeated. They were defeated by the high walls built by the brotherhood of men from the night. They were defeated by that which was written down through my own God fearing hand, using my pen which is even greater than a wielded sword.

It was on this great day, a day of feasting when the ox was slain, and we all shared in the blessed food our Lord provides for us, that I had reason to rebuke our king. It is only one who is so charged with keeping his flock on the narrow pathway to righteousness who would have the courage to challenge Our Thor, but it was I, Eathelwold, who did so. For during the feasting on the hilltop, after the killers from the North slunk away from our impenetrable walls, I saw a thing most dishonourable.

Wulfgar our greatest warrior, brother of Holt the archer, has lived with a woman for two years. The woman is Gwen who was once a novice in a nunnery in the north. 'Revered Gwen' had fallen from grace and clearly succumbed to pleasures of the flesh. This fallen woman has a child from another man, and a babe in arms to Wulfgar the warrior who uses a lance a lot. Yet at the height of the feasting on the hilltop, in our Come a Lot fortress I observed a couple fornicating against a tree at the crest of the northern embankment that side being toward the village of Cadelih. They were well away from the firelight, and it is true to say that there were others so occupied, but I wished that my eyes had deceived me. For in that pale flickering light, whilst Wulfgar was occupied with serving out meat to those present, I saw that it was Eric, our king, fornicating with Revered Gwen up against the bole of the tree in rhythmic ecstasy. The lascivious wench was grunting like a beast and both of her feet were suspended in the air on either side of Our Thor. Her left hand was gripping the top of the palisade wall, whilst her right was slung in abandonment around the neck of our leader.

I do not normally spend so much time observing such activity, although there is a duty upon a priest to observe the sins of his flock, and take steps to assist them in absolving their transgressions. This cannot be done unless the priest has a good idea of their faults, so there have been a good number of times when I have been obliged to observe such activity, despite my profound distaste. Suffice it to say that as a man of God I was obliged to watch the coupling for as long as it took for me to fully appreciate their wrongdoing, including such detail as was necessary to pray for their souls. When the two of them had finished their carnal felony they returned to the campfire by different routes. I made a point of looking at our king with a deeply disapproving stare.

I am pleased to say that the harshness of my gaze clearly had the required effect for, despite significant effort on my own part, I never again did observe these two partaking of the pleasures of the flesh in each other's arms. Sadly I saw 'Gwen the Revered' partake of those pleasures with other men during the time I was watching her closely. Yet despite my displeasure at having to follow the activity of such a wench, and observe in detail her frequent lapses, it was clear that she had no intention of deliberately causing tension between Our Thor, and the warrior who uses the lance a lot. She simply appeared to enjoy fornicating, being the lascivious harlot that she is.

I am one of the few who are privy to the truth about the heritage of Our Thor for I have been told a great deal during confessional. Our Thor was not the offspring of the Smithy (who has the given name of 'Hector' taken from a Greek story called the 'The Ill He Had') and a Norse slave girl. But it was the result of his first wife being violated by raiders two decades past. To ensure that this forced cuckolding of our village leader remained a secret, a false heritage was ingrained in all of us. This ingrained distortion of the truth creates the representation of the making of the child Eric by way of transposing the crime of a North Man with Hectors wife, into the more acceptable act of a imaginary coupling between the Smith and a Norse woman.

I digress in my record of what took place all those years ago.

Late that very night four of our number set off to the river to ascertain if the Northern murderers had left our land. I would have been asked to go, and would have done so willingly were it not for the urgent need for solace amongst the people in "Come a Lot". Despite my wish to drive the enemy from our land I stayed and assisted where I could. For some it was a restless night.

In the morning the four returned; Maerlin our wizard, a fisherman from the river and the twin warriors. The twins were our bowman and the recently cuckolded wielder of the lance. When the news arrived that the rapists from the north had left I was most pleased. I was pleased that our Lord

God had saved the day, and that I had been his instrument. Yet in my modesty I chose not to claim the credit for what had taken place.

I was told by the fisherman, whom I spoke to at some length, that Maerlin had two devices from the land of the dragon that were beyond belief. He had something that allowed him to see in the dark, like an owl or a raven, which was worrying in itself, as many birds of the night are lost dark spirits. But worst of all he had something with which he can see live flesh glowing, even when the man cannot be seen with a human eye. The fisherman said he saw how the shimmering shape of the twins could be clearly distinguished many paces away in complete darkness. I believe this was the manifestation of the souls of these two men, which only goes to justify the righteous effort I commit to saving the immortal spirits of the mortal men and women in my care. At some stage I intend to challenge Maerlin about the use of this infernal device. He may be the greatest of wizards, and of immense value to our community, but he must still answer to the One True God on his day of reckoning.

Chapter Thirteen;   The Killing Ground.

It had not been a conscious decision to remain celibate since missing my appointment at the time gate almost a year before, but it sort of turned out that way. I by now realise how deeply I had fallen in love with Monty, and despite the certainty that we would never meet again, it was quite a while before I looked at a woman and even noticed if she was attractive or not. One Eye, who now of course had two, was in fact a comely woman. Strong featured, firm shouldered, but with a good sporty shape, a bit like a modern day hockey player. Her hair was long and black, and usually held in a loose plait. Since I had moved into the hut she had been a constant help to me, assisting with tips on cooking and providing some of my meals, as well as spending time every week helping me keep my place in order, and showing how to do everything from simple needle work on a leather jerkin with a bone needle, to how to make food preserves for the winter. I had wanted to learn these skills and to remain independent. I had no idea what my future would bring in my strange new life far in the past, but I realised that my magic tricks, and modern day equipment would, sooner or later, wear thin, or wear out.

I had shown One Eye some things too, and handed over to her both of the deer carcases killed by my night-time defence systems. She acted demurely to me most of the time, but there was a real spark there that came out when she was showing me, the supposedly great wizard, how to do something a child should have already learnt. I had even demonstrated to her how to keep her teeth fresher by chewing an oak twig (thank goodness for all those CDs), and use powdered oak bark for a mouth ulcer.

In the half light of the hut, I gradually surfaced from my deep sleep and I became vaguely aware that a warm hand, which I worryingly realised was not my own, was massaging my already engorged penis through the thin material of my modern day underpants. By the time I was fully awake, presumably after only about two or three hours slumber, I was flat on my back with my knickers around my knees, my ninth century smock-like shirt pushed up to my chest, and my penis in the process of disappearing into the slippery, moist interior of One Eye's clearly welcoming vagina. Which, after a deft bit of sideways mounting on her part, had given me little time to protest. Once firmly and pleasantly 'in place' she put a hand on each of my shoulders, looked me straight in the eyes and said, "I ain't afraid of you no more. I knows you is just a person like the rest of us. Wizard or no wizard, this ere cock of yourn is goin to waste, and I is fed up of waitin fer you to use it on me. So if yer as no real objection, I is going to make the most of it, and fuck yer wizard brain out." I struggled for an erudite response. By the time I had the wits to come up with something suitable, my cock was enjoying himself far too much for me to intervene. It is odd how certain things stick in the mind and one strange thought did occur to me, and that was the revelation of just how hairy the damn things were when 'au naturel'.

Eventually I dozed off again, I was still almost asleep. The sexual activity had been greatly appreciated and much missed on my part. It had also been surprisingly intense, and then disturbingly tender. Her words spoken from somewhere in the region of my chest sort of floated into my dream like state. "You must ave luved er a great deal." I grunted. "That woman who is waitin fer yer to return to wizard country. I av erd you talk about er as you potter around the place. You said er name twice this mornin." I was silent for a while. "Yes, I loved her," I said. "I loved her far more than I thought I did, far more than I have ever loved anyone before." One Eye moved, tilting her head to look up at me, "Do yer think yer'll ever see er agin?" I moved my head slightly from side to side. "I do not see how that can happen. I cannot return to my home land. I have lost her forever.... I was once a man who had great wealth, more wealth than you can imagine, but now I have lost it all, and I have lost her. I have been reduced to almost nothing." She pushed herself up onto one elbow, her right breast resting against my left arm. There was a touch of sorrow and a glimpse of pride as she said, "But you got us, you got Kaardbury, you made em build Come a Lot and saved God knows ow many lives. I knows it's you oo pulls der strings. I seen Eric from a kid, an ee aint no king, ee aint no leader wivout you. You was sent to us fer a reason, an evry one in village is in yer debt." She clambered over me, giving me a peck on the lips half way. She was dressed in moments, and at the door before she turned to me, "I is sorry yer as lost yer Monty Izzie lady. But if yer cannot get back to er I plan to get into yer bed now and again an give dat cock o yourn summit to do. I ain't scared of yer no more, yer be a great wizard, but yer be also a man, and accordin to Father James wastefulness be a sin." And with that she was gone....

I was surprised by the depth of sorrow I felt. I suppose that was the moment when I really felt that I had lost Monty. Tears from both eyes rolled silently down to the corner of my left eye, and then onto the coarse linen covering of my grass stuffed pillow, a route via the top edge of my cheekbone. I had enjoyed the sex with One Eye, or at least my body had. But it brought back to me the complete intimacy I had felt with my Monty, my Lizzie. A connection and abandon that was based on emotions that I had never felt before and probably never would again. I fell asleep still feeling guilty. Not searing 'lump in the throat' guilt, but the sort of remorse you feel when you lose a loved one who you never had the chance to say goodbye to.

I wandered down to the village in the afternoon. There were one or two sideways looks from the women of the village, and three or four of the men came to me to enthuse about the success of the fortress. As I had hoped I managed to scrounge a bowl of soup and some bread and cheese. I was starving. I then sought out Eric and his father who were busy helping other village members to clear away the debris of a burnt hut near the Crediton road. I spoke to Eric as he was finishing piling burnt wooden panelling on to the unlit pyre that was the remains of someone's home. His hands were black, and he had clearly scratched his nose at some point after the task had begun. "We need a killing ground" I said. He carried on working and I was not sure if he had heard me. I continued, "We need to do it soon before they attack again. We also need more archers, with bigger bows. Much bigger bows!"

That evening we had another meeting of the twelve heads. I had briefed Eric on what was needed, and only intervened a couple of times as the discussion progressed. The Vikings would be back, and we had certainly pissed them off. When they returned they would know about the fort, and would come prepared. I expected them to bring some simple siege breaking equipment such as ladders. If they were allowed to spend too long at the wall they would eventually break in. We had to find an effective way of making that too dangerous and costly for them. Their armour, shields and chain mail reduced their vulnerability to arrows considerably. As it was, to do any damage when they were attacking you required a very accurate, or lucky, bow shot, one which literally struck a man in the face. So it was time for another plan.

The following day the inner embankment was started, while the Krays set about recruiting archers. I had read all that stuff about the size and power of the yew bows they found on the Mary Rose, and how they calculated the enormous draw weight they had. But it took years for a man to develop the musculature to use such a bow. A huntsman would not use a bow requiring so much effort as their quarry never wore armour, and often there was a need to stand with the bow drawn for up to a minute to enable them to pick the exact moment to release their one, surprise, accurate, first shot. I was not expecting to find anyone of such strength, certainly not with enough strength in the right places. But the brothers Kray did manage to find 15 big strong men who were powerful enough to pull our test weight using a one hand grip handle, a 100lb+ rock, on a pulley. Bracing one hand sideways against the post with the pulley attached, they were all able to lift the rock fully off the ground one handed, pulling the handle, held in just three fingers, across their chest, past their chin, to their ear. They also found the two best bow-makers in the region and bought them to Kaardbury. One of them was a local man, living in Stockleigh, the other was his uncle who had lost his first wife to the North Men 20 years ago. He had travelled from a village more than 50 miles away along the coast to join his nephew in resisting the raiders.

The discussion about what wood should be used to make the big bows was an argument cut short by my recollection of a computer wizard's very first arrival in Kaardbury over a year ago. The downed tree from beside the church had been a massive Yew, and the wood was well dried. Father James was concerned as the wood was intended for sale as building material to swell the chapel coffers, so I purchased it off him for quite a number of my silver pennies. Checking the calculated draw weights of the bows found on the Mary Rose I thought that we should have a dozen made at 100lb pull, another 12 at 120 pounds and 12 at 140 pounds. This would give us 36 bows ranging from 100–140 pound pull, and as the bowmen got stronger they could all move up in bow weight. We tested, well Reggie tested, the first ones produced. It took a nearly a week to produce six of the bows, two of each poundage. Reggie could not pull fully the 140 pounder, but the heavy arrows fired from the others all penetrated a practice dummy wearing captured chain mail, although it was noticeable that the 120 penetrated much deeper into the dummy than the 100 pounder.

Our 15 recruits, along with Ronnie and Reggie, were each given a normal bow with about a 60lb draw weight to practice accuracy each day and as soon as they had been made, one of the 100lb bows to use every night as a ninth century Bullworker to develop their strength. They were not supposed to use the big bows with arrows until they could draw the bow strings to their ear 20 times in succession. Accuracy practice was to be with the 60 pounders. I am quite a big strong man, six foot and fifteen stone, and I was still doing pull ups and press ups every single day. Yet, although I could draw the 100lb bow back to my chin, the last four inches to my ear was very difficult indeed. It was something I would work on in secret, because although I was not planning to be encumbered myself with the task of being an archer at the fortress, I certainly wanted to be able to use one of those heavy-weight bows in the future.

Another problem was stringing the biggest of the damn things. It is all very easy to string a light 30lb bow, all you do is just bend it by trapping one end inside your foot, and placing the body of the bow outside your knee and then bend the top over towards you with your hand. Even 100lb was ok, but 140 pounds is a different matter. Reggie could string one, just. But it was quite an effort even for him. Then he showed me a trick he used with the youngsters. At one end of a kid's bow he dug out from somewhere, there were two nocks for the bowstring. This bow also had two strings, one longer than the other. He showed us how with both strings nocked in the single groove at one end you could attach the long string to the outer nock point on the other end. This string was still floppy, but now attached to both ends. By trapping this loose string on the ground with one foot, all you do is lift the middle of the bow off the ground with one hand, and pull on it until the bow has bent enough for you to lean down to the double-knocked end and slip the tight, and proper string, into the lower of the two knocks. The bow has then been strung with little effort and the loose string could be removed so the bow can be used. Now why didn't I think of that?!!!

It was a month before they all had their first big bow to work with, and they had all been practising hard with the light bows and straw targets. Reggie did regular checks on the bowmen, and the results were varied. About one third were good and reasonably accurate, another third were consistent, but their overall accuracy was limited, while the last third were seriously crap. The worst five were big strong men, but with no talent for the bow at all. In the end we decided the best employment of our arrows against the Vikings would be to limit using our worst archers and make the most of our best. But I am getting ahead of myself.

Concerned that we had only a handful of decent bowmen I pondered on the use of crossbows. They were much slower, but could be used by a less skilled person and, with suitable leverage, have huge draw weights. To get a similar penetration from a crossbow you need (so my historical CD said) a weapon of about three times the draw weight of a long bow. Power is a calculation of force times a distance, so in terms of a bow this means draw weight multiplied by draw length. A crossbow with third of the draw distance of a longbow (the distance the bow string is pulled back from the 'rest' position) needs to have a draw weight three times greater to have the same penetration power.

I looked up the methods for pulling the crossbow and ruled out anything too complicated. There was also the issue of the material for the bow, as it was not until complex laminates of sinew, horn and wood were developed in the 13th century that it was possible to combine a decent distance of draw length with the shorter bow of the crossbow. Simple wood crossbows tended to have either such wide bows on the front as to be unmanageable, or such a short draw length as to be effectively too weak. As I have said, this is because the power of the bow is equal to the draw length multiplied by the draw weight. So eventually I decided to use two more of Loofah's springs.

Metal of suitable quality to make steel springs would not be produced for hundreds of years, but I still had three lengths of sprung steel from the microlight that had been produced by the best engineering of our modern world. These long flat springs were designed to handle the bouncy landing of a small aircraft. One thing we did do well in the future was to produce good quality metal and the very precise percentage of carbon content of a spring was exactly what was required for our needs. Each spring was about three and a half feet long, but shaped as they were the force required to bend them was huge. I discussed how they could be made into bows with Eric. He thought it would be quite simple. All he would do would be to heat the metal until he could cut it in half with a cold chisel. Then each half would be heated and hammered out thin at each end. As I would only let him have two of the springs, done carefully we would end up with four lengths of steel tapered at each end. He would put a curve in them so that they would have a bow shape when not under any load. He would also need to quench them to set the hardness into them, and would need to experiment to get that process just right. What draw poundage we would end up with would be was anybody's guess, but he would make one and see what it was like. He could always make the bows weaker by making them thinner or longer.

It took only two days to produce the first bow. But that was only the start of it. We had discussions with a number of people, but in the end the task of making the bow stocks was given to a man with the most impressive moustache I have ever seen. Many of the Saxons sported moustaches, often with thick stubble over the rest of their faces, as shaving was hard work with the blades available. 'Big Tash' was a specialist wood worker. He made everything from house construction and fancy doorways, to wooden halters for oxen and beautiful items of furniture. His work even graced Beouf's hall itself. Big Tash was very keen to be involved in producing something more technical for the cause than just mass producing posts for the palisade.

The trigger mechanism was an issue. Looking at pictures on my laptop I deciphered them to the point of designing a simple lever device with a pivot under the stock, with a rod of metal running vertically up through the stock to the groove for the launching of the crossbow bolt. There was a slight curve to the top of this rod to hold the bow string firmly. Pushing the lever up to the bottom of the stock dropped the rod and released the string. The string was made of dozens of lengths of hemp heavily waxed from Father James's hives. Our best efforts of pulling the string back to engage with the rod failed. But the bow was not yet fitted with a stirrup on the nose of the bow to give us something to pull against. After a metal hoop was attached to the front of the bow Eric and I were able, between us, to cock it. One standing either side with our feet in the stirrup end of the crossbow, pulling the string upwards in gloved hands until the device was set. But it was hard work. We tested the bow with a thick wood and metal fleche about a foot long. The power of the weapon was surprising.

By my calculation the bow was between 400 and 500 pounds draw weight. The strength of the bow would result in chain mail penetrating shots, but we could not afford five minutes of struggling by two big men every time we wanted to load one. Even the use of a 'goats foot' hook and a waist strap to load the bow would be very difficult for one very powerful man on his own. Further investigation of the pictures on the computer resulted in the decision to fit two metal pins, one each side of the stock, and these were the anchor points for the bottom two ends of a metal fork that sat over the bolt groove. The top of the fork was a spike, and connected by a pin at the junction between the fork and the spike was a double headed hook. With the spike fully forward the top of the fork leant towards the front of the bow, and the double headed hook could be engaged with the bow string. The spike then had a two foot handle fitted over the tip to create a long lever which when pulled back towards the top of the stock would pull the bow string back, until it slipped over the trigger rod. The weapon was then cocked and a quarrel, or bolt, could be placed in the firing groove, and the weapon would be ready to fire. (Bloody hell! that was hard work. I have added a sketch that perhaps makes the reading of the last page a waste of your time.)

The crossbow was quite heavy, and even with the lever it took some strength for one man to reload it. It also only had a fire rate, at best, of three shots in a minute. But after fitting a simple sight, the power and accuracy were very good, and it could be fired with lethal precision by any tame gorilla. (And surprise, surprise, we had a few of those.) It took nearly two weeks to make the first, but then things got quicker, and we had all four crossbows working by the end of a five weeks. At close range they were at least as effective as Reggie's 120lb longbow, just slower to load. We trained the five most incompetent longbow men in using them, but these weapons were very special bits of kit, centuries before their time. So at night they always slept in my secret store.

I was worried as I thought the Vikings would be back any day, so was glad to see the progress being made with the inner palisade. It is all very well developing the ability to injure and kill heavily armoured men, but our numbers were few, and their thick heavy Viking shields combined with the chainmail were a match for any arrow. Shooting at them head on with their shields raised would be very inefficient. It would also give them time to wear down our defences, get amongst us, and start the inevitable slaughter. If a mere 20 of them got inside the palisade and took on the whole population of Come a Lot using just their swords and axes, there would literally be a massacre. I had no illusions about our limited prowess in battle. We needed to create a situation where they were engaged and held in one direction, while we could fire our heavy artillery at them from the side, or rear. 40 or perhaps just 20 good hits from the side would cause a loss of numbers that even a force of two full ships' crews would worry about. These were raiders who wanted easy pickings. They did not come here for pitch battles and they had no desire to suffer heavy casualties.

The idea was to create a corridor inside Come a Lot, in which the Vikings would be contained. To this end the whole of the southern and eastern part of the inside the fort was to be dug out to create a new curved gully, running inside of, and parallel with, the outer wall. The success of our first encounter with the North Men seemed to have resulted in the numbers available for work on the fortress swelling considerably. This was of significance as we needed to move many tons of earth from the gulley, and to build up the banks on either side. We also needed more posts for our inner wall. Every day we worked on the gulley, but I was deeply worried that another attack would leave us still vulnerable. We could probably keep the Vikings at bay as our archers and crossbowmen were coming along well enough, and so long as we were able to maintain the integrity of the outer palisade, we would probably be able to withstand most attacks. But preventing the palisade from being breached was far from certain, and if they got inside in any numbers most of the Saxons would be trapped within our fortress, and many would die.

But they did not come, and the work progressed. By the end of the summer we had half completed the gully that was seven feet deep and 20 feet wide running around the southern curve of the fortress. By my

173

calculation our workforce had moved over 500 tons of soil and clay in three months. More than five cubic metres a day! While this was being done the inner palisade had been completed so that once inside the gate anyone entering Come a Lot would find themselves in a part finished curved gulley which disappeared to the right, but ended in a short mud wall to the left where the work continued. The gulley near the gate was where we started, and by the end of three months we had completed the earthworks to the east. We were now moving cart load after cart load from the western arm of the trench. If the North Men got in now we would be very vulnerable. The internal palisade was barely six foot high, and a concerted attack on it with the big battle axes of the Vikings would see them through the barrier within minutes. We needed the gulley and a steep slippery slope that would keep them away from the inner palisade to enable our archers to take their toll.

The plan was for the gulley to be overlooked by both the outer palisade behind them, and the inner palisade in front of them. Following the gulley either left or right would take attackers round the edge of the fortress until they reached a 'dead end' of another wooden wall set in a high bank. This was the original bank built a thousand years before which was at the end of each arm of the gulley, and beyond this was the outside of the fortress again. In creating the gulley we were losing about one third of the castle compound, but it was worth it. The remaining area was more than sufficient for the 300 it was designed to protect, and now we were creating our killing ground.

With the progress of the gulley we had a new set of problems. Our biggest difficulty was making the most of the opportunity to attack the raiders from the outer palisade walls. Arrows could easily be fired from within the main compound, over the inner palisade set into the top of the bank which was the inside curve of the gulley, as this was where everyone else would be seeking refuge. But the outer palisade was just a single fence thick. Fine if the opposition were still beyond the outer palisade, but not a good place to be when they were in the gulley. I considered putting another fence a couple of feet in from the outer wall, creating a double barrier which would hide and protect our archers as they rained arrows onto the Vikings. But the top of the outer bank was too narrow, and setting a whole new line of posts into a not very stable, steep, slope would be difficult. But I already had some ideas that were in progress.

Because of the considerable height of the big wall around the main gate, bracing was needed on a large scale. Five long, straight tree trunks had been manoeuvred into place and with the foot of each set firmly into the ground on the edge of the inner compound, they reached across the gulley to support the wall above the gate, about 15 feet from the ground. This gave us the opportunity to build two walkways, each spanning the outer two braces on each side above the gulley. Planking and simple wooden panelling gave protection from anything fired or thrown from below, and these walkways sloped upwards, but were at least 10 foot above anyone in the gulley at the lower northern end. They provided the ideal firing position above and behind any force attacking along the gulley in either direction. I then got our woodsmen to set up three tree houses in some of the larger remaining trees that were growing out of the original Iron Age outer embankment. I had originally kept these just to reinforce the outer palisade, but now they provided a significant bonus. Two tree houses were positioned above the longer western arm of the gulley, and one above the shorter eastern arm. All three tree houses were simple platforms set up in branches 20–30 feet above the gulley, with the surrounding foliage thinned to give a good field of fire.

These three tree houses, and the two walkways abutting on the high wall above the gate, provided ideal positions for lookouts, as well as excellent firing positions. But I also wanted these emplacements to have escape routes. So the walkways were connected to each other, at the high wall end, by narrow planking, this enabled defenders to escape down either walkway to the inner compound. They could do this even if attackers got onto the lower end of one of the walkways in an attempt to cut our archers off from the inner palisade.

The tree houses were more of a problem, but we strung up a stout rope high above each of the platforms, which ran down across the gulley, over an A frame set in the ground, to anchor points inside the main compound. Using loops of leather anyone manning the tree houses could reach the safety of the inner compound in seconds, and if the rope was cut any pursuer attempting the same route could always run the risk of a 30 foot drop into the gulley. My principal undertaking then was to stop them practicing these escape slides ad-nauseam. It appears that I had inadvertently introduced a craze for ninth century zip lining. We had to re-tighten all three escape ropes ... twice.

The Chronicles of Eathelwold 'James' Trefell; Monk.

Book 2 Chapter 1.

The twelve men of the night continued to meet. I made notes as requested by our young king. Again I was aware of the importance of my task, and how without it nothing would have been done to prepare for the second attack of the Northern Raiders. I continue to speak very little of my contribution, but it was me, James the priest, who recorded many of the ideas and decisions made at the round table by the Smith's fire. I was often concerned that ideas came from Maerlin who was an outsider. But I did believed in his knowledge and wisdom in the baser matters of war, and as his suggestions fitted well with what I would have proposed myself. I feel vindicated in the way I recorded what he suggested through Our Thor as our king, given my pen noted down merely what I would have demanded myself if I had chosen to take the sword from the stones.

New earth-works were started and completed at the fortress. At the same time other skills were being advanced amongst the men folk of the villages. Some were trained to use heavy longbows the like of which I have never seen. I even allowed them to use some of the holy wood from the Yew tree, that which had been felled in the church grounds by my own hand, to make the bows. This gave each of these weapons greater power, and it bestowed upon them the God given right to take heathen lives. Without this blessing I am sure we could never have prevailed against our enemies, the enemies of the Christian faith.

Maerlin also showed us how to make bows shaped as the cross on which our Lord was crucified. These bows were not of the Yew wood but were made from the melted bones of the L'uther dragon. Verily despite their being part of the beast, they were sanctified by their very shape. I also blessed each weapon when it was completed and despite the indifference of those present at the time, I know that deep in their hearts they would never have been willing to use these holy crosses to take life in battle, without them being so consecrated.

Great works were being done in Come a Lot as changes were made to the palisades and earthworks. Given the eventual purpose of these earthworks it was clear to me that they would be of great value to God fearing people such as were in our communities. I asked questions about their function only to make others believe that I did not understand their purpose. For if my people had realised that these earth workings were sanctioned by the church, and by the profound contribution of my skills with the pen, and hence were so permitted by the Good Lord, then I would have undoubtedly been drawn into a theological discussion with many of my flock as to the authority of the Church to sanction the killing of others. By my gentle and justified deception of feigned ignorance I have avoided the need to extrapolate the arguments of a Holy War and the right every Christian has to slay heathens when in extremis, or in the effort of spreading the word — therefore saving the more greatly treasured lives of the already converted.

There was a great deal of toil extended towards preparation of groups of men carrying large shields. I call these the Sacred Shields, as they were sanctified by me in person and their use was almost exclusively that of defence against the Northern killers. The Sacred Shields were held together by the Christian people of our communities to withstand the onslaught of a godless horde. My blessing made this possible, for you could see in the sideways glances of those holding the shields, as I cast holy water upon them, that they were showing deference to our Lord. The laughter they shared was an obvious expression of their joy at being so blessed.

Chapter Fourteen;   To Kill a Dragon.

My fear had been that the Vikings would return before we had completed the earthworks. That we would not be ready to use the gulley as our killing ground, and that they would overwhelm us at some point on the outer palisade. But the effort continued, and as the months passed we heard of three raids that occurred further westwards, down the coast. As the summer turned to autumn we finally finished the digging. We had reached the point where an attack would leave us less vulnerable, and I began to relax a bit. We had a big feast up at Come a Lot to which most of our people came. We roasted two pigs and a bullock, and a considerable amount of higher alcohol beer, mead and cider was consumed.

One of the staples of our diet was low alcohol beer as the brewing process sterilised the liquid, making it much safer to drink than river water that was necessarily collected from downstream of the bowel functions of other villages, or their livestock. But almost as a local custom, every time a new brew of the weak beer was made, we also made a couple of barrels of the stronger stuff. So, there was plenty to drink that evening, and a great deal of revelry took place. If those of you who think that a 21st century office party is the epitome of generic misbehaviour, you should try a ninth century autumn feast. At times it seemed like a rather uninhibited cross between a carnival in Rio, and one of the more graphic episodes of *Caligula*.

I was persuaded to show those present – those that were lucid enough to persuade me and had sufficient clothing on to be willing to approach me – some of my magical powers. My excuse is that many of those present had never seen me do anything remotely displaying my alleged talent as one of the greatest of all wizards. A grumpy old git, fretting over digging and fence building, yes, but no miraculous warlock type stuff. So I considered that ensuring their continued belief and support was sufficient justification for using up one of my special items.

I had bought with me, from twelve hundred years away, six very large fireworks. These ones were described on their labelling as 'mortars' and stated on the instructions in very large letters 'WHEN THE FUSE IS

LIT YOU MUST RETIRE A DISTANCE OF AT LEAST 30 METRES' and from this it was possible to deduce that these were exceptionally dangerous pyrotechnics. You didn't need to be 30 yards away ... not quite. But being somewhat drunk, and only two paces from the one I let off in the middle of a village which I cannot remember the name of, nearly cost me an ear-drum. They really do take off with a wallop!! I had used three of them during those dramatic days I had spent in Cornwall before I lost Loofah. But one of the remaining three had been put, along with a Verey pistol, magnesium flares, nine-bangs, smoke canisters, the double barrelled shotgun, and some other stuff, in the locker in the compound store. To keep some of my kit always ready to hand in the fort I had had my own personal emergency locker custom built, and then had it bolted against the back wall of the storeroom. Well not exactly bolted, but the foot long nails were driven through the main posts at the back of the building and into the back of this heavy wooden safe. The ends of these long nails were then hammered over on inside the locker to hold it in place and make it very difficult to carry off. This locker was then protected by not only a suitably well publicised warlock's spell, and with an associated death curse for anyone violating its contents, but it also boasted thick steel screws and hasp, with substantial hinges and one of my 21st century padlocks. That night I made the decision that the magnesium flares would be best saved in case we needed to illuminate any night-time attacks, but the firework could perhaps be most effectively used now, to raise my profile at this golden opportunity. Besides, I liked to show off as much as the next wizard.

Perhaps it was a bit naughty to pander to my desire to be viewed with awe, and to be both feared and respected, and wanting all of these at the same time. But although I was aware that I was less self obsessed than I used to be, it is quite difficult not to get hooked on being able to amaze everyone around you so easily. I still took great pleasure in simply starting fires with flames conjured from just my fingers. I had been fortunate in not only having a number of lighters with me, but also finding a box of another dozen in Monty's gifts. I used them sparingly, and always hid the lighter in my hands so it could not be seen. Since my drunken spree down in Cornwall I always kept one suspended inside one of my sleeves on a length of rubber from one of the baggage bungees. Whenever I used the lighter to light a fire to the amazement of those around me, I would theatrically open my hands and show them as empty, whilst the lighter disappeared up my forearm into my baggy cuffs. But many of the crowd had observed me doing this at some point, and it had become just everyday magic to them. Perhaps it was the right time for a show stopper....

The build up was suitably loud and extrovert. We had couples scrambling half naked back into the main compound to see what was happening. I hoped the experience would be sufficient compensation for interrupting their more carnal celebrations of the feast.

I started with dancing and chanting and calling out to the Gods, as in reality I was trying to decide how best to do this. My somewhat dismal routine was a bit like the stamping rhythm of an Indian war dance. But without music it was the best I could do without looking like a complete twat. I wanted the mortar to be more mystical than just a thick brightly coloured cylinder set on the ground that fires something into the air. So I started a story, a story about dragons. I wove a tale about how I became a dragon rider, and took the liberty of basing my tale on JRR Tolkien's *The Hobbit*. This enabled me to talk about goblins and elves and Smaug the dragon as if I was recalling it all from own memory. I adjusted things so that in this story I was playing the role of Gandalf and Bilbo at the same time, and it was me, not Bard, who shot down the dragon at the end of the story. I explained how the only way to kill a dragon is to strike it with an Exocet (again a name that just came to me), a magical missile that blows the dragon apart. A magical missile that only the most skilled wizards can create. One which takes time, and a great deal of powerful magic, to produce. I told them that as my own dragon, who had been one of Smaug's offspring, was already dead, and it was unlikely that another dragon would ever come to this land, I would still make an Exocet just to show them the power of my wizardry.

I got Little Finger to set up a large empty barrel on the ground in the middle of the compound and quarter fill it with earth. I made a big show of checking the inside of the barrel and at the same time secretly embedded the mortar upright and deep in the soil at the bottom of the cask. I then did a lot of chanting and mumbling of words and adding things to the barrel from my pockets to make it look as if I was creating some sort of potion. All this stuff was mesmerising for the crowd. I had moved them all back to the edges of the compound, and most of them had a clear and unobstructed view of what I was doing. They had no idea what I was doing of course, me neither, but it must have looked good enough. Those that were stuck at the back, and were of shorter stature, scrambled up to sit on the top of the palisade to get a clear view.

Eventually after a great deal of mystical bollocks, and many items including two pints of beer and some pigs blood carefully poured into the soil well away from the mortar, we were ready. I returned to the story, explaining again how the dragon Smaug, angered by our invasion of his nest in the lonely mountain, attacked the town on the lake, and how his fiery breath had taken many lives before I completed my magic and created the Exocet potion. At the end of this fabrication I surreptitiously lit the fuse to the mortar with my disappearing lighter. I knew there was about 15 seconds to go so I shouted, "Look, look … when the potion is ready it starts to give off the breath of the dragon, it starts to seek a dragon in the heavens above, in a moment it will leap into the sky to try to find a dragon to kill. Are you watching? Are you watching?" I faced away from the barrel towards the silent crowd, my arms were spread with the confidence of a showman. I paced sideways eyeballing the onlookers, revelling in their open mouthed anticipation. They waited in breathless silence, the only noise was the gentle hiss of the fuse. There was a slow plume of drifting smoke as it rose from the barrel to be pushed across the compound by a gentle breeze … THUUUUUMP!!!!

There were gasps and intakes of breath as the mortar went off. The barrel gave the noise a sort of drum like, ear punching quality, which was followed by the rather odd silence as the shell was thrown upwards. All eyes gazed to the heavens, but they did not know quite where to look as mortars, unlike rockets, do not leave a clear flight path in the sky. (Not that more than three of those present had ever seen a firework rocket, but I had told them that the Exocet would fly into the air like a giant arrow.) The eerie silence seemed to make the following eruption even more dramatic and, when the mortar shell exploded into a trail of green fire a quarter of a mile up and filling the whole of the sky, there were gasps everywhere. For a few moments the stars above us were obliterated by the dazzle, 50 green streams of light stretching almost from horizon to horizon radiating from a central point above us, and then just over a second later came the sound, the ear thumping CCRRUUUMPPP!!!, a noise unlike anything else they had ever heard, more akin to shellfire on a battlefield than anything else, and very different from any auditory experience any human being, outside of China, would go through for the next five hundred years. Then we had a few screams.

The light died in seconds, the screams quietened as they realised no one had been hurt. It was a strange delayed spontaneous noise. There was a mixture of shouts, of delight, some of calls for me, "Marlin, Marlin the wizard," others of loud conversation, shouts of "Did you see?" "What a noise!" "Now that is real magic." I bent into the barrel and removed the mortar tube and a couple of the items I had thrown in that I wanted to keep. I was being mobbed as I tipped the barrel up and emptied it onto the ground. I said loudly, "After the Exocet has left the potion turns into earth again. See, you are all safe, the enchantment has gone."

The noise and babble went on for some time. Eventually those couples who had unfinished business clambered out of the compound, or sneaked into the gulley out of the bright firelight, to complete what they had started. By the end of the evening, after the bulk of the meat had been consumed, many fell asleep where they lay, some in twos or threes, others in whole families, children and all. I had been offered coupling by a number of local women, something that had not happened before, and I suspected One Eye had let it slip that no serious harm befell a woman who slept with a warlock. I declined their offers as politely as I could.

I suppose in retrospect that there were a number of reasons. Primarily I still felt guilt about not being with Monty, and had sort of managed to excuse my behaviour with One Eye as sharing a need with a friend. But there were other reasons, not the least of which was that despite my olfactory gland having become accustomed to the range of body smells, this was a community where daily washing was an anathema, and in which deodorant was completely nonexistent. Yet One Eye was surprisingly fresh breathed and sweet smelling compared to most, with a body odour that was, to me, quite pleasant compared to many of these other offers. One Eye also appeared to be unable to have children, and the last thing I wanted to do was to muck up anyone's future by fathering offspring who

185

simply should not exist, and would therefore be destined to die very young.

Having secured everything away in my locker in the store house, I set off in the moonlight back to my own bed. At one point I came across a small group of revellers who had been heading back towards Thorverton, but they appeared to have decided the journey was too difficult given their drunken state, and had lain where they fell on the edge of the forest, near the main path. I almost tumbled over them and in panic turned on my powerful torch that I used very sparingly. The flood of light lit up half the hillside, and three of the bodies in front of me leapt to life and scuttled into the undergrowth quite terrified of anyone who could trap sunlight as I obviously had. Realising they were no threat I turned the lamp off, and waited for my eyes to adjust to the moonlight again. There was a drunken shout of "It is only Marlin. No one will come to harm." I set off through the woods heading directly down towards the eastern edge of Kaardbury. There were murmurings behind me as those that had slept through the blinding light were woken to be told of this new wonder. There were a few choice Saxon words that amounted to "Fuck off I'm sleeping" before I was crunching through leaves and twigs at sufficient distance to be out of clear earshot.

I was back at my hut and just about to set the outer alarms system when One Eye arrived and announced that she wanted to stay the night. She must have been watching for my departure from the fort, but the residual excitement of my theatrics and the titillation of observing some of the more overt lascivious activity for the last few hours left me feeling in need of partaking of some of the same. So I let her in, set the alarms, and took her to bed. It vaguely occurred to me that I knew someone back in the 20th century who had had three kids who were all born on dates that suggested that she only ever became really excited, and fertile, on bonfire night. I remember one year I sent them a firework in a condom, as a joke.

"How der yer capture sunslight, is it a candle frem the land of wizards?" One Eye was raised on one elbow looking at the small lamp I had left alight beside the bed. It required very little power and ran on the battery that I kept topped up by using the solar cell. I realised that up until then she had only seen my hut lit with candles and lanterns, or the flame from the fire. I was so used to keeping my 21st century light under wraps I tended to forget how little she, or anyone else, had seen of it. I looked at her naked body and was reminded again of how hairy the damn things were before depilation and the Brazilian look had taken over. I preferred the less fluffy version but did not consider it polite to raise the issue. I looked back at the lamp and realised that I did not have the energy left to create an elaborate explanation so I simply said, "Where I come from we have lights in every house, and all rooms are lit as if it is daylight, even when there is darkness outside. Our problem is that we use up too much of the resources of the earth, we do not respect the planet we live on. Money and possessions have become the new God, and saving our planet for the future is irrelevant compared to the opportunity of having power and making money there and then. Selfishness is what our government stands for."

One Eye looked at me. "What be a planet?" I realised that either the conversation was going to take a very long time, or I was going to have to improvise. "In the land of wizards there is only so much magic, and when it has all run out we will freeze in winter, and starve without food just the same as everyone else. In fact when we have used up all the magic in that land we may not even have enough air left to breathe, or water to drink. Even now there are too few fish left in the sea and too few animals to hunt on the land." She continued to look at me. "Perhaps it be good fer you that you is ere then. Perhaps dem leaders in the land of wizards aint that clever at all. Even we simple folk understand dat crops ave to be rotated or our land comes barren. Even we understand that if all yer deer is killed one year, den we will grow hungry de next."

She lowered her head to my chest and spoke again. "Perhaps you was meant to be stranded ere in dis land of ordinary people. Perhaps you werse meant to save us from de North Men, and to show us a better way to live." I replied, "I doubt it. I ended up stuck here because of either an accident, or because someone had a desire to steal from me. No one deliberately killed my dragon because they wanted me to stay. I was as guilty as any other wizard, any other computer wizard, of making too much money ... but if I can stop the North Men from killing and raping and taking captives for slaves, then at least I have done something of worth. Perhaps I will even be remembered as a good man through the fire-time stories of your people." With that I switched off the light and closed my eyes. She spoke quietly. "Our people! You is one of us now! I is sure you will be membered by many of our people."

The Chronicles of Eathelwold 'James' Trefell; Monk.

Book 2 Chapter 6.

It is now incumbent upon me to tell of something that few will believe. I can only ask you to try to do so, and understand that the ways of the Lord are wonderful, and there are times when his works are a mystery even to one as knowledgeable as myself.

It was decided, upon my own recommendation, that there should be a harvest feast in Come a Lot to celebrate the gathering of the God given crops. This feast was to be an event unto which all those who had a right to gather at the fortress in time of need, could attend. There was considerable merriment and consumption of intoxicating liquor. There was none of the honeyed mead to which I had become so partial to during my time at the monastery and of which I now produced a dozen flagons every year, as I was saving that for an even greater occasion. But I was able to gain access to a amphora of wine that was most palatable.

I deliberately limited my intake of the inebriating fluid as it was my obligation to watch over my flock at this time of weakness. I had from the outset intended to again scrutinize the behaviour of Gwen the Revered, whose salacious activity always required careful monitoring, yet perhaps because she was with child again she stayeth within the light of the fire and nursed her youngest, oblivious to my gaze. After a wander round the darker recesses of the fortress looking for sinners in need of my support, I was carefully observing two couples celebrating the evenings event in a somewhat entertaining physical activity, when it became apparent that something spectacular was about to take place. I again ask any reader of this manuscript to cast disbelief aside. I fully appreciate that scepticism is the obvious consequence of reading the following text, but I must ask you to accept upon my oath, given upon the Holy Bible itself, that what I tell you now is the truth in absolute.

I was not in any way diminished in my faculties from the imbibing of a small portion of the contents of the amphora. I am even able to recall in considerable detail the activity I was observing prior to the event I am about to relate. This is the complete truth of my witness.

Maerlin the wizard had undoubtedly been called upon to display some of his proficiency as a sorcerer. The Warlock was brazen about his ability, and it is to my understanding that the Good Lord allowed this for one reason only. Our Lord God had a purpose in this man, as reason for being that I alone saw from the very beginning. He was permitted this vanity only so that those present would believe in his powers, and in so doing enable the community to come together in the belief that they would prevail against their gruesome foe.

The Warlock created a potion in a barrel in the clearing in the middle of the fortress. This potion was an extraordinary liquid, composed of many terrible things. He told us of the purpose of this concoction, and perhaps only I, amongst the throng, having both the intellect and education to really understand such things, appreciated how this miraculous liquid was created. It is my belief that if God permitted me to do so, I could recreate this same potion and fashion the same terrible weapon in the name of our Lord.

Maerlin gave us full explanation of how he had concocted a similar potion in the protection of a town of presumably Good Christian peoples. The potion in the cauldron like container in front of us was fashioned to a recipe that, even now, I can recall in full detail, whose sole purpose was the destruction of a flying beats with breath of fire. These dragons do really exist. I have seen one myself, and it was such a beast that the Warlock rode upon when he arrived at Caardbury. It was such a beast that died so fortuitously, stranding the Wizard amongst us. In Maerlin's story he unbecomingly celebrated himself as the saviour of the people of the 'town on the lake'. Yet, although I found this self aggrandisement distasteful, I am willing to acknowledge that he had been the instrument of God in successfully saving those inhabitants.

There came a time when his magical concoction started to smoulder, as if anticipating its task. Then the cauldron gave off a noise like a giant spitting out a rock. It was a noise not unlike being placed in a wooden barrel, and having the townsfolk beat the barrel with stout staves. This is an experience from my past which was not pleasant, but was obviously one which was to prepare me for this moment. (God does his work in mysterious ways.) After the loud, resounding, deep noise from the potion as it spat skywards, I looked upwards to the stars. Moments later there was a sight such as I have never seen before. The whole heavens above us were lit with exploding flame. It was as if the Smithy had struck a red hot coal on his anvil and the flaming embers of that coal, split into a myriad of pieces, were sent flying outward in every direction, leaving tails of fire through the air. Only in truth these were not tails of fire across the width of a Smithy's forge, but trails from horizon to horizon, blotting out the stars above us. And these were not lines of red fire in the sky, but trails of wizardly green flame.

Then the noise came upon us, not the clout of a hammer upon an anvil, nor even the thud of a stave upon a barrel, but a sound which was the accumulation of every loud noise, compressed between the hands of God and released in the loudest thunderclap you have ever heard. It is small wonder that such a device can kill a dragon. My one solace is that in our greatest hour of need I, James Trefell, could now also recreate such a potion, and manufacture such a weapon, because of the God given clarity of my recollection.

Chapter Fifteen;   Roman Shields.

As autumn turned to winter the risk of a Viking attack diminished to
nothing. With storms in the channel, and clinging mud, or frozen slippery
ground everywhere, raiding was impractical, if not impossible. With the
gulley finished I turned my thoughts to how we could improve the odds in
our favour. With the short days and long nights the winter months were
filled with hearthside activity. The three old crones from Kaardbury who
still shared one of my pairs of spectacles were now able to work in poor
light conditions, and where in the past they had been unable to make
anything of any quality unless they were out in the bright sunshine, they
were now able to produce twice as many quality items every year. My
simple pair of fold down 2.5 x reading spectacles ensured they ate well all
through the winter. They were also able to make thick leather breast plates
to help protect our men. Chain mail is made up of thousands of small
metal rings, each with its own little rivet to hold the ring closed. To
produce a single chain mail coat took a good smithy many months, and we
simply did not have that sort of time available. The chain mail recovered
from the three dead Vikings would be worn by our best warriors.

Amongst the CDs I had included some books by my favourite authors. I
had no idea how much time I would have to myself during the days I had
expected to be in 831. One of them by Bernard Cornwall explained some
of the battle tactics that had been used by the Romans. It was
extraordinary to realise that although a Roman Legion when caught in the
open by Boudicca's warriors was cut to ribbons, when they were able to
pick their battleground they killed 80,000 Britons for the loss of only 400
legionnaires. A tight shield-wall with men supporting from behind,
trudging forward in a controlled manner, against a frantic horde who were
all pushing to get to the front and attack that shield-wall, resulted in
carnage. The Britons closest to the wall were pinned against it and unable
to move or swing a weapon, the Romans stabbed to their right under the
arm of the person attacking the next soldier to their right. The shield-wall,
supported by a phalanx of their men at least five deep, trudged forward
over the dead and dying bodies of the fallen Britons. Tired Romans at the
front of the shield wall were rotated with those at the back, so they did not
become too exhausted, and in doing so avoided dying unnecessarily. As

they advanced over the bodies of their enemies, any still alive were quickly finished off. It was not until the mad crush to be at the front ended, that the extent of the carnage became apparent. It was a similar process to the terrible tragedy at Hillsborough football stadium, only on this occasion the pressure from the people at the back was not fuelled by the desire to see a football match, but by the desire to be famous for killing Romans and driving them from our shores. Boudicca's failure to control this mad rush cost her dearly. The crush against the shield-wall protected the Romans from any effective blows by the Britons. It was all about organisation and tactics.

The Vikings did not use a shield-wall. From my research into their fighting methods it was not until much later, when they were involved in pitch battles, that they became so organised. We needed to find a way of luring them into the gulley and trapping them there to cause casualties. In luring them into the gulley we needed to find a way to do that without losing our own people. That would be difficult. The Norse raiders were experienced warriors. Big, heavy men who wielded swords, but more importantly wielded long battle axes. Those axes were ideal for splitting shields, or for pulling shields forward and exposing the shield carrier.

I was most concerned that the Vikings would attack the north edge of the fort and gain entry into the main compound without being caught in the gulley. I had a way of getting them to enter the gulley, but after luring them into the gulley I had to find a way of engaging them from the front while the archers did their damage from the rear. This was not so easy when you wanted whoever was challenging these big, mad, axe wielding raiders head on, to live through the day.

With the exclusion of our archers, we only had about 55 men suitable for any sort of shield wall. We had many women who wanted to be involved, and I promised them that they would be, but my main concern was an effective shield wall which held. All the work had to be discussed with the twelve village leaders, and they had to be willing to send their men-folk to Kaardbury for training. I also had to be careful that I allowed Eric, their 'Thor', to appear to be the person in charge, as he was the one who took the sword from the stones, and had been chosen by the Gods. So during the late autumn and early winter we started to look at shields.

196

The standard Anglo-Saxon shield was very similar to the Viking shields. They were round, and about two foot three inches to three feet across, although the Viking one we had turned into our oath table was a bit bigger. In the centre of each was a metal 'boss' which was cone shaped and designed to deflect blows, as well as protect the hand of the warrior. The rest of the shield was made of wood, ideally of the preferred lime or poplar wood, as they were resistant to splitting, but both these types of wood were in short supply.

In my research I looked closely at the Roman shields or 'Scuta' and the Greek 'Hoplon'. Both of these shields were heavy, but designed to protect the whole body of the soldier. Using the standard Saxon shields our inexperienced and weaker men would struggle to survive more than a couple of blows from a North Man in a battle-frenzy. Fighting in the dark ages tended to be a one-on-one, toe-to-toe affair, with the victory going to the biggest, strongest and most skilled warriors. These fights tended to end all too quickly. I needed to find a way to hold these big dangerous men in our killing ground, and at the price of as few casualties as possible on our part. It would not be much use solving the problem of these raids by getting most of the people I was trying to protect killed, would it?

An effective shield-wall needed custom built shields, and I decided the Roman design was best. In fact they were not dissimilar to the large 'Parvise' shields that were free standing individual protective walls that allowed crossbowmen to reload in relative safety during the wars with France 500 years in the future. They were heavy, about 22 pounds each, but if they did the job, who cares. They were some two and a half feet wide and four tall, but they were also curved, so that they gave the impression of being almost half of a cylinder. This size and shape impeded the use of a sword by the carrier, but deflected almost any blow apart from one which struck the very centre of the top of the shield. It took months of making shields and adjusting the boss and shield rims to get what seemed to work best. We were not expecting our shield wall to be mobile, and I was even planning for at least one shield wall to be abandoned, but when our men stood their ground I wanted them to be able to do so for at least three or four minutes. This gave us time for our 11 archers to fire about 3–400 big, heavy arrows and our four crossbows to fire up to 50 bolts into the raiders, from behind and above. With our Gulley only being 20–25 foot wide we needed only 10–12 overlapping shields to completely fill the space from embankment to embankment. The gap between the inner and outer palisades was half as much again, but the steep embankments made it very difficult to get any purchase on these, and by extending the shield wall at either side, driving the bottom edges of the outer shields partly into the embankment itself we had an almost impenetrable barrier right across the gulley. Well that's how it felt at the time.

I remembered some police tactics I had watched being practiced at an old aerodrome in Sussex, when I had allowed them to use land my company owned for their police support unit training. They used the old aerodrome buildings to practice everything from being petrol bombed to forcible house entries. Their house entry tactic involved three big plastic shields at the front, and another three shields held up by three rear men at arm's length, so that the bottom edges of these were laid over the top edges of the front three. This resulted in a vertical front wall of shields with a forward sloping roof of shields above them, which protected all the officers from anything thrown out of the building from above. Because of the spreading of the load onto the front shields, and the shock absorbing effect of the officers raised arms, I witnessed a full sized sofa shoved out of a first floor window bouncing harmlessly off them.

We experimented with a similar tactic with our Roman style shields. It worked for up to a minute or so, but the weight of the shields meant that holding the upper shields at arm's length for much longer was impossible. In the end we opted for a braced pole held in a leather sling at the waist of each of the rear men, but supported by a harness across their shoulders, much like the belt and cup used to carry a big flag on a parade. There were two shoulder straps that joined at the waist and held a thick leather cup at just below crotch level (I did not want anyone to get damaged genitals from a heavy blow on their shield). A short pole cut to fit each man meant that they could steady the shield above them with both or either hand, but with the pole set in a socket in the upper centre of the shield they could take the bulk of the weight of the shield in the yoke across their shoulders. The bottom front edge of the shield rested on the top of the front shields which were set on the ground. With these shields constructed to be about five feet tall, this meant that all the front shield bearers had to crouch a bit to give them safe clearance from the sloping shield above their heads. But so long as they were not required to lift their shields and move with them, this defensive position was very sustainable for a surprisingly protracted period. All the shields had a carrying sling, two handles and a brace to enable them to be carried on one arm. The rear shields also had a central boss of metal that ran the length of the shield to ward off blows from a downward strike on the middle, as well as a central socket for the supporting pole.

When set up together – we used 25 of these big shields, with eleven of them on top and fourteen at the front and sides – they gave the impression of an impregnable armadillo. An analogy that I made the mistake of saying out loud, before I remembered that it would be another 700 years before any modern European (whenever that collective label appeared) would step foot in South America. They started to call it their armoured pillow and I just hoped I had not buggered it up too much for Pedro Alvares Cabral, who was destined to discover South America in about 700 years time. We ran practice attacks in which they were assaulted with clubs and rocks, although I deliberately limited the attacks with the captured Viking axes themselves. We did not want to spend all our time repairing and replacing damaged shields. Attacks with swords had very little effect, but the axes were much more efficient against the shield wall. As a result of trying out the axes we added curved ribs of iron to the bottom half of the top shields. They became known as the strip-shields, and were proudly held up by the strongest of the men we had left over after the abstraction of the archers.

With a mind to dealing with injuries and loss of any shields we practiced replacing them in battle conditions, as well as replacing fallen men. In the end we positioned seven men as bracers for the front 14. These men held two of the front men by the waist a bit like second row, or locks, in a rugby scrum. They helped them keep their balance and stopped any individual being pushed back out of the wall. Four of them also had a spare shield slung sideways across their backs. It was somewhat crowded inside the 'armadillo' but with a bit of practice they were able to replace either a forward or top shield in seconds.

This left us with 19 men left for other uses. They tended to be the young and the old, as the stronger specimens were allocated shields in the armadillo. For these remaining men we produced a smaller version of the Scuta. They weighed about one third of the armadillo shields, but looked very similar. At about four feet tall and weighing less than 10 pounds they were light enough to run with. I was concerned about three of our runners as they were clearly of advancing years. I got all them to run the length of the gulley in races, carrying the shields on one arm. Surprisingly one of our elderly runners kept up with the youngsters very well, despite wind-blown grey hair and a long beard flying over his shoulder in flight, but the other two did not. We also had one of the youngsters who, despite good early muscular development, had a club foot and could only run at a fast hobble. Their enthusiasm for being involved was tremendous and identifying these three who clearly could not be in the runners left them devastated. I had Eric promise them that they would have a role of great importance, and got on with the practice with the remaining 16.

My plan was to dismantle part of the front wall of the outer palisade, close to the western side of the main gate. Anyone entering by this breach would have the walkways that ran from the inner compound to the front wall above them and to their right, with the open gulley on their left. I made the decision to put another palisade wall across the width of the gulley on the right, under the walkways, so that we could control in which direction the raiders would go. I positioned this new wall just beyond the furthest walkway so that it would not enable a nimble climber to gain access to the walkways from below. I had them make this short wall 12 foot high, and built a false bank at the foot to give the impression of it being just another section of the inner compound wall. I regretted the waste of time and effort we had put into digging out the gulley to the east, but after the experiments we had done to establish the best options for defence we simply did not have enough men to have two armadillos at the same time. What I did get them to do was to tank the east end of the gulley with clay, in the hope of collecting more rainwater. This was to enable us to better defend the fort against anyone climbing the outer banks in dry weather, as then we would need lots of water to douse the mud slopes outside the palisade.

In the end we managed to make it look as if we were in the process of rebuilding a 20 foot section of the outer wall. We had ropes and fence posts strewn on the embankment, and the slope below the breach was extended so as to be about half as steep as anywhere else around the fortress. I hoped it would be just too tempting for our enemies. We had practiced through the cold winter months, and produced a good number of the special spears I had wanted made.

In my research I found that the Romans often designed new weapons based on those used by their enemies. Amongst their most effective infantry weapons was a type of spear called a 'pilum'. These pila were about six feet long with a heavy metal head of about two foot in length, with a barbed tip. One of the clever things they did was to make these of soft un-tempered iron, so that they bent easily after one throw making them difficult to re-use, but even more interesting for me was that the barbed tip embedded in an enemy's shield made the shield so unwieldy, because that hooked barb was difficult to remove, that these shields were often discarded. I wanted the North Men to fall easy prey to our archers, so what better tactic than to force them to throw away their shields in the middle of the battle. The tip of these pila were shaped like a small pyramid, and the width down much of the length of the shaft of the head, or shank, was very narrow, less than a centimetre across. The total weight of each of these pila was between five and eight pounds, lighter that some of the Roman ones, but many of ours were going to be thrown by women. My plan was to get the Vikings into the gulley, draw them westwards towards the armadillo, shower them with spears that made some of them throw their shields away, then hit them with lots of our chain-mail piercing arrows.

Well it seemed like a good plan to me.

The last part of the groundwork of our defence was to find a way to stop the Vikings attacking the armadillo so rapidly and forcefully that it would collapse too quickly, costing us the lives of most of our men, and enable the raiders to get into the inner compound where our women and children would be trapped. Once the raiders reached the far western end of the gulley they would still be outside of the inner compound, but the slope below the inner palisade was only about 7 foot, compared with the 15–20 foot of the earth bank of the original Iron Age outer embankment. I was starting to have second thoughts about the deliberate breach we had made in the outer wall. Perhaps the best thing was to concentrate on keeping them outside the fortress altogether. Perhaps with the spears and our heavy arrows we could cause enough injuries to dissuade them from returning.

Sadly we ran out of time. To date, it had never been heard of for the Vikings to attack before full spring was upon us. The North Sea was too dangerous, the ground too wet, and the stores of food all but empty. In retrospect we had been fortunate that they had not attacked the previous summer or autumn, but this was little consolation that morning as I was shouting and swearing to myself about not closing the wall breach sooner. Their delay in attacking may have been due to a difficulty in getting the numbers together for what they had planned. Their early arrival in the year suggested that they were intending to deal very punitively with the one community that had thwarted them the previous spring. It was an early morning in March 833 when the bells rang out again.

Chapter Sixteen;   The Battle.

The procession up the hill was the same as before, just colder and wetter after a night of drizzle. Provisions and water were better organised, and the store house in the inner compound was better stocked than it had been last time. On this occasion there were only two people missing, and both were known to be away in Exeter selling livestock. What we did have were some extras.... In fact 43 extras, all of whom were additional lives to protect and mouths to feed. Some appeared to be genuine visitors in the area, extended family members staying over to help with the spring sowing. But there were a few I suspected who were just people from outside our catchment area living within distant earshot of the bells, and who decided Come a Lot was as safe a place to be as any. The bells had started at about six in the morning, just as the rising sun cleared the horizon, and when some were just setting off to the fields provisioned with their day's food. By 7.30am the last stragglers had arrived at the fort. Amongst the last arrivals were the boys from the watching post above the river, just south of Thorverton. They had taken the route back up to Come a Lot slowly, as they were the ones who had raised the alarm, and with the greater confidence of the last confrontation, had gone at a pace which enabled them to watch the progress of the raiders as they headed towards the fortress.

I remember very clearly where I was when the first of the watch boys came in and reported to myself and Eric. I was standing in the middle of the western gulley organising the big rocks being moved. I was almost exactly half way along, between the main gate and the western end. I remember it well as when I was told the news I looked upwards into the tree above me. It was one of the trees that held a firing platform, and I looked directly into the eyes of Big Tash. He had tried out with the longbows, but had eventually been singled out as one of the poor performers. I was always suspicious that he had deliberately failed the aptitude test as soon as he was aware that those who failed may get to use the crossbows. Still, as his handiwork was a key factor in their construction, and he was built like a brick shithouse, his role as a crossbowman seemed appropriate. When the boy I called 'Sticky', as he always seemed to have hands that were covered in something damp and slightly adhesive broke the news, it was the open and trusting stare of Big Tash that welcomed me back to reality. Four ships ... FOUR FUCKING SHIPS!!!!! Why the fuck have they bought four fucking ships???

Let's face it, today we are all going to die....

Sticky had given me the news with the youthful enthusiasm of all young boys about to be involved in a competitive game they cannot lose. They were in a fortress that had turned the enemy away so easily last time. The fortress was stronger than before. Some of the men had big bows that everyone talked about. They had Eric who they childishly referred to as their 'king' who had been chosen by the magic Dragon Leg sword, and they had Maerlin the great wizard on their side. What complete bollocks! I said nothing, still staring heavenward....

Sticky turned and ran back to his friends from the watch team. Because they had stayed just in front of the raiders as they headed from the river up to the fort, the watch boys, brimming with confidence, knew that the Vikings were about to arrive along the main footpath from the south. Sticky had hurried back so as not to miss the moment when they left the forest path and came into view.

All my plans and expectations had been built around a one, or at most a two ship, sustained attack. Out of 100–120 Vikings we could probably injure or kill enough to prevent a massacre, and even drive them away with only a few casualties ourselves. 200–250 of the bastards would fill the gulley from end to end, they would swarm over the walls like flies, they would be able to prop each other up to reach the inner palisade wall, even without ladders two or three could lie on the inner embankment and provide footholds for their compatriots. What was worse I was the one who had organised the dismantling of a 20 foot section of the outer fucking palisade wall. What a tosser!!!! I had underestimated our enemy. I had underestimated his desire for revenge at being made to look like fools. Perhaps I had underestimated the effect of killing three of them two years ago.

We had very little time. I had thankfully already had all the big rocks moved to the middle of the western end of the gulley. These were originally spread near the entry point close the palisade breach, but I had had them moved half way up the western arm of the gulley to provide an area of difficult footing for the raiders. I wanted them to struggle to stand up as they attacked the armadillo. To this effect I had those couple of hundred rocks we had already transported to the fort collected together and set side by side, a few inches apart. This meant that when the armadillo was in place there would be an area the full width of the floor of the gulley, and about ten foot in depth, literally covered in chunks of stone, each the size of a basket ball, and weighing between 100 and 150 pounds. These stones were deliberately rounded or oddly shaped, and set on the ground on edge, or in a way that meant they were unstable. To stand on or amongst these stones and try to strike at the armadillo would be very difficult indeed. What I now needed to do was to find a way of preventing too many of these bastards getting in the gulley at the same time.

The plan had been for the runners to put up a token defence at the breach in the outer palisade, and to then run to the armadillo, get behind it, and then throw some spears. They were to support the armadillo, and if necessary, escape up our own ladders to the inner compound to help the women defend it. I got everyone in their places and climbed to the inner compound. I walked briskly towards the footways that led to the viewing point on the high wall above the main gate. I did not look anyone in the eye. I could not, as I was the idiot that had started all this. I was the fool who had penned them all in a compound ready to be butchered. I was the one who led them into a terrible false hope. I reached the walkway. From the view point above the gate, looking down at the runners with their light shields at the wall breach, my mind was in turmoil. There was going to be a massacre. Outside the fort there were soon going to be over 200 men. 200 big, strong, highly skilled, heavily armoured, vengefully motivated, angry men. There would be almost as many of those unstoppable bastards out there as there were women, children and old men in here, inside our little fortress.

Then slowly some clarity came to me. I was scared shitless, but for some reason my mind was running through scenarios, and options, like a good computer search program. I was still scared, but for some reason felt detached, as if this disaster, which was about to unfold before me, was happening on a chess board, distant from me, hard to control, yet with some direction possible.

The wind was gentle, steady, and from the west. I had arrived at the fort that morning better prepared than I had been last time. I also had more kit stored in my locker in the store house, so I literally ran down the western walkway and up to the store room, with the stiff material of my dragon cloak slapping, in the breath held silence, against the backs of my calves. There was the store keeper, an elderly woman called Erith, who despite her greying temples was built like a barn door, with arms as muscular as mine. No one messed with Barn Door and she was the ideal storekeeper for our fort. I was the one person who she seemed to allow unquestioned access to her store, although I had always considered the way that she looked at me as somewhat predatory.

I had a total of eight bear cartridges left for the shotgun, but only four of them up at the fort. I suspected that none of the other cartridges had the penetrative power to get through chain mail at a distance of more than a few feet. But I did have some other items that may help sway the balance in the coming maelstrom. I heard shouts from the wall as I struggled out of the store with a heavy bag slung over my shoulder and my hands full. From the inner compound I could see the Vikings were massing along the southern edge of the forest on the far side of the open ground we had created over a year before. They had ladders, at least a dozen of the fucking things, and all of them were long. Long enough to reach the outer palisade wall from the ground outside, from below the Iron Age embankment. I shouted for silence. I shouted again at the top of my voice, and walked up onto the walkway above the gulley. Eventually every face was turned to me. Even Eric's, who had been cajoling the men from the armadillo at the far end of the gulley and now stood near the runners with their lighter shields.

"Listen, we do not have long and we must change our plans if we are going to live through the day." I was shouting out the words in the hope that everyone could hear me. **"All the arrows are to be saved for the battle."** Each of our longbow men had forty long heavy arrows for killing, and another forty lighter arrows for harrying the enemy at a distance. Our crossbow men had just forty iron quarrels each. With Reggie

206

and our ten longbow men, and the four crossbows we had 15 archers, a total of only just over a thousand shots, and despite what you see in the movies a less than 10 percent hit rate is the norm, even for guns with proper sights on them. Now we needed every single shot.

"No one is to fire an arrow until the enemy are through the breach, or where there are ladders against the outer wall. Use the big arrows first." "Unless you are told otherwise Acennan, Norvel and Fyren are to cover the outer walls to the east, north and west. Every shot must count, so use them wisely. Erlene and her team are to only use the fire oil on the outer wall. We must not have anyone getting over the outer wall behind us. Wulfgar you are to take charge of the outer defences. Take command of the spear women, keep some for the inner wall, and some for the outer."** A raised spear from amongst the armadillo signalled that Ronnie, our lance specialist and only professional soldier, had heard. "Wissian, leave the eastern tree, and join us at the gate."** This left no one in the eastern tree, but with three longbows committed to the outer wall we were short of archers on the walkways above the gulley. "Runners, you must hold the breach for longer. Only when the enemy are held at the top of the embankment are you to run to the armadillo. Wait for the noise like the dragon killer. Only then can you run."** There were nods from the now worried faces of the men and boys with the light shields at the top of the breach.

Eric was with them below me, to my left. "My apologies Eric Smithson, but I have had a vision of how the battle will be. Can you please keep the runners at the breach until I make the air jump with a great noise? Please then take them to safety behind the armadillo, and then lead the defence in the gulley. I will use dragon breath to confuse the enemy but you must slow them down."** I needed, as always, to give the impression that Eric was in charge but, as always, he seemed to take it with good grace.

"Erith,"** the woman mountain appeared at the side of the store, "issue every man from the new arrivals with one of the long spears, and every woman with a short one. Send them to Wulfgar to be used on the inner palisade above the gulley."** Her beaming smile and sudden disappearance back into the store told me she had heard. "Leof, get to the outer palisade of the eastern gulley with some of the water carriers and three of the new spear men. **If they try to get into the eastern gulley hold them at the outer wall as long as you can. Then get across to the main compound and hold the inner wall. Ask Wulfgar for support if you need it.**" Leof, the only one of our five trained crossbowmen who had missed out on his chosen weapon, ran down the eastern walkway to my right. I turned and watched. Wulfgar was already in the inner compound directing people to join Leof as he scaled the inner compound wall with the help of a short ladder and then scrambling down a longer one into the eastern gulley. Leof was to have been constantly at my side as a personal guard until one of the crossbowmen fell, but he took on this new role with his customary simple resolve. He was a giant of a man, not that well coordinated, and not very bright, but if I was a North Man, I would not want someone like him stabbing or throwing things at my head as I tried to scale the slope below the palisade. I heard him splashing though the two foot of water and mud that covered the bottom of the eastern gulley. I was satisfied that anyone getting over the outer wall and into that quagmire would have a bugger of a job getting into the inner compound.

One of the last things I shouted was to the men gathered beyond the stones at the far end of the gulley. **"Keep the armadillo strong and hold them back until you hear a second big noise the same as the dragon killer. Only then can you climb into the inner compound. Have one of the locking men ......, Beadwof, stay at the outer wall to watch for the enemy getting into the gulley behind you. If they attack there, use the runners with their spears to keep them out. Join the armadillo when you can."** A short stocky middle aged man raised his arm in acknowledgement and started to scale the slope on the far side of the gulley, up towards the south west outer wall. I turned to face those behind me and to my right, as well as those in the gulley below. I shouted a last few words as I looked to them all **"Everyone stick to your task. You know what to do. We must keep these bastards out of the inner compound, we must keep the children safe. This is the time when the Gods will be on our side...."** (Some fucking hope, I thought.)

Every pair of eyes were all still watching me as I walked back down the western walkway and then set off up the eastern walkway to where Reggie stood. I allowed the other longbow man and the two crossbowmen to have the western walkway as a shooting platform. Wissian had already slid down from his tree and joined us. They needed the best view of the breach and the runners below them. I went to the front wall above the closed gate, and looked across the open ground to the south. There was a strange stillness in the air, a chill breathlessness that stung the cheeks. Only the slow push of wind from the west rustled the early leaves on the trees. I raised the binoculars and got a clear view of our destiny, probably of our nemesis. I turned to Holt (Reggie's real name), and took five items from the bag slung under my left arm. "Can these be tied to an arrow and fired with your bow?" he responded with a question "How far must they fly?" I held out the smallest of the five items. "This one must fly to where the raiders now stand and these others much less." Reggie replied, "I am not sure if I can hit a man with them, but they will fly far enough." I extracted a fistful of hemp threads, and the pair of us set about tying the five items to the arrows. It was with great reluctance that Reggie used one of his heavier arrows for the longer shot, but its greater weight would carry the small tube better. All the arrows would still give him a reasonable length of draw despite the tubes now strapped to the front end of the shafts. The smallest tube was an inch in width, and about six inches long, the others were about two inches across and eight inches in length. As we hurried to the task I kept looking across the ground in front of the gate as the stragglers joined the throng of North Men readying for battle. I had handed Wissian the binoculars and with this great honour of using the magic hawk eyed device, he proceeded to give a running commentary on the progress below the fort.

At the front of the men on foot there were a dozen mounted warriors. Two of these were clearly of high status with elaborate decoration on their shields and helmets. One of the men on foot was talking with the horsemen, and he was equally well gilded. We waited. I looked around our little fortress, at the silent, concentrated faces. I could see a mixture of emotion; much of it was stoic, and determined. Some of it was forced attentiveness in the face of terror. But every glance that was thrown in my direction had a glint of trust in it, an indication of an unquestioned belief.... Oh Fuck! I thought.

I watched as the ladders were bought to the front of their men on foot, and it appeared that they were to be carried in the sword hand of the raiders, four men to a ladder. I counted fourteen ladders. Four were separated off with about forty men to the western side of the group, the other ten ladders were at the front of the remaining horde, probably about two hundred men, but at this distance and because they kept moving, the exact number was not easily determined. The horses stayed between the two groups until a signal of unknown origin set the larger group of men on foot up towards us at a steady run. My guess is that they did not want to spend longer than was absolutely necessary in the open ground, and possibly risk being subjected to archery practice. They already knew we had at least one good bowman.

I had indicated to Reggie where the first arrow with the small tube needed to go, and as soon as the raiders set off up the hill towards us, I struck the fuse of the nine-bangs attached to that first arrow. The horsemen seemed to be waiting for the men on foot to get fully under way, and the smaller group with four ladders was already angling across the slope in front of the southern wall, apparently heading round to the far side of the fort. A couple of the horses reared slightly before they came under control again, perhaps startled by the unexpected movement and drumming clanking noise of over 200 men in armour suddenly on the move. Reggie's first arrow overshot the horsemen by a good thirty yards, disappearing unnoticed, leaving the faint arc of smoke from the fuse barely visible, into the undergrowth behind them. My heart leapt into my mouth. Had the damn thing been put out? Perhaps it was plugged into thick mud, or into rotten wood at the base of a tree? Had it struck a branch so hard that it had gone flying into the woodland beyond, and would have no effect? The seconds ticked by. Probably only about two of them, considering the device had a seven second fuse. Then, without any sound at all the horses sort of took off. They reacted as if someone had simultaneously struck each of their rumps with a cricket bat. Four of the riders were left literally in the air as their mounts set off from under them. Another slid from his horse as it rose on its two hind feet. The others all set off at a full gallop fanning out onto the hillside below us. Then we heard the noise. At this distance it was less impressive than it had clearly been for those simple equine creatures who had probably never encountered anything louder than a sword striking a shield, or a heavy Norse hand striking a bare Valkyrian bum. For those of us from the modern world who have heard such things before, it was very much like listening to a slow gunfire volley on a rifle range that was a bit too close for comfort. The nine-bangs had a noise output of just over 100 decibels, repeated nine times in quick succession. I know this because on this occasion I had taken the time to read the label.

An unexpected bonus from the nine-bangs was that a good number of the men on foot at the back of the advancing throng stopped in their tracks and turned, with shields partly raised, apparently thinking they were being attacked from behind. By the time they gathered their wits and decided that they should follow their comrades the others had already reached the foot of the bank where the palisade wall was breached.

What I badly needed to happen was quite a number of things to go pretty much exactly to plan. So many things, that I realised the chance of it all actually working was a desperately slim one. Firstly I needed almost all of them to attack the breach, as that was the only way to get them into the gulley in numbers, and that was the only place where we could possibly cause enough casualties to stop them in their tracks. If they split and attacked the outer wall to the north, west and east instead, we would be simply overrun, and most of us would be dead within the hour. More probably dead within the next ten minutes!! Because there were four boat loads of the bastards (FOUR FUCKING SHIPS!!!), we simply did not have the firepower or the capacity to hold that many in the gulley at the same time. 200 men in the gulley would run up against the armadillo and tear it apart, then swarm up over the inner palisade wall before we could stop them. The other problem was the ladders. If they got enough of the ladders into the gulley there would be very little chance of holding them even if we did manage to slow them down coming through the breach. Somehow we had to get rid of the ladders.

Around the fortress there was the main embankment which was between 18 and 20 feet high. This meant that in total there was somewhere in the region of 2000 square yards (just under 2000 square metres) of steep slope on just the outer perimeter of the fort. It was not possible to douse all of that, nearly half an acre of ground, with water, in the hope that it would make the traction too difficult for the raiders to scale. We had women carrying leather buckets to hurl onto the slopes anywhere the North Men

211

started climbing the banks on foot, but the one place we had already drenched the ground properly that morning, was directly in front of 'the breach'. Worryingly the slope below the breach in the palisade was the least steep of any place anywhere around the fortress, which had originally been with the intention of ensuring that they all entered the gulley at that point.

As the first running North Men got to the bottom of the slope below our line of defenders, almost to a man they lost their footing and fell headlong forward against the slippery bank within the first few steps of their attempt to scramble up the final incline. There were jeers from above them as the struggled to their feet, and dragged their sticky shields from the wet clay. I was watching everything slowly unfold before my eyes. I had to shout at one of the bowmen in the nearest tree to hold his fire, I was surprise that he heard me above the clamour of the racket from the hoard below us, but I suspect that he had kept an eye on me as he took aim, just in case I was not happy with him firing early. My angry gesticulation was enough to stop him in mid draw.

It took a couple of minutes for the Vikings to get organised, they were a warrior race where individual prowess in battle was most highly praised. So my guess was that there was a bit of testosterone fuelled sullen disobedience related to the relinquishing of a front-line position to allow the careful placing of the scaling ladders. Eventually they had six of those long ladders laid on the bank. They clearly waited until there were enough of them in place before the front men swarmed up towards the shield wall. Once these ladders were flat in the mud they would probably stay there stuck fast, but the other four were a real worry. I could only see two of them, but knew the others were on the far side of the men massing below me, all waiting to attack the breach.

This was one of the most difficult moments. I had planned to allow the runners to flee from their line of shields above the enemy as soon as they were on their way up the bank in numbers. But this had to change. While the ladders were being organised the runners had thrown their heavy spears as instructed. I had decided that this early stage was a better point in time to use the spears (if you will pardon the pun) as the enemy would be bunched together, and almost every spear would end up in a shield.

212

Each of our runners had originally been given only two of these heavy spears for use before and during their retreat to the armadillo. But given the unexpected increase in the numbers we had to contend with, I had got them to bring all their spare heavy spears, moving them from behind the armadillo to beside their positions at the breach. I hoped they could then make the most of their elevated position. Each runner now had five spears, so during the time the North Men spent getting their ladders on the embankment about 100 heavy spears were cast down on them. I saw only one man fall to a thrown spear, as the Vikings had quickly covered their heads with their shields. The crammed gathering below us turned almost miraculously into a massive scaled limpet-like creature, which quickly evolved into a spiked carapace, like a porcupine or cactus, as the spears punched into its armoured shell. With the inherent difficulties of moving anything cumbersome amongst the crouched figures below us, I suppose it was not exactly that surprising that it took some time for them to get the ladders organised!

Six men at a time could now climb the wet bank together, and they had clearly waited to attack as one. Yet there was still the eagerness that comes with battle frenzy and a desire to be the first into the fray, so two of the men on the ladders were almost at the top before the others set off. But despite there being only two of them, the shield wall barely held the ferocity of their attack. The men and boys behind the shield were no warriors and, notwithstanding their poor footing, the assailants hacking into our shields were almost twice the size of our runners and as strong as bloody oxen.

This was the moment for something that I had not expected to use in the ninth century. Monty, bless her, had included two boxes of shotgun cartridges in the microlight casing, as a replacement for my missing rifle. She had known that I had some CS spray canisters with me for personal protection. So she had left me a mixture of shells, and included some that were for police use in house clearances. (As if they would be any use to me in 831 eh!) They were, in fact, small CS projectiles in shotgun cartridges. According to the outside of the box you needed a couple to fill a good sized room with gas and I had already used two, during my weeks in Cornwall, and in doing so causing considerable mirth for all those gathered with me. I had used them to clear a drunken group of fishermen

213

out of their hut, in a cliff-side village with an un-memorable name. They had pissed me off a bit, because after some of my usual bragging it was suggested that, considering I was an outsider, I should leave the drinking to 'real men'. I left with a number of my temporary local personal followers and made a bet with them that I could clear the hut without having to even enter it myself. They thought the effect of the cartridges, as the sailors staggered blindly into the street, was excellent magic, and very funny, but I decided not to stay the rest of the night because pissed off fishermen can be bad news. Given I had only used only two of these cartridges, I now had two in the sawn-off shotgun hanging from a lanyard inside my cape. I had no intention of firing off the last few bear cartridges unless it was to save my own skin. I did not want to lose the option to protect myself with the bear shot in my pump action shotgun, so I had loaded the sworn-off with the gas rounds and both weapons were with me now.

As the first men were attacking the runners' shield wall at the top of the bank I fired the first CS cartridge at a man standing on the far side – the windward side – of those waiting to scale the ladders. It hit him in the chest just below his ribcage and under his right arm. He didn't go down, but he did stagger sideways and his upper body instantly disappeared behind a small cloud of vapour. The ball of CS gas was pushed gently into the far side of the throng by the prevailing wind, whilst the man I had hit dropped forward to his knees, pushing his helmet from his head and scrabbling at his eyes. A group of Vikings at the far side started throwing down their shields and covering their faces as the toxic spray dissipated through the horde. There was probably only a dozen or so affected, but by then my second shot had struck a shield held by a man in the middle of the mass below me. I was trying to ensure the cartridges struck amongst and between the men below me, and not on a raised shield, where the gas would just be blown harmlessly away. Not easy, with the limited accuracy of such a weapon. As I reloaded the sawn-off I shouted to Reggie, **"Now, Holt, now!!! Aim for the far side. Only use two!!"** On the wall above the gate we had attached two clay pots. Each held rags soaked in animal fat, and the plan was for one to remain lit at all times, above the gate, during the battle. This had been a last minute arrangement as the pots had originally been there to provide light for the guards on the gate during the hours of darkness, but one was alight now. This was good news, as the last

214

thing I needed at that time was to be ferreting up my sleeve to find a bloody lighter.

The two arrows carrying their heavy load arced over the men below and struck the ground beyond. By the time I fired two more CS cartridges into the enemy they were becoming engulfed in the thick dense smoke that had not been seen since the ceremony by the lake a year and a half before. The discharge lasted just less than a minute, but whereas standing on the Perspex windscreen in the lake I had a reasonable chance of holding my breath for that long, these men had just been running up a hill. Not only that, they were carrying shields and ladders and were in full armour, so they were still literally panting for breath creating a steam that rose in a pale fog above them. I had seen exactly the same fog of breath and sweat hanging over many a rugby scrummage on cold winters days in my youth. These warriors did not have the option to hold onto a lungful of clean air until the wind cleared the smoke and I had personal knowledge of the effect of breathing the damn stuff in. By the time there were a full six men at the top of the ladders, with others hot on their tails, many of those at the bottom of the slope were temporarily incapacitated, coughing and spluttering as they spread out in panic. In the state they were in they were very vulnerable, and they knew it. They could not see through their streaming eyes, and if attacked they could not have defend themselves. They spread out blindly, shouting for each other for protection, pairing up, standing virtually sightless, back to back.

The runners' shield wall was about to collapse. I saw one of our men tumble forwards, his shield dragged from his arms, and a massive gauntleted hand pulling him off his feet to throw him down the slope between the ladders. The thunder-flash to tell them to retreat was in the air at that very moment. I wanted to save our man sliding down the slope, but was concerned that the whole shield-wall would disintegrate, I raised the pump-action and fired a round at the Viking who was about to leap through the hole he had made in our human barricade. I had no idea if I hit him or not, as I saw the raider being virtually decapitated by Eric who stepped into the breach wielding 'Dragon-Leg'. In moments the clamouring din of the battle, which you somehow don't really hear when you in the thick of it, was ruptured by an ear clapping sound. The thunder-flash went off under the feet of the men at the top of the ladders. One, startled, stepped sideways and slid tumbling down the slope, the rest stepped back to keep their balance as the runners, under the shouts of Eric, threw their shields forwards, in a well practiced move, and set off at a run towards the armadillo.

The discarded shields caused only a very temporary obstruction under the feet of the leading North Men as they dropped down into the gulley and set off westwards following our fleeing runners. It was only then that I could fully judge the effect of the delaying tactics I had used. At best guess there were only about 50 or 60 of the enemy following the runners in full flight, although it was now a couple of minutes since the smoke had cleared, and the bulk of the raiders were starting to move towards the ladders, their vision gradually returning. I could see three of those remaining ladders being carried towards the slope below me. Each only had two men carrying them, but their importance was not lost on our attackers. Men started to gather around those ladders to climb up through the breach. I looked up and could see our four men in the tree platforms above me. They had started firing almost vertically downwards into the backs of the Vikings below. They were taking carefully aimed shots, and these were already making the Vikings pay heavily. To my right, on the western walkway, the two crossbowmen and both longbows were firing as well. I pulled Holt and Bawdewyn, the two longbow men towards me. They were the two best archers we had. I shouted to them, **"We must stop the ladders reaching the gulley. Hit them when they are climbing the slope."** They nodded and turned to their task.

It is one thing hitting the backs of a dense mass of men standing side by side as they were in the gulley below us, slowed to a virtual halt as they came up against the armadillo. It was another thing to hit a man clambering up a ladder, which is so flat it can be taken almost at a run, especially when they are carrying a shield on their right side as protection against us. The first ladder almost reached the top before either of the carriers were hit. The front man dropped sideways with an arrow through his thigh, and the rear man ran on until he had to release his end of the ladder near the top of the slope because the front end was now driven into the mud at the bottom of the far side of the gulley. He stopped to pick it up again, shouting to his following comrades, but then pitched forwards and sideways as one of Holt's arrows punched through his back, leaving

216

the front of his mail shirt pushed out, like a small tent in the middle of his chest, where the heavy shaft had passed clean through his torso. I shouted to Holt, **"Wait for my signal to use the other two dragon breath arrows. I will wave a red fire stick. You will see the smoke."** I did not hang around for a reply but set off down the eastern walkway to the inner compound. I wanted to get to the armadillo.

As I ran through the compound there was intense activity all around. There were two points of commotion on the north wall of the palisade, with archers firing downwards and women heaving the long handled pots containing the precious fire oil over the palisade. The 'fire oil' was not alight, but it was the thin chicken fat and fish oil we had collected over past months, heated to boiling on the fires in the inner compound. It was an idea I had remembered from watching a film many years ago called *Straw Dogs* in which the diminutive Dustin Hoffman held off four or five men trying to get into his house. The long handles enabled the women to hurl the hot fat over the palisade with some accuracy. The fat was of course a great deal hotter than boiling water. Wulfgar was with them, and I had to trust them to prevail. I saw a group of the spear women running across in front of the store towards the eastern gulley led by James the priest, and hoped to hell that Leof was holding out. The smaller children were all gathered near the back of the store in makeshift compound of poles and ropes. Four of the oldest women watched over them. The inner compound wall above the gulley was crowded with people, some with spears, some with water buckets. I saw two of our longbow archers firing over the wall, but could not see the other two who were supposed to be there. I reached the place above the armadillo and shouted to a tall woman with a spear to move out of the way.

The inner compound wall was only five foot high. A good height if you wanted to fire or throw something onto attackers below, especially given the foot thick circular discs of felled oak trunks that lined the inner edge of the palisade that our defenders were using to stand upon. On this inner side of the gulley, the bank beyond the wall, down to the armadillo, was a mere seven foot high, so that the heads of the North Men were only six feet lower than the top of the inner palisade . Below us the gulley was swiftly filling with those big savage men whose helmeted heads and heavy axes were almost close enough to touch. Off to my left I could see a steady stream of raiders coming through the breach near the main gate. I could not see any ladders, and hoped that Holt and Bawdewyn had managed to prevent them reaching the gulley with its all too short inner embankment.

Below me the armadillo was holding well. The shape was exactly as we practiced, and the heavy blows from the long axes had not penetrated yet. Because of our relocated rocks, the poor footing in front of the armadillo meant that it was very difficult to get close to the shields in sufficient force to drive it backwards. In many ways this was where the real danger was, because if the raiders managed to get just a few feet of clear ground in front of the armadillo they would have the weight of numbers to literally tear it apart. It was all very well building a protective barrier of shields, but when the enemy stops hitting those shields and starts simply pulling them out of our hands instead, the enemy's strength and numerical supremacy would win the day and we would all die. In an ideal world the armadillo men would be able to use stabbing weapons like the Romans did with their shield walls, but it was not realistic to think that our few runners now positioned for stabbing between the shields, should they be pulled apart, would be able to cause many significant injuries. Our armadillo was defensive, it was a 'come on' to the North Men in the gulley so that our archers could take their toll. I could not in all honesty expect the formation to do more than stand their ground as long as they could. And at best that would be literally minutes!!!

The bulk of the North Men were now massing behind the rocks. Those at the front were being pushed forward so some fell over, and onto them. I saw a leg fold in a way that suggested both a fibula and tibia broke at the same time, and a big man with a bearskin cape collapse sideways in agony. Many of the men were making their way around the rocks. Some were leaping to the side, planting a foot against the bank before jumping forward to strike a single blow on the shields. This leap took them to the front of the stones. Once there they would struggle to get their footing and strike again, or try to get down the side of the armadillo by bracing against the embankment. The inner mud bank on the compound side was running with water as our water carriers hurled bucket after bucket over the palisade. On the far side it was drier and the footing was better. There I could see Eric, and a group of runners with long spears, keeping the attackers from getting alongside the armadillo.

To my left I could see that one of the ladders had made it into the gulley and was now propped against the inner palisade. The ladder was a good six foot longer than was required to reach the top of the wall, and it stuck up incongruously above the throng. There were two warriors holding the bottom of the ladder as a third was starting to climb. He stopped suddenly and fell backwards amongst the half dozen of his comrades who were waiting below for their turn to climb. Bollocks, Bollocks Bollocks!!!! We could not hang on any longer. I could see that the armadillo had just been pushed backwards a step, and there were suddenly five or six raiders directly in front of the shields. This was it ....

I pulled the bag open and started scrabbling about inside. My hand was covered in blood, but I had no idea why. I pulled out two of the smoke canisters and stood momentarily dumbfounded as I had nothing nearby to light their fuses. Then I remembered the flares, and recalled the reason why I had told Reggie that I would wave a red fire stick. Thankfully I still had the prescience of mind to drop the green one I found first back into the bag and dig out one of the red ones. They have their own striker, and the smoke and light and hissing noise cleared a space for me at the wall. I waived it once overhead hoping it would be seen. The men were massing below me now and the gulley seemed to be full from wall to wall with a heaving accumulation of seething helmeted creatures from hell. I lit both canisters and tossed them down amongst the rocks on the floor of the gulley. I went to get the last couple from the bag when the first of Reggie's landed in the midst of the men below me. Incongruously it bounced off a helmet with a laud clang, the arrow and canister going their separate ways, the one tumbling end over end between the raiders onto the mud floor beneath their feet, the other angling sideways through someone's cheek and out through their upper gum. The Norse man spat teeth through bloody lips, desperately trying to get control of the wooden shaft that was still attached, flapping frantically about his head.

The middle section of the gulley from the rocks eastwards started to fill with dense smoke. Unlike in the open ground below the breach in the palisade, here the smoke was trapped in a tunnel. The gentle wind was pushing it east along the gulley, but it was also holding it downwards so it was like a thick flowing stream. My guess is that there were at least a hundred of the North Men in the gulley when the smoke started. From the rocks eastwards they just sort of disappeared, as the flowing river of smoke completely engulfed them. The gulley that we had built as a killing ground had now turned into a tunnel of impenetrable smog. "SMOG FROM SMAUG!!" were words I heard from close by, but was taken aback when I realised I was the one who had shouted out those words, in some sort of stunned, jubilant, alliteration. I could see Reggie and the men above the gate still firing the occasional shot into the smoke below. I could see from here that these were the last few of their lighter arrows, but the Vikings were leaving, those nearest the breach were the ones who had already experienced the smoke canisters. The flow of men over the bank and out through the breach started as soon as the choking fumes reached them. By time I threw another canister amongst the rocks to keep them moving, more than half had already left the fort, and those remaining were staggering blindly in the right direction away to my left. The smoke was slowly thinning, and I saw a man fall with about a foot of feathered arrow shaft protruding upwards from his right shoulder. It was only then that I realised the ground was literally littered with bodies.

Dozens and dozens of them.

The last group of Vikings in the fort were the few that had been pushing the armadillo backwards. With a concerted effort Eric had got the armadillo to shove forward, and despite the Vikings having managed to pull two of the shields away from the front of its protective wall, the forward thrust of the shield carriers meant that the raiders had little chance of using their weapons before they were falling backwards over the rocks. Eric used Dragon-Leg to open one man's throat and was in the process of hacking at one of the men in expensive attire when I shouted to him we wanted prisoners. **"Keep him alive. Keep him alive."** I think only two of the men from that half dozen in front of the armadillo lived through the day.

The last retreating Viking staggered to the breach and slid down the bank outside. There were a good number on the ground moving weakly, or groaning, but many lay still. Apart from this moaning sound there was a strange silence ... then after what seemed like an age a single voice went up, a cry of pure elation, a battle cry from a mouth far too young for battle. It took me a good five minutes to get everyone quiet enough and that was only after the most extreme measures. Some of the runners and the armadillo men had already started to get amongst the dead and dying on the floor of the gulley. Knives were out and butchering was going to start. I took one of my precious thunder-flashes from my bag threw it over the wall at them. I missed, because that tall woman with the spear decided that was the best time to step onto one of the oak discs in front of me and give me a winning smile. My underhand throw bounced against her rather flat chest and fell at my feet....

Fuck me those things are bloody loud!!!!

When I started to shout down at the men in the gulley I was so deaf from the noise of the bloody thing that I could not hear my own words at all. It was only after a few sentences that the words became audible, and I was satisfied that the effort I was making to be heard was probably working.

"Do not kill anyone. We must have prisoners. If we are to win the day they must be kept alive." I saw men stepping back from their grisly intent and reluctantly disarming those left alive. **"Reggie,"** (he knew who I meant) **"get the archers to recover as many arrows as they can. We need to be ready for another attack. Ronnie,"** (he also knew who I meant although in the stress of the moment I did not realise that I had used the nick names I had given them) **"get the inner compound sorted, I want lookouts on the north wall. Smithy, how is Eric?"** I could see the Smith tending to his son, our famously named Thor, who was now slumped against the far bank of the gulley. His father responded. "He is injured, and cannot fight any more. We must tend his wounds quickly."

I turned to the men in the gulley below me. **"Beadwof, take command of the armadillo and have the shields set across the top of the breach. Get all those ladders off the embankment and inside the compound. Runners, I want any one of the North Men who has life still in them to be carried to the western end of the gulley. They are to be searched and disarmed. Any that can walk, or run, are to be hobbled, staked and guarded."** (This meant tying their feet as we do

221

with horses so that they can walk with only short steps, and attaching them to stakes with a leather thong. If any recovered the strength and wits to escape they would find it very difficult to do so. **"Erlene and Erith, have our wounded tended, and send some women to see to the wounds of our captives."** Things were not happening fast enough. **"MOVE ALL OF YOU!!! I want this fucking place defendable in five minutes!!!"**

The breach was filled in two, but it was closer to ten before our archers were back in their places. The fleeing North Men had gathered at the edge of the forest to our south east, around the footpath that led to Thorverton. We waited for a good half hour before I left my vantage point above the gate and handed my binoculars to Wissian again, so I could do another tour of our little fort.

Wulfgar had allowed two of his archers to descend the bank at the north wall to recover arrows, as here the enemy had already retreated with both their wounded and dead. It transpired that our inner compound defenders at the northern palisade had held off concerted attacks with water, arrows, spears and the fire oil. Their only injury was bad blistering on the right shoulder of Norvel and the left arm of one of the fire women which was due to a collision between them in the middle of the fight. We had a number of minor cuts due to badly wielded spears, and three missing fingers from one of the spear women. Leof and his team had delayed an attack by the Vikings on the eastern wall, not far from the gate, but had been forced to retreat across the eastern gulley to the inner compound. It appeared that their attackers had seen the shallow lake of mud and water between them and the inner compound and presumably had decided to try and attack elsewhere, because they had never reappeared. Sadly we lost one of our newcomers in this attack, as he had been pulled forward by his own spear when defending the wall, and a sword thrust had gone into the side of his neck. His blood was a dark pool in the mud of the gulley showing where he had fallen backwards from the palisade.

There were a number of injuries amongst the runners and the armadillo men. The man who had been pulled down the slope had been hacked open by the attackers, and had lain face up in the churned mud at the bottom of the slope below the breach until I sent three men down to collect his body. The gravest injury was to Eric who had bravely led the hand to hand battle in both defending the breach and later alongside the armadillo. He had two lesser wounds in his right arm, and a stab wound in his left thigh, but my greatest concern was a fourth wound in his side. It was not possible to see the depth of this wound, but it appeared that it may well have cut into his internal organs. I was shocked by my own emotion at the likely impending loss, as I was already having grave doubts that he would live.

The runners had, by then, not only disarmed and moved the injured enemy, but had started shifting the dead to the southern side of the gulley, between the breach and the rocks. They were lining them up along the floor of the gulley against the bottom of the inner southern bank. The priest was working his way along them, apparently giving them the Christian last rites regardless of the confusion this would cause if there really was some sort of afterlife. Think how pissed off some hulking North Man in chain mail, wielding a massive sword and spitting blood, would be thinking he was arriving at the barbarous drinking halls of Valhalla only to find he had been sent to the harps, clouds and pretty flowers place by mistake.

I counted fifty nine bodies.... Fuck me!!!!

We had eventually captured alive another 22, and from Wulfgar's estimation we had killed or badly injured another eight or so at the north wall, those who had already been taken away by their kin. So allowing for a few who had managed to escape the fort, but had probably been sufficiently injured so as to be incapacitated, and the half dozen corpses they had taken from the slope below the breach, we had probably cut their original numbers by about half. This was far better than I had hoped for. The archers had taken a terrible toll on the exposed backs of the men in the gulley. Many of the fatal wounds were from arrows through those men's backs, or down into their torsos from above. A good number of the crossbow quarrels had disappeared inside men's chests. Some bodies showed only the tip of a protruding barb, whilst others had clothing drenched in blood but, despite my brief inspection, were without any visible puncture holes in their chain mail. The arrow shafts had driven into body cavities tearing through arteries and veins, slicing into, or lodging in, vital organs. For many of the North Men their end had taken some time – time to drown in their own blood, or time to bleed out from internal wounds. Some were probably still dying, but with no outward sign, and their pulses too weak to find, it was hard to be sure who still clung on to life. Small matter, as those who were now close to death had no 21st century emergency team to keep them alive. It was only a matter of time. As I went along the line I saw one of the bodies moving weakly and ordered him to be taken up the gulley to join the other captives.

The Chronicles of Eathelwold 'James' Trefell; Monk.

Book 2 Chapter 14.

There are occasions in a man's life when one has to tell of an event of such significance that it truly is a privilege to be the teller of the tale. Modesty prohibits one such as myself, being a man of the cloth, from fully recounting one's own contribution to an episode of this magnitude.

In the year of our Lord 833 on an early spring morning the warning system of church bells rang out again across our land. I was one of those who shepherded our flock of souls up to Come a Lot to prepare for the onslaught of heathens from the north. I walked up the hill to our fortress singing the praises of the One True God, in the right and certain belief that he would hear our prayers, and protect us against our enemies on that fateful day.

When almost all had come to the fort I observed that some effort was put into the re-arranging of stones in the lower part of the castle. There was discussion amongst those about me as to their purpose. Some thought that they were to be cast at our foe, such as was done in ancient times in the land of Canaan, but I knew more than those simple folk around me, and although I did not divulge their purpose, they had a function only such as I would understand.

There was a considerable period of waiting in which I busied myself greatly blessing the weapons taken from our repository house within our fortress. The warrior known to use a lance a lot, Wulfgar, assisted me in preparing those in the upper compound for battle. I pride myself in blessing each blade and haft used on that day. Eventually the evil horde of men from the north gathered on the edge of the open ground before our Come a Lot. They had travelled to us in many ships such that there number was greater than any I had ever seen in battle before. I heard Maerlin offer up an appeal for succour from our Lord in a manner somewhat profane, but which I allowed due to the tension upon all of us.

When the enemy started to attack I observed, from the somewhat exposed position of the upper compound, that the

Good Lord assisted our purpose many times. His first act of wonder was to dismount many of the horsemen set against us. How this was done I am not sure, but it were as if he had struck a ripple of lightening in the woodland near the mounted host. This roll of thunderous noise frightened the beasts into leaving the battlefield with the speed of the wind. Then there came upon us the warriors on foot. These were monstrous creatures, slavering at the mouth, and barely human in their insane lust for blood. It was as well that I was willing to pluck up my courage and help all those around me to do likewise. I made a point of spending much time with the children who were so vulnerable to these terrible events, and I was able to offer much consolation in the dispensing of my knowledge about the delights of heaven should they be sent there that day. I heard Maerlin call out loudly and invoke the breath of dragons to spring from the ground. His dark arts, that which only I can counter through my love of God, were of great use upon that day.

I saw the Sacred Shields give way at the place close to the gate. I confess at that time I was a little anxious for the people under my care, but my trust in the Lord was absolute.

I spent time running with groups of the women as they rushed to the walls of the inner compound to hold back the invading multitude below us. I guided these women in their task, and blessed their efforts to keep the enemy from entering the inner keep of the castle. The battle went on for a great deal of time. The clamour was all around us, and I did great works in keeping up the spirit of our people, and helping the wounded. I am sure that it was only due to my swift intervention that many of them lived through the day.

I saw Our Thor the king amongst us, battling our enemies with the consecrated blade of Ex-Calliper. So great was his prowess with that holy blade, given to us by the Lady of the Lake, and won by him by the taking this sword from the stones, that all the enemy fell before him.

Eventually there came a time in the battle when it was necessary for a decision to be made. I was standing only twenty feet from Maerlin when I called out to him instructions as to what was needed to win the day. I called upon him to cause the earth to respire more of the breath of the flying beasts, although in truth there was much noise, and he may have only heard because we are connected in our holy purpose. I also admit that my request was not as specific as to what I wanted him to do as this text may suggest, but he clearly understood the underlying reasoning of my words.

So it was, through my suggestion, that Maerlin caused the earth beneath the feet of our enemies to exude that hot dank breath once more. The Dragon's rank discharge filled the lower section of the castle, and stole the very air from the lungs of our adversaries. They were put to rout and being unbelievers, and followers of false Gods, they did not have the resolve for battle as we, we who fear the true Christian God, have been blessed with. So it was, after the greatest battle in all Christendom for at least a generation, my true God fearing people prevailed.

There were so many heathens dead that it was not possible to see the ground under foot. It took many hours for me to bless each of the dead and send them to a Christian hell rather than any place of the Pagan Gods. I was also tasked with helping the injured amongst my flock. I praise the Lord that our losses were so few. It was truly a miracle of the One True God's making. Yet I can only claim small credit for the considerable number of lives I saved on the day, due to my quick action and skilful hand.

Chapter Seventeen;   The Oath.

There was a shout from above the gate and I returned to the breach to stand beside the armadillo men. There, approaching from the ranks of the Vikings, were the two men I had seen wearing fine regalia on horseback before they attacked. They halted half way to the fort and handed their swords to a servant on foot. They then advanced another 20 yards and stopped. They shouted something in their tongue, and from the far side of the armadillo our translator Pearce, or Percy as I called him, shouted out an interpretation of what had been said. "**We know that you have captives. We want our captives returned to us, and the bodies of our fallen comrades. If you give these to us we will leave this land and not attack again.**" I called Percy over to me, and he left his shield in someone else's care. "Tell them to come closer, and that we will not fire upon them."

When the riders reached the bottom of the slope I could see them clearly. They were big, strong, proud men, although they were both in their late forties at least. Their greying beards and lined faces told their age. I said to Percy, "Tell them that we will return their dead to them, but the captives remain with us. If they attack again, the first lives to be taken will be those of our captives, and they will all die without a sword or axe in their hands." I knew that this was one of the great fears of a Norse warrior. To die without a weapon in their grasp meant that they would never reach the halls of Valhalla; their warrior heaven. It was the most terrible threat I could think of at the time. The men below us looked up at us with stony faces. Their reply was translated for me. "They say that such a thing is without honour, but that they are pleased that we will allow them to take away their dead."

I have looked back at that moment and realize that I had been allowed the position of command without question. I suppose that I had always stood at Eric's side as he led our people, and with him injured there was no easy solution to the delegation of his command. As the first bodies were being lowered I went to Wissian, one of the community leaders and apologized for taking control. He waved my comments away. "Maerlin, you have had to lead us in battle, as only you can control the dragon breath and the magic that gave us victory. We have no problem with you leading us now, as perhaps we need some more of your magic to keep us, and our children, safe from our enemies."

We arranged for the bodies to be slid down the slope below the breach on some of the recovered runners' shields, attached to ropes and belayed from above. By the time this task was finished the man I had removed from their number because he had been moving, had rejoined them and he was the last to slide down the bank to be carried away. I had made a point of getting one of the runners to leave a battle axe clasped firmly in the dead warrior's hands, held closed with lengths of hemp cord. Despite this almost certainly being a posthumous addition to the corpse, it was perhaps my rather obvious attempt to convince our enemies that we were trying to do the right thing.

With so many bodies to be taken it took until the sun was at its zenith before this last North Man was returned to his brethren. During that time I had gathered the twelve community heads around Eric, and engaged them in discussion about the future. With Eric in considerable discomfort, he allowed me to chair the meeting. We decided, on my insistence, on a strategy that relied on the Vikings honour. It was risky, but was probably the only way we could prevent being attacked again. Let's face it, we had been so very lucky that day that the chances of ever luring raiders into such a successful trap again were close to zero.

Whilst we waited for the procession of the dead to finish, each being carried with some ceremony across the open area below the gate, we ate a lunch of cold meats and bread. From the edge of the woodland, the bodies were being carried away on horse drawn carts, towards the ships on the waters below. There was a tired relief amongst those in the fort. After eating I arranged to have Eric lifted onto a pallet, and propped up in a half-seated position. He had Dragon-Leg alongside him. He told me with wincing satisfaction that three Viking blades had shattered beneath its blows.

I led a procession from the Come-All fortress out through the gate, and down to the churned and bloodied ground below the breach. We waited for the Vikings to send their delegation. It took them nearly half an hour to meet with us there in the open, in front of our stronghold. Whilst we waited, the North Men were still trudging to and from their boats down on the river Exe, carrying the last of their dead. Eventually there were four leaders, and a young man who remained standing, who met us at the rough table we had set across four of the thicker discs of oak from the inner compound. Two of the discs were stacked one on top of another at either end of the table supporting it at a height of about three foot from the ground. The top surface of the table was a wide board of slit wood from the back of the store house. On the table we had laid out some food and drink, and the four raiders sat and ate the food and drank our strong ale.

Eventually I started the proceedings, introducing Eric as the leader of men and the carrier of the great sword. I saw them eyeing his blade with interest, and afterwards Pearce, our interpreter, told me that he heard them mention that they believed that Dragon-Leg was the sword that had been seen shattering more than one of their named blades in the hands their own men. Their greatest Norse warriors all carried swords that had individual names, and these were passed from father to son as the ultimate of family heirlooms. For any sword to be capable of shattering one of theirs was rare, and to break three was surely impossible without the most potent of sorcery. Eric spoke well, and appeared stronger than in truth he was. I wanted them to believe that he would live, and that he'd continue to lead his people. I hoped that the onset of infection could be delayed a few hours longer. He had lost some blood, but not a great deal. It was the infection that I was most worried about.

It appeared that the way we had dealt with their dead had been seen as honourable and they were now dealing with us as equals. During the meeting I took the opportunity to do a couple of small tricks that would help them remember that this community had the protection of a warlock who was to be feared. The first was to simply light a small amount of gunpowder taken from a thunder-flash that I had dismantled before lunch. This powder, about half of the contents of the firework, was placed at the bottom of a shallow bowl. When the food was finished I leant over the bowl and saying a few completely nonsensical words struck the artificial flint striker into the bowl with the back of my knife. The shower of sparks the striker produces is impressive enough, but the ball of smoke from the bowl was ideal for covering my sleight of hand in which I dropped four of my last few expensive boiled sweets into the basin. To all those present it appeared as if I had conjured them out of the flame. At my direction, the confectionary was taken and unwrapped in solemn silence by the four men. These muscled and hardened fellows tried not to show how truly scared they were when instructed to put the sweets into their mouths, but I took one of them myself, from the man nearest me, and put it in my own mouth. Through Percy it was explained that they were a peace offering created by the Gods who had blessed our meeting and that they would come to no harm. The evident pleasure of the three others, who were soon sucking on theirs without any adverse symptoms, even persuaded the fourth man to ask for his back. I obliged. Clearly the sharing of a little of my spittle was now not seen as too dangerous either.

I had only had a short while to contemplate how I was going to show my wizard powers. After some deliberation I had decided not to conjure up four pieces of gold instead, as the last thing we wanted was for these thieving bastards to think that we were the original alchemists and could make gold out of thin air. I could visualize the methods of torture employed in their attempts to persuade me to do so again ... and again.

The pretend magic sweets thing seemed to work well. The second bit of magic was a little more threatening. I had carried with me to the fortress my Dictaphone. It was something that was rarely used by me, but I had bought two of them from the 21st century for recording notes about my venture. I had planned, when I returned to 2006, to be able to deliver presentations on my time travels in 831, with great detail, to my adoring public. Well it would have been 2007 really, given the time lag their end. But it was now 833, and my public were still over a thousand bloody years away. Anyway, I had bought it up to the fort on a whim. I decided that I should record my thoughts throughout the day. After an initial short few minutes of recording, just after our arrival that morning, I had completely forgotten about it. In mitigation I had been convinced that we were all going to die after I was told that over 200 of the bastards had turned up, but when we decided that a parley was necessary, I remembered the Dictaphone and decided that there was still a good use for it.

After the food was finished, and we had recovered from the magical sweets incident, we started the meeting proper. It only took about 40 minutes, and even then this amount of time was really only due to the need for translation, and in taking some care to ensure that everyone knew exactly what was agreed. The Vikings had their own interpreter, a slave they had kept down with the boats during the raid, but who was an Anglo-Saxon captured some years previously. He was the boy who had not been allowed to sit down. It turned out that his name was Elmer, but the Vikings called him 'Earsling' as this apparently was suitably insulting. Having been captured as a youngster, his Saxon was excellent, and we were all satisfied that what was agreed was well understood by all.

We, of course, were in the driving seat. Eric set out our demands, and what we offered, and I checked the detail. Wissian, Wulfgar (Ronnie) and Holt (Reggie) were with us, but they barely contributed. Of the 22 we had captured there were three of our prisoners who clearly had some sort of status. One was the large man with the bearskin and the broken leg, and he was obviously from one of the leading families. His son had remained by his side defending his father until he was struck by an arrow through the shoulder. They were both very likely to live. There was another younger warrior who had apparently passed out in the smoke. He had been fighting close to the armadillo, and had delayed his retreat until it was too late. There turned out to be very little wrong with him other than the shallow wound in his forearm where someone had struck his weapon away as he had feebly tried to lift his sword when his consciousness had started to return. It was suspected that he was the son of one of the men at the table. There was a specific question about a young man of his description made by the elder of the two well dressed leaders. He had asked if he was alive, and Wulfgar said that a man of the same description was one of our captives, and his injuries were not life threatening. We did not let them know that if that young man hadn't been tied up, he would probably have jumped the outer wall and run back to their ships faster than the North Men sitting with us could get there on horseback.

The Vikings agreed to leave in their vessels at the next high tide, which was that evening. They would take their dead with them, and they would also take Wissian and another Anglo-Saxon. We had originally chosen Percy to go with Wissian but when we found the North Men had a good interpreter on their boats we chose to keep Percy with us. Good

235

interpreters were hard to find and now we had a score or so of men who only conversed in Norse, and who would be sampling our hospitality for the next few months. The choice of who would go with Wissian would have to be made when we returned to the fort. Wissian would travel with the raiders for the express purpose of searching out as many captive Anglo-Saxons originally from our region as he could, and return with them to Kaardbury. Over the last decade at least thirty had been taken from this area near Exeter, and if they wanted their kinsmen released, the Vikings would have to help Wissian on his search and return any captives they found to us. In the meantime we would treat their men well and tend their wounds. We told them that we expected Wissian to return before the end of the summer. They agreed to allow their interpreter to work with Wissian in his search, and that they would treat Wissian, and our other traveller, as honoured guests.

After the agreement was complete I made a show of taking Eric's helmet from the foot of his pallet and placing it in the middle of the table. Through the interpreters I explained that I had asked the Gods to witness the agreement and, because of the power I had been given as a warlock, I could ask the Gods to recall exactly what had been said at the meeting. I had rewound the Dictaphone about five minutes, and set it on full volume under the helmet as I placed it on the table. The voices that came from under the helmet were not very loud, but the words were clear enough to be heard by all those at the table. The shock was visible in the eyes of the men facing us, and one stood up suddenly and stumbled sideways on his bench. His comrades managed to stop his fall and they settled down to listen to their own voices which were, surprisingly enough, exactly as they had sounded as they had made their final recap on the details of the agreement in their own tongue. I had pre-warned our team of what was going to happen, but they seemed to be equally scared at first. None of them had ever heard a tape recording before, and this was the first time they had heard how their voice sounded to others. There were a couple of comments from both sides of the table along the lines of "Surely I don't really sound like that, do I?" There were looks of disbelief when their comrades broke the news that the God's skill at mimicry of their voices was perfect. The recording reached the end of the agreement summary and I carefully picked up the helmet, turned the tape off and surreptitiously pocketed the Dictaphone, as I returned the helmet to its place by Eric's feet. Even he, in his weakened state, suddenly raised his knees to give his now 'magical' head gear a little more clearance on the litter.

When we got back to the fort we had a discussion about who should be sent with Wissian. There was a young man called Grendel who was something of a musician; he played a thing a bit like a recorder, or flute, with great dexterity. He had entertained us at festival time with tunes he had learnt. He was slim built, but tall, well over six foot. Grendel had been one of our runners, and he understood the Norse language quite well, although he was much less confident with speaking it. I drew the young man 'Flute' and Wissian to one side. "There is something I want you both to do. I want you to tell no one that Grendel understands Norse, not even Earsling, their interpreter." They both looked at me a little blankly. "We have a deal with these bastards, but we need to know if they are going to keep to their end of the bargain. If they think either of you understand what they are saying they will be very careful not to mention anything of importance within earshot of you. Especially anything that suggests they will break the deal, if that is to be their intention. If Earsling knows you understand Norse then he may let it slip by accident, or even tell them deliberately to curry favour. After all, who feeds him eh? So right from the start you need to practice not showing you understand what is being said in Norse. They will probably even test you both out by shouting some sort of warning and seeing if you react. Only if you are sure they are going to stick to the deal, perhaps when you have found some of the captives, can you let them know you understand their language. Also expect them to do the same thing. Do not say anything that indicates you have understood their language, not even in front of the most illiterate North Man. Any discussion the pair of you have has to be done well away from all others." Flute and Wissian seemed happy with doing this, and understood that apart from the mission to find some of the captives taken from our region, they also had this hidden role of ensuring that the Vikings kept their side of the bargain, a task that added another considerable responsibility. Wissian had had two nieces taken five years ago, and this had been one of the considerations when choosing him. I told them to make up a fictitious, missing, close family member to explain our choice of sending Grendel.

The pair of them were then sent down to their homes to prepare for their journey. Neither of them came from Kaardbury, but they were well known by everyone who had worked on Come-All, and we were all concerned for their safety.

I made a point of not getting too involved with the prisoners that day. I had left strict instructions with Wulfgar to make sure that none of the prisoners escaped, as this was the only time they could get clean away. When the Viking ships had gone, theirs would be a very long walk home.

The leaving of the longships was a strange, almost sad affair. There was not only the delegation of our elders from Come-All at the river side as they cast off, but probably another 50 or 60 from the community. Villagers had quietly drifted down to the valley to ensure the enemy had left, and to gawp at their vessels. There was a formality about the leaving that called for us to clasp hands in a farewell with not only Wissian and Flute, but with the four men who had brokered the deal. The North Men had stacked their dead on the smallest of their ships, and as we raised a cautions hand in farewell they set this fourth ship alight and sent it down the river, following them on the ebbing tide. They had collected a considerable amount of dead wood that could be seen filling the decks under the bodies of their comrades. By the time the ship reached the turn in the watercourse over a mile away, it was a column of flame 40 feet tall, and the dark smoke pouring upwards from the top of the blaze must have been visible from the coast. I have been told since that after the ship broke up near Exeter, some of the charred dead bodies became trapped in slack water on the river, and took two days to reach the sea.

The Chronicles of Eathelwold 'James' Trefell; Monk.

Book 2 Chapter 16.

It is with some concern that I attempt to explain something of which I am only advised vicariously. This is something of which I have great concern. For although I have consented to, and to some extent permitted, the activity of Maerlin the wizard in these matters, I do not approve of what I have been since appraised.

During the time of parley with the enemy – a negotiation I was not completely happy with anyways, and without my attendance which was troubling – I understand that the warlock stepped outside of what is acceptable under the eyes of God. At one stage during the deliberations with the invaders he appears to have called upon Pagan Gods to consecrate the agreement. Not only this, but he used his trickery to convince them that the Pagan Gods were able to relate the contract back to the enemy in their own tongue. I am not sure how this was done, but I suspect that he has a similar skill to one I have seen before in a fortune-teller.

That person could appear to throw her voice into objects, and was burnt at the stake for her transgressions. I was the priest who heard her last confession, and she showed me how she did this trick which was to enable her to make money from those gullible fools wanting her advice.

Suffice it to say it was of great concern to me that Maerlin had done this thing, and in doing so had reinforced a false belief in Pagan Gods. I hope that this was done simply to ensure compliance with the oath made by the heathens. If that were so, then I may be able to persuade our Lord to forgive him. Yet even so, I have offered up in silence such a look as to have withered his soul just a little more.

Chapter Eighteen;   Prisoners and Wounds.

We did not return to the fortress but headed for Kaardbury. Eric was growing weaker, and when the travois he was on had been set carefully down in the house by the forge, he called me to his side. I was very mindful of the fact that I had no courses of antibiotics left. I had carried with me three prescriptions. One was specifically for tooth infections and the other two were broad spectrum antibiotics for general use. I had used one of these to keep the Smith alive when I had first returned to the village, and when Loofah was crushed. The other broad spectrum course of antibiotics had been used at the same time on the man who had come in from another village, the one who had that wound in his back. No problem, I had thought at the time, as I was just about to step back into the 21st century. The pills for a tooth infection had been used by me some months ago, when I had suffered from a mouth ulcer at the base of one of my wisdom teeth. With both of the broad spectrum courses there had been an intravenous booster for initial treatment. One of these remained in the cool environment of my hidden store, and I hoped it may be of some use to slow the onset of Eric's infection. Yet without a full course of antibiotics to follow the jab, all I would be doing would be delaying the inevitable. A course of antibiotics was a bit like rolling a ball uphill – you have to keep pushing until you reach the top. If you stop half-way the infection will return because, despite any initial dramatic recovery, not all of the bacteria would have been killed off. The remaining bacteria will simply start to multiply, and the infection will set in again. That jab was the equivalent of the first couple of pills, only it is fed straight into the bloodstream to give the body a flying start. To save Eric from what I suspected was significant and terminal infection, we need a full course of pills as well. That was assuming, of course, that we were able to deal with his wounds.

The injured prisoners had been treated by those women who had the best skills. But when the two most capable females arrived with dried blood on their aprons at the door of the Smithy's house, I took one look at them and decided to deal with Eric's wounds myself. I had never done any real surgery, but I did at least have a good idea about hygiene, and the need to sterilise everything. Yet it was my belief that unless we had those antibiotics with which to follow up that jab, the jab I would be giving him as soon as I could get into my secret store ....

Then it struck me. FUCK FUCK FUCK!!!! I heard mutterings from the priest who had followed the women down the hill. There were antibiotics in the bag I had left in the tree near Gloucester. I was sure of it. I did not check everything amongst the additions that Monty had put in the rifle casing, but some of it was extra first aid stuff, and there were some pots of pills with labels on them. I was sure that amongst them there must be antibiotics!!!

I gathered round everyone in the house and told them that we needed to do. I explained that hidden near Gloucester there were some pills that were so good that they were seen as the holy grail of medicine. Just as I had managed to save the Smithy's life after the attack two years ago, if we could get the contents of that bag back to Kaardbury within the next couple of days, perhaps three at the most, there was a real chance of being able to save their king's life. I called him the king as this was the term used by the more obsequious community members. He was not a king, but any role of a leader at those chaotic times seemed to permit the use of such a word. I said it to make it seem even more essential that Eric survived. He was my friend and protégée, but perhaps most importantly he was the person who held these people together. The only way that a foreigner like me had any right to tell anyone else what to do was by having a sponsor like 'Eric the King', their Thor. I was well aware that whatever good I was still trying to do in Kaardbury, in the ninth century, was dependent upon saving Eric's life.

Within the hour, and before the sun had set, I had administered the last syringe of intravenous antibiotics to Eric, and briefed the small group who were about to depart for Gloucester. There were many who wanted to go, including Percy Vale our interpreter, but he was needed to help with our prisoners. The final three who took on the journey were Holt (known as Reggie to me), Fyren one of the longbow men and a fellow we knew as Galan. Galan was a singer who had travelled the area north of Devon, and had been to Gloucester a number of times. He was a good man, and had held one of the shields in the armadillo. Galan and two of the top

242

bowmen we had, travelling on the finest horses available, stood the best chance of getting back with the antibiotics in time. I gave Reggie a sketched map, and the two electrical devices I had bought with me to locate the time gate. I had no idea if the devices I had left near the gate were still there, or even still working, but at least I was able to put two newly charged batteries into the hand held devices had I passed to Reggie with strict instructions not to turn them on until they were close to Gloucester. I tried to explain that one should help them locate the long range device at the side of the road, and the other would give a direction to the sensors I had hammered into the trees. If none of these were working I still thought that I had supplied them with enough information to have a good chance of finding the bag in its hiding place near that giant fallen branch. I had a sudden horrible vision of some woodsman having already chopped up the branch and burnt the whole damn thing, destroying the key way of identifying where the bag was located. I cast the thought out of my mind, raised my hand in farewell, and set off back to the house to start doing something with Eric's wounds.

I knew that the three who set off on the antibiotics quest were heading away from Exeter. There was a route northwards through Glastonbury, known to Reggie, which would apparently save them some time. Each man had two horses and they planned to ride three of them hard through the night, and then somewhere south of Bath to change to the spares, leaving Fyren to rest and tend the tired mounts, whilst Galan and Reggie would carry on. These two would take with them Fyren's rested horse, and when they found the bag, only Reggie would then set off back at full speed. Fyren would then be the final leg in the relay, using one of the fully recovered horses on his return to Kaardbury. It was the best plan we could come up with in the time. I just hoped they would find the bag.

I rigged up one of my own battery powered lamps in the Smithy's house to deal with Eric's injuries. There was some consternation about the lamp which had only ever been seen by One Eye and the three young men who helped me carry my kit up from the flattened microlight. But the people who were in the house were made to stay on the far side of the room, and they seemed to think that the 'out of their world' appearance of the lantern meant that it was in itself a healing device. One of the women had cleaned his wounds already. I allowed one of them to get on with stitching his right arm whilst I investigated his thigh. Eric groaned as I wiped off the crusted blood from his upper leg and explored deep into the opening with my scrubbed fingers to ensure the wound was clean. There was a flow of bright fresh blood that I staunched with a cloth that I had had them boil in clean water and had dipped in a bowl of antiseptic. I again left the women to stitch that wound as well. They were infinitely more experienced at stitching wounds than me, but I was able to ensure that, probably for the first time ever, they were administering their medicinal seamstress skills in a relatively sterile manner.

I turned my attention to the wound in Eric's side. A blade, probably a sword, had entered the lower right of his belly. It was not possible to tell exactly which direction it had entered from. If it had been from Eric's right, the blade would almost certainly have cut towards his spine, through his intestines, and be causing massive infection. This would be peritonitis on a scale that meant that even antibiotics would be of little use. On the positive side I did not think that this could be the case, as he had remained lucid for some hours after the injury. Yet his deteriorating state did suggest significant infection and I decided that the only option was to open him up and have a look.

I have never been particularly squeamish, but this was a big decision on my part. The women with some knowledge of these things all said that he would not live unless I did some of my magic, and Smithy simply handed me one of his finest cutting blades. I was tired from the most terrifying day of my life, but there was an intensity about what I was about to do, and somehow my sub-conscious mind managed to squeeze a little more adrenalin out of my body's over-worked glands. I started by giving Eric two shots of precious morphine from my 'self administer' ampoules that were identical to the ones used by the military. I had eight of them, and these were the first I had used. According to the label two was the maximum you could give anyone without risking death. I wanted Eric out cold, but I would be satisfied if he was just unable to feel any pain as a reasonable second best. I had everything cleaned using the antibacterial wash I had with me. I made up two bowls of the liquid from my concentrated solution. Having liberally swabbed the area of the wound, I carefully cut open Eric's right side where the love handles are supposed to be. These bodily protrusions were blatantly apparent on both sides of my belly, but Eric's were almost non-existent. I cut carefully, swabbing with a cloth soaked in the antiseptic fluid. I cut through a thin inner wall of flesh into the body cavity, causing a volume of bloody mucus liquid to spill onto the bedding under my patient. I opened the cut further, extending it up to meet the entry wound.... By the time I had a clear view of some of his small intestines, I had created an incision that was almost nine inches long. Some chance of keyhole surgery under these circumstances – especially as this was my first time. Eric was groaning feebly, and barely moving under the firm grip of his father and two others from our group of elders. I had made them tie clean cloths soaked in the antiseptic across their faces.

Carefully feeding the intestine closest to the entry wound between my fingers, I found a place where there was an obvious cut in the tube. Here the dark contents of his gut had seeped out. It took me a good twenty minutes to stitch that slice in the intestine tightly closed with some of the sterile stitching thread from my first aid kit. It wasn't neat, but it was not going to allow anything else to escape from my patient's innards, and I hoped that I had not inadvertently managed to sew right across the damn tube so as to prevent essential future gastric movement if he lived. I used the whole of one bowl of the antiseptic fluid to wash everything in and around the damaged gut. I did the best I could to check everything else I could inspect without actually pulling his gizzards out on the table. I was very cognisant that the longer his belly was open, the smaller was his chance of survival. I then sewed up the inner wall which again took longer that I wanted it to. I kept swabbing as I proceeded to sew the shallow section of muscle below the skin together, and then finally the skin itself, the stitches I used during closing extended across the original spear wound itself as well. I had no idea whether there were other hidden punctures in the intestine I had not found, nor if my entry by knife had caused an infection that would be fatal anyway. But I did have the satisfaction of being able to tell the boy's father, with absolute certainty, that if I had not opened him up, his son would certainly have been dead within a couple of days. Thank goodness for that paramedic style course I had been required to take, and the kit I had with me. I only hoped that the antibiotics, if there were any, could be recovered in time.

I suppose that I have always been of the view that too many people are too stupid, pathetic or lazy to take responsibility for their own lives. I detest those who cannot even be bothered to teach their own children to read, or learn basic first aid, and who expect the police to do all the behaviour management in society. For some reason if you have a child who you cannot control, or even one who you have abused in some way, for some reason it becomes a social worker's, teacher's, or police officer's fault. Everyone should take on responsibilities as a citizen, and if they cannot do that, then they should never be allowed to add to society's problems by having any kids themselves. I was musing on this point, and the belief I had just completed something somewhat 'over and above' basic first aid when I bumped my head, very hard, against the fence surrounding my little compound. I had walked into it whilst almost unconscious on my feet from fatigue.

I fell into bed exhausted. The whole operation had taken over three hours. With the Vikings gone, Eric was sleeping. He was tended by Erlene and another woman, and he was enjoying the effects of an additional dose of morphine. So despite my sore face, I closed my eyes and slept like the dead.

The Chronicles of Eathelwold 'James' Trefell; Monk.

Book 2 Chapter 19.

I now must tell of a quest that has, at its heart, the very essence of what I was trying to create at Caardbury, and within the ramparts of Come a Lot.

Our king, Our Thor was gravely hurt in the battle. I had been almost at his side at the time when the throng was most fierce, and death was as close to me then as you are now to this parchment. In this heroic place between this life and the next, our king, wielding Ex-Calliper had fought in the Glory of God, and justly smote our enemies. Yet he suffered from such wounds as to lay any man in his grave. I tried my best to prevent his passing but eventually had to relinquish this duty unto Maerlin. Although I am most skilled in the medicine of men, it is he who has greater connections to the next world through his consorting with beasts from the dark places. I am sure if I had been allowed to continue ministering the blessing of the Lord, our king would have recovered more swiftly, but given the consequence of the quest Maerlin commissioned the 'men from the night', our 'Nights'... I can again see the Good Lord's hand in what took place.

When Maerlin decided that he would open up the body of the king, and in saying this I understand that there may be incredulity amongst readers of this text, he opened up the belly of our king until all the organs of the body were revealed. I only say this to show what a miracle has taken place. But that is indeed the truth of it. I stood with others in the Smith's hall, watching what took place, and giving sage advice when needed. Yet, I saw with my own eyes that the wizard did indeed open the king's abdomen, such that his vital organs were displayed for all those present to see.

This may seem to others incredulous, but before this was done he set the Nights men a holy task. He said that the only way to save the life of Our Thor was to recover the 'Holy Grail', and allow the king to drink from the lip of that holy cup. I was not sure that I had heard the words correctly, and enquired of those about me, but that was indeed the quest upon which these men were sent. I was sure that few would return from such a journey. It was a purpose that had never occurred to me, as I assumed such a divine relic was in the Holy Land, and far too far away to assist in the recovery of Our Thor. Yet clearly Maerlin was privy to unshared information as to its whereabouts, and I was just pleased that I had not insisted on curing the king through the simple application of the blessings of our Lord. I have seen many holy things, relics that were almost always parts of the bodies of saints. I have even been blessed by kissing the remains of three of the fingers of Saint Benedict who had bought the famous Canter from Rome. This small set of bones had been retained secretly by a priest in the Northumbrian Monastery at Jarrow and he was willing to show them to me for no more than the price of a good meal.

So it was that many of the men from the night set off in pursuit of this holy artefact with my blessing. I watched the completing of the endeavour done by Maerlin on the belly of the king. It occurred to me that much of this was to impress others, as with the arrival of the Grail, any wound could be instantly healed through drinking from this most revered of objects. Yet I did not intervene, as I was aware that

Maerlin needed to maintain his mystical status amongst my people. I consoled myself by giving him a disapproving look directly to the back of his bowed head as he worked on into the darkness apparently doing something of his pretend 'magic' with a thread and needle.

Chapter Nineteen;   Recovery.

I woke to the jingle of my bell. The only way the villagers were allowed to gain my attention when I was in my hut was to pull the cord which ran from a corner of my roof, to a stout post thirty feet from the door. Doing this did not trigger any of my alarms or defensive devices. I had been so knackered the night before that I had not set any of these, but the caller did not know that. Well callers actually. It was Wulfgar and One Eye. It was my suspicion that One Eye had hoped for a bit of light physical recreation. I again got the impression that she was one of those women who were turned on by violent events, or by those occasions when I showed off my magical powers. Anyway she covered what I thought were her intentions by claiming she was there to cook me breakfast and take my clothes for washing. Wulfgar, who had met her on the pathway to my property, was reporting the situation with the captives.

I invited Wulfgar, calling him Ronnie as usual, to breakfast, and we discussed the prisoners, whilst One Eye cut bread and cheese, and heated water to boil eggs. Of the 22 captives another three had died during the night. This was no surprise, as some had suffered terrible wounds from our arrows that had been driven, with such force, into their torsos. In essence the ones with injured limbs were expected to live, and the ones with back, belly and chest wounds were unlikely to do so. He anticipated losing another three or four within the next couple of days. They had carefully splinted the leg of the man with the bearskin cloak, and he and his son were doing fine. The other important captive had had his wound stitched, but was now making a fuss about the need to remain tethered. It occurred to me that it was a bit strange that Ronnie came to me and not to one of the other community leaders, but I promised I would come up to the fort later in the day, with some of 'the twelve', and help make the decisions about our prisoners. He had the good grace not to mention the grazed nose and blackened eye I was sporting from my collision with my own fence the night before, or my bandaged forearm from the wound I had found whilst preparing to open up Eric's belly. My guess is that there were many minor injuries being discovered amongst the good people of Kaardbury in the aftermath of our little war.

I ate the breakfast quickly and headed for the smithy. I found Eric semi-conscious, still lying on the bed which was set on the table in their house. The dressing on the wound on his side had dried with blood, and I did not want to move him too much. We were able to remove the supporting trellis from under the table and lower him to the safety of the ground. I wanted him to rest as much as possible, as I anticipated him getting much worse over the next couple of days. The antibiotics in his bloodstream seemed to be doing the trick at the moment, and he did not appear to have any fever. The idea of a blood transfusion rolled through my head, but as we could not guarantee we would give him the right blood type, even from his own father, thankfully the notion trundled straight out again. I was also aware of the research suggesting that many deaths had been caused to victims of traumatic injury when blood transfusions had raised their blood pressure and caused their wounds to re-open or internal bleeding to begin again. It turns out that there is a real benefit in blood pressure dropping from a significant leakage of 'claret'. It means that if the blood pressure is low there is a much better chance of it clotting and the wound starting to heal. Considering the principles applied to the maintenance of blood pressure in all surgery during the wars of 20th century along with the number of patients probably given AIDS infected blood unnecessarily, it is rather ironic to find out that nature had the best method in the first place!

I trudged up the hill to the fort with Ronnie and three of the elders. On entering the fort I was surprised at the level of activity. The whole of the western arm of the gulley was filled with people either lying on what appeared to be beds made from the shields used in the battle, both from the armadillo and the breach, or moving purposefully amongst them administering basic nursing care. The woman who had taken responsibility was Erlene, who had been in charge of the fire oil women during the battle. She was a short stocky woman with long black hair tied in a plait. She was surprisingly handsome given that she was built like a prop forward, although she walked with that light balanced gait of someone who could move with unexpected speed. I reminded myself never to pick a fight with her – especially not her and Barn Door at the same time. Anyway, Erlene our 'Pretty Prop' came up to our group to report on what was happening with the prisoners. "The worst of the injured need to be under cover before it rains. We managed to keep them warm enough last night, but some of them will not last unless we get them inside."

There ensued a discussion amongst our group. I was aware that the priest was in the background trying to appear important, but we simply ignored him and he went back to checking on the more seriously injured. I tried to shift the lead role to Wulfgar, but it seemed he was all too aware that he was just a soldier turned woodsman, and when asked for his views he literally stepped back and demurred to the elders. I was a little surprised as Ronnie had directed our defence of the inner compound like the commander of an army. I then tried to leave the control in the hands of the three elders, but found I was soon drawn into offering ideas and solutions. I suppose that apart from the fear of my magic, there were still the manifestations of authority within me from my time running one of the most successful computer businesses in the UK. Perhaps those skills I had developed all those years in the future had really been just in preparation for what I was to do the past. (Apart from that actual computer stuff of course.) Bloody weird eh!

We carefully transported the worst injured into the store room. To do this we opened a section of the inner compound wall at the very far end of the western arm of the gulley. These were the five men who were least likely to survive, and moving them any distance would have reduced their chances even more. The space was a little tight, but by moving most of our kit outside under an awning, we managed to get them all in with enough room left to move. They used my kit locker as the support for one of the injured men's beds. Of the 14 remaining prisoners three were very mobile, and could have literally run away if they had been given the chance. There were two with broken legs, and the remaining nine had injuries caused by arrows striking shoulders or lower limbs.

One of the things about our heavy longbows, or the powerful crossbows we had been using, was the damage to bones. The heavy shafts not only punched through chain mail, but there was sufficient force behind them to shatter bones as well. So of the injured men with wounded limbs many were also carrying some sort of broken bone injury as well. The son of the man in the bearskin had suffered from a shattered clavicle and scapula (collar bone and shoulder blade) and had in fact been lucky that a major blood vessel had not been severed in the process. All but the mobile three would need some weeks, if not months, of convalescence and none of them were likely to try to break for freedom. It occurred to me that, even with just three raiders to keep secure, we would need either a great deal of time-consuming effort or a level of constraint and containment that would be seen as cruel given the deal we had struck with the North Men. So we had a light lunch and I headed off to my hut to get some kit.

Some bits of my equipment from the future had hardly seen the light of day since the demise of Loofah, so there were some interested stares as I hiked back into the fort laden with a laptop and a small rucksack. There was a bit of moisture in the air, so I arranged with Pretty Prop to have one of the badly injured men taken outside of the store room for an hour or so. We relocated him raised up on his shield bed near the door and in his semi lucid state he did not seem to mind. I then set everything up just inside the cabin, which turned out to be ideal considering the difficulty we would have had in seeing the laptop screen outside in full daylight.

Then, with the assistance of Percy Vale interpreting, I set my other kit up at the top end of the gulley and had the prisoners bought to us in turn. I spoke to each of the prisoners and asked them about their names and parentage, capturing their responses on the small video camera I had set up on a tripod. I explained that the device was just a magical way of preventing them escaping and breaking the agreement we had made with their kinsmen. The camera seemed so innocuous that they all appeared to ignore it. We asked the three mobile prisoners to come up first, and then invited all the others who were in a fit state to get there with assistance, one after another. Lastly we had the ones who were unable to walk, but were conscious and lucid, carried to the camera to say their piece.

It took me less than 10 minutes in secrecy to load the video onto the laptop, with only the laboured breathing of the four injured men behind me to disturb my thoughts. I then arranged for each of the prisoners to be bought into the store in exactly the same order as they had been in when originally spoken to. Each one was subjected to a little speech in front of the three elders, who I asked to stay in the store as witnesses to what took place. The room was tight for them, but they stood on the far side of the nearest shield bed, still close enough to see the computer screen. Each captive was told that there had been an agreement made with their fellow warriors, and if they were to be returned home they had to swear an oath that they would cause no harm amongst the Anglo-Saxon people whilst they were with us, and to promise that they would not attempt an escape. To reinforce their promises I said that as a great wizard I had captured their souls in a moving picture, and if they broke their oath I would send their soul to the Helheim. This was the worst place in Niflheim, their particular hell which was guarded by the monstrous Garm, some sort of Norse hell-hound. I hoped that the detail of their mythology I had gleaned from one of the CDs was correct. I had asked Percy, and he seemed to think I had got it about right. I followed the little speech with showing them their own bit of video on the laptop.

We had some interesting responses ranging from wide eyed rigid terror, to almost a full faint from one man who dropped to his knees, and would have pitched forward but for the close confines and my steadying hand. Suffice it to say that by the time each of them left the store room they were almost certainly scared shitless. The three elders were also quite shaken by the process, and as I was packing up my kit one of them approached me and expressed the anxiety of the three of them. They were clearly now very afraid of me, and I was concerned that this bit of showman wizardry may have made me into such a threat that I would now be seen as a pariah in what I thought was my own community.

I toyed with the idea of taking more video to put them at ease, or trying to explain about the development of television and film in the future. But I eventually just took all three aside and asked them to keep what had happened a secret. I told them that what I had done was to only capture a picture of each man's soul at that moment in time. I said that this was not enough 'data' to enable even the most powerful warlock to send them to hell, but it was just enough to scare the prisoners into not hurting any of our people (I emphasized OUR people). I also said that it was strictly against the wizard's code to send anyone's soul to hell, as it displeased the Gods who thought it was their prerogative to make such decisions. I hoped they were satisfied with my explanation. They said they were. I was not so sure.

The prisoners were allocated to families. The families were chosen so as to ensure the ongoing treatment of the prisoner's wounds. Each family was chosen as having a woman with suitable experience in dealing with injuries, in the household. They were also chosen depending on their distance from Kaardbury. Pretty Prop and Barn Door needed to do their daily rounds to keep an eye on the prisoners' recoveries and they did not want to be trekking all day just to make these visits. After some evangelical persuasion even James the priest was allocated a prisoner. He was assigned one of the uninjured ones and he had asked for a certain captive in particular. I suspected that this was because the young man in question seemed more impressionable than the others and spoke a few words of Saxon. I guess James would be trying his hardest to make a Viking Christian convert over the coming months.

By nightfall the only remaining prisoners in the fort were the five in the store being tended by Pretty Prop and another woman. One of the prisoners died as the sun set and we carefully carried him out and laid him with the three corpses of his comrades on top of the pyre being built in the open ground below the fort.

The men had built the pyre during the day to burn the remaining bodies. The pyre was considered to be the most respectful option, as the last thing we wanted was to have to dig up any dead bodies to hand them back to their kin when the ships returned. Wulfgar and Percy had discussed this with 'Bearskin' and he had agreed that his warriors should be burnt. He also insisted that they be burnt with their weapons as this way they would travel to the halls of Valhalla equipped to enjoy the battles in their afterlife. So Wulfgar had made a big show of including the weapons on the pyre. I instructed him to wait another day to see if there are any more bodies to be included, considering that the weather was sufficiently cold to slow the putrefaction enough for such a delay. I also told him to have the best of the weapons removed before the fire was lit. Waste not, want not, eh!

The wait for the return of the three men on the antibiotics quest was interminable. Within 48 hours of them leaving the infection had set in big time. Eric's wound was red and inflamed such that the stitches were stretched and now cut deeply into his flesh. I realised that a drain was usually put in at the base of a wound to allow blood, puss and other fluid to escape in a controlled manner. I carefully cut through the bottom two stitches and re-opened the end of the wound sufficiently to access the stitching of the muscle and inner membrane. I inserted a well sterilised plastic tube from the fuel system of Loofah into his body cavity, to be immediately rewarded with about a pint of bloody fluid hosing onto the floor of the Smithy's hall.

By the end of the second day, some 60 hours after the three had left I was climbing the walls. Eric was in a bad way. He was delirious, and had started rocking back and forth in the bed, so I was obliged to give him another two of the morphine jabs. I was very aware that on this occasion I was administering this very powerful drug to someone who was a great deal weaker than last time. As he slipped into motionless slumber I feared that I had killed him already. Yet he lived on.

That night I sent two men north to wait at the fords of Tiverton. I dared not send them further for fear that Fyren may have taken any number of routes to get back to the river crossing. I slept that night at Eric's bedside, curled up on straw and coarse blankets which smelt of damp and musty grass, along with the perennial odour of urine emanating from the animals penned at the back of the hall.

I thought I had stayed awake from dawn onwards, from after the cockerels had given their welcome to the shafts of early light from the east. Yet I was startled from further slumber by the gallop of horses clattering to a stop yards from the door. I stumbled to get to my feet, and fell onto my hands as I tripped on bedding still wrapped around my left ankle. By the time I was upright and awake Spots, who was now almost completely devoid of his nickname, stepped urgently through the doorway with a black waterproof canvass bag held in front of him. The bag was bigger than I remembered, about the size of a large kitbag, or good sized rucksack. I grabbed the bag from his hand and led him outside into the light. Here there were the still damp trestles we used for eating. I swung the bag onto a table and opened it. Rather than rummage through the bag in my search, I took each item out and started to arrange the contents in the order that they came to hand onto the wooden surface. The fifth item I removed was a green hard plastic box with a first aid cross on each side. The box was the size of an ice cream carton and had a list of its contents on the lid. The seal was unopened and I pulled off the tape surrounding the lid in disbelief that it was really here. After all this time it was almost like meeting an old friend, or someone from the 21st century who had just arrived for a visit. I stopped suddenly and went over to the water butt and got someone to pour water over my hands. They were still grubby with the blood from reopening Eric's wound last night. After drying them I carefully unpacked the box and took one of the syringes and a bottle of pills into the hall. I gave Spots clear instructions about how quickly anyone who touched what was on the table would be turned into a lizard. He was holding the folding wheelbarrow in one hand apparently thinking that this may also be needed, but I waved him away. I had second thoughts and went back to the table and picked up an orange coloured plastic mug that had been in the bag, and turned to the hall again.

We had done our best to keep Our Thor hydrated, as I was aware that during a fever this was always a big issue. In moments I had put the full syringe of antibiotics into a blood vessel in his left arm. I also filled the plastic cup with the boiled water we had been giving him to drink. I looked at the pot of antibiotic pills, read their use by date again, and looked heavenward. I hoped to hell these would still work. I carefully held Eric's jaw as I opened his mouth and popped in one of the pills, before I raised the cup to his semi conscious lips and made him drink. I stood staring at him for some moments, before I turned to the priest who had arrived as surreptitiously as usual at the prospect of seeing something out of the ordinary. "Look after him until one of the women arrives ... he may need a few of your prayers." With that I went out to inspect the rest of the contents of my bag.

The antibiotics still worked. I suppose if they hadn't you would not be reading this now. If Eric had died I am sure I would have been eventually driven from Kaardbury as an outsider who was feared rather than as the right-hand warlock of the 'sword chosen' leader. It was a couple of days before there was much improvement in him, but by the fourth day he was awake and able to take food. To be on the safe side I used two full sets of the antibiotics. Inside the plastic box there was a little message from Monty, which read as follows;

My apologies again Sweetheart.

By the time you open this I hope you will be less cross with me about taking your gun. I only hope that in doing so I have ensured that you return safely to me. Please forgive me. I have added to your equipment this little box of some of the wonders of modern medicine, so that you may have the opportunity to do some healing in 831. I love you.
Hugs and Kisses Monty. (PP) xxxxx

I carefully folded the message, and from that day on it was always next to my skin, in a small pouch under my smock. It was quite a while before I was able to stop the tears from running down my face.

Our three wanderers took another two days to all return. Fyren arrived later that same morning leading his exhausted mount by hand, but Reggie and Galan took another 48 hours to appear. They had rested a full day in Bath as Reggie had returned to the town to meet Galan there. I noticed a shared glance between them as they told their tale, which suggested something inappropriate may have taken place in the town. But the only person who would have given a shit about that was James the priest and he seemed oblivious to the visual world, listening to the story with eyes tightly clenched and hands clasped as if in prayer.

Galan had been the one to find the bag. When he and Holt had arrived at Cirencester they had activated the tracking devices for finding it. They referred to the bag as 'The Grail of Mecidonia', which rather amused me as they had clearly been listening very carefully to my instructions. The first device had not identified the place where they should have left the road until they were almost upon it. But when they had turned off the main thoroughfare and started searching in the woodland the signal from the second 'magical' pointer showed them the way at once. The giant branch that lay like a tree on the ground was no longer there, but the tree from which the branch had fallen was quickly found, and the remnants of the branch was seen there on the forest floor, in wood chips and a pile of smaller branches. There were even the deep marks in the soil showing where the heavy sections of the wood had been dragged to the roadway. So Galan had been the one to climb the giant oak and recover the bag and my folding barrow.

The Chronicles of Eathelwold 'James' Trefell; Monk.

Book 2 Chapter 25.

It was at this point in time that I had again cause to ponder on my essential support of the man called Maerlin. Whilst the Grail quest was in progress he went to the heathen prisoners and did unto them something of which I am concerned to relate.

Although I have no love for the Pagans, these worshippers of false Gods, my consolation is that theirs will be an afterlife in hell for daring to cause harm to true believers. Yet despite this strong sentiment against these barbaric people, I am concerned that anyone dare interfere with another's soul, and in doing so meddles with it devoid of the sanction of our Lord.

So it was that whilst I was working with the injured North Men still held in our fortress, I heard that the warlock was stealing part of each man's soul. Enraged, I went to the arsenal building in the centre of the castle where this heresy was taking place. I saw a man with an arm strapped to his chest leaving the doorway of the building ashen faced, and apparently scared for his life. Hence I went to the doorway to protest, but there another man was led in front of me to stand in the shadows inside. Standing thus I overheard exactly what I had been told. Maerlin was threatening these men, stating that he had taken by force of magic a part of their very souls. He went on to compound his evil words with threats related to some sort of heathen afterlife. He even lowered himself to putting Pagan names to the beasts of Hades and the horrors to which they would be subjected, should the captive transgress. I tried to enter the building to stop this heresy, but after considerable thought I chose to stand outside and watch until this profanity was complete. As a punishment I then stood at the doorway staring at the wizard during the time he took to put away his instruments of dread. One of the remaining Night Men had words with the warlock that were just as I would have spoken, and in doing so negated my need to further berate the wizard on behalf of our Lord.

Perhaps the only reason I did not subsequently take things

further with Maerlin, in showing him the full extent of my disapproval, was the arrival of the Holy Grail. I was not in the Smithy hall when it arrived, but was there within moments. Maerlin was clearly pleased with its discovery, for despite his magical equipment for the finding of such a relic its unearthing must have been the work of God himself. From the tales told of the terrible privations of those who embarked upon the quest, only Galan had found the Grail. Perhaps because he was the most righteous of those on the quest, perhaps because of the beauty of his voice in the praise of our Lord in church, but he was the only one virtuous enough to discover its true whereabouts. When the Grail arrived, none of the men of the night who had started on the quest had returned. I feared greatly for these lost warrior pilgrims.

So it was that I, James Trefell, Priest of Caardbury, was present as Maerlin took the holy cup, coloured as strangely as the sand touched with iron, and almost weightless as if made from the lightest of wood, to cure our king. I have to admit that some days later I entered into the Smithy and whilst Maerlin was distracted I touched the Holy Cup myself. It was resting in the top of his sack, and this was when I revealed that it was surprisingly warm to the touch and almost weightless. It was as if it were made of a wood so light as to be too fragile to be used, yet it was strong and flexible when pressed between my fingers. This Holy Grail, this cup of Christ used at the last supper with his disciples, was justifiably wondrous and of a material no man has ever seen before. In truth, I have been blessed with good health from that day onwards.

So it was that Our Thor was cured. Maerlin pretended to be still concerned, but he fed the king with liquid from the Holy Grail three times every day for fourteen days. At the end of that time our king, he who had been opened up and eviscerated such that his entrails were on display to all wishing to see, was almost fully recovered.

I confess that my reverence towards the holy vessel was such that I believed it blasphemous for it to be in the possession of an unbeliever. I therefore took it upon myself to remove the one True Holy Grail from the possessions of the warlock Maerlin. I tested the blessed cup by trying to shatter it against the alter of my church, and despite casting it with the greatest force, it would not do so. I took this as firm evidence of the truth of its provenance. I then tested it in the fire within the church. The one used to keep the Lord's house warm on cold Sundays. When I put the Holy Grail in the flames it did not blacken and burn as wood, or crack and crumble as clay, but upon my word as a priest it disappeared in a ball of flame. Transported back to the bosom of the Lord Jesus Christ once its wondrous miracle had been completed.

I have never seen the like, and these strange happenings can only be the work of our Lord. Only he can return the dead to life. Only he can do this, through the holy vessel from which his son drank during his last feast with his disciples. Only I amongst the throng could see the import of what took place in Gaardbury, and by these events the verification of the story of our Lord Jesus Christ in the Holy Land. I hope that these humble words bearing witness to these wonders, which are a true confirmation of the holy scriptures, yet scribed by a poor and modest priest, might in some small way justify my time on earth.

Chapter Twenty; The Spirit World.

During the weeks that followed life developed a new routine.

Each day I got up and went to see how our most important invalid was progressing. I then went up the hill to the fort to see how the remaining two men who had miraculously survived their torso wounds were getting on. I then returned to Kaardbury to meet with Barn Door and Pretty Prop to get an update on the other captives. Of the other 14, only one had become very ill. A long arrow had passed through that man's calf and out through his shin and had developed into a bad infection. The arrow had broken the smaller of the two bones in the leg and infection had appeared to have set in deep within the wound. On my third visit to the fellow I had decided that for him to live I would have to amputate the leg. We had Bearskin attend his accommodation which was a recent addition on the side of a house in Cadeleigh. The giant North Man had travelled on a travois due to his own injury, and turned up with Percy Vale to provide the interpreting. I had to explain what I was going to do, as the last thing I wanted was for the Vikings to think was that I was deliberately butchering them one by one. Bearskin smelt the rotting cabbage odour of the wound and agreed that the man would die. He said that if I could save his life by removing his leg the man's mother would probably travel from his homeland to fuck me personally. He had a bit of a stoic grin on his face as he said this and I appreciated that in his rough uncaring way, despite thinking it was not possible, he still wanted this man to live. It was only much later that I discovered that the injured young North Man was Bearskin's brother's bastard son.

To my great surprise the man did live. I managed to take the leg off just below the knee and presumably because of the use of good sterilisation and one of my last two broad spectrum antibiotics courses, I saved his life. Given their well over-run use by date, I decided I might as well use the antibiotics up now to good purpose, rather than wait another couple of years just to throw them away. In keeping his knee and a few inches of lower leg I hoped that the man would be able to walk with a wooden stump. I knew that if the whole leg was taken that this would be much more difficult. I had once had a Finnish man who worked for me who had a metal lower leg that sported a padded cup with straps into which a similar length of truncated lower leg fitted. He had lost the leg during his period of National Service when he had stepped on a small plastic Russian made anti personnel device that had literally blown his foot to shreds. I had no idea he had a false leg until after about our fifth meeting when we met accidentally in an office toilet, and he had removed his prosthetic to massage the stump. He had advised me that he had recently had a new one fitted and they always took longer than new shoes to wear in properly. In 833 I intended to get something similar made out of wood, and to have this man walking before the end of the summer.

My success, with both Eric and 'Legless', seemed to have raised my kudos considerably. I had been concerned that the episode with the video camera had labelled me as 'dangerous' in some sort of 'evil' way, but by saving the two of them against all the odds seemed to shift the general view of me back towards the 'nutty but nice' category. When Eric was on the mend we decided that there would be benefit in moving both Bearskin and his son, the one with the shattered collar bone, into the home next door to the smithy. This was a property owned and occupied by two of the three elderly women who still used that pair of folding spectacles to enable them to work each day. Although now, despite their reverential care of these glasses, they had evolved into two separate monocular devices, each set in a carefully shaped wooden frame, so that they could both be tied over the eye socket with a thin leather strap, just like an eye patch. This enabled two of the three women to work at any one time. The third crone lived close to the church on the other side of the lane. I guessed all three must have been in their 60s at least, although I did not dare ask, given that the privation of the dark ages seemed to subject everyone to significant wear and tear on their visage.

These new neighbours, Bearskin and 'Sling' provided company for Eric, and with the help of Percy Vale, the three of them passed much of their convalescence learning about each other and discussing everything from the best hunting to the most beddable women. It was interesting to see how their relationship developed, and although by the time they left us all three still only had the bare workings of each other's language, they had clearly become the firmest of friends. I let them get on with this without too much interference, as I was only too pleased to see relationships developing that should reduce the risk of further problems with the men from the north. I did notice that when I was with Eric, both Bearskin and Sling seemed to treat me with a wary respect. I had overheard a few questions they had asked about me, and Percy's loud translations suggested that Eric was pleased to regale them with tales of the magic he had seen me perform. The ones about the talking helmet and the stick that shot balls of fire were favourites.

The three other Smithy children had grown up quite a bit over the last two years. Elf was now a woman in the making, Short Skirt virtually ran the household, and was reaching marriageable age, and Pigtail was almost seen as an old maid. At the age of 16 she was in full womanhood, but perhaps due to her close brush with slavery and the unspoken details of what happened to her when she was captured, she was somewhat shy and spent much of her time either working in the fields, or carving the wooden handles for metal items forged by her father. Her brother Eric had done little work within the smithy since being promoted to his lofty new role.

Over the weeks of convalescence Pigtail and Sling started to spend time together. Twice I arrived at the Smith household to find them huddled together talking animatedly at the back of the hall whilst her brother and his father continued their perennial discussions in the better light near the doorway. This proximity did not go unnoticed by others, and when his shoulder had recovered enough for him to do something useful, it was no surprise that he was usually occupied in the fields alongside Pigtail or carving wooden handles next to her at the benches outside the forge. Sling was not the size of his father and disregarding the bulk he would almost certainly acquire over the next few years, he would never be as tall, or broad, as Bearskin. What he did have was an almost angelic set of facial features, and at the tender age of 19 summers he was a fine specimen of attractive young manhood.

The Smithy watched this strange courtship with a mixture of pleasure and concern. He had been worried about his eldest daughter's lack of interest in the boys from the village, and her general introverted behaviour. So although this blossoming relationship was good for him to see, he was also worried for the obvious reasons. He did not usually talk to me a great deal and I am not sure if I ever really forgave him for 'stonewalling' me at the lake, but this was one subject about which he sought my council. Who the hell was I to talk eh! I was conned into a marriage with a gold digger, stupidly left the love of my life over a thousand years away, and currently provided occasional carnal delights to an illiterate sterile woman who was more than twelve centuries older than I was. Was I the best ever relationship expert or what!

All I could do was offer a sounding board. His main concerns were for his daughter's happiness and safety, both of which may well be compromised by what was going on. Strangely both of these could also benefit by this relationship as well. Smith waited in some trepidation, yet when I gently probed the subject with Bearskin he, in contrast, remained remarkably sanguine. I suppose it is an almost universal contrast. Fathers tend to see their daughters first relationships with general concern and a paternal protectiveness, whilst they see their son's as a step into manhood, and are vicariously cheering them on from the sidelines.

There were some interesting developments in the surrounding villages that were also seen as a direct result of the presence of our captives. There were two occasions when we were called to deal with difficult situations involving a North Man and a local girl. The Vikings had been given strict instructions on their behaviour by Bearskin, and they were also still truly terrified of me and my hold over their souls. But a daughter and a young wife had clearly chosen to be somewhat more than accommodating as hosts to their captives, and a father and a husband were very unhappy. We managed to prevent any serious injury from taking place. The father had struck his offender with a large ham of a fist, only to find that the supposed deflowerer of his little girl was very competent at unarmed combat. It was the younger man who had controlled the fight and, with his older opponent beaten, persuaded the girl to admit that she had been the instigator. On investigation by both myself and Bearskin it was clear that she had been no innocent even before their tall blonde arrival. (This information had been gleaned from her brothers who regaled about their sister's not infrequent secret tumbles with local lads, not by some inappropriate physical examination on our part.)

Since the construction of the fort began, on my suggestion Eric required all disputes in the community to have a five day 'cooling off period' before being dealt with. In this case we moved things forward a bit, and managed to do a bit of investigation that solved it in two.

The other case was a little harder to resolve as although the young husband had not attacked the offending North Man, it was more difficult to establish whether the wife had been as willing as the miscreant claimed. It was clear that a confession of salacious intent on her part would probably end her marriage, and without it there had to be an appropriate response to the allegation of rape from the cuckolded husband.

Eventually we decided that there would be two elements to the solution. Firstly the offending North Man was moved to another family where the household had no women under the age of fifty. The other was that he was to be subjected to some of the most terrible magic I could do. I had decided another demonstration would be in order, just to keep these captive warriors on the back foot....

A notable aside is that after our captive North Men left us, in fact about seven or eight months after they had left us, there were two highly unexpected births in the nearby communities. One of them was to a twenty five year old woman whom we had all thought was barren, and would never be able to give birth, despite the regular and apparently (according to her neighbours) enthusiastically loud efforts of her husband. The other was from an old widow who was greying and at least fifty years of age, who lived alone on a smallholding in the valley between the fort and the hill just to the east of it. She lived close to the site of where Fursdon House would be built about 500 years from now. The twenty five year old was delighted, and thankfully no one had the heart, or understanding, to suggest her husband had had any help from their fair haired temporary farm hand. But who the hell had shagged old Moira god only knows. On the plus side she seemed very happy, and her eldest daughter moved back in with her to help her raise the boy.

The miscreant who needed to be subjected to some of my magic was apparently hung like a donkey. This physical abnormality was a great source of amusement to his comrades and presumably had been a factor in getting him into the very predicament in which he now found himself. I decided that I would use something that no one in the ninth century had ever seen before, but I was very conscious that the soul damming trick with the camera had not gone down too well with some of the community leaders. The last thing I wanted was to become that feared pariah, yet this was a real opportunity to prevent problems with the North Men, even after our captives had left our shores.

I dug out the video camera again, along with the bigger laptop and something that none of them had ever seen. In fact, I had only used it a couple of times when I was feeling a bit low during that first year and wanted to be engulfed in my 21st century memories. The item was a small projector. This was one of those small conference room projectors, the sort that would be used for PowerPoint presentations to board members, or for the occasional work related DVD that had to be shown to a larger group than could sit around a laptop screen. The projector was tiny, about six inches long and three across, with most of one end taken up with lens. The volume of the speaker was very limited, but I had an idea about that. The device would not have been suitable for a large conference hall as the brightness was constrained by the size of the apparatus, but in the Smith's hall it would be fine. The difficulty I had was to create a video that fitted with my needs, so I sat down with the laptop and, typing away, I devised my own script, just as if I was producing a film or documentary. Having finished the script, I then set about filming the sequence I wanted. It took five attempts to get it right.

On the first one the lighting was far too bright as I wanted my face well lit, but most of the rest of the background I needed to be in almost complete darkness. In the end the best option was to accept that the clarity of the picture would not be 'crystal' due to the low light, but by using an LED torch slung around my neck, facing upwards from the middle of my chest, I got the right effect. I also wore my big arrow proof cape as, with its high collar, it gave an appropriately theatrical framing for my head. I used the flickering flame from a log fire as the background light that gave the rest of me a slight halo and these flames fittingly suggested I had just returned from a rather warm environment.

I chose to try out a different voice, one that was still mine, but I deliberately attempted to give the impression of being in great pain and anguish. I tried speaking through teeth gritted into a rictus, and with eyes that remained glaring and fixed. It seemed to work OK, although I was concerned that any late night visitor may have heard my performance through the walls of my cabin. Thankfully there were very few who would dare to come to my hut uninvited, and even fewer who would take the risk of disturbing me at night. I think only Eric, or One Eye, or an assassin, would have given it a try.

It took me until the small hours of the morning to get it as I wanted. The finale was a bit difficult, as I did not want to waste any of what was left of my precious resources. In the end I took a mug full of the triple distilled grog that we had produced from fruit the previous summer and used it to create a momentary column of flame from a small open fire set against the outside wall of the hut. I took great care to position the fire in the frame of the shot so that I could blend it with the open fire in the background of the filming I had done inside. I suppose it was one of those little projects that once you get going you become completely immersed in the task. After 10 hours of solid graft, I must have eventually fallen asleep just as the sun, on it's inexorable journey, was turning the eastern horizon into that visibly glowing line.

After a couple of hours of shut eye I spent the latter part of the morning editing the film which was now stored in the memory of my computer. I also practiced my part a number of times, until I considered myself word perfect. I was so pleased with the result that I copied it to CD. I am not sure why, but I suppose I was either thinking I may have a use for it again and wanted to be able to run it on my other laptop, or my vanity about being rather clever had just got the better of me.

The loud speaker was quite straightforward. Let's face it you cannot build a computer empire without being able to do a bit of electronics yourself. The left hand speaker taken from the mounting under Loofah would give me more than enough volume for what I wanted. The big event had been arranged for the following evening, so I spent the rest of the day checking all the batteries were fully charged and going around the nearby communities making sure that the people I wanted to be there would be there.

I need not have worried. If there was ever an invitation that everyone would want to take up it would be to watch their favourite wizard do something miraculous. After the firework 'dragon killer' episode I had had regular requests for another demonstration. The main limitation for the magical event was the size of Smithy's hall. In the end I allowed Bearskin to bring along all of his men, as they were the ones I wanted to impress most. Then, with the 12 community leaders and the family of the woman who had been shagging 'Donkey' there was little room for more than about 20 others. In the end I got Little Finger and Spots to run a lottery for the places in the hall. I gave one place to One Eye (because I am soft) and others were given to Barn Door and Pretty Prop because they had helped so much with the Vikings as well as Percy Vale, of course, to translate anything that was not being understood. The rest of the places were taken up by the lucky winners, although I did notice that a number of extras had managed to squeeze in. So the following evening, with darkness upon us, every vantage point taken and the doorway crammed with faces, I started the proceedings.

To begin with, as requested, Eric, our local Thor, set the scene explaining the allegation of rape, and introducing the main players. He stood in the small space that had been cordoned off in front of the large back wall of the building. Flaming pitch covered torches threw a ghostly light on his tall frame as he held Donkey and the woman who had been raped (or willingly mounted) by the upper arm. The two parties were then sent to sit on their allocated stools in front of their supporters.

I have always loved a captive audience, and I wanted to make the most of this opportunity. It would have been all too easy to rush into the magic bit, but instead I started with a story. I had half made the story up and half plagiarised it from one I had read many years ago (before ... whatever). In essence it was a story that told of the consequence of delivering great punishment (in this case execution) on the word of one witness, only to find out years later that the witness had lied to protect themselves. I explained that this dilemma was similar to the one that we now had to consider. We could not be certain who was speaking the truth and although we wanted to trust one of our own people, if we were wrong then we ran the risk of angering the gods and damaging the agreement we had made with the Norse Men. I explained that there was only one

273

solution, and that was for one of us to go to the underworld and seek out the truth. That stopped them whispering....

I started by asking if there was a volunteer to go to the underworld and seek the truth. There was a sea of blank faces, some looked away in case I locked eyes with them and they became chosen by default. I was surprised to see James the priest start to get to his feet to volunteer, bless him, so I pre-empted him with the announced that I, Marlin the Wizard, would go because none but the greatest of wizards could make such a journey and live to tell the tale. I explained that to make the trip I would need to have a well defined place amongst the living to return to. So the only way I could find my way back here was if everyone in the room helped me by striking the palms of their hands together to make a loud noise. I showed them how to do a slow hand clap, and after a couple of minutes practice they were able to follow Eric's lead and provide a thumping rhythm that would probably wake the dead, let alone lead me back from there. I told them that they would need to keep the beat that was the same tempo as my heart so that I would be the only one who could hear it, and arranged it so that I would call out the beat of my heart, and set the rhythm, before I left the world of men.

It had taken over half an hour to get to the point in my performance where I would journey to the underworld. I lay on the floor of the hall in front of the back wall and bade Thor and Bearskin (why leave him out eh!) to cover me with a hessian cloth bleached almost white in the sun. I placed my hand on the dry baked floor of the hall beyond the edge of the hessian, and started to beat out a rhythm with my palm that I thought would be similar to a pulse. Eric took up the rhythm, and started everyone slow hand clapping, satisfied with the beat I pulled my hand back under the cloth.

It took me a few moments to get the items I needed from my pockets. The cloth covering me was deliberately stiff so that small movements could not be seen, and in a pocket in the side of my smock I took out a lighter and two small cloth wraps. Each contained a mixture of gunpowder and potassium permanganate from my kit. I had taken one of my last few bean bag shot gun cartridges and mixed the powder with a small quantity of charcoal and some of the potassium permanganate crystals I had with me for purifying water. According to my laptop it was an excellent oxidizer and would give off a good volume of smoke. I had split the mixture into three, and tested one of the three portions which I had wrapped in a cloth. The effect was excellent, and this couple of litres of purple vapour was ideal for my purposes. I had wanted to produce something different to the dense dragon's breath smoke produced from the canisters used in the battle at Come All, because everyone knew what that smelt like now. Besides, not only was there far too great a volume produced by those canisters, but this milder stuff was a great deal less toxic and I did not want to be coughing and sputtering when I returned from the dead.

I gently raised the centre of the cloth above my belly with my left hand as I lit one of the wraps on the floor beside me with the lighter. I could not see the smoke as my eyes were tightly closed, and I could not hear the fain hiss and puff as it ignited, because of the din created by the slapping palms around me. But I hear the gasps as smoke started to filter through the cloth. The effect must have been a good one as the clapping faltered, and it took a great deal of shouting from Eric to get them all back in rhythm. I waited a full three minutes before I set off the second wrap. Again there were gasps, but this time they kept the rhythm going well enough.

After the second portion of smoke had cleared I started to move as if waking from a deep sleep. I rolled onto my front and got to my knees still covered by the cloth. I took my remote control out of my pocket and stood up. I pressed the play button and the film started.

There were two main upright posts supporting the roof of the Smith's hall, each about 15 feet tall, holding up the sloping, sod covered roof. The one farthest from the doorway stood about 12 feet away from the end wall. The back wall was 20 feet across and six feet high at each side, rising in the centre to the height of these main posts. The space we had left for the theatrics, and where I was now standing under the hessian shroud, was directly in front of the middle of this large, and now almost white, end wall. Two thirds of the way up the far main post I had built a small but sturdy platform. On the platform there was an open fronted box in which there was my laptop, projector, loud speaker and a 12 volt battery. I had given Ronnie and Reggie the task of protecting the base of the post from anyone trying to climb or shake it and I knew they would perform their assignment with great diligence. The wall appeared to be almost white in the firelight because I had arranged for it to be covered by a tightly stretched, light coloured cloth that had been made whiter by being soaked in lime. So there I was standing, covered in a hessian shroud, in front of an almost triangular, 15 foot high, 20 foot wide, ninth century projector screen.

The hand clapping had now stopped and there were sharp intakes of breath and a few little whimpering screams, as a nine foot apparition came into view beside me. I could see enough detail through the hessian fabric to work out that to be in the right place I had to take a couple of small steps backwards towards the left hand side of the wall. The projection was about 11 foot square with my ghostly nine foot figure taking up the right hand side of the screen. After stepping backwards, I now stood at the left hand edge of the projection. One of the reasons I had wanted such a dark piece of filming was that I now threw almost no shadow against the back wall. We had moved all the bedding, table, bowls and equipment into the corners of the end wall so that everyone had been forced to position themselves away from the corners and had a good view of the projection and me.

Then the huge ghostly figure started to talk....

I had set the speaker so that the sound hit the end wall high up before being bounced back into the hall. The effect was that unless you strained to hear where the sound was coming from it genuinely appeared to be emanating from the projection itself. The volume was set a bit lower than I wanted, but it was easy to miscalculate when the rehearsal had been done very quietly, and with no one else in the building. Still it seemed to be going OK.

The apparition announced that he was the part of my spirit that still stood in the underworld. He was the part of Marlin the Wizard that few would ever see. He was the dangerous and vengeful part of me who now demanded to speak to the part of me that held all the kindness and goodwill. At this point I waited for the count of ten seconds before I pressed the pause for the video. Bugger me, Eric had forgotten his cue.

Perhaps he was as mesmerised as the rest of them and had forgotten to ceremoniously remove my shroud so I could talk to the spectre in front of me. I removed the shroud myself as impressively as I could, given the ungainly fumbling associated with extracting oneself from under the equivalent of a starched bed sheet.

"What has your journey to the underworld told you?"
"It was a long journey, many days in your time. But I now know the truth!" (I had resumed the video of course. Thank goodness for remote controls eh!)
"What is that truth?"
"That truth is that there is one amongst you who has told a falsehood. There is a person in this hall who has lied so as to deceive everyone. It is a person who has lied to protect themselves."
"Who is the deceiver? Who told the lies?"
"If I tell you that before the deceiver makes a confession then the underworld will demand a terrible price." (The scary voice seemed to be working a treat, although I think the torch under the chin was a bit tacky. Still, hey ho!)
"I do not understand. If you know the truth why do you not tell us?"
"When I came to the underworld the spirits gave me the truth, but said that if I divulge the truth to anyone amongst the living before the deceiver has confessed to their lie, then the ghouls of their darkest regions will demand a terrible price from the one who told the untruth."
"But we want justice. We want to know. Who lied?"

By this time I had had the opportunity to observe the reactions of the two parties involved. Donkey was as wide eyed and ashen as those around him, whereas the woman was almost curled up into a ball and shaking like a leaf.
"Angry as I am, I will allow the deceiver to confess. I will then tell you what will be their punishment. If they have confessed, their punishment will not be so great. If they have confessed I will return to the world of men without anyone having to pay the blood toll demanded by the dead."

I had allowed for about thirty seconds during which the offender would

277

confess, but once again I was obliged to pause the video to allow the simpering woman to be helped to her feet and whisper the confession, that she had willingly taken the Norse man to her bed. I resumed the video.

The nine foot giant resumed his rumblings. *"I know what the underworld wanted, but I am allowed to negotiate with them and they have agreed that although the punishment may seem to be light, they believe the punishment to be just. I will now rejoin the other part of my spirit and tell you what has been decided...."*

As you can imagine I had not been sure as to who had told the truth and needed to have to option to deal with whoever had been the liar. I had suspected the woman, but also knew of the Vikings predilection to uninvited violation on a national scale. I was rather pleased with myself (no change there then) for how I scripted the words for my apparition.

At this point the screen blazed with the fireball from the 'grog' and the nine foot spectre vanished, which, following the dark image, was almost blinding in the dimness of the hall. As the video switched off, I fell to the ground with suitable temporary convulsion. Then after a few seconds I staggered clumsily to my feet to the explosive sound of an adoring crowd exhorting my safe return to the living.

What a fucking brilliant performance eh?!!!!

As the clamour diminished, Eric eventually got me back centre stage and asked me to tell everyone what the journey had been like. I told them that the story was one that would have to be told on another night. I was being deliberately evasive for two reasons. Firstly, I wanted to deal with the issue in hand, as the woman was in a terrible state curled up in a ball again, at the feet of her husband and family. Secondly I had not thought about this possible question at all, and had no bloody idea what to tell them. So ... I am a bit of a twat sometimes!

I got the woman to her feet and stood her in front of me.
"You did a good thing confessing the truth. The underworld would have taken their price in the blood of your husband and his family. Your

courage to tell the truth has saved them from something terrible." She was unable to look at me, standing dumbfounded and crestfallen, but all around us were listening intently. "What you have done is a good thing. Do you still love your husband?" She nodded, still unable to speak. "Then the punishment that has been decided by the spirits is a simple one. It is a price that must be paid in full and if you fail the underworld will know of it." I drew the husband to me so that he could hear the judgement as well. Then holding each of them by the hand I said, "The spirits require a sacrifice. Every night for a full cycle of the moon you must light a good fire in your hearth. When the fire is well lit, then by whatever means required, you must take your husband's seed from him into your mouth. You must hold it in your mouth for the time it takes you to walk around the marriage bed three times. This will remind you of the need for only truthful words to proceed (sorry, but 'come' would have been worse) from your lips. When you have taken the seed from your husband's loins and walked three times around the bed you must spit this fluid of life into the fire. This will ensure that the spirits are appeased and your husband's seed will retain its potency. If you do not do this the spirits will take the power of making a child from both of you." (Well, a blow-job every night for a month is at least a small recompense for a cuckolded husband!)

For some time after that night the wife's 'punishment' became the subject of discussion amongst the local villagers. From what One Eye told me it was a practice that, although not unknown, was frowned upon by the church. Perhaps it had something to do with the inappropriate waste of an opportunity to procreate. Anyway, the overall view was that what the wife had to do was a task that many wives did not like and their husbands did. It was something I had sometimes heard referred to as more of a whore's talent than that of a Christian wife. The 'spitting it into a fire' bit made the whole thing make sense, as it was a clear link to the demands for sacrifice into the flames of the underworld.

It was the best option I could think of at the time.

I then turned to Donkey and his blonde compatriots. He averted his eyes from my gaze. "The spirits also told me that there was a need for the man from the North to atone. That in taking advantage of the weakness of this woman and being disrespectful to the man under whose roof you lived,

279

you have done wrong. If all men did as you there would be no shelter offered to anyone. If all men did as you did then all agreements would be broken and all promises cast into the wind."

By now Donkey was not only looking down, but he was clearly very worried for his future. I could not make his punishment too great otherwise the Vikings would feel it was unfair. I had had a number of ideas, many of which I had discarded as they would have damaged the relationship we had built with the raiders, but there was just one that may keep everyone happy.

"There are a number of women who live alone and have to tend their land and raise their crops without a man to assist them. Tomorrow at noon there will be a gathering in Kaardbury where any woman who so wishes can ask for a share of your time for the full cycle of the coming moon. If there is only one woman she will have your services for a month and if there are 29 women they will each only have you for one day."

There were surprised looks between the North Men. I continued, "And as long as you are not injured by their demands you must comply with them fully. You must sleep on the floor of their home and on pain of death make no uninvited violation of any person." There were a number of women who had heard of the special attributes of Donkey and would be most interested in sampling the service he could provide. Being required to work like a slave and bed a few ugly women would do him good.

It turned out that seven women arrived the next day. Four were getting on a bit, and two were young but ugly. Only one was young and pretty. She was a widow with two small children, but she had a fiery temper and, up until that day, had an apparent hatred of all men. So each of the women had Donkey for four days, but I let 'Temper' have that extra fifth day at end. I think, perhaps, I really was becoming too soft.

The punishment for Donkey was considered proportionate and very reasonable by everyone and we suspected that it turned out to be the source of some pleasure for three of the women who took up his dance card. The other four had simply wanted him to work hard and dig, build, plough and cut for a full 12 hours each day. Although it was always possible that these 'task mistresses' simply kept any other horizontal activity a secret from those women who had a tendency to gossip. Happily Temper was a bit of a surprise (given that I suspected her of batting for the other side). She had wanted his strength and work rate, but she also appeared to require his efforts to go well beyond the daylight hours. He did so in a manner that seemed to quell her vitriolic view of the world, and at the end of his attachment with her she offered him a more permanent position (we suspected that this was usually underneath her).

So things returned to normal, and I was viewed with a mixture of wary admiration and what I would best describe as possessive fear. Fear of what they thought I was capable of, but possessive pride as they clearly saw themselves as the recipients of my wizardly patronage. If they only knew eh!

The Chronicles of Eathelwold 'James' Trefell; Monk.

Book 3 Chapter 2.

So it came to pass that some of those captives living amongst us had transgressed. These heathens from the north, whom I had always argued should never have been allowed to reside within our community, disobeyed our Lord's commandments once again.

There was one who forsook his oath to not molest our good Christian womenfolk, and he took unto himself the young bride of Erian, a good man who worships regularly. Erian rightly challenged the offender and this matter was taken to our king, our Thor. My only regret is that I was not the one to observe these carnal acts, as in doing so I could have borne witness to the truth of this matter.

It was at this juncture I took umbrage at the continuing temerity of our Wizard Maerlin. Despite the manifest truth in what was stated by Erian, Maerlin decided that this was yet another occasion to display his unearthly powers. Powers that I have witnessed and must surely come from the hand of the one true Lord, yet for unknown reason he allows this warlock to hold sway over that which no mortal man should, and to wield strange powers far beyond that of any man I have ever witnessed in my long life.

I will tell this as best I can without the reader casting this document aside as a fiction proceeding from a fevered mind. In truth Maerlin tested that question of truth twixt the two conflicted stories by way of test. But to discern that truth he travelled to the dark lands, to the gates of hell itself. I was greatly shocked when he first suggested that he wanted one of my flock to volunteer for this journey. I felt physically sick and was rushing to the doorway to relieve myself, and for fear of being inappropriately selected by some of the more unsavoury members of our community, when the warlock relented and decided that he should go himself. In truth, there are one or two of my flock who have not yet fully taken on the Christian faith, and I am aware that it is these non believers who take some amusement from pushing me forward at times of peril.

But I am able to say with conviction, only granted in me due to my worldly knowledge, and my valuable experience in these matters, that Maerlin did in fact travel to the very gates of the underworld. There he was told the truth of the issue in question, although I am sure it was not the 'fallen angel' in person whom so advised him, but another member of the heavenly throng providing this service as penance for some wrongdoing, surely working under the guidance of our Lord himself.

As a result of this the woman showed herself to be susceptible to the pleasures of the flesh, just as Gwen the Revered has done in the past. As a result of her succumbing to temptation she was given a task that perplexed even me as an all knowing priest. I therefore took it upon myself to ensure the whenever possible over the following month, to take care to witness this punishment in person. There was a place beyond a shuttered window at their humble home that afforded me a reasonable view, albeit only lit by firelight, of her attempts to pay for her misdeed and assuage our Lord. This, for me, was an arduous task that I undertook with resolution as that which is expected of a priest caring for his flock.

The punishment of the real transgressor, the blonde heathen violator of women, was something that I was unable to verify. I decided that given the pressing need for me to be observing two of my parishioners performing a rarely seen, yet surprisingly arousing, act of contrition I would forgo that alternative task. I chose this option in part as there was genuine concern for my own welfare regarding risk of discovery by someone who may not fully understand my Christian role in watching over my flock. I therefore chose to administer my blessed observation to the succour offered to Erian.

Suffice it to say that in my unselfish commitment towards ensuring atonement through this repetitious act, albeit it providing me some interest, I was greatly concerned that in the consummation of this activity, as it did, in itself, contradict the heavenly command of 'go forth and multiply' - this higher purpose obviously being somewhat thwarted, at least in the short term. Yet it did not seem to do either of my parishioners any harm and in truth there seemed to be an unexpected amount of pleasure commensurate with the process. I consider it to be of benefit towards my own learning about of the sins of the flesh, and I have found its memory is something that I can enjoy in solitary quiet contemplation at times when I am in need of distraction from the arduous duties of the cloth.

Then came the day the bells rang once again.

The preparation for the next arrival of the North Men had continued
during the late spring and summer of 833. By the time the bells rang that
morning we had already been as prepared as we could be for the past three
months. The first thing that happened that morning was the expeditious
gathering of all the prisoners. There were three men already allocated to
each captive, and these men had been chosen for their proximity to the
homes where the Vikings were billeted. Within fifteen minutes all but two
of the sixteen captured North Men were on their way to the fortress with
their allocation of armed guards.

They were all taken, as instructed, through the front gate of the palisade,
and were herded into the south western end of the gulley where the
armadillo had been. There, under the gaze of a number of our archers,
they were sat along the north facing bank, and given breakfast. Whilst they
were sitting there they were carefully roped together at the ankles amidst
the profound apologies of their guards, who by now considered
themselves genuinely friends of their charges. There seemed to be little
fear amongst the prisoners, who clearly had a great deal more faith than
we did in the value of the promises of their kinfolk. They sat and chatted
happily as they munched through a good breakfast of bread and cold stew,
perhaps because for some this was already a second breakfast.

Above them in the inner compound the horses were gathering.

After our miraculous survival of the last onslaught I was all too aware that
if we were attacked again our chances of living through it, let alone any
sort of success, was damn nigh zero. There was no way we would be able
to lure the raiders into a killing ground again, and on an individual basis
they could wipe us out with very few losses themselves. With the
exception of Wulfgar, there was not a man amongst us apart from Eric
who could fight any one of them toe to toe. Our greatest asset was our
archers, but they were of limited use when being attacked head on by

warriors with raised shields. So the plan for this morning's confrontation had to be changed.

At the rear of the inner compound, to the northern side, we had dug a rampart through the old iron-age embankment. It was still a fair slope, but a horse could gallop down the incline quite safely. The palisade at the top of this gradient was replaced with one, quite massive, wooden structure, about 40 foot across and six foot high. From my laptop I discovered the structure was called a 'Cheval de Frise' or a 'Frisian Horse'. The central 20 foot of the construction was a line of Xs made of stout wooden poles set at right angles to each other. These X shaped wooden crosses were positioned about 30 centimetres, or 12 inches apart, along the middle of a pinewood tree trunk. These crosses sat under this central trunk which had been 'halved jointed' to provide stable recesses into which each cross was pinned. The base of each cross was then braced between the legs by another piece of wood a foot above the ground, and then along the full length of the legs of the structure, on both sides, with two narrower poles. These were pinned and bound along the line of the leg bracing joints on either side. The tops of the crosses on the outward side were tapered to wicked points. In the end the final structure looked like a centipede style version of an old fashioned saw horse with forty legs. The pinewood trunk acted as a central carrying pole which extended ten foot beyond the 'saw horse' at either end, at just over a metre above the ground. It took about ten men all their strength to squat and lift this 'one ton barrier' so that the rampart could be opened, and our riders could escape. But escape was definitely the plan. An unexpected assault from raiders would find it almost impossible to get through or over this barricade and they would have to attack the palisade set in the steeper parts of the embankment. Yet with a little organised effort this Frisian Horse, with its extended carry poles, could be moved out of the way in less than a minute, leaving the occupants of the fort with a direct, fast, and easy exit downhill to the north.

Our prisoners knew nothing of this of course. Those prisoners, now with their escorts, waited patiently in the gulley. There were one or two shouted comments from our charges asking why there were so many horses in the upper part of the fort. One asked if we planned a siege eating horse meat, and another jokingly asked if we intended to all run away. Well of course

288

we bloody did!

It was almost two hours before the boys from the watch post arrived at the edge of the woodland below the fort. They arrived amidst the throng of two Viking crews, laughing and joking with the Saxons that had returned with Wissian and Flute. Myself, Eric, Big Tash and Percy-Vale, followed by Reggie and Bearskin, walked down the hill to meet them in the middle of the open ground. 'Ronnie', or Wulfgar, had been left in charge of the captives, with Beadwof, or 'Wolf' as I called him, in charge of the horses.

We halted some five metres from the three massive men who led the procession. There was a moment of frozen formality when Eric and the leader of the Norse men looked each other in the eye. Then Eric did something I was not expecting, he stepped forward and embraced the Viking in a gorilla-like hug. They stood at a similar height, and if you did not know any better you would have thought it was a father and son being reunited. Eric by now spoke Norse well enough to offer a suitable welcome, and motioned to Bearskin to come forward and join them. The atmosphere was lightened by the clear shouts of delight of the watch boys, as one of them walked towards us with his arm round his mother's waist – a mother that he did not believe he would ever see again. The ceremony of the meeting, and the acceptance that the bargain had been kept, soon flowed into a relaxed melee in the open ground below the fort. Eric gave the signal for the release the our prisoners rather sooner that I would have wished, but within minutes there was a carnival feeling as greetings, laughter and back slapping filled the hillside.

There were 11 captives that had been found by Wissian and Flute, although they later told us that they had found a further seven from our stretch of the south coast who had chosen to stay with their Norse captors. It took some time before things quietened down and we were able to go through the more formal process of returning each of the captives to their Viking comrades. We called them together into a group, whose number had now increased to fifteen with the surreptitious arrival of Sling. He had avoided capture that morning, and had escaped with Pigtail into the woods. They must have been observing the meeting on the hillside, and decided it was safe to join in. Sling was reintroduced to the warrior chief who turned out to be a second cousin, or something similar, so they hugged in that brash hard way that warriors seem to do, but followed it with a conversation, that I could barely understand the gist of, about the welfare of other family members. Then Sling pulled Pigtail in front of this warlord and announced that he wanted his father's permission to wed the girl, and to return north with her.

I looked at Bearskin who evidently already knew of this plan and was beaming his approval. I looked for the Smithy but he was nowhere to be seen. Then Eric walked up to Sling and held out his hand. They clasped each other's hands in that more intimate manner where each man's grip held the other's forearm and Eric said loudly, "I embrace you as a brother, care well for my sister for she is much loved," repeating it again in the language of the North Men. It turned out that Eric had persuaded the Smithy that such a union would be a good thing for our community. Despite losing his daughter it was pointed out to his father that she would be at least as safe with Sling as she was here, and the bonus was that the rest of us would be much safer as well. These conversations had gone on, unbeknown to me, that morning. When Sling had fled with Pigtail in tow, as the bells started ringing, he had told his father of his intentions. Bearskin had told Eric on the way up to the fort, and Eric had told his father whilst we waited for the raiders to arrive.

The one thing we had not prepared for was feeding over one hundred hungry Vikings. (Well I couldn't be expected to plan for everything!) Luckily there had been a significant amount of 'slow time' preparation by the likes of Pretty Prop and Barn Door. Over the summer months, despite the extra demand on the local resources caused by our captives, they had been able to build reserves of dried meats, cheese and fruit. We slaughtered two pigs and four goats knowing they would cook quicker that a whole oxen and managed to assuaged the early pangs of our visitors hunger with the dried meats and cheese. We gathered in as much bread as the local villages had to hand, and set ten women to baking like mad during the day in preparation for a feast that evening.

The hill below the fort became something like a fairground. We carried all the wooden discs of tree trunk from the inner compound to create a giant seating circle. Inside this we set up a half a dozen broad planks strapped at each end to pairs of stakes driven into the ground. After the first of these was flatted by three warriors involved in horseplay, and the food upon it spilled across the trodden grass, we made the area within the circle a place for good behaviour only. This seemed to work well enough with the roasting of the animals taking place at four fires, down-wind, and to the east of this seating circle. The revelry and macho games resulted in two occasions when the cooking carcases needed to be re-set on their 'spit roast' frames, and there was one significant combustive collision episode that set fire to a man's hair and caused third degree burns on his head face and hands. Thankfully as he rolled off the fire someone had had the presence of mind to dose him with a jug of beer. The shouts and laughter that followed had almost nothing to do with empathy for the injured, but a great deal to do with the wasting of good drink.

The carnival atmosphere was a little high spirited for my taste, and I was constantly wary of a genuine fight breaking out in which one our people would get hurt, or even killed. You know when you are in charge of a party, perhaps in your parents' house, or an office, and you can see that there are too many people there who you do not really know, who are getting progressively more drunk, and you are sure they will start damaging your mum and dad's house at any moment – well that's how it felt. Only under these circumstances there was the potential for not merely damaged furniture, broken glasses and cigarette holes in the carpet. Here we were likely to have someone maimed, raped or killed.

I had been persuaded to light the fires for roasting the carcases using my usual lighter up the sleeve trick. I still always kept one of the lighters on a length of plaited rubber fibres from one of Loofah's bungee straps dangling against my left forearm, just out of sight. By now I had dismantled two of the original bungees completely and had started to wonder how long before they all rotted. Miraculously lighting the fires with my bare hands had probably been seen by almost everyone in our communities and remained a defining piece of real wizardry as far as they were all concerned. The raiders thought it was great magic, but clearly were in considerably less awe of me than our own people. They perhaps had not been made fully aware that it was my magic that had conjured up the smoke during the battle. Perhaps the story of the talking helmet, or even my journey to the underworld, had either not become common knowledge amongst the newly arrived crews, or they simply did not believe such nonsense.

On the third occasion a somewhat drunk, large, blonde man had demanded that I perform another trick for his edification, I set off down the hill to get some kit. I had asked that Eric require everyone to leave their weapons up in the fort for safekeeping. But although they had managed to collect most of those carried by our own people, with the progress of the alcohol our 'guests' were becoming increasingly more difficult to persuade.

I was back in less than half an hour, but in the meantime there had been two significant incidents. Ronnie, who had been trying to collect weapons with his brother, had been thrown to the ground and had a blade held to his throat by one North Man, and Pretty Prop had had to intervene when two raiders were in the process of carrying one of the young girls off into the woods. Bearskin had started to try to control the crews, but even he was having difficulty.

I returned wearing my high collared cape, despite the heat. This enabled me to carry a number of items hidden about my person. In my right hand I held the two fire tubes from Loofah that I had taped together with some of my remaining, and very precious, 'duck tape'. In the middle of the tubes I had taped the sawn-off shotgun, angling the barrel slightly away from the line of the piping with a piece of wood. I had a bag over my shoulder and my pump-action shotgun dangling down my left side under the cape, loaded with all the remaining solid shot rounds. If push came to shove I would use it.

I walked into the centre of the seating circle. Only half of the seats were taken, and the revelry was going on all over the place. Some of the knots of revellers were grouped around wrestling contests, trials of strength or gambling games. There was a small group with Flute trying to make music that was loud enough to be heard amidst the throng. Their plaintive notes rose with the smoke from the cooking fires and drifted eastwards over the trees.

I called Eric, Ronnie and Reggie to my side and then shouted at the top of my voice to get everyone's attention. The revelry continued. I tried again to no avail. I told Eric and the twins to cover their ears and then turned on the loud speaker from Loofah that was hanging round my neck. It was connected to the 12 volt battery slung under my coat on my right hip. When I had gone down to my hut to collect the kit I wanted I had decided not to do anything too clever or subtle. The siren from Loofah was truly deafening. It made the loudspeaker vibrate against my chest and the wail it gave out was literally ear-splitting. Thankfully at the last minute I had remembered to put on my leather flying helmet which had built in mufflers on the side flaps. With the chin strap pulled tight I only experienced moderate discomfort during the 10 seconds that I allowed the noise to scream out across the hill.

Most of the people in front of me showed real distress, some falling to the ground, others holding their hands over their ears. Everyone stopped what they were doing. I switched the loudspeaker from siren to microphone and announced, in both Saxon and Norse, that everyone must come to the open ground by the fires. (I did not know the Norse for 'circle of seats' but the fires were close enough). My voice boomed out at over 100 decibels, and now everyone bloody well heard it.

I turned the volume down to a more reasonable level and waited for the gathering to complete its journey inwards to the fires. In a matter of minutes there were some 400 souls standing around the four of us. They had gathered in a rough circle around the roasting food with me standing at the western side of the circle. Using the loudspeaker I told Percy Vale to stand with the Norse men, the bulk of whom were at the far side of the ring of faces, and to translate my words.

"OUR FRIENDS FROM THE NORTH, YOU ARE MOST WELCOME TO BE HERE TO SHARE FOOD WITH OUR PEOPLE … (Percy shouted out my words so that they all heard) … AND WE ARE PLEASED TO RETURN TO YOU THOSE WHO HAVE LIVED UNHARMED AMONGST US, AND BEEN HEALED OF THEIR WOUNDS BY OUR HANDS…. BUT I, MARLIN THE WIZARD, HAVE GREAT CONCERN FOR THE SAFETY OF EVERYONE HERE TODAY. WE HAVE ALREADY SEEN SOME OF THOSE PRESENT BEING HURT … THERE IS A REASON FOR US

ASKING YOU TO GIVE UP YOUR WEAPONS DURING THE TIME OF FEASTING ... I HAVE BEEN TOLD THAT SOMEONE HELD WULFGAR TO THE SWORD WHEN HE ASKED FOR YOUR WEAPONS....

There were turned heads amongst the Vikings as they looked at the culprit.

WOULD THE MAN WHO HELD WULFGAR TO THE SWORD COME FORWARD PLEASE.

There was an awkward silence and the shuffling of feet before a very broad man walked to the front, on the opposite side of the circle to me.

TELL ME WARRIOR, WHAT IS YOUR NAME? (I decided to play nice)

"'Randver the Hawk' is my name," came the reply translated through Percy. They both had to shout to be heard clearly, despite a respectful expectant silence from the encircling throng.

IT IS MY UNDERSTANDING THAT YOU DID NOT WISH TO HAND OVER YOUR WEAPONS TO WULFGAR. WHY IS THAT? (I on the other hand did not need to shout and everyone had heard what I had said – even old Eowen whom many believed to be completely deaf.)

"I am a warrior, a Viking, and I do not have to hand over my weapons to any man."

"BUT YOU ARE OUR GUESTS, WE HAVE KEPT OUR SIDE OF THE BARGAIN, AND WE ARE OFFERING YOU FOOD AND DRINK ... IF THERE ARE WEAPONS IN THE HANDS OF DRUNK MEN SOMEONE WILL BE HURT OR KILLED."

"I have no wish to hand over my sword"

"I CAN SHOW YOU HOW POWERFUL MY MAGIC IS. I CAN MAKE ANY MAN HAND OVER HIS WEAPONS BY FORCE ... I

DO NOT WISH TO HURT ANYONE, BUT I AM ASKING ALL OF YOU TO ALLOW YOUR WEAPONS TO BE KEPT SAFE DURING THE FEAST."

The conversation had started with 'Randy' originally appearing very unsure of himself, but by now he was obviously back to close to his belligerent self as his reply was

"I have seen you make fire with your hands, a great conjuring trick. But if you are so powerful you will need to remove my sword from my hand yourself. That would be a trick that many have tried and many failed to perform."

There were murmurs amongst his peers, even a low grunting laugh. A mixture of cautious disapproval and open interest was apparent at the prospect of a spectacle. Vikings love a fight. I needed to do this in a way that solved the problem without making enemies. If they suddenly chose to do so the North Men could still easily wipe us out.

"I COULD TAKE YOUR SWORD FROM YOUR CHARRED LIFELESS HAND, BUT I WILL NOT DO SO, YOU ARE OUR GUEST AND OUR FRIEND ... BUT DO NOT MISTAKE THIS FOR WEAKNESS BECAUSE I COULD KILL ANY MAN WITH A WAVE OF MY STAFF...."

I had been holding my composite 'staff' upright in my right hand, at these words I lowered the tip of the fire tubes to forty five degrees and released one of them into the air over the roasting food. A blaze jumped from the tip of one of those tubes and threw a huge ball of flame into the air directly above the gathered North Men. This angle was ideal for the release of the fluid, and with the extra weight of the duck taped bundle, the recoil of the composite weapon was greatly reduced.

There were very few who had seen this effect before, and the gasps of surprise and fear were very real. Randy was still looking upwards to where the ball of fire had evaporated above his head as he drew out his sword and threw it onto the ground in front of him. I walked slowly across the circle, between the cooking fires. He stood there clearly not knowing what to expect. I stopped 10 feet in front of him and asked him through the loud speaker

"ARE YOU A STRONG MAN, 'RANDVER THE HAWK'?" (Percy continued to translate) Randvar held my gaze and nodded warily. "IF I CAN MAKE YOU DROP YOUR SWORD BY THE MEREST TOUCH OF MY STAFF, WILL YOU BE WILLING TO WATCH OVER ALL THE WEAPONS OF YOUR BRETHEREN, AND TAKE NO MORE DRINK DURING THIS FEAST?" He nodded again equally warily. I picked up his sword carefully by the blade, the loudspeaker momentarily scraping on the ground between my feet. I straightened and held it out to him handle foremost. After a few moments he reluctantly took it.

"HOLD IT AS FIRMLY AS YOU CAN, AND LET US SEE IF I AM JUST A CONJOURER...."

At this I slowly lifted my combination staff high in front of me and turned on the electrical stunner attached on the base. This was that hand-held equivalent of a Taser which I had once used on Beof's men. I had duck taped this zapper onto the bottom of my staff and only had to remove the cap from the device and turn it on for it to become the business end of a five foot cattle prod.

I had my proper Taser gun fully charged in the shoulder bag, and given the choice I think it would have been even more impressive to incapacitate him from ten yards away. But Randy was wearing a jerkin of very stout looking material and I did not wish to put my life at risk because of the high quality, thorn resistant properties of clothing produced by their Norse womenfolk.

I swung the staff in my hand and tucked the central section of the shaft with my attached sawn-off shotgun under my right arm, so that the zapper was pointing to the now visibly worried Randy. He held the sword in front of him in both hands. The blade was held vertically in front of him and the bulging muscles of his forearms glistened like knotted ropes covered in oil as with gritted teeth and wide eyes he rooted himself to the ground. It was a good job I wasn't going to have to wrestle with him for real. I stepped forward and slightly to the left and carefully pressed the tips of the Taser against the sweaty sheen of his sternum and his protruding left pectoral muscle which were clearly visible through his partly open clothing.

The effect was instantaneous. His sword fell from grasp as his fingers went into paroxysmic convulsion, and as he tried to pull backwards I maintained contact with the tips of the cattle prod by pushing it forward. He appeared to try to turn and step away, but his feet seemed stuck to the ground. His knees buckled under him as he sagged backwards onto the trodden grass, his face in a rictus of muscular spasm. I pulled the staff away from his chest and Randy flopped onto his back before turning onto his side in a foetal position as if to nurse his upper torso. I looked to the circle of faces that had crowded closer. As I turned, deliberately panning the crown with the tip of my horizontal staff, they fell back in stunned silence.

"'RANDVER THE HAWK' AND WULFGAR WILL COLLECT ALL THE WEAPONS AND GUARD THEM AT THE FORTRESS. EVERONE ELSE WILL EAT, DRINK AND MAKE MERRY. BUT NO ONE WILL CAUSE HARM TO ANYONE. NO WOMAN WILL BE TAKEN AGAINST HER WILL. NO SAXON WILL HURT ANY NORTH MAN AND NO NORTH MAN WILL HURT ANY SAXON MAN DURING THIS DAY OF FEASTING. YOU CAN ONLY FIGHT OR COMPETE AGAINST SOMEONE FROM YOUR OWN PEOPLES TODAY. I DO NOT WISH TO BE OBLIGED TO INTERVENE AGAIN."

The silence endured as I turned and helped Randy to his feet.

As it turned out I did intervene again that day, well night really. The festivities continued in a somewhat more subdued fashion after the Randy affair. Wherever I went there seemed to be an invisible barrier that prevented anyone getting in my way or very close to me, unless I walked up to someone from behind and they had had no chance to move. Or unless they were a person who knew me well, like Eric, who came to talk to me. Happily the contests of strength resulted in only one man being injured with a dislocated shoulder and finger. The finger I put back quite easily, but the shoulder required me to lay on my back to brace my feet against his neck and ribs to extend the joint before returning it into the socket.

To do this required me to remove some of my kit, and I left Spots in charge of it for a few moments. When I went to pick up my kit and put on the cloak again I could not see well enough to check on the ground properly, because the fireside where I had tended the injured man had been some 20 feet away. I was concerned that one of the smaller items had fallen out and would lie hidden in the grass. So I called for everyone to move backwards and connected the tungsten bulb ark lamp I had in my bag to the big battery on my hip, and to the crowd's amazement, I bought sunlight back to the hill for a minute or two. I searched the ground and checked my kit carefully before turning the lamp off and returning everyone to blinding darkness. I could not be sure, but I thought one of my thunder-flashes was missing. As my eyesight returned and everyone grew accustomed to the firelight again I was approached by Bearskin and the blonde giant who was the leader of the crews. I was introduced in the broken Saxon tongue that Bearskin now partially commanded. I called over Flute who had long since given away the game about his own linguistic ability and got him to translate their request that had started to sound like rather a big deal to me.

A dozen men from one of the crews had moved down into the woodland away from the fire and Bearskin had been told that a fight to the death was likely to take place. It was something to do with *sansorðinn* (thank goodness I had an interpreter as I would have got it all wrong), which was an extreme insult suggesting a man had been sodomised. One of the crews had seen Sling with his arm around Pigtail and suggested that they were both so pretty that he would not know which to fuck first. When challenged over this, his level of alcohol intake combined with the jealousy of the less wealthy family and an old unsettled score from their time as children in the same village, resulted in a development of the insult that led to a death challenge. Sling had recovered from his injury but had not held a weapon in months. Bearskin did not want his son killed over such a matter, and they were not sure where the fight was going to happen.

I called over Spots, Wolf and Little Finger and told them to spread out

298

with Bearskin and Giant so that when I turn night into day they can find where the fight was going to take place. The North Men clearly did not fully understanding what I was going to do, but were by now ready to believe I was capable of almost anything. They pulled in another couple of their men and in a few moments were scanning the dark woodland that surrounded us on three sides.

I changed the red distress signal flare in the Vary pistol from my bag to a white-light magnesium one with its own little parachute. I pointed it directly upwards and lit up the sky. Once again everyone and everything stopped and gasped. To these people what I had done was change night to day. Only those who were ready for it, and were watching the woodland, did not look up to be blinded by the slowly falling brilliance above us. There was a shout from over at the eastern edge of the clearing and some of those nearby set off at a run into the woods.

I arrived amid great confusion. There were men in the woodland in front of me but the flare had just died out, and we were now all thrown into that deeper darkness of eyes temporarily sightless. I turned on the floodlight and held it high with my left hand holding my composite staff in my right. Two men, with knives glinting in the light, rolled across the forest floor to my right. I could not see if there was blood, but the colours under the arc-light were hard to distinguish. I had come prepared and lowering the tip of the staff fired one barrel from the sawn-off at the rolling bodies. I had originally hoped that the one I hit would have had chain mail on, or at least one of those thick leather jerkins some of the crew were wearing. A CS cartridge is not delivered with the same force as a normal shotgun load, but it is designed to punch through a window and explode in the room beyond. It exploded all right – engulfing the two wrestlers in their own little cloud of thick white vapour – but it turned out there was no chain mail being worn, and the cartridge broke two ribs of Sling's opponent and left a stinging deep gash across his side. But there were some positives. The panting breath of the two combatants caused the CS gas to have a pretty much instantaneous effect on both of them, and they fell apart leaving their blades in the leaf mould as they scrabbled at their eyes.

I shouted to everyone to stay back, but five others were contaminated and were spluttering sightless before everything slowed down. Those affected by the gas were taken up to the fort and sat in the gulley to be kept under the watchful gaze of Bearskin and Wolf. By the time everyone had recovered enough to make their way down to the fires again Sling and 'Insult' had resolved their differences, and Sling was making enquiries about who would stitch up his bleeding friend. Apart from the CS wound they had a couple of small injuries each. Thank goodness the fight had lasted only a minute or so before the flare had literally 'gone up'. Probably the most put out were Wulfgar and Randy whose naked appearance at the inner palisade above the gas victims suggested that they had been partaking of the pleasures of one of the professional women from Crediton. She and three others had joined us in the afternoon looking for business, and I had directed that particular lady up towards the fort before dealing with the shoulder dislocation. Being a bit of a softie, I had even paid her a couple of coins to cover the cost of pleasuring the two men who were stuck with the sober task of guarding the weapons. I do hope they appreciated that.

By the small hours of the morning the party was over. There was a chill in the air and a touch of mist developing between the numerous bodies strewn across the hillside in their positions of slumber or intoxicated unconsciousness. There were some couples lying naked in the developing chill, and I covered one pair with a discarded cloak as I made my way down the hillside and home. Thank fuck no one had died eh!

One Eye had not been able to get in to my hut due to the alarm systems and locks I had made sure were set before I had left all those hours before. She was curled up in a borrowed blanket, fast asleep on the path down the hill, just before the gate which would trip the first alarm when opened. I switched off the alarms, opened the hut, and then went back and picked her up. She only half woke, as the beer had taken its considerable toll on her faculties. She was not a big woman, but strong and long limbed. By the time I virtually dropped her onto the bed, and sat panting on the edge of it next to her, I had promised myself to do a bit more muscular exercise. All this magic stuff was not keeping me as fit as I wanted to be.

The Chronicles of Eathelwold 'James' Trefell; Monk.

Book 3 Chapter 13.

So it came to pass that the vessels of the sea sailed by the men from the North returned, carrying those raiders to our God fearing community. I was the only one amongst our people who counselled against allowing these barbarians to our shores once more. Yet my wise words remained unheeded and they permitted these heathens, who worship their false Gods, to eat and drink with us on the land below the Come a Lot fortress.

I was pleased to see that this was where we dealt with them, and it was right and proper that the location reminded them of our great victory, in which I had no small part, and which was given to us by the one true Lord. We returned to them their prisoners whom I had been instrumental in ensuring were tended most carefully. I am sure that almost all of those returning to the barren lands of the North were now doing so as believers in our Lord Jesus Christ. I contend that my very example of honest and simple priesthood has transformed their view of the only one true religion and that they henceforth will travel northwards and spread the word of God.

We held a great feast for the Northern horde and at that feast I was able to persuade Maerlin our wizard to control the excess behaviour of the Viking beasts. I was present when one of these men, a man of such stature that it would have taken a giant or a man of the cloth to best him, was disarmed with the lightest of a touch. This man mountain held his weapon with all his strength, yet when the tip of the staff of our wizard, a staff that I myself had blessed, was held but gently to him, it caused that man to fall prostrate on the ground in realisation of his sins, and in penitence to the Lord.

I was not best pleased that Maerlin flaunted his powers that night. He set fire to the air once again, and briefly turned night into day to show that the good Lord can control the appearance of the sun. But I was present when he decided to offer respect for the penitence of the man who had been so aggravated in vain by the touch of his staff. I set great store by my powers of hearing, and by standing close to those who have matters of import to discuss, I was able to ascertain that this sinner was to be sent a woman of doubtful virtue as recompense for his pledge to take no drink that night, and to protect the weaponry of his comrades. I therefore took it upon myself to ensure that this bargain was kept, and I was able to find a vantage point from which I could observe the impressively strenuous activity which was a consummation of this token of appreciation.

Some might question the veracity of this task I willingly undertook, given that the sinner in question was not a Christian and the woman a person of low virtue. But I can simply direct one to the scriptures themselves, in which the Good Lord demands that all sinners 'come unto him' and that the holy personage of Mary Magdalene was once a fallen woman by occupation. Yet as a regular and committed observer of sins I can comment on the little difference between the efforts of a professional woman, and those partaking of the sins of the flesh through carnal desire. I do note that payment in some form is usually a prerequisite of any such activity, and that the professional woman somewhat lacks the intimacy and care of the amateur.

Thus, this leads me to believe that the recent arrangement I had with two of the less provided for womenfolk of the community of Bickleigh, in which they were allowed to partake fully of the altar wine as a precursor to me asking deep and searching questions relating to their personal experiences in the pleasures of the flesh, was wholly acceptable. This ploy enabled me, an inexperienced priest, to obtain great detail of the feeling and sensation of these acts through vicarious appreciation — the sacramental alcohol being a blessed libation for loosening their reticent tongues.

Chapter Twenty Two;   Trouble on The Run.

The North Men stayed for two days. Thank goodness it was not longer. By the time we waved them farewell from the riverside below the lookout hill to the south of Thorverton, they had drunk almost all of our beer, eaten a great deal of our meat, and lain with rather too many of our women. They departed with Pigtail who had been quickly wed to Sling, but left behind Donkey who had clearly become deeply enamoured with the delights of Temper and was perhaps a little cautious of returning homeward to deal with some of the domestic issues I understood he had left unresolved in the North.

I could include in this narrative a long list of the events that happened over the following years. Most of them were of little consequence compared to those surrounding our dealings with the North Men. What the small community of Kaardbury achieved was quite extraordinary. The use of the old Iron-Age forts in the south west was copied by others, although I do not believe they had the startling success we had in that great battle at the fortress above our village.

The Vikings did return, but only to trade and visit. The friendships built over the months they spent with us stood the test of time. There were even voyages by some of our own people to visit relatives now living in the North. Smithy and Eric went to see Pigtail only to discover they were living near the coast in a Viking community in Northumberland.

With the North Men gone life returned to something approaching normal. The normal life of the fourth decade of the ninth century in the small village of Kaadbury, just north of Exanton, had been very far from normal for a few years, so it was hard to compare. There was less frenetic work to be done, as although I was conscious of the need to maintain the fort until we were sure that the relationship with the Vikings held true, there was little more to do than regular maintenance.

I started running again. This was something that I had enjoyed as a great way of de-stressing and keeping fit for many years. But since my arrival in the dark ages I had only run when the circumstances urgently required me to do so and certainly not for my own recreation. I had brought two pairs of good walking boots with me, and I had recovered the pair I had originally refused to take back due to their odour. This pair was now cleaned up and would only become my regular footwear when the pair that were on my feet, and were already starting to fall apart, completed their demise. I had also brought a pair of light climbing boots that were far too tight to wear with any comfort for a long period, and anyway they had metal rods inside the sole to enable you to brace your foot in a crevice, making them unusable for walking over any distance. I did have a pair of modern trainers that I had been using as slippers in my hut, but I was loath to get them muddy three times a week, and spend much of my time cleaning them for reuse and having to wear them wet on my feet at home. Besides they were fast wearing out anyway and running in them would have finished them off very quickly. So I turned to the three crones and asked them to make me some thick moccasin style running pumps. This they did with a great deal of pride and considerable skill. (Thank goodness for those little old specs eh!) They provided me with three pairs, as they insisted on completing one pair each, and were then competing with each other to see which ones I would choose to wear.

I solved that conundrum by taking all three pairs with great gratitude. I wanted to pay them, but they refused, so the only thing I could persuade them to take was the opportunity to watch a DVD played for them on the wall of my hut. I told them that they could not tell anyone that they had come to my hut, but that they could say that I took them on a secret journey to see some of the wonders of the world. I found the DVD of *Reign of Fire* which I had bought with me as something I might be able to use to promote the legend of dragons. I was going to take great care to warn the three old dears how scary it would be, and even decided to keep the volume of the film very low. I was also going to let One Eye watch as well and told her so. But I started to have second thoughts. The dragons in the film did not look at all like Loofah and the chances of the four of them keeping such an experience to themselves were statistically infinitesimal. I would almost certainly be put in a position where I would eventually have to show the damn thing to the whole community, and then what would happen when Beouf turned up?

In the end I showed them a video of the rugby world cup final from 2003 when England beat Australia 20 points to 17 in extra time. I had it stored on the hard-drive of my laptop. I explained that this was one of the great sports in my country, and although I had played it myself for a number of years I was not that good at it, and this was a match between the best players alive. They were fascinated. But although they were interested in the game itself, they were literally awestruck by the enormous numbers of people watching the game, the size of the stadium, the clothing people were wearing and all those other things that we take for granted. Anyway, it seemed a little safer than showing them a film with guns, dragons and aircraft in it.

The running went better than anticipated and I was fitter than I thought I was. I suppose the very task of walking everywhere had kept me fitter than I had expected. The moccasins had no real shock absorbency, so right from the start I used what was being referred to in the modern world as the 'Tarahumara Indian' or 'barefoot' running style. The Tarahumara Indians live in Copper Canyon area on north west Mexico, and some journalist long distance runner was there when he noticed that the Indians ran many miles, to and from work, over their rocky mountain footpaths, without proper running shoes. Yet they did not seem to suffer from the injuries that almost all long distance runners succumb to. He noticed that they ran on the balls of their feet, all the time. This meant that their stride length was a little shorter, but that by not 'heel striking' on the ground the whole leg became a giant spring and that meant that there was almost no shock through the joints of the leg, hip and spine as they ran. This made sense to me as we humans evolved, running and hunting barefoot on the baked earth of Africa, at a time when we had no footwear at all.

I found that for the first month or so it felt a bit odd, almost effeminate, constantly running on the balls of my feet. It also took a couple of months for my calves to get used to the greater workload. But within a matter of eight or nine weeks I did not even have to think about it, and to return to the so called 'normal' running gait of someone on expensive, shock absorbing, footwear, was not an option anyway. I did make a point of always running with the sawn-off, a nine-bangs and a can of mace with me. I became very used to the weight of the gun in my hand, and found it an added element of the exercise which worked my forearms and arms quite a bit. By the time I had been doing this for five years or more, you could feel the slight hollowing of the wooden fore-end of the sawn-off, where I held it one handed at the balance point as I ran. It was not only good exercise, but it was also a great way of exploring the countryside, and I used these runs as a way of staying connected to all those little communities that had been a part of the 'All Can Come' venture.

In all the years and all the miles I ran, I discharged the shotgun only twice. Once was by mistake as I tripped over a tree root and went sprawling headlong. My hand had been round both the barrel and fore-end wood in my normal grip, but I had either forgotten to put the safety on, or my right forearm pressed against it, pushing it forward and off as I hit the ground. In either case the end result was one of the barrels was discharged when the gun was slapped to the ground in my fall. It gave me one hell of a shock, and afterwards I was always very careful to double check the safety was on. I had decided that there was no point in carrying an unloaded weapon as any real danger would happen fast – too fast to load the gun anyway. I always carried a pouch on my hip with three spare cartridges, with the mace can and a nine-bangs. My Lizzie, my Monty, had left me some rock salt cartridges which were supposed to be a non lethal round for use in a shotgun and these had been recovered with the antibiotics from the time gate site near Gloucester. I always had one of these, along with one of my last few precious single slug bear cartridges in the barrels. The second time the weapon was discharged was when I was confronted by Garr the son of Beouf. It turns out that Garr means 'spear' but due to his petulant nature he was affectionately known as 'Moire Garr' as the name Moire is a woman's name for 'bitter'. Anyway this spoilt, arrogant, petulant youth, along with three of his father's henchmen were riding down a footpath on which I was running one brisk morning. I always stopped and avoided contact with strangers when I was out running on my own, I usually hid somewhere away from sight as I did not want any sort of confrontation. But in this case they had seen me from some distance due to a straight section of bridleway with good visibility, and they shouted for me to stop. I had no choice. If I ran into the woods, off the path, they would follow and ride me down, so I stood facing them, getting my breath back as they approached.

I had had few problems with Beouf since the sword test, and although he sent the occasional emissary to make some sort of demand, or just to find out what the hell we were doing, he avoided turning up at Kaardbury himself. This suited me fine, and the success we had had in dealing with the Vikings became known in the south west as a great victory. A victory which, because he was able to feed whatever bollocks he wanted to back to the court of King Egbert, resulted in an enhancement of his own War Lord status. So, perhaps because of this, he had left us alone.

But this event with Garr was five years after the battle at the fortress. Enough time for the burnish to wear off and the gloves to be removed once again.

The horses had broken into a canter when I had been seen, but had slowed to a walk as they approached me. Two could ride abreast at that point, and Garr was alongside a larger older man with impressive facial hair when they halted 20 feet in front of me. My guess is that they chose to stop at that moment as I had raised the shotgun to point directly at them, and although they had had no personal experience of what it could do, word does tend to get around.

"Is it safe for an old wizard to be out on his own?" (Fucking cheek! ... I was only in my mid forties.) "Should you not be hiding safely away behind your magic killing fence?" (So it was his father who sent that assassin who died all those years ago.) I said nothing, and this seemed to annoy the little shit.

"Perhaps you need a lesson on how dangerous these pathways are, and how lucky you are to live under the protection of my father, the Lord Boeuf." I decided I needed to respond to that. "Your father does not protect his people. He hides in Crediton when the North Men raid. It was the people of Kaardbury who saved themselves and who now have an agreement with the raiders. If you like, we can ask them to lay siege to your father's little fortress and see if he is brave enough to come out of hiding and fight?" That threw them. They knew we had a deal of some sort with the Vikings and that we now traded with them twice a year. Our arrangement had taken the pressure off the whole region, and there had been no attacks in the Exeter area since our battle in 833. But I decided I needed to offer them a way out with a bit of dignity. This little shit clearly wanted to show off in front of his father's henchmen and I knew I ran a real risk of injury, or worse. "Yet if your father and you, as his warrior son, are willing to really protect the people hereabouts, I am very grateful. We do not need protection from the North Men any more, but there are many villains on the highways that need capturing and punishing. If your father would do that for us we would be eternally grateful." (I knew full well that the worst thieves and robbers were Beouf's men themselves.) "If he did that for us I would not need to use any of my magic. In fact, I would be willing to show you how to do some of this magic for yourself."

He seemed a little taken aback at that, but responded, "I am not willing to lower myself to learning your magic, wizard. I only need my weapons, and my men, to deal with any foe." "As you wish," I replied, "but I can show you how to make it so this man cannot see." I twitched the barrel towards the man beside him. "Think what value such a power would be to a warrior like yourself in the midst of a battle." 'Hairy face' looked suitably worried as he glanced from me to his master. "I do not believe you," he said, "but if you can show me this, I will allow you to leave without my men giving you a good thrashing." He was smirking at the thought.

I said to Hairy Face "Do not worry, the blindness will not last long, I promise. Here, take my hand on it." I lowered the shotgun and walked to the side of his horse. I held out my hand, and when I did not lower it he reluctantly shook hands with me. I had noted that he did not wear gloves as Garr did. I stepped back and the youth moved his horse toward me. I said, "Turn to your man, say 'Abracadabra', and spit into his face." He looked a little surprised, and reluctant. He may be his father's son, but the man at his side was twice his size. "Go on, it will do no real harm. It would only be dangerous for him if he was attacked when he cannot see, and you are not going to do that are you!" He turned to his man saying, "If this doesn't work you can kill him for me" and then from a couple of feet he drew his head back and spat a good volume of spittle straight at his hirsute target. There was stillness for a good few seconds. Everyone was looking at Hairy Face, but nothing happened.

Garr turned to me smiling, "You will pay for your silly game with your life, you trick playing peasant." At this moment the man on the horse beside him started to double up, clutching at his eyes. He had, after a few

310

moments of dumbfound shock, tried to wipe the spittle off his dripping visage with his hand. His hand, the one I had shaken with my hand, my hand, the one which had mace on it. Mace from when I had sprayed the can into my palm whilst waiting for them to approach. It was a trick I had used twice before, and this time I had not even had to add an explanation that the spit would not become 'a blinding venom' until someone attempted to remove it. And with my connections it was, of course, the industrial strength stuff, 'the real McCoy', so to speak.

Garr backed his horse away as Hairy Face half dismounted, half fell from his horse. He staggered into the woodland uphill from the pathway and sort of curled up in the undergrowth, clawing at his face and trying to protect himself with a flailing arm from an unseen enemy. I said, "He will be fine in a little while. Tell him not to rub his eyes." By now I had backed up that 20 feet again, and Garr refocused on me. He suddenly dropped his heels into his horse's flanks. He was obviously intending to ride me down, to use the weight of the horse to knock me over and trample me.

The shotgun was held around the middle, at the balance point, in my mace covered right hand, with my left hand on the front trigger. I had done that to help prevent me touching my face with that right hand until I could clean it thoroughly. I was a bit ambidextrous, and had always used a rifle left handed despite being naturally right handed, as my left eye was the better eye. This meant that I could fire a gun from either side. All I had to do was to make sure I used the front trigger, as that set off the right barrel, the one with the salt cartridge in it. I did not want to kill Garr, despite him being a complete little shit.

I had already had plenty of time, (nearly seven years by then), to ponder on my unexpected continued survival in the ninth century. One would have thought that surely my interventions were sufficiently significant to warrant time itself to crave, and orchestrate, my demise. So in many ways I wondered how the hell I was still alive. My only conclusion was that somehow time had found a way to fit me into history. Perhaps the legend of dragons would actually work? Perhaps someone would find a manuscript at some future time that confirmed that dragons had been seen in Cornwall, and that a 'dragon rider' had become involved in helping to turn the Vikings from raiders into traders and settlers? Perhaps there was some unknown, unheard of, legend that would be discovered many years in the future and I would fit in, somehow? Anyway, I had no intention of cutting my corporeal chronometer unnecessarily short by pulling the wrong bloody trigger and doing something that time would simply not permit.

The salt sprayed out in an explosive cloud, directly into the face and eyes of both horse and rider, and with some considerable force. The horse bolted uphill to my left, almost directly over Hairy Face but somehow managing to leave him unscathed. His rider-less steed set off downhill to the right followed by both of the other two, each with their occupants clinging on for dear life. In moments the noise of their departure was fading into the distance. I walked up to within a few feet of Hairy Face where he was on his knees trying to see out of streaming eyes. I said to him, "Do not worry, in a few minutes you will be able to see again. Stand up and let the wind blow upon your face. I Marlin wish you no harm." I continued "Your master broke his word and has shown that he lacks honour. Tell Beouf that this was why this has happened. Tell him that I chose not to kill his son, but tell him to leave the people of Kaardbury alone. This incident was caused by Garr. If Beouf wishes to speak to me about this, tell him to send a messenger to Kaardbury and we will arrange a meeting."

I set off again at a jog, angling away from the footpath through woodland unsuitable for their horses to follow. My pulse was going like the clappers, and not from the run. Stress eh!!

The Chronicles of Eathelwold 'James' Trefell; Monk.

Book 7 Chapter 5.

There have been few events worthy of note over the last few months. Not since Our Thor returned from the North lands, and his visit to his sister. There was a death in the village last week of one of the older womenfolk. She had been ill for some time and had grown a belly as if she were with child. I was with her as her breath began to race faster and faster. There came a time in the middle of the night when I knew she had lost the race, and death was going to outpace her. Her breathing became slower as if she had relinquished her hold and had started to let go. I gave her the sacraments and by morning there was no breath left in her. It was a great sadness as this was one of the few women who had shown me kindness on my arrival in Caardbury those many years past.

Twas that same day that I was near the forge when I overheard the converse between our Smithy and Maerlin our wizard. It was with great concern that I was obliged to move closer to enable me to ascertain fully every detail of that which was being related.

It transpired that Maerlin had met with Moire Garr and had given that callow youth a lesson in wizardry. It had been viewed for some time that this boy, the son of Beouf, was responsible for much of the evil that had transpired in the last year. There had been many robberies and beatings, one of which had resulted in the death of a young man from a village to the north west. The victims, fearing these evil men, would not take the risk of openly naming their attacker as Moire Garr, nor dared to complain to Beouf as it was the War Lord's son who was believed to be the culprit. Hence one can imagine my displeasure at hearing this news - that Maerlin was teaching Moire Garr how to do magic.

Maerlin and Our Thor were sitting at the round shield table outside the Smithy. The men from the night did not meet each week as they had done. In fact it had been some months since they had last had a gathering at the little round table to discuss the protection of our community. Theirs was the responsibility to protect the people, and here was Maerlin teaching our enemy magical powers. I stood back in the shadows and delivered unto him the strongest of disapproving stares.

It was my belief that this recklessness on the part of Maerlin offered an indication of his gradual demise. He was perhaps aware that he was becoming less powerful. I have always taken great interest in his wizardry and he had done little in the preceding years to indicate that he still retained his powers. I had considered that our Lord and Father perhaps had finished with his use for this man. For he was only a man, of that I am sure. I have taken confession from some of my flock who talk with the fallen woman Etheswitha who sometimes beds with Maerlin. From the details I have obtained through judicious enquiry I discovered he is very much a man, with a man's needs. I have even heard that he requests the woman to bathe before spending time within his embrace. This being something that astounds me as the very act of fornication is one that is of its very essence is degrading and of filth. Yet had I ever lowered myself to perform this carnal act in full, before I became ordained, I would never have taken the very aroma from the body of the woman first. I have found myself that the odour *left by a healthy young woman, when seated in a church pew, is a rare and tumescent pleasure.*

Chapter Twenty Three;   Flying Beast.

I knew that the incident with Garr and Hairy Face would come back to haunt me. I perhaps should have been less bloody clever! Anyway, it was two days before a dozen men with full weaponry arrived. None of them were on horseback, and my suspicion was that they had come to the conclusion that I had too many ways to scare the shit out of a dumb animal. Maybe they should have been a little more introspective, if not aware of the irony associated with that thought.

Perhaps because they had been on foot, and because all the youngsters thereabouts knew me quite well by then, I had three different messages relating to their arrival. The first was from some kids playing near their family's farm alongside the road to Crediton. They were sent by their parents to tell both Eric and myself that the soldiers were heading in our direction. The children had run the mile that the men were walking, so I left my buckets at the side of one of the houses and had plenty of time to hurry back to my place. I had been collecting urine at the time, (I know, one should not take the piss!) and had just started my twice weekly collection. The second warning was one of the same group of children, one called Buck Teeth who, having run back to the Crediton road, had waited until the soldiers turned at the junction onto the Thorverton road into our village. Then Buck Teeth had run all the way to my little abode, shouting to me from my gate the news that the men were coming into Kaardbury. The third warning was given as I was leaving my front door. There must have been half a dozen of the youngsters by now, and they were all announcing in excited voices that Beouf's men were just about to appear at my hut. And sure enough, they were.

By this time I had no bean bag cartridges left at all. But I had two solid slug bear cartridges, 11 salt, and five CS gas left. This was not much in the way of protection if things got really nasty. I still had quite a few litres of the napalm like Loofah breath, but had not had time to test the tubes for a while. The last time I had loaded them had been nearly a year ago, and having been left untouched for all that time the air pressure had slowly dropped to nothing. I had re-pressurised them quickly with the hand pump, and just hoped that the liquid that had sat inside them for 12 months or more would still ignite when released. But I had been very busy in the 10 minutes that the children's alarm had given me before they arrived. I still had six nine-bangs, and three thunder-flashes, but all that stuff would not actually cause much in the way of injury. Especially as the approaching men were not on horseback!

But I had been experimenting a bit.

I had somehow managed to avoid using the diesel fuel oil from the microlight, as over the years I had always worried about wasting anything from the 21st century unnecessarily. As a result of this I had habitually found time to recharge all of my batteries by either the solar cells, manual effort, or the little wind powered charger I had positioned high in the trees above my hut.

Given I was becoming less able to surprise/entertain/terrify everyone I had intended to attempt to make gunpowder, so I had started experimenting with evaporating off the urine I collected to create the potassium nitrate crystals as the oxidising agent I needed. (Thank goodness for those survivalist CDs that my lovely Monty had left for me!) I only had time to 'play' like this because I was looked after by the village rather well. I had no land to farm, but I did have two first rate and highly efficient ploughs to lend out for payment in kind, (or in my case provisions) so I really did not need to work all hours like everyone else. I therefore spent much of my time trying to do useful things, and this included a bit of experimentation on stuff that I hoped one day would replace my 21st century wonders. Of course, I claimed that urine was for the purpose of tanning animal skins, as I did not want to cock up history by showing anyone how to invent gunpowder some 400 years before it was first ever used in Britain. Hence, in truth, I lied a bit to make sure that no one knew what I was actually doing. Well, lied quite a bit, or perhaps quite a lot ... even....

My problem, apart from the time it took to produce any real quantity of the saltpetre crystals from the evaporated urine, had been the lack of sulphur. There was bugger all of the stuff about in Britain at that time. Its addition to the mix is apparently as a 'combustion temperature reducing agent' as well as being something that is 'fuel' in the burn of the gunpowder. The old fashioned name for sulphur was 'Brimstone' but the islands of Britain are on what is known as a 'craton' – an old and stable part of the earth's crust. Hence we have no volcanoes, and not much in the way of surface sulphur. The CDs told me that there would be a significant sulphur mine at the side of a river in North Wales a few miles south of Colwyn Bay. But the mine would not exist for nearly a thousand years, and the only stuff available in the ninth century was tiny amounts bought by travellers from volcanic places like Sicily. (Which, under the circumstances, would have been a bit of a long walk really.) However I had managed to get hold of a piece the size of a golf ball, which had been the treasured possession of a roaming medicine lady who wandered from village to village festooned with a truly extraordinary array of things which she scraped, dipped and poured into her various potions. Potions for the treatment of any ailment known to man, and each brew guaranteed to be unique to the customer and probably to the size of his purse as well. My sulphur ball cost me a quarter silver piece, which was all I had had with me at the time, and worth a good week's wages.

But sulphur was 10 percent of the required mix, and from the quantity of sulphur I had I would only be able to produce just over half a pound, 300 grams of good gunpowder. So I experimented without it, and found the blend I produced with just finely ground alder-wood charcoal and saltpetre would not burn quickly enough to go 'bang'. I tried it in clay pots and wooden tubes, but could barely get enough force from the burn to blow the pot apart, at best leaving a small pile of fizzing powder smouldering away amidst the shards of the vessel.

From further searching through my survivalist CDs I came across ANFO, Ammonium Nitrate and Fuel Oil. This was a 'blasting' material, or a poor man's explosive. It combined 6 percent 'number two' type fuel oil with 94 percent Ammonium Nitrate as the oxidizing agent. Diesel is a number two type of fuel oil so I tried it with the saltpetre. I had experimented a bit to get it right, and I did have some real problems with the fuses, but I guess you are starting to see where I was going that morning with Beouf's men. Again, I did not want to kill or maim anyone, but I needed to find a way to scare them off for a few more years. Paradoxically I was back at the same location, in front of my hut, trying to frighten the living daylights out men employed by the same arsehole War Lord as last time.

I did still have a couple of those mini claymore mines left that I now kept in my safe room. I had managed to accidentally kill four deer, as well as seriously injuring one assassin, before I stopped using them on the perimeter fence. The free meat had been welcome, but I did not want to waste such an irreplaceable resource on inadvertent ungulate executions. This did not seem stop my alarm going off now and again, and worryingly it tended to happen more often when One Eye was visiting, but although it caused 'coitus interruptus' I am sure that was only coincidence. Eventually I built a bloody big fence.

The problem with the ANFO was ignition. In the text about this stuff it explained that the normal way of igniting the ANFO was by using a couple of sticks of dynamite. This is a bit like the need for an atom bomb (which is a fission process breaking large atomic elements like plutonium 235 down into smaller elements like barium, as energy is given off, a lot of energy of course) as the trigger for a hydrogen bomb. (Here the clue is in the title, this is a fusion process, so when a high enough temperature is achieved with the A bomb you can then start to fuse hydrogen atoms together to make larger elements, and so get even more energy). Thankfully my problem was on a much smaller scale of course.

Anyway, I digress.... I did not want to blow people up, but I did manage to get them to stand on the other side of my now reasonably substantial fence to discuss matters further. Garr was now at the forefront of the men crowded in the space between the trees and my enclosure, to the side of where the pathway entered my wooded clearing.

"My father wants to see you personally, and we are going to take you to him right now!"
I raised my arms wide. There was a nervous stepping back by three or four of the men opposite me, perhaps because my hands held items that to them looked dangerous. One was the shotgun, and the other held the two fire tubes, and these had been seen in action before. I was very aware that if I went to Crediton there was a good chance I would never leave the place alive. So I had absolutely no intention of going there.

"I said that I would meet with your father, not that I would go to his castle and be killed by him. Do you wish to arrange a meeting at a mutually agreed safe location?" I questioned. He sneered at me and then responded with "My father is the Lord of this land, and you will come to his beck and call. Drop your weapons and we will allow you to keep your ears."I felt almost disconnected with the process. I should have been very scared indeed, but for some reason I was not. It was a feeling a bit like the one I experienced during the battle up at the fort. So I replied, "I am Marlin the wizard. I answer to no lord other than the dark lords of magic. I am sorry that your father does not wish that to be so, but he had the opportunity to be our leader, as chosen by the enchanted sword, but he was not the one chosen. I am happy to talk to the great Beouf, War Lord of Crediton, but my magic holds sway here. I can take any man's soul and condemn him to an existence of misery and unending pain in the afterlife. You must have heard what I did to the North Men when they were here." (There were some exchanged glances. I was well aware that Beouf been kept fully informed about all that had happened).

He responded, "Conjuring tricks ... you have no real powers against genuine warriors, men with swords and shields." At this he turned to the men beside him and with a jerk of his head indicated that they should hack their way through the fence to get me. (I did vaguely wonder how many of them had been spat in the face by Garr in an attempt to recreate his own little bit of magic during the last couple of days?)
I raised my arms again (perhaps I had been overdoing the ego thing a bit) and said, "Wait, I have no wish to kill you and your men. I have no wish to demonstrate my supernatural powers by tearing a man limb from limb and scattered him in bloody pieces amongst these trees. But, if I can show you just how dangerous I am, will you go back to your Beouf, your father, and ask him to meet me at a place where we will both be safe?"
From the concern on the faces of the men around him I could tell that the consensus of opinion, if there ever was going to be one established, would be for a safe demonstration before they attacked. I could see Garr shrug and then staring straight at me, from the safety of the other side of the fence, he said, "I do not believe you, but I will give you a chance to show us what a charlatan you really are."

I turned to Spots, who was now a full grown man of considerable stature and with barely a blemish on his handsome visage, and said "Is it on its way?"

"Yes, Maerlin, it will be here in a few moments."

As he spoke Little Finger arrived at the gate leading a full grown bullock. It had occurred to me that he may have brought a large sheep instead. A big moton (the Saxon word for a sheep, and where in English we get the word 'mutton' from) may have worked ok but this should be much better, assuming it all went to plan. This was one of the animals that had been in the field below the village, and was about the age when it would be butchered. It did not belong to me, but I had told Little Finger to grab any beast from the field that could be slaughtered, and if anyone asks, tell them that I will pay for it handsomely. Some of these beasts were to be gelded and turned into draft oxen for work on the farms. I just hoped that this one had not already chosen for that purpose. What was about to happen to it would be rather more than a little bit of gentle neutering.

The animal was fairly skittish, probably because of the number of humans around him, but when Little Finger led him through the gate he seemed to calm down a bit. I decided that the men on the other side of the fence would probably stay put until they had seen what was going to happen, so I turned and led Little finger and his bovine follower to the far side of my compound.

Since the days when the assassins had tried their luck I had improved my defences quite a bit. My compound was about 50 yards across (just under 50 metres in new money) and was surrounded by a wooden fence that stood about eight feet tall. It was made of 231 coppiced posts, each about two inches in diameter and sharpened to a wicked point. The posts were about four inches apart and were braced by long iron nails fed through holes in the poles. I had wanted wire, but that had yet to be invented, (or at least the quality of metal required and the drawing process had yet to be invented) so I had got Eric to produce about 700 nine inch iron nails. Three of these ran across the gap between each of the posts, with their ends of the nails turned over to prevent them from being removed. These posts were set three foot deep into the ground and the whole barrier had a number of braces that held the structure rigid. The fence could be hacked down if you were willing to make a mess of your sword, and make a great deal of noise at the same time. But that was the point.... Anyway, this prevented any deer triggering the remaining dangerous or loud alarm systems that were now positioned inside the compound. I had few of these left and only set them, on the posts close up to my hut, at night.

I led the young man and bullock to the far side of the compound from the spectators, and I then tied the animal to the fence. I positioned it so that he stood over a dip in the ground where a tree stump had been removed. I then walked with Little Finger back to my hut which was at the north eastern side of the clearing. I told him to go out of the gate and join the others. When he was reluctant I said, "Do you want to live?" I clearly meant it, so he left.

I turned to face the onlookers. With my back to the hut they were to my right, and they had spread from the gate by the pathway to some third of the way round the fence. To my left, and farthest from the spectators, was the bullock. The animal had turned so that it was now facing towards me. I had attached its head to the fence with only a foot or so of rope and originally with its arse towards the hut, but the bugger had turned so that it was now the wrong way round. I needed it to be facing away from me, standing over the dip in the ground.

I turned to the people on the outside of the compound again and started to throw my voice. "WOULD YOU SAY THAT THIS IS A REAL BEAST, A LIVE ANIMAL?"
There was a general look of 'failure to understand the question', but it was rhetorical and I was on a roll anyway. "IS THIS CREATURE NOT MADE OF FLESH AND BONE, JUST AS YOU ARE?"
The soldiers made up the central phalanx of audience, but there must have been at least 20 others as well. I saw that a group of children were edging themselves away from the rest of the crowd along the far side of the fence, towards the tethered creature.
I shouted at them "STOP AND GO BACK. YOU WILL GET YOURSELVES KILLED!!!"
They slunk back to stand just the other side of Garr's men. I waited for them, before I continued.
"IS THIS BRUTE NOT AS STRONG AS ANY MAN? HOW POWERFUL MUST A WIZARD BE TO BE ABLE TO TEAR SUCH A CREATURE LIMB FROM LIMB?"

323

I took a flare from my shoulder bag, struck it, and then tossed it across the compound to my left, so that it lay near the fence on the far side, not too distant from where the startled animal stood. Thankfully this meant that to enable it to keep a wary eye on the hissing flare the bullock had reverted to it's original position, with it's backside towards me, standing over the stump hole once again.

I said "I AM SOMETIMES ACCUSED OF MERE TRICKERY," (I looked at Garr pointedly), "AND THAT STICK IS JUST FIRE AND SMOKE...." It was fizzing away with a bright green light in the shadow of the clearing, with its smoke drifting high over the onlookers.

"IF I AM ANGRY I CAN JUST RAISE MY HAND AND DO THIS!!!!" at that point I threw out my left hand. I had already stood the two fire tubes and the shotgun against the hut, so my left hand was empty as it swung toward the bullock, which promptly, on queue … blew up.

The shock wave from the explosion was cushioned by the earthen hollow and thrown mostly upwards because the pot of ANFO had been set in the loose earth at the bottom of it. The blast threw soil and pieces of clay upwards and outwards, showering the compound and well beyond. The blast was truly deafening, and I could feel the shock wave thump into my body, throwing me backwards against the hut wall. Thankfully I had had the presence of mind to put ear plugs in before the confrontation started, (perhaps that was why I was shouting a bit too loudly from the start) but now my head was literally ringing as I got to my feet. I had had only a momentary vision of the bullock as it disintegrated because I had turned away in a reflex action to protect myself. In the modern world I had become so used to being able to watch everything on replay, often slow motion replay, that I sometimes, even then, forgot how fast things happen, and how suddenly it is all over.

One of the hind quarters of the beast landed with a thump in the middle of the compound, while the bulk of the eviscerated carcass ended up on the far side from me, where the flying weight of it had broken the fence down, so that the head and upper torso, along with one and a bit legs attached, came to rest on top of a flattened section of my perimeter fence. The right hand semi-circle of fence from where I stood was still intact, with some of the onlookers still on their feet beyond it, but with a red cloud of vaporised blood and dust starting to settle over everyone. Smaller parts of the dismembered innards and clumps of soil were still coming down through the trees, with a swish of leaves and small thuds as they landed. The fence where the animal had stood was gone, completely. Thank fuck that pot hadn't been any bigger eh?!

I had attached one of my last two mini claymores to the pot of ANFO in the hope that it would set it off. At worst the bullock would have only been given a very limited, but probably fatal blast of little metal ball bearings into its belly from the claymore. But that would not have been as impressive as the occasion required. As I have said, I had had problems setting off the ANFO, but this had been an idea that had been wandering around at the back of my mind for quite a while, and I considered it would almost certainly work. Diesel is a compression fuel, so if you hit it hard enough, like with a small explosion, it should go off with a bit of a bang....

The best thing, of course, was having the audience. It would have been a crying shame to have choreographed such a successful demonstration without anyone being there to see it. The fence now needed quite a bit of work, and most of the watchers would be deaf for a while. But on the plus side, as far as the bullock was concerned, it had met its end faster than any other bullock in the whole bovine history of the world, ever. Well, so far anyway, plus there was the added benefit that some of the butchering had already been done ... bonus!

I started to walk toward the people to my right, who were outside the fence. I realised that I still had the little clip from the end of the claymore lanyard in my right hand. The 'trip wire' connected to the claymore was about 10 metres long, and I had fed it through the fence behind where the bullock would stand at the same time as setting the ANFO pot in the ground. From the fence I had led the thin dark line to a post near my hut so that I could give it a good 'yank' at the right moment. I dropped the clip, still attached to quite a length of the line, and turned to pick up my two weapons. By the time I had walked, a little unsteadily, to the fence directly opposite Beouf's men, there were only three of them still there. The others had run. The standing two were helping the third to his feet. According to one of the boys, a lump of clay the size of a fist had hit one of the soldiers in the face, stunning him and costing him a couple of teeth. The three walked away, almost deliberately slowly as if in some sort of limited act of defiance, two supporting their spitting, snorting comrade, as he tried to clear his mouth of debris.

The kids were 'cock-a-hoop', if it is appropriate to use any description that did not exist at the time and would not appear in print for about 800 years. But they had recovered from the shock surprisingly quickly, and the mutilation and gore involved was to them a true delight. They all jumped around the torso, and blooded each other's faces. In the end I needed some peace and quiet to sort things out a bit, so I had Spots drag them away. I then asked Little Finger to find the owner of the animal only to discover he was already there, amongst the locals that had set off towards my hut soon after the Beouf's men had passed through the village. He was a man known to me, and had farmed the land near the church for many years. I apologised for taking his bullock and killing it, but he did not seem worried about that at all. What he clearly wanted most of all was to get the pieces of the animal back to Kaardbury so that he could show it off. I suspected that it would spend the next week in his barn with him charging a handsome fee from anyone who wished to see it.

Well, beef does need to be tenderised for quite a while before consumption. Bleeding and disembowelling the carcass had already been done. It occurred to me that before I left the modern world I was aware that steaks for sale in supermarkets have to be left on a cold shelf to rot a bit for about a month before going on sale. I wonder if those people who are so paranoid about sell-by dates are aware of that?

The Chronicles of Eathelwold 'James' Trefell; Monk.

Book 7 Chapter 8.

As a consequence of the reckless behaviour of Maerlin our village, my flock, were subjected to yet another worrying experience at the hands of the War Lord Beouf and his now magically gifted son Moire Garr. It is a terrible thing for dark forces to be used in battle, but I was witness yet again to the powers involved and for once began to question the appropriateness of such behaviour.

In truth I was sorely tempted to step between Moire Garr and Maerlin and demand that they put aside their differences and come to a peace. Was it not Maerlin himself that persuaded Our Thor to require five days to pass from when a dispute was reported unto him, until the time when his judgement would take place. This Maerlin called a 'cooling period' as if the protagonists were cooking pots on the boil, and an idea of some merit. But here the pots had no time to cool. I reluctantly chose not to intervene and watched as their posturing reached a climax in the compound beside the wizard's habitation.

I knew this place well, and had walked up to this place a number of time during the hours of darkness, in truth on nights when I knew that the barren and lascivious woman Etheswitha had gone to him in his weakness. I had been able to listen to them in their coupling and asked the Good Lord to forgive them of their sins. But after a number of failed attempts to get closer to their sinfulness, when each time a great noise was made by Maerlin's wizardry requiring me to leave at great speed, The Good Lord showed me his blessing, in my endeavour to test this licentious behaviour, by one night preventing the noise from happening, and allowing me to stand close beside the hut and find a crevice through which to observe their behaviour

Sure enough what took place is something that perhaps should not be put into the written word. Suffice it to say that I saw the shameless wretches feast upon each other in a way that only wild animals would do. It was a view into their dark world of depravity, and when the woman cried out as if in pain, the brute Maerlin took pleasure in attacking her person, with his mouth, again and then yet again. I thought the poor woman would die from her repeated agony. I can only wonder with what evil enchantment he has trapped her soul and somehow forces her to go reluctantly to him and suffer so. It was with some regret that I found he had built a palisade around his habitation preventing me from doing the Lord's work and watching these terrible events in my habitual penitence as a man of the cloth.

The day of the confrontation between the wizard and his apprentice Moire Garr was one of great consequence. I reached the gathering at the gate in time to hear the posturing of these two warlocks. Maerlin had been able to hold the power of the apprentice in check and demanded that he and his men stand to watch something truly terrible. It was clear to me that Maerlin considered the young upstart as an adversary posing threat to us all, and it is in that context, and that context only, that I can forgive what was done, and what took place.

I must say again should this text be read by any man liable to disbelieve my words. I swear on the holy book and the lives of all my flock, that the following is a true account of what took place.

Moire Garr was held as if by sorcery with his multitude of armed men on the outside of Maerlin's 'magic circle'. This palisade of wood was built not to allow others to see the terrible practice of witchcraft within, but to prevent us mere mortals from getting close to his lair. Although I was, at one time, willing to take those risks, I am now not sure that even a holy man such as myself would be safe.

The Wizard Maerlin drew into his compound a massive beast of burden. An ox of gigantic proportions that he had subdued with his dark powers. He took the creature to the far side of this magic circle, and then with the mere cast of his hand he made the beast be torn asunder. Yes, I tell you it happened ... in a single moment of time, and from many paces away he had the power to rip the animal to pieces. The body of the stricken giant was thrown into the air and its limbs torn from it in a manner which makes one's blood run cold. And blood there was, so much of it as covered everyone present. The noise made, as this terrible act of barbarity was

performed, was so loud as to strike all those nearby deaf. I
myself am not sure my hearing, which has always been so
acute, was not affected that day such that it has never fully
returned.

Suffice it to record the fact that this took place, and that the
upstart, the wizard pretender Moire Garr, withdrew to the
safety of his father's unholy den of iniquity. Thereby giving
notice to the supremacy of our warlock Maerlin. From my
own knowledge of the scriptures I am sure that under the
right circumstances a righteous and holy man would be able
to overcome such magic and prevail. I can only say that it is
Maerlin's good fortune that his work, dark as it may be, has
been blessed by our Lord, the one true God. For there may
come a time when I am called upon to defeat this shaman, this
wizard, this trickster. But that time was not upon us, so I
allowed him to live on and continue to protect my people.

Chapter Twenty Four;   Sacrifice.

The following day a single emissary, a servant, came to Kaardbury to ask where I was willing to meet with Beouf. Sending the servant was an insult, but the request being made suggested that the demonstration had worked as well as anyone could have possibly hoped.

I had had time to think about where the best place would be, on the assumption that there was this possibility of Beouf wanting to meet. I had considered the church, but it was in the village and I wanted to arrange a bit of protection. Having such a meeting close to habitation would make it difficult to deal robustly with any dirty tricks on Beouf's part. In the end I decided that the best place was up at the fort. It had become a bit overgrown, but a farmer was now grazing sheep and goats in the compound as it was already fenced for him. So the grass was short, albeit somewhat peppered with sheep shit.

We arranged the meeting for the following Sunday. It was believed that Beouf, although not Christian, had some concern over angering any God, so the choice of day for the meeting was to reduce the likelihood of bloodshed.

When Beouf arrived at the All Can Come fortress he was, as agreed, with an escort of four mounted men, and his son Garr. I had considered getting all 12 of our village elders involved at the meeting, so that Beouf could hear how the people, who he was supposed to look after, felt about his efforts. But I decided that this would seem like a dirty trick, and may result in reprisals on the 12. So it was that just six of us sat down at the table in the gully where we had trapped the Vikings all those years ago. Beer and refreshments were laid out for us, a fire heating some mead, and warming a pot of stew, stood to one side.

Beouf seemed a bit surprised at our hospitality. After a formal hand shake, in which there was only a momentary concerned glance towards my open palm, we sat down with Eric, Smithy and myself facing Beouf, Garr and a scribe.

"I am not happy with your rebellion. I am the lord of this land. I am the representative of Egbert the king of Wessex. I demand that you subject yourself to my control in the name of our king!" These were the first words from Beouf's lips. Well it was at least direct and to the point! I should have deferred to either the Smithy, or to his son. But Beouf had spoken directly to me, and he clearly saw me as the threat to his position. So I said "I understand that you feel you have not been obeyed as you may have wished. But the people of Kaardbury and the people of the villages hereabouts have been killed and taken prisoner by the Norse raiders, and you had done nothing to protect them. All we have done is find a way to protect these people. Are you not pleased that we have protected your people for you?"

He stared at me. "But when I give you an order I expect to be obeyed!"
"I understand. But I am not from this land, and if you try to force me to obey I can use my powers to take your life. I have not done so because you are important to your people."
"Do you threaten me?"
"No, I do not. But it is the simple truth that I can kill any man I wish." He glanced at his son who looked down. The events with the bullock must been a considerable reality check for them all. My guess is that they believed in my powers a great deal more than I did myself.

I continued, "What I would like is for you to take control of looking after these people again. They are your people, not mine. You have been given the responsibility for this by King Egbert and you are the chosen and deserving War Lord." (This was a bit of sycophantic bollocks, but I needed him to feel he was winning, and for him to refrain from any retribution on the villagers.) These conciliatory words seemed to throw him a bit. He had arrived all bluster and indignation but things must have seemed to him to be going unexpectedly his way.
"Why did you deny me the sword? I had ordered you to give it to me!" He was looking straight at me but there seemed to be a little less menace, or perhaps less fear, in his gaze.
"I had no choice. If the Gods are disobeyed they become angry. Angry Gods can kill us all with plague, pestilence or famine. Without their good will none of us will live for long. All I did was obey the Gods. You yourself saw how Eric was able to take the sword from the cage under the

rocks with no difficulty at all – yet no other man, however strong, could open it. That was not my magic, that was the will of the Gods! Their powers are far beyond mine."

"But I am the War Lord, the Thane! You should have given me the sword when I commanded you to do so!"

"The sword's intention, its very purpose, was to choose someone to lead the people to build this fortress, and to defeat the North Men. That has been done, and I believe the Gods have played their game with the sword and it has pleased them. To them we are but pieces on a board, and their amusement with the sword is now finished."

There was a pretty universal popular notion that the Gods played with the lives of humans much like a game of chess. (Although the only popular board game seemed to be one called 'Hnefatafl', but you know what I mean.) This was a good way to explain the trials, tribulations and generally shitty experiences of real life. It is a notion that seems to me to have much more merit than the pathetic adage of "but God works in mysterious ways," which appears to be the universal answer when it becomes clear that if there is a God, he/she clearly doesn't give a monkey's. Anyway, I had already discussed the issue of the sword with Eric. Although he was reticent to give it up, I persuaded him that this was necessary, as handing over the weapon may be that the only way to make peace with Beouf. So I concluded my little speech with "If we come to a suitable agreement during this meeting the Gods have agreed that you, our War Lord, should be keeper of the sword called 'Dragon Leg'."

He was silent for a few moments. Then he said, "How do we know that the Gods have agreed this? Many people claim to speak to the Gods, even your Christian priest! I have yet to see proof of this."

I responded; "There will be real proof if you wish. Firstly I will tell you of a prophesy the Gods have already told me. From searching their runes of the future they tell me that later this year there will be a great battle between our king Egbert and a combined force of the North Men and the Britons from the south west. This battle will take place only ten miles from Crediton. You are to tell Egbert to take the high ground to the east of the Hampstead of Moreton. There he will have a great victory, and if you were the one to have advised him, you will be seen as a great War Lord and tactician." (Thank goodness for the quality archaeology and detailed history that Monty had researched and cobbled together for me. The battle of Hingston Down would take place there that year, in 838, at exactly that location, come what may.) Beouf seemed very interested in that information and looked over the scribes shoulder to make sure the details were being recorded. He was apparently only partly literate, but then I was only partly a wizard.

The discussion progressed and, despite my anxiety, seemed to be going rather well. Suddenly there was a commotion in the woodland beyond the wall of the fort to the east. The section of palisade that had been taken down to lure the Vikings into our killing ground had long since been replaced. So in response to a shout from in front of the gate in the southern wall Eric stood on the wooden beam which acted as our fire-step that ran along the bottom of the outer fence, to shout down to those outside. The agreement had been that there should only be an escort of four soldiers with Beouf, and that these four would stay close by, but out of earshot. These men were in the upper compound with Wulfgar, being fed and watered by Pretty Prop and Barn Door. If any of them decided to try their luck with either of these two ladies I am sure we would have been willing to send their dismembered remains back to Crediton. But because I am the distrusting type, not only due to Beouf and Garr's previous convictions, but because of my experiences in the cut-throat business world of the 21st century, I also had other insurance.

Our archers had been re-convened, and led by Holt they had been sweeping the woods around the fortress for the last couple of hours. They had come across six of Beouf's men creeping towards the eastern wall. Interestingly if they had climbed into the fortress at that point they would have been stuck in the still very muddy enclosure of the eastern end of the gulley. But it was the thought that counted. There were then a few accusations banded about. But eventually having convinced the War Lord that our men had been told to keep well away from the fort, but had been tasked with challenging anyone approaching it, and after Beouf had sort of convinced us that it was all his son's doing, we sat down once again. His men were sent marching back to Crediton, and told not to return.

We managed to pick up where we left off, and had roughed out an agreement within an hour. We paused to drink some mead and eat the

335

stew before continuing. We got to the point when I asked Smithy and Beouf to say what they thought the agreement was in their own words. It included the sword going to Beouf, some villagers doing the equivalent of national service in the oncoming war against the combined armies of the Britons and the North Men. Some protection for travellers, and punishment for offenders, even if the offenders were proven to be in the employ of Beouf. (He was denying they had been involved at all so it was difficult for him to get out of that one.) An agreement on protection of witnesses, response to further Viking attacks, and so on. It even included making my idea for a cooling off period in local disputes semi-official. At the end of this I said to Beouf and Garr;

"Do you wish to hear the Gods speak? Do you wish to hear them confirm your agreement?" Eric and Smithy looked at each other. They knew what was about to happen, and although worried stayed seated. Beouf and Garr sort of laughed it off, but their bravado sounded somewhat forced.

"Can I borrow your helmet, War Lord?" I held out my hand and he reluctantly lifted it from the ground beside him and handed it to me, saying; "I had heard you did this ventriloquist trick with the North Men." I responded. "It is no trick and I will prove it. I will ask the Gods to mimic your voices exactly, and whilst they speak to you I will walk away. If you think it is either of these men (I indicated the two Smiths) playing a voice game, please just ask them to drink whilst the Gods are speaking. No man can talk properly with his mouth full of beer. I will ask the Gods to confirm our agreement exactly as you said it, so that not only you will believe me, but you will know the Gods consider this a 'blood binding contract'."

I did a bit of mumbo jumbo over the cooking fire during which I made some overt references to contacting those Gods who specialise in retribution from the more fiery regions of the afterlife, and in doing so gave myself time to rewind the Dictaphone and change the batteries. By now none of the remaining batteries held their charge particularly well, and the full agreement had taken almost 10 minutes for each man to recap. The tiny button microphone had been set in the middle of the table sticking up between the planks and was almost invisible between two plates. The Dictaphone cable was left attached to the underside of the table top. I hoped I had managed to get a better, and louder, soundtrack than last time. I ended my routine by putting the helmet upside down in the fire for a few moments whilst pretending to stir it with a flaming piece of wood, before returning to the table. I hoped that would at least deter anyone from touching the helmet too soon.

This time the Dictaphone was loud enough to be heard clearly by everyone. Beouf and his son sat aghast, and in silence, as the words were returned to them. I walked to the gate and back, slowly, twice, making sure that I was on hand as the recorded discourse drew to a close. I took the risk with my Dictaphone of allowing it to drop down into the longer grass at my feet as I gathered up the helmet from the table. The rest of the tape was silent and I was probably the only one of the six of us who heard the faint hiss as the tape cassette wound slowly on.

I solemnly handed the helmet back to its owner. He took it gingerly and could not stop himself from peering surreptitiously inside it before returning it to the ground near his feet. The meeting lasted another half an hour, and at the end Smithy, Eric, Beouf and Garr all made their mark at the bottom of the two documents produced by the scribe. I was not that skilled at reading Anglo-Saxon, as there had not been much call for those skills to date, but I was able to read them well enough to see that they were almost certainly duplicates of the agreement as stated on the Dictaphone. They left carrying Eric's precious sword wrapped in crimson coloured leather and their right hands streaked red from the minor cuts required for the blood oath.

I was pleased that they had never realised that there had been our four crossbowmen in the tree houses high above our heads. Big Tash and the three others had been given strict instructions to lie down out of sight behind the low wooden walls of their arboreal nests and to not move during the meeting unless I shouted out the word "CROSSBOWS." Their bows had been cocked and loaded, and if push had come to shove I would have used them. A War Lord dying during a sudden and unexpected Viking attack was not that unreasonable a story. It turned out that our discussion had been interesting enough for none of them to become bored, although after Beouf had left, two proceeded to spectacularly relieve the pressure on their bladders whilst still up in the tree tops. I was not sure if they were attempting to demonstrate how desperate they had become over the previous three hours, or if they were just showing off in a literal pissing contest. Probably a bit of both.

When the four of them reached the ground and their bows were made safe, they expressed great concern over the loss of Dragon Leg. They were so incensed that I knew that this was going to be a bigger issue for everyone than I had anticipated. I drew Eric to one side. "Eric, we have one more calliper spring left from the Loofah dragon. Could you make another identical sword? I could ask the Gods if they will allow this." This seemed to mollify him, and he clearly liked the idea, although I had to insist on absolute secrecy, just as before.

I gathered the four crossbowmen and Smithy. "The weapon the War Lord has taken is not the real Dragon Leg. No one must ever be told of this, as Beouf must always believe he has possession of the true magic sword from the Gods. No one from the village is to be told he has taken the sword at all. If you tell anyone this secret, that person will become at risk of death. There is to be no discussion whatsoever with anyone about it. If Beouf thinks we have tricked him he will come back with his soldiers and slaughter our women and children. Beouf must believe he has Dragon Leg, and no one from our communities is to be told anything at all. The real sword is hidden in Kaardbury and it remains with our chosen leader Eric. I will ask the Gods what they want for the future of the sword." (I had decided that the best thing to do would be to get rid of it before there were any further problems. Perhaps it should be returned to the Gods at the next harvest festival.) "It has done its work and our Eric has completed his task well. It is only right that the Gods be asked what they want done with their magical sword now that its purpose is complete. I think that is the right thing to do. We would not want the real Dragon Leg to end up in the hands of someone like Beouf." Eric was standing close to the group, and was a bit quiet, but everyone agreed that this was the correct course of action. At some stage I would tell Beouf that the villagers had been so upset at the idea of Eric losing the special sword that we had pretended that another similar one was the real thing. I thought perhaps by then I would be able to tell him that this fake sword had already been thrown back into the lake just to keep the community happy.

So that's what I did.

338

Book 7 Chapter 10

It was with great concern that I heard of a meeting in the Come a Lot fortress. This meeting was between Our Thor, our rightful leader, chosen by the Lord God to do his work, and Moire Garr and his un-chosen father. The undeserving Thane, the man who tried to wrest the sword from the stones yet failed. He who failed, where our true king, despite his ignoble heritage, did succeed. Not only was this undeserving Thane there, but also his wicked son, the man who wanted to be a wielder of magic, yet was defeated in a battle of witchcraft by our own warlock.

Verily I was yet also concerned that the sorcerer Maerlin was involved once again. In my informed view he should have no voice in the decisions of our Christian peoples. He has never come to my church, nor joined with our flock before the alter of our Lord Jesus Christ. When challenged about this he laughs at me. He says that foolish people, people who refuse to see the evidence of their own eyes, will follow without question religious books like the Holy Bible, and will do so for time immemorial. He says that 'faith' is real and is of great value. But faith in anything works equally well. What heresy! If I could cast him down without hurting my people I would. I would call upon the Lord to cease looking favourably upon this terrible sinner and take away his powers of sorcery.

Maerlin even claims that the world was not made in seven days, and that at some stage this will be proven by something called Sky Ants. He says that in countries where knowledge and proof of how the world was formed is there for everyone to see, many will still blindly believe whatever they are told by those who want to keep control of them. Control by those that want to make money or retain power over others, by using their faith and fear of the afterlife to get them to do terrible things. He states that in truth there is only one way to make a good person do something of great evil, and that is to use religion to get them to do it.

These are terrible things to say, and all I ask is that when the Lord Almighty has finally finished with this blaspheming sorcerer, this mere mortal man of magic and spells, he must make him go through a purgatory beyond hell itself.

So it was that at this meeting within the fortress and away from the eyes of those of us who watch over our flock, an agreement was reached. An agreement in which the Holy Church took no part, yet it is my belief t'was still guided by the Good Lord himself. How else could a reconciliation take place of such magnitude? A reconciliation in the Come a Lot castle which made all of my parishioners safer than they had even been in living memory. This starting a time of safety for all, unparalleled in our history. A safe time when the Norse raiders did not attack, and were even called friend by some. Even a time when our journeying far and near became safe, and the terrible Moire Garr caused us no harm.

I had heard a rumour that the terrible Moire Garr had fought for the Ex-calliper sword and that at one time it was thought to be lost unto him. Yet I know differently and saw the same blade, unblemished as any weapon of sanctified purpose must surely be. Unmarked by the task of battle as it was our Holy Lord who sanction the blood spilt under its blade. His blessing makes the taking of heathen and pagan lives a right and proper thing to do. His blessing permits the taking of any life not devoted to his church.

Chapter Twenty Five;   Returned to The Gods.

Eric made the new Dragon Leg sword in secret. It was much easier for him to do this than it was when making the original weapon, as his father was semi retired and now left the bulk of the hard hammer work to his son and another young man who was as ugly as a warthog. Much of the work in a smithy requires two men, and as ever, the constant ring of hammer on metal was the perennial sound that emanated from the village. But 'Warthog' didn't ask any questions, and until the finished product, one bit of red hot iron tends to look much like the rest. The old Smith now concentrated on the production of charcoal for the forge and although that was still hard graft he had help from Short Skirt's husband, a squat stocky young man with a constant smile on his face. I was never sure if his expression indicated happiness or mild stupidity, but so long as Short Skirt was content I did not care.

When it was finished Eric kept the sword well away from public gaze although I know he did show it to the men who had been at the fortress meeting, and who needed to be satisfied that the sword was the real one. They commented on the fact that it was such a magical weapon that despite being used against the North Men there was not a single mark upon the blade. Funny that!

The battle at Hingston Down took place as predicted. This had two consequences. Firstly the people of Kaardbury and surrounding areas had even less to fear from the Vikings, as now the other raiders who had been attacking further along the coast would be licking their wounds for a few years. Secondly the warning I had given to Beouf had enabled him to gain a great deal of kudos with Egbert, and so he spent much of the next year either at the royal court in Winchester or with the mobile court the king used to travel around his domain and keep his finger on his nation's pulse.

Following the death of Egbert, Beouf returned the next year to Crediton as a confirmed Christian. Garr had been left in charge much of the time, but he must have been under strict instructions to leave me, and us, alone. Which suited everyone just fine. On Beouf's return Garr went off the rails a bit and turned to drinking.

By the middle of September I broke the news to Eric that I had spent a night in deep commune with the Gods. In truth I had got hold of a quantity of the priest's mead, something he tended to hoard in a miserly fashion. Hence my communion with these spectral beings was rather intoxicant focused, and the resultant details flagrantly elaborated upon. Interestingly (to me anyway) I find I always struggle to remember exactly what was said when I am pissed, but I am always very good at remembering the meaning behind the words. I had, of course, got to the stage where I talked to myself, well Monty really, far more often than was considered healthy.

I said to him; "The Gods want the sword returned to them. They appreciate that the one you have is only a copy of the one they originally blessed, but they say that they require a sacrifice. You made these swords, and you have been a great leader for your people. But the Gods now demand a special sacrifice from you. They ask that you return the sword to them yourself. They say that at the harvest thanksgiving you are to return the sword to the Gods through their watery portal."
He replied; "But it is not the right sword. It is not the one I was given by the Gods when I was able to open the door in the stones. Why would they want this one?"
"I have asked them that very question. They say that it is the sacrifice that is all important. When you return the new sword to the water the old sword will cease to have any power or magic within it. If any man then uses that original Dragon Leg sword, it will be as if it is cursed. The Gods would not state the nature of the evil in that enchantment, but the very casting of your weapon into the lake will be a blow to Garr and Beouf, from which they will never fully recover." Eric did seem to like that bit.

So it was that at the festival for the harvest in the year 838, in front of the gathered villagers from our community, the magical 'ex-spring' Dragon Leg sword was returned to the Gods. Eric cast it out into the deep water amidst the deathly hush of all those crowded at the lake. It hit the surface point first so that it seemed to disappear instantly and with barely any sound or ripple. Even to me that seemed a little spooky. For everyone else it was simply a confirmation of the magic embodied in the blade, and an affirmation of the merit of returning it whence it came.

345

The Chronicles of Eathelwold 'James' Trefell; Monk.

Book 7 Chapter 14.

There came a time when the sacred blade, the Ex-Calliper sword, had completed its purpose, and the Good Lord called for it to be taken from Our Thor's hand. Our saviour permitted this to be done in a manner that fitted with some of the misguided beliefs of the more wayward members of my flock. I was witness to this event myself and had prime position at the water's edge when the blade was returned whence it came. I was probably the only one amidst the throng who observed with such care that I had a momentary glimpse of those two pale hands, the hands of an angel in the water, those same hands that had given us this holy weapon, as she once again took the blade from the air, swifting it beneath the surface, into the darkness below.

This was surely the only way for this sword to leave the world of men. I am sure if Eric had been allowed to die under the knife of the wizard Maerlin that this was always the one true place where he would have demanded the blade be cast. It was only by drinking from the Cup of Chirst itself that he was bought back from death to enable him to cast his weapon into the deep water himself.

Two years later Garr was hamstrung in a fight with a man in a tavern in Exanton. The man from the tavern was later killed by Beouf's men, but only Eric knew that his downward spiral into drink, as well as this crippling blow, had been directly caused by the curse of the Dragon Leg sword.

Egbert was succeeded by his son Aethelwulf as king of Wessex. Beouf spent a lot of time praying and being sickeningly righteous. Garr stayed in his dad's fortress getting drunk and having sex with a number of servants and slaves he had retained in the premises for that very purpose, much to his father's now sanctimonious displeasure. Eric married a young woman from Thorverton, the daughter of a fisherman, who insisted on carrying on helping her father work his nets along the river, and whom I suspected simply could not handle the constant noise at home.

Me, well I just got to the stage where I ran out of things to do in Kaardbury. I managed to persuade Spots to do a bit of travelling with me. It transpired that although communities were, in general, static and stable, a good many people travelled around quite a bit. So I decided I might as well see some of the 'old' world. I could not persuade One Eye to travel with me and it always made sense to go with at least one other person for safety reasons. Spots was my height and build, although he was better looking than I ever was, (the bastard) so he could have been mistaken for my son. We were both pretty good with the 100 pound longbows and had had a good deal of practice with the other weapons of the age. As always, I wanted an 'ace' up my sleeve, so I converted 10 of the remaining salt cartridges into something more lethal. I got Eric to melt some lead, and mould some ball shot for the cartridges. With the salt removed and replaced with three lumps of lead, each the size of a .38 calibre bullet, I had something to really defend us with again. I was tempted to take the fire tubes but I decided they were too cumbersome, and would draw too much attention. I told Spots that I did not want to be known as a wizard on our travels. I said that I would be able to learn much more if I was seen as an ordinary man, and I would also not have to keep on showing everyone my magical powers. Spots was a very nice guy, and surprisingly intelligent. He agreed that this was a good idea.

By this time I was usually using the black 'cramp balls' from Ash trees as tinder alongside my slowly thinning flint striker. I had another one left for me by Monty, but I wanted mine to last as long as possible. The cramp ball 'amadou' was used by many people at the time, but I made the mistake of describing them as 'King Alfred's balls' to Eric. Worryingly the name stuck, and was used frequently amongst my companions, despite there having never been a King called Alfred – as yet anyway.

By the time I went on my first trip around Britain I had four thunder-flashes and two nine-bangs left, so I took literally half of my stock with me. I had created a few pyrotechnics with the little sulphur I possessed, so I also took three kilos (six and a half pounds in old money) of ground saltpetre crystals and just over half a kilo of high quality, finely ground, alder-wood charcoal as well. If I found half a kilo of sulphur somewhere I was in the gunpowder business. So in case I got lucky, I had also produced some saltpetre encrusted string as fuse, and a few narrow necked fired clay pots as grenade containers.

I placed all the valuable modern-day stuff in the hidden cave at the back of the safe room in my hut. No one knew this secret store was there, and One Eye was willing to live in my hut whilst I was away. I placed the padlocked locker from the fortress in the safe room beside my bed, and filled it with things that were of little consequence. I told her that no one was to be allowed in the safe room at all, to keep it locked at all times, and that she was only to go in there to sleep. She promised that she would look after the place well, and I considered that even if it burnt to the ground I did not think the equipment from Loofah would be harmed. I also hoped that if anyone made a real attempt to get hold of some of my wizardry kit they would only find the contents of the locker, and be suitably unimpressed.

So it was that in the summer of the year 839 Spots and I, both of us riding a horse and leading another, set off on our first journey. The many journeys we had will be documented elsewhere, assuming someone is daft enough to want me to do so. But we did travel most of the length and breadth of the country. We even spent some time on the continent of

Europe. To get anywhere took a great deal longer than it does in the modern world, and we were away from Kaardbury for literally a year at a time. Our trips began to have something of a pattern about them. We would be gone for about a year, from summer to summer. Habitually we would obtain interesting or valuable items on our journey and we would sell and trade with them en route. We would usually stay in Kaardbury for one full year planning the next trip, and then set off again in the early summer. We would travel for the warm months of the year, winter somewhere different, and return by an alternative route.

So it was eventually, when over sixteen years had passed since I had arrived through the time-gate, something happened that turned this all upon its head. That something was a young woman. A young woman with auburn hair.

It was a time when I was in Kaardbury, during the early spring. One Eye had told me that she could not look after my hut any more. She had been asked by a man from Crediton to become his wife. She was very old now to be taken as a wife, but she was unhappy when I was away on my trips, and had fallen in with the father of Warthog who had been visiting the village on a more and more regular basis. Supposedly this was to visit his son, but in fact it was to surreptitiously court One Eye. She had decided she wanted more security and comfort in her old age, and she was going to move to Crediton, jump over the broom, and live with him. He was a widower with some property and he traded in vegetables. I do hope he kept a couple of his root vegetables in the house at all times. He was going to need them!!!

Well the best of luck to her! She was a good woman, and although it had always been very much her choice I had always felt a bit guilty, as if I was using her. I had never been able to give myself fully in our relationship. It was not just that we were from very different worlds, (well times really) but there was very little intellectual connection between us despite me teaching her to read and write. Plus, of course, there was the most significant block of all to any genuine emotional connection because, despite the impossibility of ever seeing her again, I was still very much in love with someone else.

I knew that Monty would be involved in the archaeological side of any research related to the originally planned 'find sites' for items I would bury for posterity. So I left her a couple of personalised items. I suppose it was just something I wanted her to know. One Eye could never have replaced the absolute love of my life.

The Chronicles of Eathelwold 'James' Trefell; Monk.

Book 11 Chapter 4

So it was, that there came a time when the warlock Maerlin ceased to partake of the sinful cup of the woman Etheswitha, and this woman of low repute took steps to be returned to the Christian fold. She left Maerlin, as she knew was right, and joined in holy matrimony with a good man whose work praises the bounty of our Lord and shares these fruits of the earth amongst his people. I was told that this good man frequents the chapel in Crediton and I hoped that he may lead this fallen woman fully back to Christ.

But at this time a wielder of great sorcery came amongst us. There came amongst us 'Mord-red'. She was of the devil's kin herself, and she looked at me as if she could see into my very soul. She looked at me with a distaste for the very holy clothing, the simple monk's habit I wear in servitude to our Lord. She watched me like a hawk, and saw me keeping a close and caring eye on my parishioners. At one time she even followed me at night and made it impossible for me to do my rounds, my checks and observations, upon the sins of my flock.

This Mord-red woman was an apprentice in sorcery. She took control of the life of Maerlin and devoured him of his knowledge and skills. This evil apparition who treats me, a man of the cloth, like vermin, was here to do no good. I at once saw a profound change in our Wizard. He was transformed by the potions she plied him with. He was unable to resist her unholy wiles. She bewitched him so that he held his arm around her as a lover, yet she had such a terrible control of him that his hands would not move to the places on her body I would have wished to see them travel if theirs had been a true relationship of the flesh. She had him helpless within her control, and in his pathetic stupor under her spells and potions I beheld in him a happiness such as that of a man believing himself to be reunited with his greatest love.

What unholy sort of Pagan hex she placed upon him I do not know. Such a spell would turn the hardest man to nothing. I am glad that I am not susceptible to such weakness, and that I can stand back and observe the sins of *man and woman without this consummate vulnerability.*

Chapter Twenty Six; A New Arrival.

It was a bright crisp morning with a touch of frost in the shadows of the trees, and a light breeze carrying the sharp air of the new day, when I wandered into the middle of the village to see if I could scrounge some milk. I mainly drank pine needle tea in the mornings. With milk added it was the closest thing I could get to a morning beverage that reflected my old life. The bulk of Eric wandered out of the smithy where, behind him, Warthog was hard at work on the bellows, trying to get something metal sufficiently hot to work upon.

"Greetings Marlin I hope you have slept well. Have you broken your fast yet?" He seemed in good spirits.
"I am after a cup of milk my friend. I will eat after I have found some, and slaked my thirst." I replied.
"Well you had best get away back to your home as quickly as you can. There is a woman here asking after a wizard, there is something most strange about her. She has clothes that tell me that she is from across the water, from far away. She has the face of an angel with not a mark upon her skin, yet she has a sharpness of tongue that suggests she needs to be either taken, or beaten, or both. She also has a strange accent, perhaps as bad as yours had been when you first came unto Kaardbury."

Over the years there had been a number of enquiries about me, Marlin the Wizard. Some of these had been from foreign lands, especially the Norse lands. I had even had an envoy from the court of Aethelwulf asking about me. I had given strict instructions that no-one was to be told where I lived, and everyone had to be told that I lived somewhere else and that it was known I was travelling in Europe. Well, sometimes I was.

Eric continued; "I sent her packing, but the arrogant cow just wanted to know where the fort was. Someone must have told her about the All Can Come castle. She set off up the hill half an hour ago. Oh, and she gave me this!" I had always thought the description 'castle' was overdoing it a bit, but the passage of time seemed to elaborate stories and progressively increased the proportions of any monsters slain. Oh fuck! The last thing I needed was to have some smart arse spying on me. Perhaps she was from some Southern European country where they desperately wanted some bit of magic to win a war, or to heal a dying king!

He handed me the piece of parchment he had been holding in his hand. It was a tube of about six inches (15 centimetres) in length, and had originally been sealed with wax. The seal had been broken. Eric said, "My apologies Marlin, I did not want you to receive a summons from anyone who wants to hang you from a tree. I have tried to read it, but although I can see one or two words similar to our own, it must be in a foreign language. Perhaps so only you can read it." He handed it to me, I unrolled it and read a poem, written in bold letters, that it contained.

I looked up at Eric and demanded; "What did this woman look like? Was she tall, almost as tall as me?" There must have been an edge of desperation in my voice as he became at once visibly concerned.
"Is everything all right Marlin? You look as if you have been back to the spirit world."
I could not give a fuck about how I looked. I virtually shouted. "WHAT DID SHE LOOK LIKE?"
"She is a mature woman of normal stature ... unusually pretty ... probably the best looking woman I have seen in many years. Hair the blood colour, like some North Men."
I was crestfallen, It was not who I had suddenly hoped against hope for, but I urgently wanted to know where this stranger had gone.
"Up to the fort" was his reply, and before his words had dissipated in the morning air I was running uphill between the smithy and what had originally been the crones' house, through the woods, and directly up the hill.

I had missed my Monty so much over the years that it was like a physical blow in my belly when I had read the poem. The reason I had never really got close to One Eye was my enduring love for my Monty, my Lizzie, despite the impossibility of ever seeing her again. My feelings were such that at one time I had gone to my original departure site outside Gloucester, to the time gate I had been too late to get through, and I had buried there a beautiful glazed clay pot alongside the items I had been supposed to leave for evidential and archaeological reasons back in 831.

On the outside of the pot I had written in darker clay, before the glazing had been added, a short poem.

I live in darkness here my love,
time's shadow, oh so deep.
It had to be a thousand years,
for you, from me, to keep.
But know this truth my one true love,
for every night I weep.
It is you I think of every day,
and when I go to sleep. DD (842 AD) xx

As I said, I knew that Monty would be involved in the archaeological side of things, and she would understand. I was her Dick Dastardly, and she was my Penelope Pitstop. Silly names we had given each other playing a Wacky Races memory game in the canyon lands of America. I suppose it was just something I wanted her to know.

That very same poem was written on the parchment I had just read.

I was completely out of breath by the time I broke out into the open area below the fort and had to stand, hands on knees, gasping for air. I was approaching our citadel from the west and as the main pathway to All Can Come ran up from the south, my route had taken me though quite a bit of thick undergrowth and over a dry-stone wall. I was quite fit, but trust me, if you run up a steep enough hill (and this really was one), with the level of desperation I was experiencing, you will be going somewhat faster than your body feels comfortable with. (In modern parlance it is called going seriously anaerobic.) On the way up the hill I had been thinking that to Eric everyone looked small, and to him a mature woman could be any age over 14. There was still hope, so my heart was aching for more than one reason as I set off again.

I could see no one as I approached the steep slope of the original iron-age construction. Below the outer palisade I came across the beaten path that now circumnavigated the outside of the fort. I turned right, slowing to a more reasonable jog, made easy by the slight downhill gradient towards the gate. The sweat was pouring off me as I had not gone to the village dressed for uphill sprinting. I stopped and shouted. "HELLO, CAN YOU HEAR ME?" There was no response. The breeze was stronger on the hill top, and the sweat was starting to cool very quickly in the sharp cold air. "ARE YOU HERE? I AM MARLIN – BILL MARLIN!"

I had by now I slowed to a walk, and entered the fortress through the main gate. The gate was still more of a doorway in a large wooden wall than a gate, but you know what I mean. The grass in the western end of the gulley was a good two feet tall and dotted with bushes of various sizes. The sheep were in the inner compound above me, and were never grazed in the 'killing ground' of this outer fortress, as getting them through the gate was too difficult. The steep banks of the gulley were a bit less steep than they had been 15 years ago, because time had started to wear things down a bit. The palisades were still in good order because they were repaired every spring, just in case, but the rest had been allowed to go fallow. In an emergency the fort, as it now was, would still be as good a place to run to as it had ever been. We were just rather less well prepared now.

There was a ladder that led directly up and over the inner palisade close to the walkways above my head. I climbed it and shouted across the animals in the main compound. Two leapt away from the wall close to the ladder. The rest turned to look at me, and then resumed their perennial feast.

I heard the gate behind me and turned on the ladder to look. I was taken aback as through the doorway stepped a woman. I had seen this woman before, or someone very like her. I froze on the ladder looking down. I froze for two reasons. Firstly, I stopped because I remembered where I had seen this woman, or someone very like her. Secondly I stopped because of what she had just said;

"Dad, Dad is that you?" …And she said it in fucking English!!!!!!

Maud, my own daughter, looked the spitting image of her mother when I had first met her in the year 2000. In terms of the chronological progress of my own life, my child should only be 21, but she was in fact 27 years old. The time gate she had travelled through had taken 22 years to re-open. It was the strangest of reunions. I asked her so many questions, many of them about Monty. I could go into a great deal of detail at this point, but instead I will try to summarise as best I can.

When I had not returned through the time-gate it had been huge news. What followed were a number of things. Firstly the excavation took place to see if I had buried the archaeological stuff I was supposed to. Along with the recovered items was my special pot, with the date on it that told everyone that I had survived at least eleven years. This meant that the legal profession went into overdrive. My ex's lawyers wanted me declared dead as there was no way of getting me back, and in their argument I was therefore, of course, actually dead already. My team responded with the 'seven year' rule that I had to be missing seven years before I could be declared actually dead. There was a great deal of expensive game playing by solicitors (what an appropriate name for them eh!) which was more about dragging out the legal arguments for as long as they could, rather than solving the problem.

This apparently triggered Monty into action as she then took up a sort of personal quest on my behalf. She wanted to prove that it would be possible to open another time-gate to get me back, and to do this she was engaged in a consultancy role within the Einstein Group. It took most of those seven years, seven very well funded years, thanks to *moi*, for the group's research to get to the point where it could prove they would be able to build into the time-gate device an increase in power commensurate with opening another window to get me back. This allowed the courts to put my assets on some sort of extended ice. In the meantime they had sanctioned a handsome allowance for my ex. She was also allowed to divorce me 'in absentia', to enable her to get on with her life. Over the following years three significant developments took place.

Firstly the Einstein Group continued to work towards building the paradigm shift in power system into the time gate equipment. As they were doing this they found those power requirements, which had risen sharply over the first two years following my disappearance, had levelled off. This was despite my apparent continued survival in the ninth century. They also began a search for two time-gates in the years from 843 onwards that would be suitable for getting me back before I simply died of old age. This was a search for two very small needles in a thousand haystacks.

Secondly, Monty started doing what she was best at. (Actually, second best, because I, of all people, knew what she was really best at.) So she began an archaeological search across the South West of England. She needed to find out where I was living, so that whoever travelled back in time to get me would know where the hell to look. This search was done by a team she had put together, and was part funded by my business capital which was being shrewdly invested in my absence by Cyril and my business manager. I had wisely written a will before I had left that gave considerable powers to Monty and Cyril regarding my residual estate, which thankfully the courts read as permission for them to manage things in my unusual absence.

Thirdly Maud had started to grow up. She was five when I left. By the time she was 15 she had met Monty and they started to develop a bond. By the time Maud had finished her degree in Archaeology she was an almost permanent fixture with Monty's historical investigation team. There had been extensive document research followed by a number of digs. The breakthrough had been about six years ago, just after Maud had graduated. There were some documents that talked of a burial mound holding the remains of an Anglo-Saxon warrior who was interred with a special sword. A headstone set in a wall led to a description of the sword that was obviously nonsense, as it spoke of its magical powers, but it was stated as having been taken 'by right' from a wizard called Maerlin.

Maud had never felt close to her mother, who was clearly more obsessed with finding a way of getting 'her money' as she always referred to it, from her un-dead ex-husband's estate. The allowance still paid for a big house with two staff, plus a full time nanny. When Maud had been sent to a boarding school at a very young age, her mother had gone off the rails for a while using drink and drugs. But she had managed to get through rehab and then find a man who was willing to put up with her bullying ways. Maud's guess was that although he was both dumb and pretty, he was even more of a gold digger than her mother was. Eventually her mother managed to get a court order that allowed her to make a claim from my estate when I returned, or when I was proven dead, even though she was already re-married. Her allowance, in the meantime, continued. Of course.

Maud started to spend school holidays with Monty. Eventually, she barely saw her mother at all. Monty treated Maud like the daughter she never had, and Maud considered that Monty was the mother that she had always wanted to have. Their search now focussed on the town of Crediton.

Two years ago a small church in a nearby village was checked with ground imaging equipment and it was discovered that the church had been rebuilt at least twice. Under the church there were sealed catacombs, and in one of these there was a document found that took the archaeological world by storm.

Maud explained to me about the chronicle they had discovered. Apparently it rivalled Bede's work in its importance and volume. The only thing against this new find, this extraordinary record from the past, was its partly fictitious content. One aspect, the description of one person and what that person did, read like the tale of a fantasy novel – a 'dark ages' version of Harry Potter, perhaps written by a deluded fool. A literate fool, who made things up and then wrote them down as if they were fact. Pure nonsense … unless, of course, there was such a thing as a time gate. She said that she was unable to tell me who wrote the document and was a bit evasive. But my guess is that it was Eric, or someone writing for Eric, and the document would be written at some time in the future.

Maud was a bit circumspect about some other matters as well. She said that the Einstein Group were of the opinion that there was a danger of 'flux' in the power requirement of the return time-gate if I was told things by her that would make me change my behaviour or decisions. For instance, the person who wrote the manuscript must still be allowed to do so, and this 'fact' of history needed to be permitted to run its course.
"Did I ever manage to create a legend? Did this person write about Loofah?" I asked.
"Yes, he documented your arrival as the dragon rider, and chronicled your history here, along with much else."
"Did it prove the legend of dragons?"
"Well sort of.... We had supposed that 'time' had found some way to fit you into history without causing progressively further damage. It seems to have done that. If it had not done so, then the power requirement for me

to get here would have been astronomic, and way beyond our capabilities."

I probed no further at that point. I was just happy I was going to get back to the present, back to my Monty. It felt as if a huge weight (and wait) was being lifted from my soul.

I had been told some bits about Monty, but I was desperate to know more. She must be about the same age as me now. It turned out that when I did the mathematics she was, in real terms, a year older than I was. She had dedicated over two decades of her life towards finding me and was apparently looking forward to my return. Maud said that Monty had not come through the gate in person as she was now a bit long in the tooth for this sort of adventure and physically would have found it difficult. Maud was a bit vague on that one as well, but I didn't press her. Her search, or research, had made my Monty, my Lizzie, the foremost authority on Anglo-Saxon Britain in the world.

I had forgotten about breakfast, and it was midday when we wandered down the hill and into the village again. I decided that it would be better if no one knew that Maud was my daughter as there was the ongoing risk of someone wanting leverage over me. It was apparently seven weeks before we were due to leave through the return time-portal, and I did not want her kidnapped and ransomed by someone who wanted to know my magical spells. I decided that she would be a wizard's apprentice who had travelled from my homeland to learn my skills. This would cover a proliferation of issues from shared confidentialities, to sleeping in the same hut. She did also have with her some new, fresh and very real bits of wizardry kit we could play with over the next few weeks. The arrival of an apprentice seemed to work very well as our explanation.

Maud was fascinated with my account and how I had used items to amaze and bamboozle everyone. She seemed to know quite a lot about my story, and asked questions that indicated that the writer of the manuscript had gone to some length to describe the goings on at Kaardbury. When I told her about the ANFO she gave a giggle of delight and declared "So that's how you did it!" I showed her my secret store behind the rock wall, and my now meagre remaining equipment from the 21st century. I had not thrown things away when they had stopped working, but before that had happened I had gone to great lengths writing down the important stuff from the CDs. My 'hard copy' was literally hand written books of information. But, because of this, when the laptops had finally given up the ghost I still had a great advantage over any adversary or fellow traveller. I had eventually been able to produce some really good quality gunpowder that I had used for noise, smoke and distraction 'magic'. I had even used it to blow a few things up. But that is another story.

Over the following weeks Maud was my constant companion, meeting everyone I knew and surreptitiously recording video of interviews with them. She asked them many questions about their lives, a priceless record for any historian. But they all knew she was my apprentice, so my 'amazing' exploits featured somewhat heavily in these personal tales. Photos were taken, items collected, and preparations were made for my final departure.

The departure gate was only 35 miles away from Kaardbury as the crow flies, just north of the hamlet of Sutton Montis, south of where the A303 will run through Somerset, north east of Yeovil. There was apparently another large Iron Age fort there that they had been investigating following the finding of the now somewhat famous 'Chronicle'. On the off chance they had done some gate tests and found a suitable portal in the one of the south facing earthen walls of this large old fortress. (What irony, on so many levels!)

Some of the stuff I had with me was worth taking back. The hard drives of my laptops contained some valuable bits of video and lots of pictures that I had thought would never be recoverable. I removed these, and added the remaining carcasses of these machines to my 'for destruction' pile. Some great artefacts I had collected would be the envy of any museum, assuming a pot or piece of jewellery, or handmade item of clothing that looked, and was, as good as if it had been produced in the last few months, was acceptable. It would be an interesting question as to whether these pristine objects would still be acceptable in an establishment that exists solely for the display of items of antiquity that have, by definition, gone through the normal trauma caused by the actual passage of time.

My 'baggage limits' were the proportions of the time-gate itself, and I had to get a very clear picture from Maud of the dimensions of the return portal. We reckoned that as long as we carried the most important pieces ourselves, and pushed through something on wheels, if the gate opened close enough to the ground we would be OK. They had told Maud that the return trip was less of a problem in terms of the time-healing issue as a few extra items missing from the past was neither here nor there in the great scheme of things. A person from the past coming through the gate with us would be a problem as all their future in the ninth century would just not happen from that time onwards – their children would not be born, and so on. Spots wanted to join us but was told in no uncertain terms it was impossible. I told him that the journey would kill him.

One of the last things I did before we left was to spend an afternoon with Maud on the oxbow lake – the one where the harvest festivals took place. She took lots of photos and some video, but I was not quite sure why the place was such a big deal to her. I dived to the bed of the lake a dozen times before I found the sword, buried in a couple of inches in the soft mud at the bottom. Maud took a load of pictures of it for some reason, and I wrapped it up and kept it safe for our departure. I made sure she could locate the position of the lake when we returned to modern times. In the 21st century I was sure it would be filled with silt and be dried out to form part of the landscape, but its contents would be a fabulous treasure trove for her and Monty when we got back.

My final journey in the year 848 was with an entourage of 11 people. I said my farewells in Kaardbury before we set off south to Exanton, heading south west first to visit One Eye and her husband in Crediton. He was somewhat frosty towards me, but my guess is that when One Eye showed him the gold coins I gave her he would be quite happy with my visit. My fellow travellers were Maud, of course, Eric, the old Smith, Spots, Short Skirt and her husband Warthog, Wulfgar and his wife Revered Gwen, Elf, Holt, and tagging along as ever, Father James the priest.

We arrived below the return portal a whole day before it was due to open. We had left plenty of time and had taken three days to cover the 50 miles at a steady amble. Walking was something that everyone did a great deal of in those days. The provisions for the journey, and all the stuff we hoped to get through the time gate, were on pack horses and in little donkey carts. We set up camp on that last night in the field next to the outer embankment of the Iron Age fort close to the northern edge of Sutton Montis. That night we made a large camp fire and had ourselves a fun little festival all of our own. We shared out the few modern day delicacies that Maud still had with her, and everyone agreed that chocolate was the firm favourite. I slept a slightly drunken but reasonable night of sleep. I was only woken briefly by an argument between Eric and Wulfgar, which happily seemed to sort itself out. So, I closed my eyes and drifted off again.

As luck would have it I was awoken by Holt, because a group of armed men were approaching us across the fields. There were about a dozen of them with one man on horseback. They entered the field we were in, and the mounted leader demanded to know who we were and what we were doing. I took it upon myself to reply.
"We are doing no harm. We are travellers from a village near Exanton. We will be gone by the morrow."
The horse rider dismounted and left his animal with one of his entourage. Then he walked up to within a few feet of me. His men had followed, so that they formed a solid phalanx behind and either side of him.
"I am Graeme, War Lord and Thane of this place, friend to Aethelwulf our King. I have heard rumours that a wizard comes to my land. One who has made a treaty with our enemies the North Men." (Oh fuck! I thought). I responded; "We are simple folk who have done no harm."
"Are you the wizard?" He demanded. "You fit the description well and my king has been searching for you for many years. If it is you, then the rest of these people can go free. It is only you that the Kings wants."
Before I answered Maud stepped to my side; "I am the daughter of this man, and I am a sorceress of great power. If you turn and leave now none of you will be harmed!" (A bold statement, under the circumstances, I thought.)

At this the Graeme the local chieftain started to unsheathe his sword. All the men with him started to do the same, when suddenly they were in trouble. The noise from Maud's sonic weapon was quite painful to me, and I was, by now, well behind her. She had stepped forward as she raised her arm and fired the damn thing. I noticed later that she was already wearing earplugs, so she must have prepared herself as soon as the men had been seen. Three or four of the soldiers just crumpled where they stood. Unconsciousness was apparently a regular effect of this bit of kit at close range. A bit of kit that I had never seen in action, and would only be available to police forces after the year 2020. It was the size of a small handgun, but with a more rounded shape, it had a bell like delivery end which was about two inches across. With the thing still on she swept it back and forth across the width of the line of men in front of us. Those that did not simply crumple unconscious, folded up with their hands over their ears, some literally screaming in pain, as they fell over sideways. The boffins of the future had found a way of using sound to incapacitate and disrupt the inner ear's balance system, without causing any long term damage to ear drums. Boy, did I wish I had had one of those.

The horse did not keel over, but it did clear the stone wall southwards, and kept galloping flat out until he could neither be seen nor heard any more. Maud turned the device off and everyone in our group moved back away from the pole-axed men. I was handed one of the heavy bows and a sheaf of arrows by Reggie, and by the time there were half of them back on their feet they were facing a number of old fashioned weapons as well as Maud and her 'noise maker'. I determined that I should be the one to re-open communication, but decided it needed to be loud. "CAN YOU HEAR ME? CAN YOU HEAR ME GRAEME?" He was on his feet, white faced and shocked. "Yes, I can hear you wizard." He was shaking his head as if to clear water from his ears. He started opening and closing his mouth to work his jaw. "What was that, what did you do to me?" I continued to shout "YOU AND YOUR MEN ARE UNHARMED. BUT YOU WERE ABOUT TO ATTACK US. I WILL NOT COME WITH YOU AGAINST MY WILL, AND AS YOU CAN SEE, UNLESS I COME WILLINGLY NOTHING ON THIS EARTH CAN MAKE ME SO DO. I WILL DECIDE WHEN I TRAVEL TO SEE YOUR KING." He chose not to come closer again, and his men were starting to reassemble on either side of him. "The king has given orders that if you are found you are to be taken to him unharmed. He is a Christian King and he wants to know your magic, and how you forged an agreement with the North Men."

We exchanged a few more questions before I made a decision; "IF

YOUR MEN LEAVE, YOU CAN STAY AND BE WITNESS TO
WHAT HAPPENS HERE. IN A FEW HOURS TIME YOU WILL SEE
SOME MAGIC THAT WILL ASTOUND YOU, AND YOU CAN
TELL YOUR KING WHAT YOU HAVE SEEN WITH YOUR OWN
EYES.... YOU WILL COME TO NO HARM, I PROMISE."

So that was that. There was an addition to our entourage for the final
hours of my time in the ninth century. It took an hour or so to set up the
flat trolley, with its big wheels which we had built specifically for this
purpose. It was designed such that the bed of the trolley had a good three
feet of clearance beneath it. I wanted everything to be that elevation above
ground to provide a sufficient margin of error in case the gate opened
higher off the deck than planned. Maud had originally planted some
tracking devices on a visit to the site when she first arrived, just as I had
done. These were positioned with some accuracy, and she reckoned that
the return gate would appear within a couple of feet of where she had
marked it would be.

With 15 minutes to go I started to say my goodbyes. I had brought with
me a number of gifts, some of which were items brought to us by Maud
only a few weeks ago. I gave Ronnie the cut down jerkin I had made from
my arrow-proof cape. (I had tailored it with a red hot blade from the
forge, and produced a wearable jerkin that was lighter than mail, but better
at stopping blades.) I gave Reggie Maud's brand new flint striker stick, so
he would be able to start a fire more easily than any woodsman alive. (My
last two remaining lighters would travel with me forward in time as they
were so obviously from another world.) I gave Spots, my companion of
many years, a whole box of Maud's new thunder-flashes and two cans of
mace, plus a number of small items including my remaining silver coins. I
had small items for Short Skirt and Elf, a somewhat battered telescope for
the priest, a pair of spectacles and a monocular for the Smith, and finally a
wrapped item for Eric. I said; "This is for you my friend. I believe we have
done some good in the time we have been together. Keep this and
remember me, but please, no man may examine this, and it must go with
you into the ground." I stayed his hand as he started to unwrap the sword
and told him it was for his eyes only.

I stood beside Maud with one hand on the trolley-cart and my other holding hers. The earthen bank in front of us started to shimmer and turn the iridescent blue that showed the gate opening. I glanced at Maud, and she at me. She said "I need to tell you something. Monty is very ill, that is why she could not make the trip here to find you. I just need to tell you that before we go through. I am so sorry Dad!" As my heart leapt into my throat, and my legs started to give way as the dread of what she had just said to me struck home, Maud dragged me and the cart back into the 21st century....

The Chronicles of Eathelwold 'James' Trefell; Monk.

Book 11 Chapter 6.

So it was that the arrival of this witch 'Mord of the Red Hair' heralded the untimely demise of the Wizard Maerlin. A sorcerer who had surely gained his powers through the Good Lord, and whom with my modest yet significant assistance, delivered our communities from the decimation of the Norse invaders and the deprivations of Moire Garr. With deliberation I play down my role in these things, as it is only right and proper for a man of the cloth, such as myself, to display humility and a meek manner despite the key role I have played, and all the personal risks I have taken.

There came the time of supposed departure and I wondered if they would mount again a dragon, such as the Luther dragon on which the wizard arrived at this place. But that was not to be. We travelled a great distance, such that I was sore of foot, until we came to the great walls of an old fortress. One greater earthen work than even the Come A Lot fortress of

Gaardbury. There I was witness to three events of significance to my journal.

The night we stayed beneath the earthen walls of this place of fortress from the time of history, I was simply checking upon the few members of my flock - some being couples who may have wished to partake of the flesh following the revelry of that evening. I found that the rhythmic grunting and squealing commensurate this activity which I was trying to observe was interrupted by Wulfgar, he who uses the Lance, and Our Thor. Their disagreement of purpose was that of a misunderstanding - in that Our Thor had been looking for a place to pass water, not to find Gwen the Revered to impale her in secret, as was the challenge of Wulfgar. It was at this time it came clear unto me that the brazen hussy, Gwen, had at some time admitted her indiscretion with our king. This confession had given rise to constant suspicion of indulgence in further opportunity should it arise. A doubt that clearly still simmered within him.

I gave silent thanks to our Lord when they did not come to

blows and each continued on to his place of rest for the night. In so doing the healthy coupling that had been rudely interrupted could continue between Rosanna and her husband. I had, perhaps, been fortunate with this distraction as it enabled me to reach a better place for the rarely experienced observation of the sins of my flock in clear moonlight. This being a task I take most seriously, and one in which a number of my holy brethren have confessed they themselves also partake with almost equal diligence.

On the morrow we were witness to the second of these worthy events, being observer to the terrible powers of the witch 'Mord-red', when we were confronted by the better part of five score warriors in full armour. A prodigious force, had we not been protected by our faith in the Holy Scriptures. I heard these men had been charged with taking of our sorcerer Maerlin. He was to be taken to the King Aethelwulf. This being the true Saxon Christian King, not Our Thor the one chosen to by the Holy Sword to lead us against the North Men at the castle above Caardbury.

I was about to intervene. I was about to place myself before these men of blood intent, for I was willing to offer myself as hostage to Maerlin's custody. Something he was never grateful for, albeit there was scant time left for him on this world had he known it. With an awful suddenness the witch Mord of the red hair raised her hand and cast at these men of the sword a piercing spell, one which assailed the senses, and cast them all to the ground writhing in their torment. If I had called upon the Lord to do this same debilitating act he would have done so for me. But he, like myself, is not taken with show. He is not willing to display his supreme powers in this way. Yet, in his wisdom, he was willing to stand aside and allow this wretched woman to strut like a cockerel and make these men kneel before her.

So it was that we were joined with Sir Garweme, War Lord and Thane of these parts, to witness the passing of Maerlin. I have said many things about his sinful ways. Yet I must at this juncture give thanks to our Lord for choosing to send him to us and allowing him his sorcery and magic powers. These have been of benefit to my people, my flock. And I only take the credit as the man with the vision to sanctify these things and allow them to happen. It was a choice I made with some difficulty, yet I have now few regrets. For in his extraordinary interventions the true hand of our Lord God has been clearly seen. The Heavenly Father even saw fit to direct Maerlin, before his eternal entombment, to surrender unto me a gift which has assisted me greatly in my ongoing efforts to keep check on the sins of my flock. It is a gift that has given me great satisfaction over the years.

So it came to pass that we were standing close to the earthen wall of the old fort when a hole into the ground opened directly before our Warlock Maerlin and the Witch Mord-red. This hole led into a cave of the underworld, a place of damnation that only I, as the true Christian amongst us, could see with clarity. At the moment of the devilish spell opening this pathway to a cave of despair I could tell that the witch Mord-red told Maerlin of her true intent, and that he would be locked in the hillside for all eternity. At her words he seemed to crumble, as if at last he sees the terror of his future and the emptiness of everything for him to come. At that moment of realisation, the first moment of time in which perhaps the Warlock was allowed to see his awful fate, she dragged him listless into the darkness, never to return. There went with them a cart of goods to appease their heathen Gods of the underworld. It is my view that the Lord Almighty allowed this thing to happen as a warning to others, and as a justified retribution for the Wizards lack of faith.

Twas a surprise to all, that when these two sinful people went into this cave of despair, the bottom of the wheels from their wagon were cut off by the sharp edge of the mouth of the cave. They were cut as clean as a knife passing through butter in a barrel, leaving parts of spokes and pieces of wheel rim that even today I keep in the church, to show disbelievers that sins are always punished.

The Chronicles of Eathelwold 'James' Trefell; Monk.

Book 23 Chapter 17.

I write now as my life comes to a close. I think back and see moments of redirection of purpose. Moments where there is a turning of my path in the serving of our Lord.

Having witnessed the internment of the wizard Maerlin, tricked by the witch Mord-red as they disappeared for all time into the earth I remember that I spoke unto the armoured Garweme, and in that converse I seeded a direction in my life that was full of adventure. I, in time, became the tutor to the King's youngest child Alfred who was born but a year after the loss of Maerlin, and as a consequence I went with the royal entourage on the pilgrimage to Rome. What joy!

It was I who taught the Great Alfred to read and write, and he has become the most blessed king of our land. He had many years in hiding, but in this year, the year of our lord Eight Hundred and Seventy Eight, he has defeated the

Danes in a mighty battle. A battle at Ethandon, where he used the old earthen fortress on the hill and a shield wall, to defeat his unbelieving foe. This was just as Our Thor had done all those years ago, in that battle when I led the people of Caardbury to victory over the heathen hoard of raiders. Well I remember the tales I had told the young Alfred, of dragon slayers, and battles in the old fortresses, and how a wall of shields can hold against the greatest of warriors. Perhaps in doing so I even had a hand in the battle just won.

My thoughts wander back in time, and muse upon those years before I came to the king's court. Our little village, our community, was blessed in such a strange way. A man came to us as an unbeliever, and yet his presence amongst us was such an unusual benediction. It makes me wonder at the power of our Lord God Almighty to direct the future using such strange instruments as the wizard dragon rider and his ungodly powers. The changes made to our lives through his meddling and his spells, the magic of this man made of the devil, were so often for the good, despite the sin within him, and despite his terrible end at the hands of Mord-red. I think back to those days as perhaps the best of all. They were the days when I did the most for those people who relied upon me, their priest, to save them. If truth be told, if I had not cut down that tree, the sorcerer would never have stayed with us, and history would have been so greatly changed. It is my belief that it was the will of our Lord, and in truth one of his better choices - an act of such consequence that I changed my name.

Addendum;

(The following words are translated from 14th century French script, written in a bold hand and added to Father James work at a later date.)

My thanks to you ancient Priest. I am but a wandering poet, and have travelled this land for some years. Finding your tale to read has inspired me greatly, and your fanciful ideas are already formulating a story full of wonder within the eye of my mind. I will secretly dedicate this book unto you. If all madness led to such wonderful tales, then our illiterate world would be so full of stories and legends that every man would demand to be skilled in reading, and every home would be filled with books.

You will have to forgive me for sealing these volumes away so deep within this crypt. I would not wish another man so skilled with a quill as to take what is now mine to write.

Signed ; Chretien de Troyes.
Ninth day of June 1168

Author's Notes.

Where do I start these? Perhaps with an apology.

My apologies that I am about to now make you suffer further by telling the sad tale of this book's strange journey.

It began in 2006. I was fascinated by certain things that seemed worthy of exploration. Alfred the Great won the battle of Edington (Ethandon) by using shield walls and the strong position he gained from arranging his forces in a good defensive location on the earthen ramparts of an old Iron Age fort. I had always thought of the Vikings as individual warriors who fought much like the Scots, on bravery and individual prowess rather than an organised attack or defence. In my limited research I have not found any evidence that 'shield walls' were much in use before this date. So the idea that a smaller scale battle inspired King Alfred did appeal to me. Then seeing Tom Hanks strike a lighter at the end of the film *Castaway* made me think of how magical the simplest of modern day conveniences would have appeared to people from the past.

I have always had an interest in science, but when I read a book I expect everything that is not obviously 'fantasy' – such as a time-gate – to be as accurate as possible. I have read in books, by some well known authors, unnecessary untruths that simply piss me off. Lies such as describing the hero as using a 'Judo chop' (given there are no blows in Judo, at all!), or a claim that sumo wrestlers are selected in their youth and with practice, for their later protection, can push their testicles back into their abdomen by stretching the tubes down which they descended. (This is bollocks, literally, the male testes descend by the age of 6 months. To force them back is impossible, and if it was possible, it would be very dangerous) ... I digress.

So, with the exception of the need to make the story interesting I have tried to ensure all the anecdotes from longbows on the Mary Rose, to the quality of the steel in vehicle springs and the placebo research in acupuncture, as accurate as possible. I have deliberately used much of what I know of personally, including locations I have been to, and courses I have undertaken.

I was aware that the Iron Age fortress at South Cadbury, (just north east of Sutton Montis, but mentioning South Cadbury in the story would have been a bit obvious), was thought to be a possible location of Arthur's Camelot. When I found out there was another smaller Cadbury in Devon, and that there was an Iron Age fort on the hill above that village, the idea for the story started to take form. I had Bill Marlin use the name Kaadbury as a simple diversion for those who know of the possible sites for Camelot. Besides, Bill Marlin would probably have never seen the village name written down anywhere.

Despite being a smaller venue, the fort above the Devon Cadbury has a truly impressive earthwork outer wall, and the description, and sketch, in the book are accurate. There is a strange gully around the southern side, inside the fort, that I have explained as being built by Eric and Marlin as their 'killing ground'. If this had been a defensive inner gulley it is now well worn down. But if you ever visit the fort you will see what I mean.

Some of the characters have evolved on the page. I had no intention that the priest would behave as he did. But that just sort of happened. I liked the idea of allowing his continual excuses (called cognitive distortions by psychologists) for his licentious and lascivious behaviour to mingle with his sanctimonious pontificating in his part of the text. (A simile perhaps?) I was also keen to play on the idea that history is what the winner, or the writer, says it is. For one person to tell such a long and detailed story and fail to see how another would describe it, is perhaps of interest.

The Arthurian legend appears to have had a number of early references suggesting he was a Welsh leader who fought against the Saxon invaders after the Romans left Britain, although 'Camelot' did not appear until the writings of a French poet Chretien De Troyes (Christian of Troyes – a French city) in the 1170s. I rather liked the idea that a historical document telling of the exploits of 'Our Thor' would have been the source of inspiration for his stories, and that perhaps he had deliberately hidden this original text in order to avoid others writing similar tales.

I started this book in 2006 as a long term relationship I was in was falling apart. My wife had left me with four children to raise in 1998, and after a couple of years on my own, another woman and her two children began living with me. When this partner left in 2006 I began searching for a lady I had met many years before, and who for some reason I had never been able to forget. We had met only briefly, but her personality was a delight, and in truth I fell head over heels for her. They say there is no such thing as love at first sight. Maybe not, but from my experience there can be love at a prolonged or second viewing. Anyway, we were both married, and neither of us wanted to hurt anyone, so we had gone our separate ways for 16 years. I started to write this book with Monty being this character from my past. Yes, the lady I had met, and fallen in love with, was tall and broad shouldered and gorgeous and, by the time I met her again, she had a first class degree in Geology, along with a doctorate in Forensic Sedimentolgy. And when I did find her again she became truly the love of my life. The picture on the front of this book is of 'Monty in The Narrows', although perhaps you have now guessed that it is actually of my Lizzie in The Narrows at the head of Zion valley, exactly as described on page 41.

So, it was after this book had already been started, I found my Lizzie again at the beginning of 2007. We were both single by then, and so began a great life 'going steady' and spending a lot of our time together.

The day we walked to the bottom of the Grand Canyon and back in 2009, we noticed a slight change in her right breast. By the following spring she had had a double mastectomy, chemotherapy and radiotherapy, and the doctors had told her that they had done a 'belt and braces' job on her and all should be well. In April 2010 she asked me if I still wanted to marry a woman with no breasts. An easy question if it is someone you completely adore. In May the cancer had come back in her skin, so we brought the wedding forward to the 28th of July 2010 so that she would still have hair for our wedding. After the new chemotherapy was over there was no sign of the cancer and so we got on with life, a truly fabulous life, together. This book became something I did now and again for fun.

In November 2011 the cancer came back in her brain and liver, and on the 11th of May 2012 the love of my life, my soul mate, my gorgeous wonderful Lizzie, died. It was three days before her 49th birthday. I have written a great deal of this book over the last few months just to keep myself sane.

So, there are analogies at many different levels in this story. I hope you have found it fun to read, and perhaps thought provoking. You will have noticed that I am not a believer in God any more. No higher being with any sort of positive purpose would have done what was done to my Lizzie. I believe that when we die our light simply gets turned off, forever. I believe that this is not a rehearsal, and that this is our one chance at life.

If you are religious, and you believe you may be offended by someone suggesting there is no God, please do not read the remaining couple of pages of this book. I hope you have enjoyed this story. It was good therapy for me.

Now you have chosen to continue, I would have to start with the fact that interestingly it appears that all religions are continually reinforced by the significantly beneficial placebo effect of 'faith'. Faith is great stuff, and I would always support others faiths as there are such significant benefits. They have recently found that the reason the placebo effect works so well is that it plugs in to our own internal chemistry set, and can deliver drugs, from pain killers to euphoria, better than most registered medicines. Faith and being positive really does move internal mountains. It is something every medical doctor learns very early on in their training.

As a personal example of the power of these internal drugs I remember a game of rugby I played some years ago when I tackled a very large player very hard, before the end of the first half of the match. From then on in the game, although I knew there was something not quite right with my left shoulder, I was in no pain. At the end of the match I discovered that the top end of my left clavicle was completely torn away from the top of my left scapula... An hour later I was in absolute agony.

I personally think it is unethical for any religion to seek to manage our behaviour by threats of what will, or will not, be done to us as a punishment or reward in any supposed afterlife. And for me it is probably worse that they claim the moral high ground within this process. You do not have to be religious to be a good person. We should all be good to others because it is the right thing to do, not out of fear. Those who only behave well towards other people because of being blackmailed by a religious threat are certainly not any better than those who do so because they are just nice human beings.

All the major religions appear to be competitive and exclusive claiming they are the only one true religion, praising the one true 'God'. Well, what about all those faiths that must have got it wrong then? Surely they should not be damned for being born in the wrong country, or having the wrong parents? Surely no 'worthy' God would damn people to eternal hell when obviously it is not their fault? To be fair to the human race, would it not be the obvious thing to do, to openly 'prove' which is the correct faith to follow? And, if the world was made in just a week, then why lie about it? Why try to deceive everyone by planting 4,500,000,000 years of unimpeachable false evidence of the evolution of this planet, and even build in a perfect historical Deoxyribonucleic Acid link between all living things, just to con us into getting it all wrong! Oh, and please do not respond with 'God moves in mysterious ways' or 'it is just something sent to test the strength of our faith'.

Having possibly upset some people who did not take heed of my warning, please accept my apologies. (Perhaps they are of the view that warnings written in books are just nonsense!). But what I have just done is no worse than anyone from any religion expressing their views on the benefits of becoming a believer in their particular deity. If anyone is genuinely upset, I am sorry, as I said I do not want anyone to lose their faith because of me. If you think my views are nonsense then how can you continue to be troubled by my obvious gibberish? At least I am not claiming to follow another, and perhaps therefore in your view false, deity. (God forbid eh!)

As for me, I have no idea what direction my life will now take now. I plan to do a bit more writing. Handling the loss of Lizzie has been very hard for me. It has also been very hard for her family and her many good friends. I wonder if it will be possible for me to feel as completely in love with anyone ever again. I just do not know. When I first wrote this page it was 214 days after she died. At this final belated edit it is now 919 days. It was truly my privilege to have known her, to be in love with her and to have had the time we had together. I hope that Bill Marlin has some quality time left to be with his true love Monty as well.